By the Pricking of Her Thumb

A Real-Town Murder

ADAM ROBERTS

This paperback published in Great Britain in 2019 by Gollancz

First published in Great Britain in 2018 by Gollancz
an imprint of the Orion Publishing Group Ltd
Carmelite House, 50 Victoria Embankment
London EC4Y 0DZ

An Hachette UK Company

1 3 5 7 9 10 8 6 4 2

A CIP catalogue record for this book is
available from the British Library.

ISBN 978 1 473 22151 2

Typeset at The Spartan Press Ltd,
Lymington, Hants

Printed and bound in Great Britain by Clays Ltd,
Elcograf S.p.A.

www.orionbooks.co.uk
www.gollancz.co.uk

'There's something in the human personality which resents things that are clear, and conversely, something which is attracted to puzzles, enigmas, and allegories'

Stanley Kubrick. Quoted in Thomas Allen Nelson, *Kubrick: Inside a Film Artist's Maze* (2000), p.10

'Include utter banalities'

Stanley Kubrick, notes on *Full Metal Jacket* screenplay

Contents

PART 1

Eighteen Months Later

1: *The Thumb Itself*

Alma couldn't make sense of it until she met the monkeys. Don't blame her for that. It wasn't a simple business – first the Howdunnit, then the Whodunnit-to, and both together a real tangle, inhospitable to solution. A darker time for Alma than any she had previously known. A confounding puzzle.

Until, that is, she met the monkeys and was finally able to piece the whole thing together.

Well, I *say* 'met'. It wasn't what you'd call a conventional meeting.

Well, I *say* 'monkeys'.

At any rate, first there was the Howdunnit. That was the one with the needle. Then afterwards, as a quite separate matter, was the Whodunnit-to. But first things first. *How* is always primary. *Who-to* has to be a secondary consideration.

It proved easy to be mistaken about such things as who actually was employing her, and to solve which crime. There was a howdunnit in place of the whodunnit, and then a whodunnit-to in place of the same thing.

'Take me through it one more time,' said Alma.

'As many times as you like, sweetheart,' said Officer Maupo.

'The woman is dead?'

'Dead as dial-up,' the officer confirmed.

Maupo was not physically present in the room with Alma, of course, but the latest iteration telephonics were so realistic it would have been easy to think she was. Fact of the matter: Alma was beginning to feel old. They hadn't had this new hyperreal hologrammer, all these creepily precise visualisations of people hundreds of miles away, when *she* was a girl. Back then a hologram looked like a hologram, scratches and blips and all.

Alma cleared her throat. 'And she has a needle in her thumb. Like Aurora.'

Maupo hesitated. 'Aurora? My feed is giving me a disambigua-
tion list as long as my overtime claim sheet on *that* one.'

'*Sleeping Beauty*,' Alma said.

'I see what you— No, though. Because, you see, Aurora got
a needle in her thumb and fell asleep, where Alexa Lund got
a needle in her thumb and fell *dead*.' Out of nowhere, Maupo
grinned. 'Less Aurora, more Aurigormortis.'

Oh, she was a sparky one, this Officer Maupo.

'You are sure the needle in the thumb killed her?' Alma asked.

'Indeed we're not,' said Maupo. 'We're not sure of anything.
Which is why Pu Sto has sent me to ask you to assist.'

'Being,' Alma said, 'too busy to come herself.'

'Ah,' said the officer. 'About that. Pu Sto herself asked me to
say—'

Alma put her hand up like she was directing traffic in antique
times.

'It doesn't matter. Really it doesn't. I'm assuming there's a
reason you mention the needle in the thumb? You would hardly
bring it up if it were wholly unrelated.'

'We've honestly no idea. No *needle's*-eye, dear.'

Maupo gave Alma the benefit of her loopy grin a second time.
It crossed Alma's mind that the policewoman might be flirting
with her. She put the notion to one side.

'Let me summarise what you're telling me,' Alma said. 'Just so
I'm clear. Ms Lund, a thirty-nine-year-old woman in good health,
was found dead in her apartment, and the only thing out of the
ordinary about her condition – apart, of course, from the fact
that she was dead – is that she had a six-centimetre-long *sewing*
needle stuck in her thumb.'

'That's the nub of it.'

'Is there,' Alma prompted, 'anything else I ought to know?'

'That I get off duty at ten?' Maupo offered.

'Anything else I need to know about the case. Surveillance
footage?'

'Not that we can find. Normally the apartment would have
footage, of course, but it just so happens the program was offline
for fifteen minutes, on a diagnostic and rebooting protocol. It
doesn't know who ordered the diagnostic and reboot, although
whoever it was had good enough bona fides to convince a level-7
AI.'

'Those can be forged,' Alma said. 'Though it isn't cheap.'

'This implies that somebody with a lot of money wanted Lund dead, and was able to sideline the apartment for long enough to make that happen.'

'Or perhaps Lund herself ordered the diagnosis and reboot?'

'Unlikely,' said the officer. 'Why wouldn't she just tell her apartment to undertake the diagnostic? I mean, if it was *her*, then why hide the fact? All we know is that the program recognised valid command codes, and switched itself to diagnostic mode. When it switched back to its regular duties, fifteen minutes later, Lund was dead on the floor.'

'With a needle in her thumb.'

'Through her thumb. Pushed in through the back of the thumbnail, right through the joint and out the other side.'

'Painful sounding,' said Alma. 'But not in itself fatal. And there was no poison, or nanotech, on the tip of this needle?'

'Nothing. Nothing on the needle, nothing in Lund's system.'

'What does your coroner say about cause of death?'

'She says circulatory shock.'

'Having a needle pushed through your thumb would certainly *be* a shock.'

'No,' said Maupo. 'Not that. Circulatory shock is medical terminology. It has nothing to do with common or garden shock. There are four main types of it, each one defined by the underlying cause. It might be, for instance, that your body goes into shock because of a large-scale haemorrhage. Or because the heart stops. Or there's some blockage in the circulation. Or it might be that a massive infection simply overloads your body, or trauma of some kind, allergy – you've heard of anaphylactic shock, I guess. Lots of possible causes, but the same result. The body, in effect, shuts off.'

'Death.'

'Death.'

'Maybe,' said Alma, 'she died of fright. That's a thing, isn't it?'

Maupo shook her head. 'No, not really. Not a thing, generally speaking. And that's super unlikely to have been what happened here, because her adrenaline and cortisol levels would have been way higher. There was evidence of adrenaline residue, so something startled her. But whatever it was had time to settle down, physiologically, before she died.'

'Died,' Alma prompted, once more, 'of?'

'Her circulation went into a specific, medically defined form of shock. Oxygen was not being delivered to her organs. It was probably the cerebral hypoxia that actually killed her.'

'But circulatory shock can't be caused by getting jabbed in the thumb with a needle,' said Alma, who was checking her own feed on the condition. 'Or people would be dropping dead at sewing classes and acupuncturists and tattoo studios in their thousands daily.'

'That is a perfectly accurate summary of the state of play.'

'Why would somebody want to kill her?' Alma asked.

'Why,' Maupo countered, 'does anybody want to kill anyone?'

'You ask that like it's a rhetorical question. Actually, it's not. It admits of quite a straightforward answer. Most people *don't* want to kill other people. When murder happens it's almost always either hot or cold, and if it's cold then the reason is almost always one of two things.'

'Speaking as a police officer,' said Maupo, arching a simulated eyebrow, 'I feel it would be in my professional interest to know what those two things are.'

'Money,' said Alma, as if it were the most obvious thing in the world, 'or psychopathy. Including genocide in the latter category. If it's psychopathy, individual or collective, then the death of Ms Lund will already be, or will soon prove to be, part of a larger pattern of murder.'

'And what about the hot murders?'

'Passion, sex, drunkenness, a flare-up of rage or resentment – all those. Whoever did this took pains to close down surveillance, and left no other clues or pointers. They were meticulous. They knew what they were doing, and planned it carefully. So this one was cold.'

'Money, then.'

'Was Ms Lund wealthy?'

'Not rich-rich. She was well-to-do, I suppose. Worked for a private company, spent most of her time in-Shine, liked classic culture, drank only twentieth-century wine. That level of rich.'

'What was her job?'

'Details are hard to get – it's a privately owned company, and not under obligation to post anything publicly. Owned by a firm that's owned by a firm that's owned by one of the ultra-rich.

You know how it is. Best as we can tell she was working on consciousness. Modelling human consciousness.'

'Full AI?'

'That's our assumption. One of those people who hadn't given up on that dream – actual artificial consciousness, the real-deal AI.'

'Maybe she had got close, and was killed to stop the research going any further?'

'Maybe.'

'Or maybe she had broken through, and was tortured to obtain her work, and then killed to cover traces? Either way, actual AI has the potential to generate prodigious amounts of money, and money is a very solid reason to kill.'

'Not much of a torture, though, is it? One pinprick in the thumb?'

'Maybe she had a phobia about such things. Maybe a childhood viewing of the fate of Princess Aurora in *Sleeping Beauty* traumatised her.'

'At any rate, if we get any more details on her employment,' said Maupo, 'I'll let you know.'

'Can I see the body?'

'Pu Sto said you'd ask that. I'll have to get clearance. This is an official police investigation, you know, and however tight you are with Pu, you are not actually police. But I dare say it can be arranged. Maybe tomorrow. Until then, I'm authorised to share all official files and data with you, and any assistance you can render will be—' She broke off. 'There are rules, you know,' she went on, in a different tone of voice, 'rules against police officers entering into relationships with the members of the public with whom they come into contact during the course of their investigations. But you're not strictly speaking a member of the public, are you?'

'I'm not, strictly speaking,' Alma replied, 'single.'

'Oh,' said Maupo. 'I mean, of course.'

'Of course in the sense of OK? Or in the sense that you had previously checked my confidential files and already knew that? And that, given the state of health of my partner, you figured you might have a shot?'

For the first time in their encounter Maupo looked actually uncomfortable.

'You know very well that it's against police rules to go poking around files not immediately relevant to the investigation. Against the rules means against the law. And— Look – this specific thing. This dead person, Lund. I'm police and we have instincts, and my instinct tells me this whole *thumb* thing is surely, surely irrelevant.'

'Either the needle in the thumb is related, in some way, to Lund's death, however hard it is to see how, or it is *un*related. If it is the latter, the needle is either purely adventitious, which seems unlikely, or else is part of some red herring game, some attempt at distraction. And if *that's* what we're dealing with, then there must be something the killer is trying to distract us *from*. Or I should say, something *from which* the killer is trying,' Alma smiled one of her rare smiles, 'to distract us.'

'And what are you trying to distract *me* from, Ms Alma,' said Maupo, recovering her composure with another of her weird off-kilter grins, and essaying, Alma suddenly heart-sinkingly understood, a waggishly direct form of flirtation. 'Might you be a tiny bit more single than you said? A little tiny bit more open to going on a date with an interested, attentive and, if I may say so without sounding vainglorious, attractive police officer who—'

'No,' said Alma.

Maupo waited for more.

There was no more.

'Goodbye,' said Alma.

'That's ... That's abrupt.'

'Very much the kind of person I am,' agreed Alma. 'Not just abrupt. *The* brupt.'

Maupo looked blank for a moment, but then, in a manner evidently unconnected with any notion of mirth, moved her facial muscles into a smile. Joining the game was joining the game, after all.

'OK then,' she said, heartily. 'Oh jay, oh kay *and* oh ell – I shall take that,' and she paused, and bowed with old-school courtesy, 'as a definite no-no-maybe. *À tout à l'heure*, Ms Alma.'

She ended the call, and the sim vanished.

It was time for Marguerite's next bout of treatment. Alma went through to the bedroom and settled to the business of determining which fractal iteration her lover's polyform pathology was taking this time. Every four hours and four minutes, without fail. Never quite the same from one appearance to the next, never predictable – designed that way by persons unknown, to torment and likely to kill.

Alma watched the antibodies spread, like smoke through the blood, watched the little spikes run up and down on the toximeter. As with chess, no combination of moves was ever precisely like any previous pattern, but sometimes fell into more broadly recognisable strategies. So absorbed was she in constellating the dosage trifecta and inspraying the antipyre in the right places that she barely noticed how uncharacteristically withdrawn Marguerite was being.

'What's up with you?' she asked, washing her hands afterwards.

Marguerite was staring at a point on the ceiling.

'That young police officer,' she said, in a haughty voice, 'seemed unusually interested in you.'

'And why wouldn't she be?' Alma said, coming to the bedside and kissing Marguerite's cliff face cheek. 'I'm hot.'

'You are so attentive to my physical hurt,' Marguerite replied, affecting a tragic-heroine voice, 'yet so careless of my emotional suffering.'

'Don't be a bloke about this, Rita. If you don't trust me by now then you're being seriously stubborn in your insecurity. I'm quite tempted to tell you to get over yourself.'

'Have you *seen* myself?' Marguerite returned. 'You realise what manner of Alpine Hannibal I'd have to be to traverse that?'

Alma kissed her again. 'That's better. And you have nothing to worry about, you know. The flirty copper ... That was just her manner, I think. I don't think it was anything personal. More to the point, she was bringing me a case – a paying gig, from Pu Sto herself. You were eavesdropping, so you know all about it.'

'A ridiculous case,' said Marguerite, taking a long sip from her straw. 'A trivial case. A waste of your time and my genius.'

'You've solved it then?'

'There was something on the needle, of course.'

'Flirty copper says not.'

'The police officer in question,' said Marguerite, her left eyebrow arching like a willow branch, 'clearly knows nothing, and cares not that this is so. A human being doesn't die of being pricked in the thumb – doesn't die, that is, on account of the prick itself. Ergo there was something on the needle. It injected some lethal toxin into the body. If the toxin hasn't shown up on their post-mortem scans, that means it erased itself, or metabolised into something inert. It means they're looking for the wrong thing. Which means it's not a conventional toxin, or an easily identifiable nanotech agent – so, they need to look again. They need to look harder and look smarter.'

'I shall go see the body, its needle still in situ. Perhaps you could give me some pointers on what this super-subtle, so-hard-to-detect toxin might be.'

'I was adored once too,' said Marguerite, suddenly. 'And more than once, you know? There are *plenty* of people mooning about the world nursing broken hearts on my account, you know.'

Alma waited a moment, to give her a space to expand on this observation. When nothing more emerged, she prompted her, gently enough. 'I don't doubt it for a moment.'

'Maybe *you* are the one who should be touched by insecurity,' Marguerite said, turning her huge face towards the window. 'Is all I'm saying.'

'My love,' said Alma, kissing her, 'is made perfect in jealousy. There's nobody else in the whole wide web of the world for me except you, dear.'

And, after a short and sulky pause, Marguerite said, 'I do know it,' in a small voice. 'Ignore me.'

'Ignore you? Easier said than done. Have you *seen* you?'

'I should tell you more often that I love you. And say how much I— Oh, *appreciate* is a wormy and underpowered word, a nothing sort of word. But what else can I say? How much I *appreciate* what you do for me. Why is speech so under-adequate to these things?'

'You don't need to say what I already know.' Alma kissed her again, and went through to the front room for a nap.

2: *The Whodunnit-To*

Alma slept for three full hours, and woke feeling slightly less bone-deep exhausted than she usually did. She washed, settled down to a cup of coffee, and reviewed the files Officer Maupo had sent through on the murder of Ms Alexa Lund. There was a lot of irrelevant quotidiana, and a lack of useful specific detail: her actual line of work, for instance.

Another slurp of the black stuff, and Alma dipped her toe into the online world of Actually Intelligent Artificial Intelligence – AIAI, as the movement had named itself. Supposedly, a step beyond the merely reactive AIs that ran mundane business in the Real and populated the Shine with such density. Impossible, said some. Not only possible but inevitable, said others.

Surveying the present state of debate was far from edifying: one influential sub-group within the AIAI movement were convinced genuine artificial intelligence would be more than a matter of consciousness – it would be the creation of new *souls* to glorify God's creation. For a second, larger group, philosophy, or psychology, or programming logic, or theology, absolutely proved that AIAI was simply impossible, a non-thing, a contradiction in terms.

Was this the world Alexa Lund had inhabited? There was certainly enough animus swirling around to suggest a degree of murderousness. Then again, there was no proof this was even what Lund's job entailed, let alone any indication she'd got close enough to the holy grail of a properly conscious AI to stir up the hornets.

Alma checked again: a flat fee for undertaking the case, a national minimum bonus if her advice led to an arrest and conviction. Chicken feed, really.

Alma put Alexa Lund to one side and sorted through her admin in-feed. The thing was: money. The thing was: their lack thereof. The need for unpredictable and often unusual medicines was a constant pressure making their joint supply of money lackier and lackier. The government-mandated flat fee for acting as an adviser to the police would make little dent in the debt. A trivial debt-dent.

Better than nothing, yes. Only a tiny bit better, though.

Money. The oldest problem.

And then, as if conjured into being by her need, an offer of work came through, slinking in wrapped firework sparkles of gold and silver and a muted jazz-bugle honk. Fireflies swirled like neon smoke and assembled themselves into the words 'An unusual case!'

Alma waited.

Finally an avatar poked its golden head into her feed and shunted a permissions request to manifest in the flat. Alma, assuming that a troll with malicious intent would hardly announce themselves so flamboyantly, ran a basic scan and was about to OK the request when she had a second thought. Something tickling her suspicion gland. So she put up a smiling major-domo, cat's-cradling his hands, and dug swiftly into the metadata of the request. Direct from the office of Jupita. Direct. She double-checked, and it was true. From her penthouse in the Blade Tower, Jupita herself was offering her work.

Alma needed money. If there was one thing Jupita had to a plethoric degree, it was money.

The avatar finally materialised: a slim young male, tightly but not extravagantly muscled, angelic-faced, naked, genital-less and with all-gold skin, like an actor auditioning for the role of Ariel in an especially kitsch production of *The Tempest*.

'So,' he said. 'You're Alma.'

'And you're Jupita?'

'Me? Ho, no. Nono, *she* doesn't venture this far out of the Shine. And you—' (the avatar smiled an excessive and dazzlingly silver-toothy smile) '—never step *into* the Shine. Oh, your reputation precedes you.'

Alma said nothing.

'No, I'm not Jupita, rising. I am but a messenger, come to invite you to the Blade Tower to meet my employer in person. She would like to offer you a case. She is, you know, *very* wealthy.'

'Rumours are,' Alma replied, 'that she is absolutely wealthy.'

That smile again, like a headache in facial-expression-form. 'We don't comment on the rumours that absolute wealth has been achieved. But my employer is certainly wealthy enough to pay you handsomely – *if* you take her case.'

'Shunt the details into my feed,' said Alma, who didn't like being bounced into things, 'and I'll consider whether it falls within my bailiwick. I don't, as you say, go into the Shine, so if the case requires doing that you'd be better off hiring a different investigator.'

The avatar held up one golden finger. 'We've been right through you, and your history. We have the resources to do a deep search on anyone at all, and we know what we're getting. There's a flitter outside and we'd very much appreciate it if you came with us.'

'Came where?'

'To meet my employer.'

'You just said she never leaves the Shine.'

'No more does she. But she wants to meet you in as close to the flesh as possible. Which means – and believe me, she wouldn't do this for just anybody – she *is* willing to step into the antechamber, where her body is plugged, and you can meet the two of them, which is to say the one of them.'

Alma reflexively checked her feed. 'I need to be back here in fifty-nine minutes.'

'I am placing a bond for a million euros in your porch,' said the golden avatar, 'redeemable if we don't have you back here in forty minutes precisely.'

'Well, that's,' said Alma, actually startled, 'certainly an ... an unusual ... uh.' A million would eliminate her debt with a healthy sum left over. The downside, of course, was that if she did not get back to the flat before Marguerite's next treatment was due, her partner would die. But, Alma thought, even if the forty minutes expired, she would still have a further nineteen minutes to hurry home under her own power, and the Blade was not so very far away.

She looked in her feed's porch. There was the package.

'Well, all right, then.'

The golden avatar rode the elevator down with Alma, and ushered her with several elaborately florid bows towards the flitter – not, Alma was a little surprised to discover, a gold one, but a regular plasmetal model, though larger and more luxuriously appointed than the standard models. The inside smelled of elder-berry.

The car rose so gently into the air she hardly felt the accel-eration. The avatar, having vanished from Alma's apartment, remanifested inside the car.

'Have you ever been inside the Blade before?'

'Stepped into the lobby once or twice.'

'No higher than the ground floor?'

'No.'

'My employer doesn't like the word *penthouse*,' said the avatar, as the flitter sped up and Alma's shoulders and head were pressed into the blue suede upholstery by the acceleration. 'She insists she is in no sense pent. She is at liberty to travel anywhere, real or in-Shine. But what are the alternatives? Free-house has entirely the wrong connotations. Ah! We're here!'

The flitter settled onto a landing pad, external to the building, and the passenger door swung up as if pointing the way towards the starry firmament itself. Or heiling a führer.

Alma stepped out. The platform was high above the city, which meant that the whole of R!-town was arranged below: its empty streets and voltaic roofs, its towers and arcades. Behind her the Kennet throw a trapezoid loop around King's Island, and to the north the broader stripe of the Thames, grape-coloured and gleaming, eased its doubled *U* course. It was strange to look *down* upon the drones, small as hornets, as they drifted here and there. The air smelled fresh. The breeze, frisky, rubbed its fingers through Alma's hair.

The golden avatar led Alma inside: a wide interior space over-supplied with cream sofas and red-and-gold wall patterns. There were low tables and a range of items that, her feed assured her as if nudged to do so by some exterior app, were all *absurdly* rare and expensive: vases and little sculptures; an actual skull blistered all over with diamonds; on the wall, a painting from the Dutch medieval period of a sombre-faced man in brown standing stiffly alongside his serenely bald-headed bride in green. The whole room was arrayed precisely according to the aesthetic logic of Plutocratic Chic.

There were two human beings in the space, neither of whose identities was openly available to Alma's feed. There were also three private myrmidrones, one by the elevator and two more standing to attention beside a further, inner door. The two humans eyed her with unalarmed but attentive gazes. She cast a surreptitious line out from her feed, and was immediately, if politely, rebuffed. Identities not to be disclosed without a warrant; private security, licensed to carry firearms, legal and approved, please move on.

'Through here,' said the avatar, beckoning Alma in between the two myrmidrones and through the inner door.

Alma passed into a chamber narrower than the outer sitting room, but taller. And in the middle a triple-width bed, upon which, recumbent but floating, somehow, a centimetre or so above the actual mattress, was the ample corpus of Veronica von Polenz, known as Jupita. Why Jupita? Alma checked; the reference was, it seemed, to some antique movie about the acquisition of absolute wealth.

So, thought Alma. Here I am physically proximate to one of the richest people in Europe. That's not something that happens every day.

Jupita's body was wrapped in a silver onesie, leaving her hands, feet and face free. Alma checked the specs of this tech on her feed; induction loop-thread meant that the body could be massaged, moved, levitated, stretched and compressed more-or-less continually while the consciousness was in-Shine. It was a more elegant (and of course more expensive) solution to stopping atrophy and bedsores than the mesh regular people wore, the noisy and awkward suits that plonked them like zombies up and down the stairs in their houses, or up and down the streets outside if they couldn't afford more than a single room.

Alma surveyed her surroundings. The induction loops doubtless ran through everywhere: floor, walls, ceiling. Jupita's physical body could move about the whole room, probably – dance, jog, do aerobics – while her mental attention was absorbed in the Shine.

Alma took a step towards the bed, and the body on it flexed sinuously. There was a *parp-parp* of artificial trumpets, rising on a cheesy crescendo, and a new avatar appeared in the room. Ultradef, smooth, recognisably the same person as the body floating over the bed.

'Alma,' said Jupita. 'Such a *pleasure* to meet you.'

'Likewise,' said Alma.

Jupita raised an avatar hand in greeting. Her real hand twitched and lifted beside its supine body.

'That's not something you see every day,' Alma observed. 'Are you about to slip out of the Shine altogether?'

'It does feel a little odd,' Jupita agreed, with a smile, 'being so close to the real. Usually I'm deep and deeper in the nested paradises. It's an odd thing to shift from the richness of the Shine to the – frankly – coarse-grain crudeness of the Real. It feels a bit like being on the edge of waking up. The protocols for exiting the Shine tickling my consciousness.'

'Also, evidently, tickling your body too.'

The body twitched again. 'It's an unusual sensation,' said Jupita, distantly. 'I certainly wouldn't manifest an avatar anywhere outside this building. I have at least fitted my house with the sorts of projectors you can't buy in the regular shops, and that mitigates the sensation a little.'

'Mitigates?'

'You could say, the tech I have fitted in *this* building enShine-ifies my appearances in the Real. From my point of view, I mean.'

'I appreciate you coming into the Real at all – to meet me. Since I never go in-Shine. It's kind of you.'

The avatar smiled, as if kindness was so utterly alien a concept to her that Alma mentioning it must have been a sort of joke.

'You're very *popular*, you know.'

This took Alma entirely by surprise. 'I don't mean directly to contradict you but – I'm not.'

'Oh, I don't mean *out here*. I mean in-Shine. Fan groups and followers. Your partner's narratives of your most famous cases. She-lock Holmes and Dr Watsdaughter.'

'Since I am almost entirely ignorant of what happens in-Shine,' Alma said, 'this is both a surprise, and simultaneously an irrelevance. I don't mean to sound snotty. I mean it's not something that will ever impact my life. Unless I could monetise it somehow, of course. *That* could be useful.'

Jupita's smile, now, was of a more indulgent kind. Monetising was *her* superpower. The thought that Alma could wield such a Thor's hammer was almost quaint.

'Popularity interests me,' Jupita said, expansively. 'The logics of it. Put a hundred children, from a range of backgrounds and families, in a school and some will become more popular and others won't. Popularity clumps around some, and not others. Isn't that interesting? What's more interesting is that this popularity doesn't particularly correlate to background, family or anything else, really. It just is.'

Alma said nothing.

'It's not that the richest kids get to be the most popular, say. It's not even that the *nicest* kids get to be the most popular, you see.'

'I suppose that's true.'

'Indeed, sometimes kids can be real bastards without impacting their popularity. In fact, they can be real bastards and *increase* their popularity. When others can be bastards and find themselves shunned. And that's true more broadly – true in the grown-up world, I mean. Think of how many fans there are of Jack the Ripper. Or Hannibal Lecter.'

Alma's feed supplied the necessary info on these names.

'Is this why you asked me to meet you? To discuss how mass murderers end up with their fan base?'

This time Jupita's smile was a goofy grin. 'Dear me no. I have an actual case for you. Something a little out of the ordinary.'

Alma waited.

'I've been following your career. You've done some interesting work, in terms of investigating, solving. De-puzzling puzzles. You say that you're unaware how large your in-Shine fan base is. But I wonder about that. I mean, you must have some sense of it?'

'I can honestly say I'm not bothered, either way. My priorities are focused on one particular person. Anything else is... an irrelevance. I don't care what people other than her think of me.'

'Well, that's nonsense. Patently. You're a human being, and human beings are social animals, so of course you care how popular you are.'

Alma said nothing. This obsession with being popular, like an insecure teenager at a new school, seemed a strange character trait in a woman so rich she cleared more money annually than the GDP of the country in which she lived. But people have their odd little eccentricities.

'You're sure you won't try the Shine, some day?' Jupita asked. 'I'm perfectly genuine when I say it is the destiny of humankind – it is the transcendence that will perfect our species, by liberating us from all the petty irritations of mundane life.'

Alma smiled thinly, but didn't reply.

17

'No? Honestly? Ah well. Not to badger you. Maybe you'll come round in time – my conviction is that everyone will. In time. The advantages,' she added, stretching her avatar's arms luxuriantly, while her body twitched like a lucid dreamer, 'being so manifold and palpable. The only downside is that if I want to investigate something real-world, I need to hire a proxy.'

'Procks see,' Alma said, 'procks do.'

'*You've* investigated all sorts of crimes and puzzles, I know. Including murders. You have solved what they call whodunnits?'

'I have,' Alma said.

'I'm offering you your first whodunnit-to.' Jupita's avatar put its not-there head to one side and waited. When Alma didn't bite, she added, 'Somebody has been murdered, I just don't know who. I want you to find out.'

'That would be a first, certainly. You mean to say, there is a mystery corpse and you don't know who it is? A case of tracking down their identity?'

'Nothing so straightforward. I know it is one of three people – and none of the three are strangers. I just don't know which of the three it is.'

'Forgive me,' said Alma. 'But how can you know a person has been murdered without knowing *who*?'

'You can sit, you know.' Jupita indicated a padded chair across the top-back of which solid gold knobs in the shape of Walnut Whips were situated, like a row of tiny aureate turds.

'I'll stand,' said Alma.

'So. You know that I'm beyond rich. I don't mean beyond in a loose or merely idiomatic way. I am one of a select group who are so rich that we have left rich behind.' Jupita's actual body rolled a little in its field, like a dolphin in the salt flood. The motion pushed a little air out of its lungs, which sounded to Alma – though of course she knew it was purely reflex – like a sigh of contentment. 'Now, my personal path to wealth,' Jupita's avatar was saying, 'has been lengthy. Naturally it mostly happened in-Shine, because that's where all the money is made nowadays. All the serious money, I mean. I have investments in the Real, since I'm massively diversified. But the lion's share of the money is made in-Shine. The lion's share. I'm the lion.'

Alma said nothing.

'There are various groups of beyond-rich around the world, and a few solitary figures as well, but for myself I belong to a group of equally, more-or-less, wealthy people. We're called the Fab Four.'

Alma's feed prompted her with a definition of Fab Four that gaped, alarmingly, down a rabbit hole of proliferating definition into a vast roiling sea of data and fan-text. No need to go down *there*. She narrowed it to a definition: Fab, short for fabulous. Highly esteemed. Mythical, legendary, non-existent. Which of those two meanings was more relevant?

'Fab Four,' she repeated.

'You have heard rumours of the search for absolute wealth, I suppose?'

'Everybody has heard those rumours.'

'They're true. They're not just rumours. It's a fact. I'm not giving anything away by saying so. I mean, it's a logical extrapolation of the desire to accrue wealth in the first place, isn't it? Poor leads to moderately wealthy, which leads to very wealthy, which leads to ultra-wealthy, which is where I am now. Extrapolate that trajectory, you end up at absolutely wealthy.'

'It has not been my personal experience that poverty leads to moderate wealth.'

Jupita chuckled at this, as though Alma had made a joke. 'I don't want you to think that I *trust* the other three members of our Fab little group either. Nothing so foolish – we're all competing *against* each other to be the first to reach our goal. But we're pooling our resources too. And though none of us *trusts* the others in the least, we trust the rest of humanity even less. So that's a bond. Regular people simply don't understand what it means to be as rich as we are.'

'I see,' said Alma.

'One of them is dead.'

'And you don't know which?'

'Exactly.'

Alma stared at the avatar. 'Really?'

Jupita chose to misunderstand her. 'A good way of putting it. Yes, dead in the Real. The reason I don't know who is that the death is being covered up by some manner of trickery or imposition in-Shine.'

'I meant – are you serious? Are you not, rather, kidding me? You think one of three people – with whom you interact daily – is dead?'

19

'Yes.'

'And you don't know which one?'

'That's right.'

'And you want *me* to identify the dead person?'

'Yes.'

Alma said, 'Might I suggest you contact the police? Or just check the news feeds? If one of a group of the wealthiest individuals in all Europe has died, it's bound to get coverage.'

Jupita shook her head. 'I have to assume you're smarter than you're pretending to be here, Alma, or I'll just be wasting my time hiring you. *Obviously* the death has not been officially logged.'

'I'm afraid I have to return to my original question. How do you know they are dead?'

'The Fab Four do all our business in-Shine, of course. I have known these people for decades. I could go further and say that nobody in the world knows them as well as I do. And what I know *now* is that something is wrong – I mean, with regards to their in-Shine personas I can't put it more precisely than that. Something is not right. One of them, or possibly more than one, have been replaced in-Shine with imposters. Very clever copies. But I can tell.'

As if to a child, Alma asked, 'So *which one* do you feel has been replaced? That would narrow down who might, or might not, have been killed.'

'It's not so simple. It's really not so simple. Do you think we all sit round a table, in-Shine, and *chat*? No. We hide from one another. We game the group. We clone and winnow. We cache-cache. Of course we do. Each of us has to, or the others would steal our ideas and beat us to the goal.'

'You hide?'

'We use masks. Misdirection. We play games. It's very hard to explain to somebody not familiar with the worlds of the Shine. Or indeed, not familiar with the habits of the ultra rich.'

Alma said nothing.

'Naturally,' Jupita drawled, 'none of us trusts the others. Our holy grail is absolute wealth – I mean, that's what the group as a whole is dedicated to achieving. But of course I want to be the one who actually achieves that, which means by definition I want my three fellow Fabs *not* to achieve it. And they all feel the same way. We share some strategies, pool some resources, collaborate to fight off or bankrupt external threats. We've handled that part of the process pretty well. But none of us is so foolish as to make ourselves *vulnerable* to any of the other three. For example I shan't be making myself vulnerable to the others by poking around this issue. That's why I'm hiring you.'

'I still don't see why it is you think one of these three is dead.'

'The group has a gestalt. You understand the term? In point of fact, that's what makes it valuable. And something is... off... about that gestalt.'

This still sounded screwy to Alma, but she thought back to her and Marguerite's debt and nodded slowly. She checked her clock. There was still time.

'If one of them has changed,' she said, 'if one of them has replaced their in-Shine presence with an imposter – I still don't see why that would mean they've been *killed*. Maybe they have been kidnapped.'

'Which would also be a crime. Though I don't think that's what has happened.'

'Or maybe one of them has simply stepped down, without telling you. Isn't that more likely? Given what you say, they might not want you and the others to know they had stepped down.'

'Leave the group voluntarily? You don't understand our manner of working. The dedication to our notionally shared goal. Our interactions are... It's hard to explain.'

'You don't want to give away how you do business,' said Alma. 'I understand. But once I'm hired, client confidentiality will mean that—'

Jupita interrupted her a little crossly. 'Gracious! Of course I'm not going to share my business secrets with *you*, client confidentiality or not. The very idea! Obviously I know who the three of them are, where they live, their real-world names, histories and identities. It's just that it can be tricky working out which of the individuals I'm interacting with in-Shine correlates to which person. It may be that *more* than one of them has been killed – that would certainly explain my uncertainty in pinning down what's going on. Conceivably – I mean, I don't know, but conceivably – all of them are dead.' She pondered this for a while. 'It's a real mystery, isn't it? I mean, death and so on. Human beings are *mortal* creatures.'

'We are,' Alma agreed.

'At any rate, kidnapping makes no sense in this context. Kidnapping to what end?'

'As you've already said, more than once, they're all beyond wealthy,' Alma noted.

'And a kidnapper's plan to tap that wealth would be – ransom?' Jupita chuckled. 'You'd never live to collect! Perhaps you don't understand how much power our level of wealth brings with it. No, of course you *do* understand. You're just being thorough, ticking off the various possibilities. I understand. Ransom is a non-starter. Besides, why settle for a ransom when you can *be* one of the super-rich – gain access to all their wealth.'

'So you suspect somebody, somehow, has murdered one of the world's super-rich, somebody from among the wealthiest people in the world, and taken their place in-Shine. And you think they have done this to get their hands on that person's wealth.'

'I don't know. That's why I'm hiring you.'

'Wouldn't the murdered person's staff notice? I assume some of them have family – wouldn't *they* notice? People such as yourself have the finest software, AI, monitoring and so on money can buy – somebody would notice something.'

'You'd think so. And yet, here we are.'

' "Here" being – your hunch?'

'I *know* something is wrong. I can *feel* it. Calling it a hunch is to misunderstand the nature of how we are known and how we know in-Shine. It is to misunderstand the nature of the gestalt of this group. It's a perfectly unique gang, it really is. Out where you are, it's all glass darkly – but inside is … Ah, but listen to me, I'm preaching again.'

'If your suspicion is correct,' said Alma, 'somebody has killed a member of your Fab Four group, and also managed to hack their feed into the Shine. That's some remarkable level of tech-fu right there. And now they're impersonating that person in-Shine. OK. But why hang around? Why don't they grab the money and get away?'

'Wealth at our level isn't some sack of gold coins to be lifted and carried away. It's massively distributed, and complexly committed. Besides, as you say, whoever this person is, they have superior tech skills. Embezzling funds would be a doddle to such a person, and there would many easier marks than we four. No.

They want access to the *whole* fortune, and plan to use it in some way. That's what gives this investigation its urgency.'

'You want me,' Alma said, to clarify, 'to check on three of the wealthiest individuals in Europe and see which, if any of them, has been murdered?'

'One of them *has*,' Jupita said, adamantly. 'And I want you to find out which.'

'To be absolutely clear, for my own benefit – you can't just *ask* them?'

'If their in-Shine identity is a forgery they're hardly going to admit to it, are they?'

'I mean ask them in the real world?'

'I'm never taking a single step in that place ever again,' said Jupita, with asperity.

'But surely you have people who could deputise for you?'

'Well, of course I do. Of *course*. I have many. And once you sign my contract, you will be one of them.'

Alma hesitated. Something about this gig smelled fishy to her – something told her it would be best avoided. At best it was the bizarre paranoia of a super-wealthy individual who was losing touch with reality, and that would lead her nowhere. At worst it would lead Alma into some very dangerous territory. Then again, Jupita was egregiously wealthy, and Alma really, really needed the money. She tried one last time, for the benefit of her conscience.

'Ms Jupita, I'm really not sure I'm the best person for this job.'

'Not the best person to investigate a murder? Pull the other one, it's got bells on, and by *bells* I mean a massive in-Shine fan following. Popularity! Popularity!'

'You understand that if I discover a murder I will be legally obliged to report it to the police.'

'It would be immensely disruptive to *any* of the Fab Four, and to their entire organisations, to have legally sanctioned police investigating them,' said Jupita smoothly.

'I see,' said Alma. Because she did.

'Good! All friends together, then. You'd best be getting home. I know you're tied to this short timescale, on account of your partner. One of my people will shunt all necessary paperwork into your feed, and negotiate fees and so on. Goodbye. There will be no need for us to meet again, my dear. Not, that is, until you have *solved* the mystery. Not until you can explain death to me.'

'Explain who it is who has died.'

'Exactly.'

And with that, Alma was being escorted back out to the flitter. In moments she was back at her apartment block. As she rode, solus, up the elevator she checked the porch of her feed. The million euro package was gone.

3: *Tim Tym*

Back home, and into the familiar routine of Marguerite's four-hourly health intervention – a routine overfamiliar, so far past familiar as to have transcended familiarity and become effectively an autonomous nervous reaction, like breathing or flinching.

Marguerite was excited at the prospect of the new job, and she chaffed throughout her treatment.

'Hurry up, I want to start seeing what I can find about the Fab Four.'

'The treatment takes as long as it takes,' Alma insisted. 'Quiet down, now.'

Alma's latex-sheathed fingers probed in under Marguerite's ear; the lymph node seemed to palpably swell under her pressure. She spray-injected a detusion agent, and put some drops in Marguerite's eyes. The screens displayed their alarming data, and Alma watched, and slowly the vitals settled into steadier grooves. Marguerite's temperature was still stubbornly high, and there was a low-level flu-like illness lurking in her system. It wasn't part of the four-hour designer pathology, though. Hopefully it would settle itself.

'Now that you've concluded your fussing,' said Marguerite, briskly, 'I can get to *work* on these rich-oids who have *hired* us. We can milk 'em! Milk 'em of their flowing money – their creamy cash – their buttery billions.'

'Billions is small change to these four,' said Alma. 'Though it's only one of them has hired us.'

'Then we'll milk *her.*'

'I don't have any good feeling about this gig, Rita,' Alma confessed. 'It's screwy. I foresee us putting a huge amount of work into it, uncovering nothing because there's nothing to be uncovered, and not getting paid at the end.'

'Ye of little faith.'

'Calling me *ye*, now, are you? That's a slippery slope, Rita. Before you know it'll be *thee*.'

'*Thee* one and own-*lee*.'

'You poke around online for details about these Four, and their search for absolute wealth. I'll send out requests to them for a meeting – which they will decline.'

'Don't do yourself down! I think they'd be honoured to meet you. We have a big in-Shine fan club, remember. And if they're dead, then meeting them in the flesh will soon reveal that fact!'

But Alma was right. She sent requests to meet the three Fabs in person, and received three politely firm denials. She pressed; all her messages diverted to underlings. It was a sure thing that none of these possible murderees – if such an entity were even conceivable – were even personally aware that Alma wanted to talk with them. It would be a circumstance massively beneath them.

She pressed again, and dropped hints as to her police connections. Meetings could be arranged with underlings, it seemed, but there was no possibility that Alma would be allowed into the actual physical presence of any of the three.

'Hardly a surprise,' said Marguerite.

'*You* were the one who said they'd want to talk to me!'

'I hardly think so.' Marguerite looked with affectionate disdain at her partner. 'Of course they're not going to let a scruffy little private investigator into their bedrooms to poke and prod at their sleeping human bodies.'

'Scruffy?' Alma retorted.

'Not *physically* scruffy,' said Marguerite, gravely. 'But you have to look at matters from their point of view. I have had my dealings with the ultra-rich, you know.'

'In your youth.'

'In,' Marguerite agreed, 'my youth. I moved for a time in a most exclusive set. Did I ever tell you about my adventures with Countess Stylo and her gilded blimp? Never mind. But it gave me an insight into them. *You* can wash, as you do, and dress tidily, as you do, and still appear to them like the filthiest homeless tramp. And that's because you're washing with soap and dressing in clothes, where they wash with and dress in money. And you don't have any of that.'

'*We* don't,' Alma said.

'It's an intriguing sort of nonsense anyway. How can you know somebody's dead without knowing *who*? I like it. It stretches my Mycrofty mind.'

'More of a what's-on sort of mind. Surely.'

'*Not* on, that Watson,' said Marguerite. 'You're just envious of my superior ratiocinative powers. Of course we should, to be thorough, at least consider the possibility that Madame Jupita is playing her own double-game. Or conceivably that she's just off her rocker.'

'I don't mind if she's playing me so long as she's paying me.'

'If there's no mystery to uncover then you can't uncover the mystery. She's hardly going to pay you for failure.'

'She'll still have to pay me a *per diem* and a basic fee.'

'Solve the case, though,' Marguerite pointed out, 'and you get a bonus. Maybe a generous one – maybe enough to settle our debts.'

'Then I'll do my best to solve it,' said Alma.

It occurred to Alma that she should not neglect the woman who died with a needle in her thumb. But the problem was the police were paying her so little, and the ultra-rich might pay her so very much more. Money drew her attention away. She told herself that she was a professional, and spent half an hour working through possible angles of attack. She messaged the police officer, Maupo, but got no immediate reply. She scoped around for information on Lund herself, but there was very little there. She sat and stared into space, trying to intuit how sticking a small needle into the flesh could kill. Marguerite might be right – there would have to have been something *on* the needle. So the problem then became – how did one make a fatal toxin vanish after the victim into which it had been injected was dead?

That was a bigger puzzle than the first one.

Her attention wandered.

Their debt called to her, like a primal megasaur issuing its mournful howl in some faraway tar pit.

So she parked Lund for the time being, and spent the rest of that blue afternoon and into the grey evening probing the online reputation of the Fab Four.

Three of them maintained remarkably low online profiles. The exception was Jupita herself, who ran a whole series of online friends-and-influence networks, and whose name popped-up, according to Alma's search protocols, in uncountably vast numbers of in-Shine contexts. The other three, though, kept themselves to themselves, presumably because they had more important things to worry about than interacting with strangers. The more important thing being *money*. All four of the Fabs were breath-stoppingly rich, wealthy beyond the dreams of individuals, of corporations, even of nation states. They were so wealthy that online estimates of just how wealthy they were could only offer minimum guesses, with riders that their actual wealth – massively distributed through the Shine and the Real, all directly personally owned – was certainly several and probably a great many times that baseline.

Still, Alma had a job to do. She rechecked and reflagged the responses to her formal requests for interview. She hadn't expected to be invited immediately into physical proximity with the Fabs themselves, but meetings with representatives were a reasonable place to start.

Two were less promising: Jay Cernowicz and the individual who was known only as 'the Stirk of Stirk' had both sent through a cliff face of prefab responses, smoothly programmed AI and junior staff.

Cernowicz had made her super-fortune metafinancially. The Stirk of Stirk was a more traditional sort of quintillionare. He had started his empire with the extraordinary success of Orgas-matropolis, the in-Shine sex simulation location, also known as Screwtopia, Sessex and various other names. That had started him off, although he had subsequently massively reinvested and acquired many times his original fortune in a variety of diverse ways.

Neither were likely to let an unknown private investigator into their personal space. But with a little persistence, Alma figured she would be offered a meeting with a senior manager, perhaps a personal assistant.

There was less obstruction from the other Fab: Melissa Herford, known popularly as 'the GM', short for Golden Meteor. The name (Alma's feed offered conflicting explanations) reflected the shooting-star rapidity of her rise into ultra-wealth, or else rumours that her company of submarine drones had happened upon a solid gold meteorite on the Atlantic seabed, or various other less likely explanations.

The elegantly programmed AI who handled the GM's diary paused its algorithmic responses in mid-conversation – Alma had a sneaky bit of code monitoring their exchange that noted a tentacle of communication checking official police records, presumably confirming her bona fides – and changed tack.

'As a sign of the GM's respect for the rule of law,' the AI said, 'we might be able to arrange a meeting with one of the GM's personal private secretaries.'

'I would appreciate that,' said Alma, politely.

So Alma took a cab to one of Herford's commercial properties in Wokingham, and had a ten-minute conversation with a slender and extremely well-dressed man called Tim Tym.

'Short for Timothy?' Alma asked.

'Yes,' said Tym.

'And the surname?'

'Indeed.'

'No, I meant—'

'Altogether *something* to do with how little I like the syllables *oth* and *y*. How can I help you, Ms Alma?'

'I'm checking on the Golden Meteor's well-being.'

'Checking on it?'

'I'm working on behalf of one of the other members of her in-Shine consortium, the so-called "Fab Four",' said Alma.

'Almost everything you read about that group is myth and mendacity,' said Tym. 'In truth they're a respectable pro-business cadre dedicating to improving the store of human happiness. You're working for one of the other Fabs?'

Alma nodded.

'Which one?'

'You are the GM's personal secretary?' Alma asked.

'One of them.'

'Well, this is going to sound like a strange request, but I have to ask: can I meet her?'

'Not so much *strange* as *surreal*. Of course it's absolutely out of the question,' said Tym. 'And of course you know that it is. My employer is very protective of her privacy.'

'*You* have met her, of course?'

Tym beamed, and said, 'Of course.'

'How often do you see her? I mean, personally see her, in the flesh? Did you see her this morning, for instance?'

Tim Tym sighed. 'This is Jupita, isn't it? Another of her *lunatic* ideas. Last week it was something about bees. The week before that it was about resurgent royalty. What does she think this time – that the GM's sick and not telling the world? Losing her mind?'

'Dead,' said Alma.

She was watching the fellow's reaction, and it certainly appeared genuine. He looked momentarily nonplussed and then, easily, began to chuckle.

'The J thinks my boss is *dead*? Oho, that's a new one.'

'To be strictly accurate,' Alma said, 'she's not sure if your boss is dead or not. She has asked me to find out.'

'My dear woman,' Tym said, haughtily, fiddling with the knot of his (ostentatiously tagged for Alma's feed to see) €30,000, raspberry-coloured, spider-silk tie. 'To answer your – frankly impertinent – question: yes, the GM is alive and well. In fact I saw her in the flesh this morning – her real-world body, I mean, and it is very much in the pink. Is that all you wanted to know?'

'It would be good to know if your boss shared Jupita's suspicions.'

'Suspicions?'

'That one of the group to which they both belong has been hacked. Or replaced. That something is wrong in the group.'

'Something wrong in the group is the very *definition* of the group,' said Tym, smiling. His suit was a unicorn-thread unique weave, and it glimmered nicely as he shifted position. It positively *thrust* its six figure price tag upon Alma's feed. 'These are four people trying to collaborate on a collective effort while also, every one of them, hoping the other three fail. It's no easy thing.'

'Absolute wealth.'

'I think I've been all the help I can be, Ms Alma,' said Tym, shaking her hand.

Security showed her out. It was time to be getting back to tend to Marguerite, anyway.

On the cab ride home Alma raked through her feed with a few of her more specialised programs. Her sense of the oddness of the job was only growing. There was, her instinct told her, *something* there – but she didn't know what, and it was surely nothing to do with the bizarre specifics of her employment.

She sifted through some of the online gossip about the Four, and about the likelihood, impossibility, inevitability and other iterations of the dream of achieving 'absolute wealth'. Alma went through quite a lot of this chatter and emerged without a clear sense of what such a phrase would even mean.

Absolute wealth? Wasn't wealth by definition the *relative* index of access to resources? An absolute relativity was a contradiction in terms.

Two of the Four, it seemed, 'lived' locally – in that attenuated sense that their physical bodies were located in particular places nearby. Jupita, as Alma knew, lived in R!-Town. The Golden Meteor's material corpus resided in north London, in a towering palace constructed on the top of Highgate Hill. Both had holdings of real-world properties all over the south-east, which seemed to Alma an odd financial play, given the continuing wane of the Real and the continuing ascendency of the Shine. But then again, such records as Alma could access only touched the iceberg tip of the prodigiously complex and capacious financial holdings both held in-Shine, so maybe the strategy was one of total domination.

Of the remaining two, the Stirk of Stirk was on a luxury yacht that sailed on a continuous clockwise voyage around the North Sea, up the east coast of the UK-EU, across to the Bergen littoral of Norway-EU and down past Denmark, Germany and the Netherlands. There was no reliable news as to where Cernowicz might be staying – some said London, others Helsinki, others again in a deep-delved bunker, a hangover from the Age of Nuclear Anxiety, in the Alps.

Checking on whether those two human bodies were still breathing, or not, was going to be a challenge.

4: *The Man Who Calls Himself Stanley*

Alma steered Marguerite through another complex, life-threatening bout of her malign designer pathology. Afterwards, as her patient slumbered, she went through to the front room and sat. She was too exhausted to sleep. For a while she pondered the frank contradiction of that state of mind. Then, for a long time, she did nothing but stare at the wall.

She needed fresh air.

She went for a walk.

R!-Town, never crowded, was emptier than ever these days. Rumours were circulating that an airborne nanotoxin that turned one's innards to slush was about to be released any day now. Any day! People, in the mass, are easily spooked, and this rumour spooked them. Counter-rumours mocked the very idea of a nanotoxin as fake news.

Alma knew better than that.

She walked, the innards of her head foggy, down deserted streets, under the communal hum of flying drones. From time to time she passed trundling cleaning bots. Once, only, she encountered another human being – asleep, in a clunking mesh-suit.

She walked down to the female of R!-town's two rivers, and along it for a while. She passed some willow trees trailing their green dreadlocks in the water, and turned to follow a path through a dull green lawn, trimmed but intermittently bald and spotted with splotches of duck excrement. Then, with a pang that was almost welcome, she felt the urge to lie down and sleep. She turned and started back home. Pine needles, she thought. Fir needles. Fur coat. Pine furniture. *Für Elise*.

The needle and the damage done. Something was trying to come up to the light, where she could consider it. Some octopoid hypothesis deep in her subconscious that was pulsing and writhing in the attempt to reach her conscious mind. What, though?

No – it was gone.

She was turning the corner, into the road on which her apartment block was situated, when a small, bearded man started walking towards her.

Always the flinch. Always the possibility that an attack was coming. He came closer. Small of stature. Shoulders like the McDonald's logo. A nervy manner that revealed itself, on closer acquaintance, to be actual eccentricity.

'Hello!' he called.

He was wearing no sort of mask, not even a handkerchief knotted around his chin, so presumably he was either unaware of, or uncaring about, the prevailing rumour swarm.

He pinged her, and she ignored it.

He doubled his pace to match hers.

'Hello, there!'

He had a quaint, clever-looking face, with slightly protuberant eyes. His black beard ran thickly under his chin and up both sides of his face to connect with his thick black hair, which made his high forehead and round-eyed face look as though it was framed in the middle of pulling-on a shaggy black sweater.

Then he said, 'Alma!'

'Do I know you?' she replied, in that specifically English way that meant *I don't know you*.

'Sorry, to, you know, flag you down. Alma, Alma, if I may,' he said, in a rapid, twitchy sort of voice. 'If I may. I'm a big fan. A big fan!'

'A fan?' Alma increduled.

'I'm Stan – how do you do?'

'You're Stan, a fan?'

'Though Stan is, *obviously*, not my real name.'

Alma thought about this for a moment, and took her thumb off the dettack in her pocket. Being harmlessly odd was not a reason to burst a man's eardrums, after all. She did not get the vibe from this little fellow that he was going to attack her. And she had been in her line of work long enough to come to trust her instincts.

'I don't understand,' she said. 'You're a fan? A fan of whom?'

'Of you, of course! Of *course* of you!'

Alma took a step backwards. 'You're a fan of me?'

'Of you and of Stanley Kubrick.'

This was just bizarre.

'Who?'

The bearded fellow looked carefully at her, as if trying to confirm what he felt must surely be true: that Alma was joking.

'Only the greatest maker of motion pictures in history. You're— You're not a connoisseur of the old film idiom? Lights – camera – action?'

'I'm not a connoisseur of *any* weight of camera action.'

Puzzlement momentarily manifested in Stan's eyes. Then he decided to believe she was joking.

'Very funny. *You're* funny. Kubrick!' he said. 'A true artist. One of the few.'

He did a happy little dance with his feet, back-forth, back-forth. Alma looked him up and down. He must be in his fifties. A loon, evidently.

'It's why I go by the name Stan,' he was explaining. 'In homage to his montage. And to hide my true identity from,' he leaned in and gave Alma a co-conspiratorial look, '*them*. But I'm not here to talk about Stanley Kubrick. I'm here to talk about *you*. Big fan, Ms Alma. Big fan.'

His face was, it seemed, prone to odd little twerks and twitches. Perhaps he had a nervous condition of some kind.

'I'm finding this conversation rather difficult to process,' said Alma. 'So, without wishing to offend you, I think I'll just—'

'In-Shine,' Stan said urgently, 'and I appreciate you don't go in there, but *in-Shine*, you know, there are whole fan clubs devoted to you, you know. Solving crimes and so on. I mean, if I'm completely honest there are fan clubs for almost everything in-Shine. And following true crime, and so on, is pretty niche. But niche in the Shine can be *huche*.' He coughed. 'Huge. It's where the majority live nowadays, after all. And your partner—'

Alma said, a little too quickly, 'What about her?'

'Nothing – nothing – only you do *know* she parcels datapacks of your more choice investigations and punts them in-Shine? She's no doctor, but she knows what's on, if you see what I mean, and what's on is you. Big star. Big!'

'I did know,' said Alma, which was at least a part-truth. She knew Marguerite liked to archive some of their cases, and to make them available online to people she called 'friends'.

'I mean,' she clarified, 'I didn't realise until recently that fan groups, plural, had accrued.'

'One main group. And a number of satellite groups. But still. I mean, the only thing she's not doing is monetising this material. People wonder if that's because you two just don't need the money, or—'

'Mr Fan,' said Alma, 'pleasant though it is to chat, I'm afraid I have a pressing appointment.'

'Oh, but I don't mean to keep you! Only – I have information. It's why I'm here.'

'Information?'

'I used to know a friend of yours. By the name of Pu Sto.'

Alma put her head a little to one side. 'Friend is not exactly the word I would choose. How did you know her?'

'I ran into her, through my work.'

'You were police?'

'Dear me no.' Stan did his little foot-shuffle dance again. 'But the stuff I did... I don't want to bore you with my boring old life story, but stuff I did meant that our two paths crossed, from time to time. All in the past now.'

'You're not doing that work any more?'

'Retired. Spending more time with my fannery.'

'If, by that...' Alma started, but ran out of steam before going any further. Who *was* this peculiar fellow?

'Anyway, the point is – I know you're currently working on something.' Some new look of wariness in Alma's expression prompted Stan to add, hurriedly, 'I mean, it's not *public* knowledge – it's not that your partner is providing a running commentary on cases as they are in the process of being investigated. That would be... No, obviously. I mean, I know about it, because... Look, the point is, the *point* is, the point really is, I can help you wrap up this case. And, as a fan, that would be just tremendous, for me. Tremendous.'

This was almost certainly mere blather, of course, but Alma saw no reason to ignore the possibility that there might be something in it.

'I really do have to go, right now.'

'Surely, surely.'

'But perhaps we could talk later?'

'Gladly.'

35

The man who called himself Stanley pinged her his details, and she stowed them in her porch, and went on her way.

And with that peculiar encounter behind her, Alma made her way home.

5: *Debt Tu, Brute*

As she washed up, having administered Marguerite's latest medical intervention, Alma said: 'I met a fan this morning.'

'Fan of whom?'

'Of us. Our work.'

'Well,' said Marguerite, stretching luxuriously upon her bed like a tonne of dough expanding in a vast oven, 'it's good to know that there are people in the world with both taste and good sense.'

'Did you know we have a fan club, in-Shine?'

'I did, as a matter of fact.'

Alma pounced. 'I know you did! Because this fan informed me you have been supplying datapacks of various of our cases to them.'

'Oh, not just to *them.*' Marguerite made a circular gesture with her dainty left hand. 'There are various people who lap it up, in-Shine. Not just our *affiliated* fans. The problem is in finding a way of monetising it. That, I confess, I have yet to crack. But, you see, I am at least *trying* to address the Marianas Trench of our debt.'

Alma did something she rarely did, these days, and climbed onto the edge of Marguerite's bed, and cuddled against her right arm and shoulder.

'I know,' she said, 'that you feel guilty about the money thing.'

'Not at all,' purred Marguerite. 'I repudiate guilt. Guilt is the mind-killer. Guilt is the little-death. I will not permit guilt to pass through me. When it has gone, I will have finished. Only the guilt will remain. No, wait. Strike that. Reverse it.'

'Maybe just a little bit of guilt?' Alma prompted.

'Well, perhaps a marginal quantity. Guilt-edged, let us say.'

'We're a team, you and I. This is us, not you.'

'Except that I am disproportionately the drain on our resources. They're my medical expenses, not yours. And except that I do not directly *contribute* to our income. Believe me, my dear, I am always aware of these facts – acutely so. My thinking was: perhaps by using my leisure time to parcel up one or two of our old cases in attractive packages, I could *sell* them, and so go some way towards at least the second of those issues. And what I'm doing at the moment is priming the pump. Creating a demand. Giving it away for free, so I can charge in the future. Well, that was the theory, at any rate. It doesn't seem to be working out so well in practice.'

'It's sweet of you to try. But we'll be all right, my love. Really we will!'

'The debt grows, month on month, Mah-mah. The negative number increases, the positive one becomes increasingly under-positive.'

'It's not so under-positive, really.'

'What I have discovered, to my annoyance,' Marguerite said peevishly, 'is how hard it is to make money by peddling anything in-Shine. It's awash with free content! If I put a price ticket on my little curated datasets, then people just ignore them. By putting it out free I at least attract the interest of a small group – and, once they have grown accustomed to my supply, perhaps then I can moon-et-*ise*. But my skills as a shaper are not au courant, my dear. What people in-Shine are prepared to pay for is fully immersive enviroes. If I had that skill set, and the time, and, you know, industrial levels of code-crunching hardware, I could recreate R!-town as an in-Shine enviro, and paint you in three-dee as Botticelli painted *Primavera*. Bring the whole thing to life. Make it all fully interactive – which, since my life is more inter*passive*, would mean bringing the whole thing to more-than-life. Bringing it to superlife. *Then* people would pay! They'd gobble up our cases and the money would flow into our account.'

'It's sweet that you're trying, Rita,' said Alma. 'You know what, though? A better bet would be: apply your superior intellect to this group-of-four problem. If we can pull together a satisfactory solution to this Jupita case – this super-wealthy person – the bonus alone would clear us entirely of debt.'

'For now, it would,' said Marguerite, warily. 'The debt would just start growing again, though.' But Alma could see that she was considering this.

'I've got a few things to sort out, first. Give me an hour, or so.'

'In an hour,' said Marguerite, smiling again, 'I will have cracked this case wide open, my dear.'

There was – at last! – a reply from the flirty police officer, Maupo, in her porch. It seemed it would be possible, perhaps as soon as the following day, to go and see the dead body of Alexa Lund, whose thumb had been so strangely punctured. Alma sent a generic reply, a prefab emoji indicating acceptance. Wouldn't do to be over-encouraging.

There was a call from Lez the Mis. That was odd: Lez *never* called – he didn't trust the system. But since Lez was one of their oldest friends, she accepted the call.

It was an old-fashioned call: no avatar, a strange whining noise behind the words which, Alma's sweeper filter told her, was a disruption app run by Lez himself. He always had been a paranoid old twit, and she would have been suspicious if he started manifesting any less paranoia now.

—Hello, Lez.

—Alma, replied Lez, in a sepulchral voice. You all right?

—Right enough, if not all. To what do we owe the pleasure?

—Owe, that's funny, said Lez, in a tone of voice as far removed from the conventional human response to something funny as can be imagined.

Alma owed Lez quite a lot of money, a debt incurred on a previous case that she had, as yet, been unable to repay.

—You'll get your money, Lez. It's just a question of time.

—Time, said Lez, I see. Question. Yes.

—Is that really why you called? To badger me about the money we owe?

—Things are tight, said Lez. Really I'm checking if you had any money invested in the AI investment pot.

—Money invested? Alma scoffed.

—It pays to spread your liability, and stocks can go down as well as up, Lez intoned, drearily. Lots of people invest, you know.

—No, Lez, said Alma. We're living hand to mouth here. We don't have spare cash sitting in little piles for us to dispose into an investment portfolio.

—Well, that's probably for the best, said Lez. The whole AI futures market has just crashed.

—You called to tell me this? Alma asked. Really?

—You didn't know?

—I don't follow the ups and downs of investment markets,

said Alma. I've better things to be doing. All that stuff happens in-Shine anyway.

—It's good to keep a weather eye on these things, Lez said, sulkily. Keep your ear to the ground.

—Sounds like an uncomfortable sort of posture.

Belatedly it occurred to Alma that Lez might have had a stake in this game.

—Wait, she said. Have you lost money in this tumble, Lez?

—It's a downer, drawled Lez, miserably. But then the entire vector of the universe is down, isn't it. I've been reading Heraclitus. Know much about Heraclitus?

—I've never even Heardaclitus, said Alma.

—Oh, you should read him. Everything is flow. Nothing retains its value, everything rushes away. Also Lucretius. *He* said every atom in the universe is plunging downwards into some vast and pitiless abyss. He was ancient, you see, early on in the history of philosophy, but he understood the reality of things. Understood it bone-deep.

—What happened, Lez? Did you lose a lot of money?

—I'm diversified, said Lez, gloomily, so the hit isn't *quite* as catastrophic as it might have been. He sighed, or else just breathed, since with Lez the two things tended to sound alike. It's depressing, though, he added. The last six months, stocks on Actual AI futures have been going up and up. Then – boom. *Down* they go.

—What happened?

—Rumours. Deflationary whirlpool. Investors believed the creation of genuine artificial consciousnesses was just around the corner and then, abruptly, investors stopped believing that. Something has *gone down*, Lez added, pronouncing those two words with relish, in the research arenas dedicated to this topic.

—There have always been people who argued Actual AI is simply impossible, said Alma.

—Maybe that's been proved true, agreed Lez. Or maybe some new approach has gazumped the old-fashioned approaches in which all the money has been invested. Either way the result is: I am placed in the awkward position of having to call in all my old debts.

—We will pay you, Lez, you know we're good for it, said Alma,

a sinking sensation in her gut. I've just picked up two quite promising new gigs, and when I'm paid *you* will be.

—We're friends, said Lez, you and I and Marguerite. But money
flows stronger than friendship's eddies. That's just the way of
things.

—You'll get paid, Alma insisted.

—If *you* get paid, Lez added, with the grim satisfaction of a
pessimist who thought that prospect unlikely.

—Solve the crimes and I get a bonus, Alma insisted. In fact,
I'm pursuing a valuable lead right now.

—Don't let me hold you up, said Lez, and rang off.

Alma washed, had a coffee, sorted through some files. A ping
in her feed told her it was time to go and meet her strange
Kubrickophile contact. Valuable lead, she told herself.

Yeah. Right.

She stepped through the main entrance of her block to the
smell of something harshly chemical, perhaps something burning
a long way off upwind. Alma stood in the deserted street outside
her apartment building and paused. Was she wasting her time?

Probably. But what was time, if not a resource to be frittered
away? She walked off.

Alma met the person who called himself Stan by the deserted
Oracle centre.

'We could sit somewhere,' he suggested. 'If you like. But if it's
all the same to you, I'd like to walk along the river. I don't get
out as much as I ought, really.'

'Happy to walk,' said Alma.

So they walked.

There are two rivers in R!-Town, the Thames and the Kennet,
and it was the former along which the two of them strolled. The
town itself, like any town, figures as an excrescence upon the
stream that first gave it a reason to exist: a palimpsest of bridges
and buildings, of overlays and stony redirections in the path of
the flow. It was a blue-sky day, brisk and bright. It had rained
only a few hours previously and the air was still in motion. Trees
shuddered and shook their hoary masses of leafage. The water slid
down its calcified channel as smoothly as silk blown by the wind.

'Do you sometimes get the urge,' Stan said, 'to vent a barbaric
yawp?'

'I do not,' said Alma.

'Just to cry *whoop*.' Stan started doing that, loudly, 'Whoop! Whoop!' and dancing around. 'Get it all out of your system! Whoop!'

'Please stop whooping,' Alma said.

The man who called himself Stan hunched over. It took a moment for Alma to realise that he was crying. But he really was – tears were visible on his cheeks.

'I'm sorry,' he said. 'I'm sorry! I know what you think. You think I'm touched – unbalanced – unhinged.'

'I don't make assumptions,' said Alma, debating with herself whether to abort the whole meeting. 'It's the nature of my work not to jump to conclusions.'

'That's good,' said Stan, smiling again. The unwiped tears still glittered on his face, but he seemed suddenly much cheerier. 'What can I do for you?'

'You offered,' Alma told him. 'You said you can help me with my current investigation.'

'That's right. And I think I can.'

'I'm puzzled as to how you even know what my investigation is. It's not public knowledge.'

'Oh, well, no.' Stan looked away. Was he blushing? Was he about to cry again? He seemed to be chewing the inside of his cheek.

Alma ran a discreet picking exercise, shunting the veiled hook of an app at Stan's porch, where his feed presented itself for interaction with the world. It was an expensive app, and designed to fit seamlessly with Alma's own feed; she had used it several times before, and had a good record of unzipping people's encysted feeds. Stan, though, presented a smooth surface to her careful poke. Nothing.

She reappraised the situation. However eccentric Stan appeared in the flesh, his feed was, in effect, wrapped in stainless steel. And that meant he was a pro.

'So, you said your line of work brought you into contact with Pu Sto?'

'A while ago, if I'm honest.'

'Has *she* put you up to this?'

'Dear me! The very idea.'

'Stanley, I'm going to be honest. I sometimes need to infiltrate or unpick people's feeds, in the line of my work. I just had a discreet look at yours, and—'

'I know you did.' He looked at her and grinned, his black mane of beard bristling as his cheeks bulged. 'I'm not offended – it's prudent of you. It's fine. And in a way I'm honoured. Really, I'm *such* a fan.'

'Those are some industrial level professional counter-measures you have there, Stanley. What was it you did?'

'I did... oh, various things. For a highly monetised company that dealt with... let's say, security. But then I became persona non grata.'

'Did you break the law?'

'Much worse. I fell in love with somebody from a different company.'

'Oh.'

'I know, right? Montagues and Capulets of the money-making classes. All that kerfuffle, and my love life caught in the middle of it. Foolish, really. It didn't matter – I was ready to go. So go is what I did. I went. Don't miss it.'

'You've clearly not left it entirely behind.'

'What?' said Stanley, looking distracted. 'Say – who? What?'

Alma wondered if this was the real person, or only an act. If it was the latter it was bizarrely clumsily performed, which inclined her to the belief that it might be the former.

'I'm guessing,' she said, 'you have contacts, or in-Shine skills, and maybe both. And I'm thinking I'm going to need a deep clean of all my protection protocols when I get home.'

'Oh, I haven't hacked *you*, Alma. That would be terribly bad manners, don't you think? I'm a true fan – really! I respect what you do so very much. No, no. When a person has a personal meeting, an actual face-to-face, with one of the Four, word gets about. In certain circles. That's all.'

'I see.'

'You're in a dangerous place, Alma. It's why I decided to break cover.'

'Break cover?'

He nodded, emphatically.

'Fan cover?' Alma pressed.

'Could we sit down for a bit?' Stan asked. 'My legs aren't what they were.'

They found a bench, kept scrupulously clean by R!-Town council bots for an almost complete absence of R!-Town bottoms, and sat. The view was across the Thames to an expensive-looking apartment block on the far side, with many well-apportioned river-view balconies that none of the occupants ever took advantage of. A person (man or woman, it wasn't possible to determine) in a mesh-suit was attempting to climb an exterior staircase, but the passageway was blocked by a closed-up gate that the suit's software was, evidently, not expecting. For some reason, instead of turning about and finding another way, it walked up to the shut gate, stopped, walked down backwards, and then walked up again. Alma watched the figure's progress and regress for a while.

'Some glitch in the suit's ware,' was Stan's opinion.

'Presumably.'

'It's a strange business,' said Stan, shortly. 'When you're in that world – I mean, security. You're a sort of go-between. On the one hand, wealthy private citizens. On the other, governance. Civil Service. The security services, in the broadest sense. And then – Health. There are departments supposedly dedicated to in-Shine governance, and tax collection, and so on. But really it's Health. Because it was Health who grasped, early on, that everything hinges on the bodies. People in-Shine don't want to be bothered with their corporeality, not more than they have to be. And Health is the department that looks after those bodies, which gives them tremendous power. Add to that the freak of our criminal justice system that means felons serve their time in-Shine, in virtual prisons, which gives control of their bodies to Health as well... I'm sure I'm not telling you anything you don't know.'

'No,' said Alma.

'No-no. No. I know-know *you* had... personal experiences with Pu Sto. I mean, I had dealings with her, once or twice. I did my best to keep myself and my clients out of her way. But I never had anything that amounted to a *personal* experience with her.'

Alma said nothing.

'As I said – I happened to fall in love with... Well, I don't want to make something big and melodramatic out of it. Happens all the time.' Stanley stared across the Thames for a while. 'And stepping down from the position I'd held... I had plenty of offers of work. I was freelance for a while. But even when you stop working for *it*, you discover it's almost impossible to avoid the gravitational zone of *it*,' and he paused. Then he made a strange expression, a wide-eyed open-mouthed surprise face like a human emoji.

'"It"?' Alma prompted.

He looked at her as though he was surprised to see her still there. Then he said, 'Money.'

Alma said nothing.

'Oh, sure. There once was ... I mean, if you're interested in *history* – there probably once was a time when the people with the overt power – I mean, the politicians, monarchs and emperors and so on – there probably was a time when *they* had the money. I guess the ruler of imperial China, or the Egyptian pharaohs, or whatever, had all the money there was to have, back then. All the money there was to have in their kingdoms, at any rate. But that stopped being true, I suppose, a thousand years ago. By the Middle Ages, monarchs were no longer rich. Powerful in a secular sense, sure. Could raise armies and invade countries, yes, order castles built and swan about wearing fine clothes, sure. But to pay for all that the monarchs had to borrow money from bankers. So though the monarchs might be powerful, only the bankers were rich. And since money underlies all the other sorts of power, money turns out to be the only sort of powerful. In the long run.'

Alma was watching the interference pattern of ripples on the Thames as it flowed past. Stanley seemed to have calmed down, somewhat.

'Obviously politicians do have *power*,' he went on. 'The law gives them leverage. They command the police and the army. But their power only goes so far. And governments now exclusively operate as debt-driven entities. The more ambitious the government, the bigger the debt. Every now and again a politician will talk about the need to pay down the debt, but that never happens. I mean, it never does, does it?'

Alma said nothing.

'It's like *Eyes Wide Shut*. Wealth, hidden behind weird masks.'

Her feed was giving her a series of links pertaining to this title, and also its director, whose look – Alma now saw – 'Stanley' was mimicking. A quick summary of the movie: images, links to visuals if she wanted to follow them up.

She didn't. 'I'm really not much of a one for antique movies,' she told him.

His mouth made a moue so severe it briefly gave him a harelip. But then he settled into a smile that said *you are joking, of course*.

'There are lots of interesting directors,' he told her, as if confiding a great truth. 'But only one Kubrick.'

She tried to bring him back to the matter in hand. 'So you worked for Money.'

'We both did.'

'You and the person with whom you fell in love?'

'Both of us.'

'But you don't work for money any more?'

'Neither of us, any more. For different reasons.'

'I assume we are talking,' Alma prompted, 'about the Big Four? I assume that's how you know the case I'm on? And why you think you can assist me?'

Was that a nod? Or just another weird twitch of Stan's head? For a while he sat silently, watching the river flow. Eventually he spoke.

'Well, that's the thing about *money*, you see. It's a much more thorough-going hierarchy than any democracy ever was. There are the majority of people, and their lives are debt. And then there are the wealthy, with modest reserves, a much smaller group. Then there are the ultra-wealthy – the Four, the Fab Four, let's call them whatever. But you can't make money without speculating, and borrowing, and so on: it's all in the *flow*. S-s-so even the modestly wealthy are in hock to the top hounds. You know?'

'If I understand you correctly, that's a very roundabout way of answering my question with a yes.'

'Yes I said yes I did yes.'

'Yes you worked for one of the four?'

'Yes yes yes,' said Stanley, shifting his position on the bench, 'which, backwards, is *sey, sey, sey*.' He sang the last three syllables on three rising notes, the root, minor third and fifth of a minor chord.

He was, Alma reflected, fairly bonkers.

'Stanley—' she started.

But he was singing lustily now. '*Sey sey sey what you want, Bert*,' then a deep breath, then, '*Don't, play agames awith my affliction*.'

'Stanley!'

He stopped singing. 'What?'

'Which one?'

'Which one? Which of the four? Well, I'll tell you. Understand, I was no *personal* assistant or anything. I was never part of any inner sanctum. But I was useful to her. For my security expertise. My contacts in government. And private industry research.'

'Not for your encyclopaedic knowledge of the films of Stanley Kubrick?'

Stanley turned his head and looked at her. He was scowling. But then he smiled – genuinely.

'Your deadpan is very good, Ms Alma. Very good. It's one of the things that makes being a fan of yours so rewarding. Your deadpan-handling.'

Her feed gave her no alternatives for the meaning of that word, so she ignored it.

'Which one, Stanley?' she pressed. 'Which of the Four?'

Stanley turned his face back towards the river. For a while Alma wondered if he simply wasn't going to answer.

But then he said, 'The one they call the Golden Meteor.'

'I was speaking to one of her underlings only this morning. He assured me the GM is alive.'

'Alive, yes,' muttered Stanley.

'You think that's right?'

'In what sense are any of us truly alive, though? We give birth astride the grave. The light flickers for an instant, and then – what? What? Oh yes. You should *talk* to her, you know.'

'I was told a face-to-face would be out of the question.'

'Oh, I could arrange that,' said Stanley offhand. 'Easily.'

Alma didn't reply. Was this an actual offer, or just another example of Stanley's unhinged manner? His in-Real manner suggested he might be delusional. But his feed suggested a steely sanity, or at least a professionalism. The walls of Troy were not higher or more cyclopean than his defensive set-up. It was not the set-up of a crank. It was the feed set-up of somebody who knew what they were doing, and didn't like to take risks.

He was humming another song now – 'Mull of Kintyre', her feed informed her.

Then he stopped. 'You should . . . you know,' he said. Then he stood up and performed a theatrical double-shoulder shrug, exaggerated and peculiar. 'Should *follow the money*. Follow the

47

money is good advice for a private investigator, investigating a crime, don't you think?'

'If a crime has been committed,' Alma said, by way of agreeing.

'Oh, there's always a crime. That's the thing about money. It and crime are conjoined.' And he started off, along the river.

She watched him go.

6: *Tym Flies*

Whether it was a direct consequence of Stan's promised intervention – the seriousness of which Alma rather doubted – or just a coincidence, by the time she had finished Marguerite's next treatment there was a message from the GM's personal assistant, Mr Tym, suggesting a second face-to-face meeting. Was there a restaurant or coffee emporium convenient to Alma's habitation? There are several, Alma replied, and they agreed on one.

'Well,' she told Marguerite, 'that's unexpected. Him actively seeking me out, I mean.'

'Something's changed,' said Marguerite. 'That can only be good.'

Alma tugged the tag on her socks and they hardened into shoes. 'We'll see.'

'I have hacked one of your Fab Four,' said Marguerite, with calculated offhandedness as Alma took a step towards the door.

Alma stopped. 'What?'

'The Stirk one. Lives on a boat, you know.'

'You *hacked* him?'

'Surely.'

'Marguerite, what are you doing? I mean, apart from playing with fire and endangering us all?'

'Not *illegal* hacking,' said Marguerite, haughtily. 'You think me a child? No, no. I have an old friend who works for the coastal services. There's long-standing legislation on platforms that opt for non-national affiliation – sealands and blimpworlds and so on. It makes their people rather easier to monitor than regular EU citizens, strangely enough, although I'm sure that wasn't the intention of the people who set up these semi-independent little princedoms. I mean, I can't see *inside* the boat. But I can tell you that a doctorbot, accompanied by a human being with medical training, was flown out to the boat four days ago.'

'Somebody as wealthy as the Stirk surely has his own doctorbot.'

'Presumably there's one on the boat, yes. But, for whatever reason, they needed another. A specialist perhaps, or perhaps the one on board malfunctioned, I *don't* know. But I do know this – no death was certified, as it would must needs have been if anybody on the boat had stopped living.'

'Four days ago,' Alma mused. 'Strangely contiguous timing for the boat's own doctorbot to go down, don't you think?'

'The human being might be bribed to lie, of course,' Marguerite was saying. 'We are dealing with ultra-wealth here. But the doctorbot – not.'

'So we assume the Stirk of Stirk is alive. That's two we can tick off the list. And if we can trust Tym, then the GM is alive too, so that only leaves Cernowicz.'

'I'm not sure he is to be trusted,' was Marguerite's opinion. 'This Tym chap.'

'My hunch,' said Alma, leaning over the bed and kissing her on the cheek, 'is that all four are alive and well and this whole nonsense is a pointed pointlessness.'

'A case that promised so much,' wailed Marguerite, in mock-distress. 'Turning out to be nothing but a squib! Ah well, there's always the Punctured Thumb. She's *definitely* dead, and that's definitely a case to solve.'

'One thing at a time,' Alma said.

By the time Alma got to the coffee shop Tim Tym was already there. He was wearing a different shirt from the morning meeting, together with a gold-and-silver tartan jacket and trousers. The red-purple tie was the same, though, and there was the faintest sheen of unshaved stubble on his fashionably pale cheeks.

As she sat down, a number of discreet alarms pinged in Alma's feed.

Tym, watching her, said, 'I assume alerts will be going off in your feed. I have Faraday-caged the shop – just for the ten minutes or so it will take to have a conversation. Not the full cage, nothing crass, nothing to get the police worried. But I don't want to be eavesdropped upon. Not by any Tomboy, Dick or Harriet.'

Alma said nothing.

A bot trundled over and peed out a cup of black coffee from its nozzle. When it had trundled away again, Tym nodded and offered his hand. She stared at it, and then shook it. It was warmly moist, and not particularly pleasant. She squeezed a little antibac gel out of a pouch inside her jacket and rubbed her hands together.

Tym seemed nervous.

'Thank you for meeting me,' he said.

'I was a little surprised to get your call,' she said. 'If I'm honest.'

'How so?'

'You weren't exactly *forthcoming* at our previous meeting.'

'Oh, it's nothing personal, absolutely nothing personal,' drawled Tym. 'One gets used to treating the unrich as ... Look, I don't mean to be offensive, but – really. I mean, look at you! I don't mean the blood-and-bone you. That seems fine. I mean, look at the *fiduciary* you. I don't mean to be condescending, but your debt – your whole public feed just *reeks* of it.'

Alma smiled a hard smile. 'You'll find me an unwelcome condescendee, I promise you.'

'Sure, sure. Money isn't ...' Finding the right word with which to conclude his sentence seemed to be taxing him to a remarkable degree. 'Everything,' he finished, and looked slightly scared, like a priest uttering a blasphemy.

Alma waited.

'You know the old song, money can't buy me love?' Tym asked. He was running a manicured forefinger around the square block of his tie's knot. 'If you think about it for half a second you can see it's not true. The only person who would say money can't buy you love is a person who doesn't have enough money. It's not actually a song about love, that one. It's a song about poverty.'

'I wouldn't call myself a connoisseur of antique music.'

'Money *can* of course buy you anything at all,' Tym went on. 'Really. Actually, love is one of the easiest things to buy. If only you have enough money, people *will* love you. And I mean any kind of love. Rich people have been paying poor people to make love to them, to *pretend* to love them, for as long as there have been rich people and poor people. You'll say, but that's only an act. And I'll say, the act is what you get if you don't pay enough. Pay the proper rate and you get the reality.'

He sipped his coffee, and stared past Alma's shoulder.

'You don't have money,' he said eventually, as if he had summed her up in a single phrase.

'We can go further. I have less than money. If I wanted to be more precise, I could say I have quite a large amount of unmoney.'

'Debt,' said Tym. 'Credit. You know where the word credit comes from? *Credere*, Latin for belief. Money is not gold coins, or paper notes, or the manifestation of surplus value, or externalised labour, or a ratio of supply to demand, or anything like that. Money is belief. Simple as that. What is the whole of human society? A complicated network that subsists from month to month because people believe in it. What is politics? Belief. What is love? Love is what you believe about another person. What is God? That in which people believe. And what *is* belief? It's another word for credit – for money.'

Alma said nothing. He was working his way round to saying something important, she could see. Whatever he was trying to say was making him pretty nervous. Best not to interrupt him.

'I find it amusing that Jupita calls the group the Fab Four. Fabulous. Legendary. Mythical. Wizards and demigods and magic. Since magic happens when we suspend our disbelief, in that sense it's apt. You know what my boss calls Jupita?'

'Nothing flattering, I'm sure.'

'She calls her Twenty-five. She means cents. You know? A quarter. She calls all the other members of the group "quarters". Together the three of them add up to *less* than one dollar. It's money, you see – it's just not very much money, compared to what the GM commands.'

'But even the GM hasn't achieved *absolute* wealth,' said Alma.

Tym shook his head slowly. 'Do you know what absolute wealth means, Ms Alma?'

'My feed supplies a number of, frankly, conflicting definitions.'

'In the old days, before the Shine, there were rich people and poor people. There was a global economy, of which local econom-ies were subsets. To be absolutely rich in such a situation wasn't a tenable dream. It would have meant, I suppose, one person owning the entire wealth of the globe. But how would such a state of affairs work? Other people would still need money to buy and sell, to trade and save. So it would mean one person would own all the money, and everybody else would borrow little bits from her. It would mean a global economy in which everybody on the planet was a debtor to one person.'

'Wouldn't people opt out? Set up private independent barter systems and so on.'

'They might try. But it would be straws. One person would

own all the forests. She might shut down independent barter systems – she could certainly afford the muscle to do that. She might simply ignore it.'

'Hard to see such a set-up working.'

'It came closer than you might think, in the early twenty-first century, although with the Chinese government instead of one individual person. But that's ancient history now.' He fiddled at the knot of his tie again. 'Through the twentieth century the gap between the rich and the poor got narrower. Then, through the twenty-first, it widened sharply again. But all that was predicated on the antique economies. The Shine has changed everything. The Shine is where almost all the wealth is being generated nowadays. You see, economics works differently there.'

'Everything works differently there.'

'You solve crimes. I'll save you a whole lot of bother where your job is concerned. I'll solve all your past and future crimes here, now. I'll get to the bottom of every case you'll ever work. It's always money.'

'The motive, you mean? I'm not sure I agree. Sometimes it's money, sure. Sometimes other things – power, maybe. Jealousy.'

'No, no – I don't mean motive. The *whole crime*. It's the murderer and the motive and there is no other. Power is just a word for what money gives you – and without money power is impossible.'

'Tell that to Gandhi.'

'You think Gandhi wasn't wealthy? Just because he wore a loincloth? If he'd told his followers "every one of you must give me ten rupees", you think they wouldn't have done it? If he'd said to them "give me all your money", they'd have done it. He held India in his palm, and India was a superbly wealthy country back in the nineteenth...' A flicker as he checked his own feed, 'eh, *twentieth* century. That was why Britain assimilated it into their empire, after all.'

'He didn't, though,' said Alma. 'He didn't do what you said.'

'Didn't have to! Being wealthy doesn't mean rolling a barrel full of dollar bills through the desert – it means having *access* to wealth. It's the access, not the conspicuous display. Access is power. Gandhi had access to pretty much the entire wealth of India in ways the British colonial administration didn't, as they discovered, to their cost.'

'I feel like we're splitting hairs.'

'We're not. It's very important you understand this, if you want to solve the case. This case – all your cases. It's always money. Maybe there was once a time when there was a total set sum of money in the world – the total amount of gold that exists, say. And theoretically one person could have owned all that gold. But money hasn't been a static scale for a very long time now. For half a millennium. Money is fluid, and it grows. It can be created ex nihilo. It's in constant flux, and constantly expanding – in the Shine above all. How could one person ever possess all that?'

'So,' said Alma, 'you're saying your boss's dream of absolute wealth is a chimera?'

'You're coming at this the wrong way,' said Tym. Behind his suavity there was, Alma thought, a quantity of panicky desperation, and it was closer to the surface than she had at first realised. 'You're not thinking in the right way. Imagine you're one of the world's ultra-super-rich, Europe's four wealthiest people. You have spent your life making money. Now you understand that money has made you. You have more money than you could ever spend. What are you going to do – give it up and pass your time playing games? Collecting stamps? Not if you're a person of the calibre of my boss.'

He was fingering his tie-knot again. His Cary Grant manner was failing to disguise how perilously on-edge he was.

What was he scared of?

'So,' said Alma, deciding it was time to bring things to a point. 'What's on your mind, Mr Tym?'

'What do you *really* know about the Four?' Tym asked.

'I know that they're exceptionally wealthy, but that they're not wealthy enough for their own satisfaction. I know that they are collectively – which in fact means individually – working towards what they call absolute wealth.'

'OK. So, that's what everybody knows. So, I'm going to tell you something that very few people know. It's why I'm here.'

'You're telling me this with your boss's permission? At her instigation?'

The look Tym gave her made it clear that neither circumstance obtained.

'What do you think,' he asked, fiddling with his tie knot, 'their planned route to absolute wealth involves?'

'I've honestly no idea. I'm not sure I even understand what absolute wealth is.'

'Shall I tell you?'

Alma looked at him.

He met her gaze, but only for a moment. Then he stared over her shoulder, into the middle distance.

'I'm going to say monetising the Shine, and you're going to misunderstand me.'

Alma waited, but Tym looked, almost, as if he had shocked himself into silence.

'I was talking about this with my partner a few hours ago,' said Alma, when it became apparent Tym wasn't going on. 'She for one would like to find a way of monetising the Shine – to generate an income out of the stuff she posts there. Stuff about our cases and so on. So monetising in the sense of persuading people to pay for things they're not currently paying for. Yes?'

'So it is you misunderstand what I mean,' said Tym, in a low voice.

'Edify me.'

'I don't mean monetise in the sense of extracting money *from* the Shine,' said Tym, in a tired voice. 'Millions do that already, some of them quite effectively. I mean, to reconfigure the structure of the Shine itself. I mean, to turn the Shine *into* money.'

Alma waited.

'The Four – they are engaged in today's biggest project. Biggest and most important. They are seeking properly to understand money for the first time in human history. To redefine it for the age of the Shine, to get under its skin. And the person who can do that…' He left this hanging.

'I'm afraid you're going to have to spell that out for me, Mr Tym. In what sense, *redefine?*'

'We're getting hot, Ms Alma. You and me. You know that? Closer to the centre of the heat. And it could melt our faces. There's a ruthlessness here that's—'

He blew out his cheeks like a jazz trumpeter and let the air go with the sound of a distant explosion, accompanying the noise with a gesture with both his hands, pulling them apart from one another.

Alma said nothing.

'You want to solve your puzzle, Ms Alma? Follow the money.'

'That is the proverbial phrase,' Alma agreed.

'The smart money. Yes? The smart money.'

'OK.'

'I'm serious. Keep your eye on the smart money.'

'I will keep,' Alma returned, puzzled at the vehemence with which he said this, 'my eye on the smart money.'

He fell silent, and appeared to be musing. 'In the old world,' Tym said, shortly, 'or in the real-world as it used to be, money was a function of scarcity. Some things are more abundant than other things. If there are lots of some things and only a few of others, then the first kind of thing will be cheaper and the second kind more expensive. So you need a scale to measure cheaper and expensive, and to allocate those resources. Money begins as an index of scarcity.'

Alma said nothing. She didn't want to put him off. He was working round to telling her something big, she knew it.

'There are lots of berries and roots, but it's not often the tribe gets meat. Or, many go barefoot, some wear clogs, but only a few people can afford the leather and cobbler's expertise to wear elegantly designed shoes. Or, no, a better example, from the last iteration of the old economy – the one the Shine has replaced. Housing. Really, it's hard to overstate how crazy people became where the housing market was concerned, back in the day. So, all right, think back. There are only a few really nice mansions; there are rather more ordinary two-up-two-downs, and many more shitty rooms and slums and run-down flats in bad areas. The first cost a fortune, the second cost a lot, the last cost less. So people with lots of money can afford to buy mansions, and the rest bid against one another for the nice houses, or else reconcile themselves with living in shitholes, or else – you know: sleep on the street. Owning a mansion is a way of saying "this person is wealthy". Yes?'

Alma nodded.

'The whole old-world economy was predicated upon scarcity. But the Shine is not like that. Anybody can log on, and once you're *in* scarcity simply doesn't exist. In the Real, there are only a few mansions because there's a limited amount of land, and raw materials are expensive and so on. But in the Shine there's an infinite amount of virtual space and raw materials are, in effect, free. You want to live in a mansion? Go right ahead. You want to conjure up an entire planet and be the sole inhabitant and world-leader-pretend? Sure. Do what you like. So the economy of the Shine is necessarily radically different from the economy of the real world.'

'This,' said Alma, 'is hardly buzz-buzz news.'

'And you might say – great. You *might* say – this means we don't need to worry about money any more. The Shine can be an actual utopia, that ancient human dream. But we've lived with it for many decades now and, clearly, it's not working out that way.'

'You spend more time in-Shine than I. I'll take your word.'

'For thousands of years money has been a way of parsing scarcity – a way of allocating scarce resources. What happens to money when scarcity is no longer a thing?'

'And that's what the Four are trying to settle?'

'Because if any one of them can establish that – then they will be establishing the grounds of *wealth as such* in the Shine. Do you see how important that would be? In the antique world you might become absolutely wealthy by, I don't know, seizing control of all the gold mines. But that strategy's not going to work in an environment without any such objective correlative to wealth. An environment in which wealth is constantly shifting and expanding. What *might* work is if you *become the gold mine*. If you define what wealth is as such, and everybody else in the Shine is excavating *your* resource – playing by your rules. If everyone in the Shine is in your debt.'

'Become the gold mine,' said Alma. 'Right.'

'I mean, at the moment, the Shine is in transition. It's still sort-of tied to the real world, at least to some extent. It's tied less than it was ten years ago, but still. We all have bodies in reality, and that means we have to maintain property, pay taxes and the like. So old-world actual money mixes with the various protocols and clubcard points and specialist tokens and so on. But it won't be like that for much longer. We can be honest – eventually everyone will migrate wholesale to the Shine. Because it's better.'

'Not I,' said Alma.

Tim Tym smiled. 'My feed is suggesting Samuel Beckett as a line to pursue. Which is pretty stonkingly apt, I'd say. Of course not *you*, my dear woman. I understand your situation. And of course a rump will remain, in-Real. But the centre of gravity of humanity will transfer to the Shine – has already transferred, to be honest. Pretty much all the people who matter. Do you know what Leper Colony Money was?'

'You want that I should check my feed?'

'It's not the raw facts of the phenomenon – it's the way it signifies that's important. In the days before there was a cure, lepers were grouped together into colonies, to keep them away from uninfected populations. Each leper colony was a community, with houses and shops and so on, sealed away from the larger world. And each had its own dedicated coins and banknotes, because people didn't like the idea of handling money that had been handled by lepers. There was no basis for this – you can't catch leprosy from a banknote. But they didn't know that back then, so each colony had a unique currency. And now there are no more leper colonies, which means their currency is of interest only to collectors. It's not worthless, you understand, but it is only valuable insofar as history buffs and collectors will expend real money on it. And that's what's going to happen to the euro and the dollar and the yen. Sooner than you think, too.'

'What is going to replace the traditional currencies?'

'Each of the Four has their own approach,' said Tym, fingering his tie-knot. He was becoming more evidently nervous the longer they talked. 'And naturally they want to keep a close eye on what the other three are about. In case their idea is better. None of them want to be gazumped. And of course each of the Four want to stop the others from getting too close to realising *their* idea.'

'They're all trying to identify the scarcity in an environment, like the Shine, in which nothing is scarce.'

'Adequately put,' said Tym, smiling for the first time during their meeting. 'My boss has a sense of the others' strategies, of course. Broadly speaking.'

Alma waited.

'There's the Stirk of Stirk – the Scot, you know? His idea is the oldest. An antique idea, the GM calls it, for an antique individual. He made the first of his money the old-fashioned way, by serving sexual desires. You know Orgasmatropolis?'

'I've never visited.'

'Oh, you should. It's very good. Although I know you don't venture in-Shine. Anyway, not to get distracted. Back when the Internet was getting going there was a thing called Bitcoin – your feed will supply all the ins-and-outs, if you're interested. The idea was, basically, a processing chain that released coins to people prepared to work their way along the processing algorithm. It was costly in terms of time and processing power, and became more costly the further along the chain one worked. Mining, they called it. Each individual miner would verify the whole chain prior to excavating more coins – or fractions of coins. You see, early on Bitcoins were easy to come by, and later they were much harder, and there was an asymptote that meant that... I mean, I don't need to get into it, since history overtook it. Processing became so vastly more rapid, it meant the entire chain was swamped. The mine got mined out. But that, or a variant of it, is the philosophy of money that the Stirk is pursuing. He reckons he can forge a Shine-friendly version of blockchain, and that everyone in-Shine will gravitate towards it, such that it becomes the key mode of currency. My boss thinks he's barking up the wrong tree. I tend to agree. As you'd expect of somebody who likes porn, the Stirk's mind is a linear sort of thing. He's not terribly imaginative.'

'So, Blockchain,' said Alma. 'That's one. What about the others?'

'There's Cernowicz. Her line is that there are scarcity indices online, even if only very very minor ones. The Shine needs power to run, and even though power generation nowadays is laughably cheap, compared with the historical baseline, it is still a cost. She thinks the future is in finding a mutually agreed and objectively fair way of scaling those costs up. My boss thinks this the most daft of suggestions, but Cerno made an absolute fortune by micro-programs that traded stocks and shares on a vast scale in fractal interstices of the usual trading chronometry, so she's no fool.'

'And what about your boss? What's her theory?'

There was no mistaking the change that came over Tym when Alma asked this question. He grew manifestly more nervous.

'Of course you ask that.'

'I'm not attempting industrial espionage,' said Alma. 'I'm on a case. And it's a case you clearly think has enough merit to be worth seeking me out, and telling me all this.'

'Yes,' said Tym, looking doleful. 'I know you are on a case. Well, I can share something about the broader shape of the GM's theory. None of this stuff is *particularly* secret, if you know where to look. It's just that most people aren't interested. Too many in-Shine distractions and attention sinks. And let me say this before I go any further. One reason I'm working for the GM rather than anybody else is that she is the smartest of any of the Four. Easily the smartest. The Stirk has a linear mind, Cernowicz a devious one, Jupita is too eager to be liked, bouncing around like a puppy. The GM's intelligence has clarity and depth.'

Alma waited.

Eventually Tym said, 'Time.'

'Time.'

'It's the one scarcity that's unavoidable. It's baked into existence itself, in-Shine just the same as in-Real. Because we're mortal beings. Put it this way – you can, in the Shine, pretty much coin anything, with this one exception. You can't coin *time*.'

'Wingéd chariot,' agreed Alma.

Again, the merest pause while Tym checked his feed for the reference.

'Oh, that's good. I hadn't seen that before. Oh, I like that.'

'Time,' Alma prompted him.

'So my boss's thinking is: it's the one non-negotiable. That's not to say it's an absolute and objective benchmark. Some people have more time before them, some less. The conventionally rich can afford the best medical and other interventions to stretch out their time, for instance. The conventionally poor die younger. I mean, your partner – she only has, what, four hours and four minutes at any given moment?'

Alma sat up straighter, restrained her knee-jerk hostility.

'Your point?'

'I'm sorry,' said Tym. 'I didn't mean to rile you up. Touch on a sensitive spot. But you see what I mean? I won't go into all the ins and outs, but that's my boss's strategy, her broad approach. Time is the only scarcity in-Shine, so time will prove the ground of any new in-Shine currency.'

'Mr Tym, I have been hired by Jupita to investigate what she believes is a crime. I appreciate you meeting with me, but I can't honestly say that what you've said helps me do that.'

'Have you...' said Tym, a kind of anguish becoming visible in his face, 'have you been paying attention *at all*?'

'Mr Tym—'

'My boss really is alive and well. I really did see her this morning. I can't speak for the other two. But do you understand what we're talking about? We're talking about *all the money in the world* – in the world as it is coming into being, the only world

60

that matters now, the in-Shine world. Only imagine the level of incitement to crime this represents!'

'What about Jupita? What's her strategy for establishing money in the Shine?'

'That's a little harder to summarise. It has to do with flows and intensities and pools and nodes and fluid dynamics. A concoction of physics and cultural theory. She's obsessed with things like friendship networks, social status, the way those ebb and flow. It's something to do with that, so far as we can tell. She thinks that old money required static markers – a gold mine exists in a certain place and can't move. The same thing with a house, or a farm. Banks were static structures, and although the *contents* of a gold mine might be moved, it was laborious and expensive, so it wasn't done very often. But, she thinks, the Shine is not fixed like that. It is a place of perfect, frictionless flow. And so far as we can see, Jupita's theory is to try and ground the new money *in that flow.*'

'How?'

'We're not sure. It's not clear that such a thing is even possible, actually. Obviously we have theories, but that's all they are at this point – theories. Something to do with aping friendship networks, the old valences of social media, likes and whatnot.'

'Likes instead of coins?'

'Presumably nothing so crass. But in that ballpark. The point is – you remember what I said about the smart money?'

'To keep my eye on it.'

'There you have it. With the sorts of people we're dealing with, the crucial thing is to keep a close eye on what the smart money is doing.'

Tym put both his hands to his tie. He straightened the length of it, making it more perfectly vertical, and untightened the knot a fraction. Then he dropped his hands to his sides and winked at Alma.

Winked.

What?

'Mr Tym,' Alma pressed, 'at our last meeting, you called Jupita's suspicions groundless, and now you're ...' She stopped. Tym was going red in the face. Embarrassment?

Some sixth sense provoked Alma to select the only really

important question, at that time, in that place, and presented it to her consciousness.

'Just now you said *money isn't everything,*' she said. 'Just now. What did you mean?'

Tym opened his eyes wide in what looked to Alma like a confirmation. But his red face was now tinged with purple. His eyes were bulging like button mushrooms. The veins were painfully visible on his neck, creepers wrapped around a tree trunk.

'Money,' he gasped, his voice like sandpaper rubbed on tarmac. 'Will be. Everything.'

'What do you mean?'

'Smart money,' said Tym, gasping. 'Where the *smart money* goes—'

Alma had been stuck in her seat by some inertia of surprise. But the spell broke, and she threw herself across the table at Tym.

'How do I loosen it?'

'Hhhhhh,' said Tym, his tongue coming out of his mouth like a stub of liquorice.

Alma tried to dig her fingers in under the circle the tie made around the man's throat, but it was like a hoop of steel, and digging deeper into the flesh. She scrabbled, struggled, tried to pull the tie back. It had vanished into his flesh. His face was black. No air was going to his lungs. No blood was getting to his brain.

'Get me a knife,' she bellowed at the bot that had trundled over to see what the commotion was. 'Or some scissors!'

There was a crunching sound, as of bones breaking.

It was too late. Tym was dead.

7: *Change is as Good as Arrest*

It took four minutes for the police to arrive on the scene – two myrmidrones and a *very* young-looking human officer with a surprised look on her face.

'Golly,' she said, on entering the coffee shop. 'Gracious me.' The surprised look, it quickly became apparent, was a permanent aspect of her manner.

Before the police arrived Alma had had long minutes alone with a corpse. In that time she discovered a couple of things. One was that the same drones who served coffee, and who were (she knew) liable to sprout metalcord lassos and electrical prod-rods if a customer attempted to leave without paying for their drinks, were simply not programmed to deal with a death on the premises. They didn't even seem to recognise that Tym *was* a corpse, and kept trundling up to him to offer him a top-up of his drink.

Tym's face was now as black as his coffee, his tongue leered like a devil pulling a face and his eyes protruded in a most distressing fashion. The tie was sunk so deep into the flesh of his neck that the loop of it was no longer visible. The dangling length of the tie now appeared to sprout directly from his puckered flesh.

The other thing Alma had discovered was that Tym's wealth was no mere show. A quick frisk showed that everything he had about him, from watch to clothes, from shoes to Shine-link in his jacket pocket, was absolutely the most expensive brand the market had to offer. Now that he was dead she could not, of course, check his feed; using hers to match his clothes and possessions with online marts produced an eye-watering scroll-down of very large numbers.

The fact that he had muted the coffee shop's larger connectivity spoke to a top-of-the-range set of software parcels, bots and apps. Those things weren't cheap.

Otherwise there was nothing on him. She shooed the coffee bot away for the third time and took as close a look as she dared at his body. A comma on the skin by his hand revealed itself, as she loosed the cuff of his sleeve and pulled it up, to be an old-style tattoo on the inside of his wrist. It was a snake, curled into an S-shape, but dead – because it was pinioned right through on two sharp vertical skewers. It was, Alma realised, a dollar sign. It was a money sign made of snakes and death.

And here were the police, and the fresh-faced young officer, her ingenuous features, wide head and cropped hair giving her the look of a face drawn on a thumb in pen.

'Did you do this?' she demanded.

'"Do" this?' said Alma. 'No.'

'Oh, good grief. He's *very* dead, isn't he? Good gravy indeed. Who did this? Did you see who did it?'

'So far as I could tell, he did it to himself.'

The police officer shook her head. 'Won't do, you know.' How squeaky was her voice! 'This won't do at all. The shop's surveil-lance feed has been compromised, you know.'

'That's nothing to do with me,' said Alma. 'He did that.'

'How do you know he did that?'

'Because he told me.'

'Which we only have your word on, because the shop's *surveil-lance* feed has been compromised. Won't do at all, you know. Simply won't do. You'd better come with me.'

The officer prodded the necessary official notification into Alma's feed: name Officer Newport, force BARTOC – Berkshire and R!-Town Constabulary – licensed and legally permitted to, and so on and so forth.

'Am I under arrest?' Alma asked, startled.

The face crumpled into a look of annoyance. 'Did I say "arrest"? I mean, did you hear me *say* "arrest"? Has that word so much as emerged from my mouth? Did you *hear* it?'

'You've just said it twice,' Alma pointed out.

Newport narrowed her eyes. 'Assisting us with enquiries. And would you look at that?' Through the glass front of the coffee shop an ambulance was settling onto the road in a small flurry of briefly aerial dust and detritus. 'What's the use of an ambulance when the fellow's dead as all get out?'

As Officer Newport led Alma out of the shop a second car arrived, this time with two human police officers inside. Officer

Maupo was one of the two. Alma nodded at her and Maupo nodded back, but neither said anything.

Newport fussed around Alma, nudging her on and along: into the car with her, and off in short order to the central station.

As they touched down on the roof of the station, Alma told Officer Newport, 'I've put all my official necessaries into your feed. You'll see that I have an affiliate status with the police. You'll also see that I need to be back at my flat in a little over an hour.'

'I am not wasting my time examining any goshed-diggedy *non*-crime-scene-related documentation,' said Newport, waving open the door of the police flitter. 'And – golly – really? Telling *me* when I'm supposed to be letting *you* go? You do understand here that you're the civilian, and I'm the police officer? I mean – ser*yeo*usly?'

Alma felt the first stirring of unease. She flipped a cam tab, to ensure her own record of the encounter would be uploaded so as to stand alongside the police records.

'I am co-operating in every respect,' she told the police officer. 'You explained to me, in the cafe, that I am not under arrest. All I am doing is informing you that my partner requires medical attention every—'

'Good gravity but you're a *gabbler*, though, aren't you?' Newport broke in. 'Are you getting out, or am I going to have to jab you?'

Alma, assuredly not wanting to be jabbed, got out, and sent a blizzard of notifications of location: to a dozen or more to her contacts, to Marguerite herself, to three law firms, and to a raft of small-circ media outlets. That was all legal. Also legal was her parcelled and coded message shoved discreetly to Pu Sto – her friend, in a manner of speaking (or perhaps not), and an individual with the effective rank of Regional Commander in the relevant police authority. Alma didn't want the fact that she had sent such a message noticed, for fear that some overzealous bot would park it to check for malware, or some such nonsense. So she covered its traces with a fractal chaff message.

'Oh, *good* golly,' said Officer Newport, speaking either with real outrage, or else a damn fine impression of it. 'Are you sending fractal chaff from your feed? From *the very roof* of a police station? Are you trying to *get* arrested?'

'I apologise, Officer,' said Alma, straight-faced. 'I accidentally triggered it while contacting my—'

'Would be achingly grateful if you'd just *button* your lip.' Newport pointed her towards a door.

Alma was led down, and into the building's innards. The air smelled faintly of disinfectant. She was put in a small room and left for a quarter of an hour. Her feed was, of course, being monitored. Alma decided not to check it anyway. Watching the minutes tick away was only going to make her anxious.

She tried some breathing strategies. They didn't help.

She had forty-five minutes before Marguerite needed her. A lot could happen in forty-five minutes. She would give herself another ten and if nobody came to see her, she would try walking out of the station on the grounds that she wasn't under arrest. Newport might try to stop her, in which case it might be worth asking a lawyer to manifest. An avatar appearance would cost less than an in-flesh one, although either way it was not going to be cheap – and Alma really didn't have any money. But needs must: if she didn't get back to Marguerite, then Marguerite would die.

But then Officer Newport entered the room, accompanied by another police officer. Alma, since her feed was still active, dropped a discreet line to the official station feed. Nothing more than that, no attempt to peer behind the official facade of the station online presence.

'So, golly, you know I said you *weren't* under arrest?' Newport said, taking her seat.

'I do remember that.'

'Strike that. It seems we're in the process *of*,' said Newport cheerily, 'activating a warrant to change *that* goshed old state of affairs, and no mistake.'

'I'm being arrested?' Alma asked, her gut clenching.

'You will be,' said the other officer (Alma's feed said her name was Coffman), 'as soon as the warrant has been processed.'

'Tickety-boo,' said Newport, apparently thereby affirming her colleague's pronouncement.

'Why do you *talk* like that?' Alma asked her.

And with that, for just a moment, it looked as though the sheen of mannerisms and attitudes veiling the true Officer Newport – whatever *she* might be like – trembled on the edge of falling away.

But Newport pressed her mouth so tightly shut that little pastry-rolls of flesh bulged above and below the actual lips, and glared at Alma and said, 'Let's look at what the warrant requires,

66

our reasonable grounds for suspecting you have been involved in a crime, shall we?'

'I have not been involved in a crime.'

'And yet, here we are. Let's begin at the beginning, shall we? You harass three of the wealthiest people in the world—'

'Harass,' Alma put in, 'is not right—'

'Harassment is *definitely* not right,' said Newport. 'I'm glad your moral compass is at least able to recognise that basic fact of blimming *ethics*. And thank you for confirming your contrition on the official police feed.'

'I wasn't expressing contrition,' said Alma.

'Hardened,' said Newport. 'Exactly as I suspected.'

'You are deliberately misunderstanding me. What I mean is, the word "harass" does not describe what I was doing.'

Newport waved this away. 'Shall we continue? In the course of your harassment of these upstanding and important citizens you interacted with a certain individual called T. Tym. Do you deny you interacted with him?'

'We talked.'

'So you're confessing.'

'No. Words are not actions, inter- or otherwise.'

'Jesting Pilate,' sneered Newport, and, without access to her feed, Alma couldn't check the reference. 'So now T. Tym is dead. You were the last person to see him alive, and now he has been throttled. Since *somebody* jinxed the cafe feeds, we have no footage of how he died.'

'He did that to the feeds,' Alma said. 'He wanted privacy for our conversation.'

'He shut down the cafe feeds? I see. He was the person who performed that – I'm sure I don't need to remind you – *illegal* thing? How handy for you. I'll have to check with him, of course, ask him to confirm your story, and then you can... No, no, wait a moment, I can't. Because he's dead.'

'I thought his tie was a handmade special, old-school cloth, silk. But evidently it was smartcloth, and evidently its protection protocols had been overridden. I wouldn't have the first clue how to hack smartcloth. I don't suppose you would either, Officer. But somebody clearly did. They could have been anywhere, and committed the crime remotely.'

'Or you could have been *right there* and done it. You could have got to your feet, walked round to the back of the unfortunate Mr Tym, hauled on his tie with your gloved hands and killed him, the old-fashioned way.'

'I don't have any gloves.'

'Gloves would be a necessity,' said Newport, as if this contradicted what Alma was saying. 'You'd hardly be so darnéd foolish as to leave your DNA on the murder weapon. We give you at least *that* much credit.'

'If I had gloves, how did I dispose of them? You guys were on the scene within minutes of Tym dying.'

'Why don't you give us,' Newport instructed, 'your version of why you wanted to meet with Tym?'

'He wanted to meet with *me*. Look, this is absurd. You should be running a diagnostic on the smartcloth – tracing the command code back to its source. I'd expect it was run through some shells, possibly through a fractal maze to disguise its origin point. But there are people who can excavate pretty much any false trail, if you—'

'Oh, I'm sure you would absolutely *love* that,' said Newport, loudly. 'I'm sure that would make you just fuzzily-wuzzily in your tummy, wouldn't it? Sending us off chasing phantoms, covering your own traces with smoke and mirrors. Why would we?'

'Why,' said the other police officer, smiling, 'would we?'

'Why should we waste time on that,' Newport leaned in, 'when we have the murderer right here? A full confession, here and now, and it will go better for you down the line.'

Alma said, 'I didn't kill Tym.'

'You are stubborn, I see.' Newport sat back in her chair. 'In other circumstances I'd admire that quality in a person. I'm capable of stubbornness myself, sometimes. In point of fact, I'm going to propose a contest. You sit there, being stubborn. And I'll sit here, being stubborn. And we'll see who cracks first. Top tip – it won't be me.'

Alma felt the first prickings of what would, if she allowed it, become panic.

'My partner's need for medical attention is an absolute. Check her file. Check mine. I have to administer it in person, or she will die.'

'Confess,' suggested Newport, 'and we can talk about maybe

letting you go back to your flat to attend to her. Under police escort, of course.'

'I didn't kill Tym.'

'So we're back to the stubbornness Olympics, are we?' Newport folded her arms.

The door crackled, and slid back. It was Officer Maupo.

'Time to cut her loose, boss,' Maupo said.

'Looseboss?' snapped Newport. 'That's no talk. That's not even talk.'

'Word has come down, boss,' Maupo insisted. 'She's free to walk.'

Newport scowled an impressively ugly scowl.

'There's a warrant to hold her pending,' she told Maupo. 'In quarter of an hour I'll have a case to prosecute her for murder.'

'Warrant's nixed,' said Maupo.

Newport hesitated, evidently checking her own feed.

'There's a glitch on its processing, is all. Patience, and it will come through.'

'Afraid not, boss. It's been actively nixed.'

Newport checked her feeds more carefully. The expression on her face was enough to let Alma know that Maupo was telling the truth. As the police officer gurned, Alma got to her feet, straining to prevent the trembling in her legs being too obvious.

'Do let me know,' she said, 'if I can in any other way assist you with your inquiries.'

8: *Cognac-ered*

Alma got home and drank a thumb's thickness of brandy in a straight glass. She had thirteen minutes before Marguerite needed another treatment. Too close. Always cutting it too close.

Alma wondered if she had ever felt this exhausted in her life before. But she was too tired to undertake the rummaging around in her memory that would have been required to determine if she'd ever been so tired before.

She went through to tell Marguerite what had happened, but found her sleeping. Also exhausted. The pair of them, absolutely worn down. A genuinely end of tether situation.

Her hands were trembling: with shock, with exhaustion, with the onset of some horrible pathology. Who knew?

She took four long, slow breaths to calm her still shimmering hand, and then she washed and put on gloves, and sat down to check the machines and their various read-outs.

The news wasn't good. Quite apart from the four-hour attacks, Marguerite's general health was worse than it had been the previous month, which had itself been considerably worse than the month before. Her heart was struggling, and her platelets and white cells were cycling between too high and too low like a ski-lift. She was having some kind of dermatological reaction on her neck and chest. Little red bumps constellated her upper body, like rivets, each capped with a tiny hard squirl of a scab.

Alma did a quick triage among possible treatments, ordered up a brand of ointment that was the best balance she could manage between likely effectiveness and affordability. Though the latter term applied, strictly speaking, to nothing at all. They needed money very badly.

She spent the four minutes before the medication was delivered sorting through her feed for possible offers of extra work. There was nothing that paid, and only a couple of avenues that might lead, eventually, to paying work.

Then, with the feeling that she was giving in to a slightly base impulse, she put in an in-Shine skimsearch for her own identity via fan groups.

A little branching tree of lit-up possibilities appeared, in among the stargate plummeting downscape that the Shine offered to her online visualisation. It seemed to be true: there were indeed fan groups dedicated to what she and Marguerite got up to. It was, of course, a minuscule fraction of a fraction of the total number of fan groups that existed – but, still, it was something.

If only, Alma told herself, they could be encouraged to donate a little money – to draw on these people's interest, and sympathy, with some kind of virtual begging bowl. To reduce Rita's and her catastrophic indebtedness.

A bing in her feed told her the drone had arrived with the medical cream.

She collected the pack, washed her hands and began applying the ointment to the dolphin-back curves of Marguerite's chest and collarbones and shoulders. When the two of them had first started dating, Alma had found an endless source of astonished joy in the smoothness and clarity of Marguerite's skin. She could stroke and kiss it for hours – literally, for hours on end – without growing tired of it. And now here it was: red and scabby.

And now Alma's eyes were wet, and she couldn't wipe them because she had medicated cream all over her hands. Wasn't that just typical?

She dried her tears in the fabric at the crook of her right elbow, finished up applying the ointment and washed her hands again. Alma's knuckles were crusty with lines of red irritation, hard and hot tomato-coloured scabs, where the constant washing was provoking her skin.

She pulled a handkerchief out of the fabric of her shirt and wiped her face properly. And then she reached a second time for the brandy. Very rare, this, for her – to guzzle a second alcoholic drink so soon after another. *But then again*, she thought, *I need it*, and poured two thumbs' worth into the glass.

'Drinking in the day,' Marguerite said sleepily. 'That's a slippery slope, you know, my dear.'

'Want some? I've just been released from police custody, and for about ten minutes I was literally shaking with fear they weren't going to let me out in time to get back to you. Literally shaking. And they wouldn't have, either, if the warrant had been processed as they planned it. It got stopped, though – the warrant, I mean. So here I am, and a tiny *tiny* little part of me thinks: if these jolts keep arriving the wheels are going to get entirely shaken *off* the chassis of my sanity.'

'I stopped listening after the first two words, dearest,' said Marguerite, 'because my reaction to them was *yes, yes*, very firmly.'

Alma scooped a slight meniscus of salt water from the underside of each of her own eyes with swift strokes of her index finger.

'Brandy? Or your usual?'

'Do you know what? I have a hankering for brandy.'

So Alma put some brandy into the system for Marguerite to enjoy, and pulled a chair over and sat down beside her bed.

'I don't mean to vent,' she said, a little sullenly. 'I was scared, though. I spoke to this fellow, Tym, and he died. He died right in front of me.'

'I saw something about that in-feed – a local death. Strangled! Didn't mention you, though.'

'I don't know what happened. I don't know if it is connected to this Fab Four investigation. Presumably it *is* connected. If so, then it's not the ludicrous goose chase we both assumed it was. If so, then there's something there worth killing for. But more alarming even than that was believing the police were going to hold me for longer than four hours.'

'Who blocked the warrant from being activated?' Marguerite asked. 'Presumably your friend in the high place.'

'I haven't seen Pu Sto, in the flesh, in six months. I only ever hear from her at second hand. To be honest I'd be surprised if she was behind it. From the news, I'd say she has bigger fish to fry.'

'Bigger salmon to sauté,' said Marguerite, as the first of the brandy slipped into her system. 'Bigger bream to bake.'

'Too many *b*s, that one.'

'Bigger minnows to microwave.'

'Fish, wave,' said Alma, saluting her with the glass. 'Very good.'

'Isn't it odd that one can buy fish fingers but not fish toes? And talking of toes, or at least, stoes – I think you underestimate Pu Sto's interest in you.'

'I consider it good policy not to get into the habit of relying on other people.'

'I would expect, at the very least, that Pu Sto has an alert on any arrest warrants issued in your name. Probably she has a list of such names. And it would be a simple matter for her to block implementation. Besides,' said Marguerite, chuckling to herself, 'if not Pu Sto, then whom?'

'I don't know. I'm getting the sense ...' Alma broke off, because she found it actually quite hard to articulate what the sense was that she was getting.

Something awry somewhere.

'Your gut reaction,' said Marguerite approvingly. 'Your ability to pick up a vibe, which combines so well with my superior powers of ratiocination. *That's* what makes us such a formidable investigative team.'

'Getting the sense that ...' Alma tried again. 'That since I took on Jupita's bizarre case, something is – I don't know. That there's some force being applied from behind the curtain ... or something. I don't know.'

'Money,' said Marguerite, simply.

'You think that's it?'

'Money exerts its influence everywhere. Money is like water, in that it flows into every crevice and crack. Politics and the law build their little houses, but money is the wind and the rain, the ground on which they build, the occasional tornado that comes to tear everything down. Money is elemental.'

'How poetical you sound.'

'I'm just saying: follow the money. It's an old proverb. Tell me about this Tym fellow. Throttled! Horrible way to go.'

So Alma told her all about her strange encounter with Tym, and all the things he had said, and his strange demise, and soon enough she had finished her brandy and was beginning to feel sleepy. Seven minutes to go until Marguerite's next treatment became due.

'One thing I did do while you were out,' Marguerite said brightly. 'I put down feelers round and about to find out what I could about Ms Thumb, the dead woman. Lund.'

Alma adjusted mentally. She was so tired it took a distinct effort.

'The other case. OK. And what did you find out?'

73

'Well, for one thing, I discovered that somebody, or somebodies, is trying to bury her data. Throwing a tonne of soil on top of anything – false trails, fractal fictions, redirects to other people called Lund. A real maze. I'm not one to blow my own trumpet,' Marguerite said, looking pleased with herself, 'but it would be enough to baffle a person of lesser searching ability.'

'She was killed. The killer, or people associated with the killer, want to make it harder to investigate her death. That's not rocket science.'

'She was a researcher. She worked for an institute called the Fugit Foundation.'

'Researching what?'

'Something to do with brain chemistry.'

'Maupo wondered if maybe she was working on a *biological* model for machine AI.'

'Hard to say. Details are the opposite of forthcoming. Unforth-coming. Forthgoing. One-quarterth-coming. I like that one best. Anyway, there are a great many copyright and IP protection bar-riers erected around the actual research, and the foundation is not publicly listed – no prospectuses, no sales catalogues or anything like that. So I delved a little deeper.'

'With your famous searchability skills.'

'Search, search, search,' agreed Marguerite, 'searchability, that's the beauty of – me.'

'And?'

'Oh, I was curious how they were being funded. That's all. It's hard to be sure, but the residual dataflows suggest that it's all being paid for from one source, rather than drawing revenue from many different directions.'

'So, it's not selling its products to many buyers and drawing income that way? The funding comes all from one place?'

'Which,' said Marguerite, 'might mean the foundation is a wholly-owned subsidiary of whoever is funding it, or it might mean that the foundation is independent but has struck a deal to sell only to one buyer.'

She was becoming excited, and that in turn was putting stress on her system. Alma set her empty glass on the side, and moved closer to the screens to check the read-outs.

Time to prep.

'Does any of that,' she said, going over to the sink and washing her hands, 'tell us what she was working on?'

'It does not. But we can assume that if the entire foundation is being funded by one individual, then that individual must be one of the Four.'

'Assume makes an ass of you and me,' said Alma, pulling the latex over her fingers.

'That's what the information implies!'

'Imply makes, uh, a lie come out of an imp. No, never mind. Lie still, dear heart, and let me treat you.'

Marguerite fidgeted, tried to settle, grew more agitated.

'I still think there must have been something *on* the needle that was pushed through her thumb, you know.'

'Uh-huh,' said Alma, her eyes on the read-outs.

A pause, immediately before the latest iteration of the pathology revealed itself. Alma's least favourite part of the whole horrible experience. And, then: there – a crystalline plaque creeping up the vagus nerve, and an associated swarm of deplateletised virions. Alma tried to clear her mind, and visualise her path through. Wafts of cognac fumes drifted through the grid of neurones. Why had she drunk so much? A prick of adrenaline, and actual fear, as it occurred to her that she might have degraded her cued-in reactions to the level where she could no longer see how to treat Marguerite. A hollowed-out nothing in her gut, and a rapid running of her heart. But, there it was – and as Marguerite's eyes rolled over white she was in.

The virions were chased down to the lymph nodes, and by applying a particular pharmakon Alma began to diminish their number. She was able to stop the advance of the plaque, and saw how to strip it from the nerves altogether. Put in a purchase order with the – much more expensive – emergency delivery tag, and took a long breath to prepare for the thirty seconds it would take.

Bong bong. The combination of medications could be sold to her, but delivery would have to be standard rather than instantaneous.

'No,' said Alma aloud. Her rapidly running heart ran more rapidly still. Priority message:

—I need it immediately, medical emergency.

—Instant delivery cannot be authorised. Standard delivery only.

—Why not, you great arse— (even in her ire she knew it wasn't a good idea to risk getting locked out of the purchase system altogether for profanity, so she changed this to) Asclepius?

—Insufficient funds.

And just like that, from sprinting like an Olympian on the final straight, Alma's heart flopped over and stopped dead.

Oh, dear God.

—Request upgrade of credit scale.

—Request, said the purchase system, brightly, denied.

Alma spent a desperate thirty seconds trawling for instant credit. But she'd been here before, and already exhausted all possibilities. Algorithms were only prepared to enter into agreement after assessment and interview, and she didn't have time for that.

—Send the medication, said Alma, to the original purchase algorithm. I can at least afford that, can't I?

—Standard delivery.

—Do it!

She checked the vitals. The plaque was quivering, bulking at the epineurium. It was about to explode, regrow at twice the rate. This was a very serious threat to Marguerite indeed. This was something that could kill her.

Swearing aloud, Alma tried two interventions with stuff she had to hand. Neither did anything to reduce the density of crystallisation suspension. Marguerite's breathing was shallow, and her fingers' ends were going blue. As Alma watched, she shifted her considerable weight and passed an unusual quantity of flatus. The read-outs suggested that something extinction-level was happening in her gut flora. Was that connected to the neural plaque? Alma rapidly addressed the intestinal situation. It took two long minutes, and occupied her attention, but at least it distracted Alma from the car-alarm voice inside her brain that was shrieking *what are we going to do?*

What are we going to do?

The intestinal issue was a separate thing, it seemed. And Marguerite, despite being unconscious, was making odd little moaning sounds, and the neural plaque was beginning to reform on her vagus nerve.

'Not good,' said Alma. 'Not good.'

Where was the damn delivery?

What are we going to do? meant not only, *how am I going to handle this situation?* It also meant: *what happens next time?*

What if Marguerite's next treatment disclosed a need for some rare and expensive medicine at the very last minute? Of course, maybe that wouldn't happen. Say, to play the optimist for once, Marguerite's next breakdown could be handled with pharmakons Alma happened to have to hand. What about the one after that? And the one after that?

Eventually there was going to come a time when Alma would again need to call emergency delivery of some unusual medication. What then?

What if she not only lacked the funds to pay for instant delivery; what if she couldn't even pay for the drugs themselves?

One thing at a time, Alma told herself. When this is sorted, I shall try and track down some more credit. But for now – and, *bing bing*, there was notification of the delivery of the necessary.

Alma's hands trembled anew as she administered the pharmakon, and then, with her eyes pricking yet again with tears, she watched the plaque retreat and then break up.

She sank back in the chair she had placed beside the bed, and fell, without intermission, into deep sleep.

9: *Lez the Mis in Person*

Alma woke with a jolt. Four hours had passed. She scrambled to the screens, but Marguerite was slumbering peacefully enough. Everything seemed OK. She pored over the read-outs. Rita's health was not as ruddy as Alma might have liked, but at least she was still breathing.

Three hours had passed, not four. Alma double-checked her timeline. She was panicking unnecessarily.

She went through and washed her face and hands in cold water.

A woman is killed by having a needle through her thumb. Marguerite was probably right: there had to be something *on* the needle, or some strange feature *of* the needle, to explain such a death. I mean, that was the impossible-eliminated, improbable-remaining only conclusion. Wasn't it?

Unless the needle was a mere red herring.

One of the four wealthiest people in Europe may or may not be dead, and I've been asked to find out if it's true, and if so, which of them is the murderee. And now Lund – who certainly *is* dead – seems to have been working for a company that was either bankrolled by, or else was doing exclusive business with, a super-rich organisation or individual.

Maybe with one of the Fab Four.

She couldn't be sure of that, though. The professional danger Alma ran, when investigating, was assuming connections where there was none. Trying to connect elements that had no connection. As an old friend of Alma's had once put it: the human brain has a hard-on for patterns. Which was bad news for Alma since puzzles, including crimes, are solved with the brain, not the genitals.

Especially crimes.

So far as Alma knew, these two things – Lund and the Fab Four – had absolutely nothing to do with one another. Until she had actual evidence that there was a connection, the sensible thing to do was to treat them as separate.

Still, her gut told her there was a connection.

She went back through to find Marguerite awake again.

'Feeling much better, dear heart,' she said. 'Just a little peckish.'

'I'll rustle up some food.'

'What kind of food rustles? Sounds a little dry. Can't we have something a bit more juicy?'

'Rita,' said Alma, as she summoned a variety of comestibles, 'we need to have a serious conversation about money.'

'Do you mean professionally speaking? Because it is my considered and immoveable belief that the murderer we seek is, very precisely, money.'

'Has money, you mean.'

'I know what I mean.'

'If the murderer already has money, why kill?'

'To get more money. To prevent her money being taken away. Who knows? But I'm not sure I mean *has* money. I'm getting the sense that the person we are looking for more than *has* money.'

'I had to give you a new cocktail of pharmakons, to treat the latest flare-up,' said Alma. 'I think it might be muddling up your brain. I'll get some food.'

As they ate together, Alma tried again to draw Marguerite into a discussion of funds.

'We've borrowed up to the allowed limit from all the regular sources,' she said. 'And we are in hock to a number of rather irregular ones. I'm not sure where to ask next. But we absolutely need money, and we need it sooner rather than later.' She decided not to mention that the company's refusal of further credit had resulted in a delay in the arrival of the drugs, a delay that had nearly killed Marguerite. No point in worrying her unnecessarily. 'Is there nobody you can think of who might lend us a little ready cash?'

'Light of my life, I've asked anybody I know who has *any* money at all. The only people left are deeper in debt even than we.'

Again, Alma held back from saying: *ask them anyway, this is a matter of life and death*. Instead she said, 'It's a function of the drying-up of wealth in the Real. The world's finances have all migrated to the Shine, now.'

'Well,' said Marguerite. '*In*deed.'

A tinkling bell sounded in Alma's feed.

'It's Lez again,' she said. And then, 'Good grief – he's asking if he can come say hello.'

'Lez pay a house call?' said Marguerite. And then again, in a more hilariously outraged tone, 'Lez the Mis, come here in person? Good golly Miss Moly, and all the magical herbs, you're right – he's knocking on my feed too.'

'Come here in person. That's a first, I think.'

'Let him in,' urged Marguerite. 'Maybe he can lend us a bit of brass.'

'You forget that I already owe him quite a lot of money, love.'

'*We* owe him,' Marguerite corrected her. 'What's yours is mine, and vice versa, and that holds as much for the things absent as things present.'

'It's probably why he's here. I dare say he's reassuring himself that we are still living in a place he can monitor, with objects he can repossess in lieu of payment.'

Lez was not what one might call an optimist about human nature, even the human nature of those he knew well. And though Alma had been paying him back in increments ever since she had incurred her debt, they had not been very large increments, and there was every chance, as Alma's financial situation deteriorated, that they would grow smaller and less frequent.

At any rate, they sent an accept to Lez's feed, and four minutes later he was knocking on their actual door with an actual, flexibly jointed set of knuckles. Alma went through to the front room and let him in.

'Hello, Lez,' she said. 'Cup of tea?'

Lez peered dolefully at her for a moment, as if trying to decide whether 'T' was short for *toxins*.

'It's really Marguerite I've come to see,' he said. 'Just to check up on... you know. Check up on how she's, you know. Doing. You know.' He looked gloomily into the middle distance for a while. 'So, how *is* she doing?'

'For a person only ever four hours away from painful and ignominious death, she's doing spiffing, thank you for asking. Your commendable humanitarian interest in Marguerite notwithstanding, I assume you're here to check on the money I owe you. As I explained on the phone, I'm working a couple of gigs right now.

I should be able to pay off another chunk of the debt by the end of the week.'

Lez's expression made it seem as if the prospect of receiving money caused him actual physical discomfort.

'Great,' he said.

'Well, if you're really here to see Marguerite, then come through. You'll have to put this hat on, and this mask.' Alma ran a hygiene skein quickly over Lez's clothes. 'And roll up your sleeves, please – you can wash at this sink.'

'Didn't have to do all this last time I visited,' Lez complained.

'Her lymphocyte levels weren't quite so basement, back then, and her general health was better. She's had a bad series of months, I'm sorry to say. Her immune system is basically down to nothing at all. Barely an immune system.' Alma knew all this, intimately, of course, but saying it out loud brought a sense of horrible sinking to her heart. She forced a grin, and tried a goofy joke. 'More an im-none system, now.'

Her heart did not lift.

Lez scowled, and sniffed, and then twitched his hands. His left sleeve shrank up his arm, but his right sleeve didn't move.

'The fabric's bust on that side,' he said, as if stating an existential truth about the cosmos.

'Maybe you should buy a new shirt?'

'Maybe when you pay me back I'll be able to,' he said sharply.

Alma made a pff-ing noise. 'You got plenty of money, Lez. Plenty! No way you had all your funds in one AI futures pot. You'll have other monies. You're just a miser, is all. Wash there, please. Not that soap, the one next to it.'

A little resentfully, Lez complied.

They went through to the bedroom.

'Lez the Mis,' said Marguerite, 'as I live and breathe!'

'Both of which you are barely managing, it seems,' said Lez, with gloomy satisfaction.

'And lovely to see *you* again too,' said Marguerite. 'Park your arse at ninety degrees in *that* very chair, and tell me how you've been.'

Lez sat down, a little gingerly, as Alma took up a position next to Marguerite's bed.

'How have I been?' he said. 'Dreadful. How has the world been? Dreadful. You see the correlation, I'm sure.'

'Hullo, clouds, hullo, sky,' said Marguerite brightly. 'Are you here to chase us regarding our unpaid debt to you, as Alma thinks? Or maybe things have gone beyond such chivvying. Have you come to *evict* me?' She laughed, a long and gurgly sound, and Alma reflexively checked the screen for her vitals – prolonged laughing was not good for her health. 'Good luck with that.'

'I consider it, Marguerite,' said Lez, fussily, 'Alma's debt. Not yours. For one thing, she would at least be easier to evict.'

'Don't count on it,' said Alma.

'We have a new case – did mah-mah tell you?' Lez's eyes, above his mask, looked profoundly sad. But then they always did. 'You know the Fab Four?' Marguerite asked. 'Come along, Lez, you know everything that goes on. You keep your ear to the ground.'

'The Quartet,' said Lez, grudgingly. 'Also known as the Tetrawealthy, the Fab Four. A mutually loathing group of some of Europe's richest people, each of them desperate to become *absolutely* rich. Yeah. I know a little something about them.'

'One of them has been murdered!' said Marguerite, and laughed again.

'I'm not sure, Rita,' Alma put in, 'it's ethical to discuss our client's private matters with outsiders.'

'It's Lez, he's hardly *L'Étranger*.' Marguerite sounded a little giddy, and sometimes got rather hyper if the minor glabe infections hadn't been purged properly.

Alma shuffled over to the screens and checked her vitals again.

'Even so,' she said.

'Oh, tsh,' said Marguerite.

'Which one?' Lez asked. And when Alma didn't reply he pressed, 'Which one of the four is dead, then? I mean, that's huge news. Why isn't it all over every newsfeed?'

'We're not sure,' said Marguerite. 'Isn't that a hoot? We're not sure which one has gone from suspiring to expiring. One of them has, we think – but whoever it is, their team and family and whatnot are keeping it very quiet, or are perhaps collaborating in the crime. And somebody is impersonating the dead person in-Shine. Hacked their feed maybe – imagine such a thing!'

'Such a thing is impossible,' said Lez lugubriously, inserting a finger under his mask and scratching his nose. 'And I cannot imagine impossible things.'

'There's no proof *anybody* is dead,' said Alma. 'Mostly likely, none of them are. And Marguerite shouldn't be sharing our private investigative business with you, Lez. I hope your discretion is not in doubt?'

'I am quiet,' said Lez slowly, 'as the grave.'

'You're *everything* as the grave, Lez.' Marguerite started burbling with low laughter. Alma gave her a sharp look; this giddiness was not normal Rita. 'But come now, have you heard anything about this kerfuffle? Out on the street? What with you having your ear to the ground and everything?'

'About one of the Four being bumped off? No, I have not. But—' He held up one forefinger. 'It'll happen. One day.'

Alma waited. Marguerite was humming quietly to herself. Eventually Lez went on.

'Like, you know they're working towards absolute wealth, yes?'

'I've heard as much,' said Alma, 'although I'll confess I'm still a little hazy on what that concept even means.'

'It means absolute misery,' said Lez, with a dour satisfaction. 'Though *they* don't see that, of course. But that's the rich, see? Imagine it, only. Just try. Let's say you start out poor – say you don't have enough to eat, say your opportunities are curtailed. Imagine you work, or graft, or con, and get rich. You're thinking to yourself – I'm never going hungry again. Yeah? Motivation, see.'

'Motivation,' echoed Marguerite, and giggled again.

'So you're rich. You'll never go hungry again. So, what motivates you to keep working at getting richer? Inertia? Pride, is it?' He shook his head, slowly. 'Not that. It's money. Money itself. Money is a parasite, see? It enters its host and drives her, him. On they go. You want to be richer than other people. Who? Richer than ordinary people. Well, OK, you are. So you say to yourself: *I want to be richer than other* rich *people*. That's a thing to aim for. So you manage that. *Then* it's: *I want to be richer than everybody else*. Soon enough you want it all – all the money, every other breathing *Homo sapiens* on this cold world in *your* debt. It's the working of money inside the human soul. It's a virus that breeds until it has killed everything else. It's a parasite, and it creeps inside your brain and hollows it out, as a spoon scoops the meat out of a boiled egg. And then it's just your hollow body and money, inside, pushing you on with its virus hunger, more, and more, and more.'

There was a silence.

83

'I don't think I've ever heard you so,' Alma observed, '*mm*, eloquent, Lez.'

'Sorry,' Lez mumbled. 'It's something I *feel* about. I have feelings. I feel that...' But he shook his head. 'Not that I'm letting you off the money you owe *me*.'

'I'll pay,' said Alma. 'Don't worry about that.'

'What I'm saying is,' he added, 'these four, they're all infected, as it were. Money has got hold of their souls. And they're super-rich, ultra-rich and for *them* – that's simply not rich enough. They'll never want for anything, materially speaking, so long as they live. But that's not enough. They got to be richer than everybody, and as it stands they are richer than almost everyone – *except* the other three in their little Quartet. So I can tell you, and without benefit of telepathy, what each of them is thinking. Each of them is thinking: I could get richer than those other three, or I could just kill those other three – either way I'd then be the Richest of our little group. So what I'm saying is: they will get round to killing one another and when that happens it won't – surprise me – in – the – least.'

Alma and Marguerite looked at Lez.

'Anyhow. Never mind that.' He made to change the subject of the conversation to something more agreeable. 'I heard that you were arrested. On the street I heard that. With,' he glowered at her, 'my ear to the ground.'

'Arrested?' Alma might have been Snow White talking to forest birds. 'Me?'

'You were, though,' Lez said.

'It's true I assisted the police with their enquiries. Just a chat. No warrant was filed.'

'I heard there was a murder, and the police took *you* away. A man got throttled in the *Coffee-fi-fo-fum* is what I heard. Arse *fix*-iated, it seems.'

'Well,' said Alma, 'bad things do happen in this world.'

'Oh, I am *Moses*,' Marguerite broke out, suddenly, loudly. She had gone from being full of hilarity to incipient weepiness. Symptoms of a chronic feverishness. 'I am Moses.'

Lez peered at her, over his mask. 'Horns, is it?'

'I'll maybe *see* the promised land – but I'll not *get* there with you – everything you say, Lez, has been true of this real-world. But the Shine is different. The Shine will be different. No need for money there – we can root out money, root out the root of all evil, make a clean new moneyless world. Root the root!' Tears were glass-beading down her impressive cheeks now. 'Root!'

'I'm going to give you a xanex-xfaux, Rita,' Alma told her. 'You're upsetting yourself.'

'Root-root!'

'Well, anyway, I'll be off,' muttered Lez, getting to his feet. 'Good to see you again, Marguerite. But I've got to be—'

'Root!'

'Off,' said Lez. 'Going. See myself out, I will.'

Alma came with him into the front room and relieved him of his cap and mask.

'Terrible to see her like that,' he said, with his usual morose satisfaction at, yet again, having his life-philosophy confirmed. 'She was the smartest person I ever did meet, in all the world. Once upon a time.'

'She still is,' said Alma, loyally.

Lez looked at the floor, and then stood straighter. But before he told the front door to open itself he said, 'That geezer who got throttled.'

'Yes?'

'He was a very different feller before he got the fancy clothes. Before he got the gig working for that Golden Meteor corporation.'

'You *knew* him?'

'Not personal. Friend of a friend. In point of fact,' Lez sighed, 'friend of an enemy of a friend of mine. Proper small-time crookednesses. That was him, as was. Low-rent stuff. When my newsfeed brought him up I couldn't believe it was the same breezy *geezer*, to be honest with you. I mean, the money fairy tickled *his* nuts and no mistake. But did it make him happy? All that money? Did it heck. It got him murdered.'

'It might have been suicide,' Alma said.

'Auto-erotic?' Lez said, eyes wide.

'Not that. Bloody hell, Lez! I meant, just ordinary suicide.'

'Oh,' said Lez, his interest diminishing.

'What I'm asking is,' Alma pressed, 'was he the sort of person to do such a thing? From what you knew of him? Was such a thing in his character?'

'Like I said,' said Lez, gloomily. 'I didn't know him well. You never can tell who's liable to top they-selves. Comes in waves, in my experience. Monkey misery, monkey miser-do. The only thing that I knew about Hartwell...'

'Told me his name was Tim.'

'Oh.' Lez rounded his lips as though sucking a marble. 'That's what the newsfeed called him too. But back when I knew of him he was Hartwell Lowndes. And everybody said the same thing about him. He wanted money. He wanted money more than anything else – more than sex, or status, or revenge, or any of the usual things.'

'Judging by how expensively he was dressed, I'd say he got it.'

'So your theory is he *got* exactly what he wanted all his life,' said Lez, nodding slowly, 'and then he topped his-self. Exactly what I've been saying. Good day, Alma. Tell you what though – *I'm* carrying fuzzdar. You know it? Not cheap.'

'Bully for you, Lez.'

'Only it alerts me to the proximity of licensed police officers, and it's telling me there's one on the other side of your door, right now. Which is less than my optimum state of affairs. So good day to you, Alma. Don't forget to pay me the *money* you owe me.'

'All the moany, Lez.'

And he opened the door to reveal that what he had said was true – for there was indeed a police officer on the far side of Alma's door. Lez slipped past this individual without meeting her eye and was gone before Alma could say goodbye.

It was Officer Maupo.

10: *The Slabmiralty*

'Is this an inconvenient time?' Officer Maupo asked. 'I messaged you a couple of times, but I'm not sure any of them got through.'

Alma checked her feed's receptivity. Somebody had put a block on receiving any messages from this one particular individual. Marguerite, of course. Only she had the access, and only she might be secretly jealous enough to do it. This symptom of how deep her insecurity ran, combined with the fact that she had been too proud simply to tell her partner about it, smacked Alma's heart painfully. She told herself: *Rita hasn't really been herself, lately* – but still. This was a deeply uncharacteristic thing to do.

'Sorry about that,' Alma told Maupo. 'Some glitch, I guess. What were you messaging me about?'

'You wanted to see Lund. Which is to say, you wanted to see her body.'

'And so I did.'

The whole nonsense of this non-case with the Fab Four, and the bizarre death of Tim Tym – or Hartwell Lowndes, if that was what he was actually called – had temporarily pushed it out of her mind.

'I checked with the higher-ups,' Maupo said. 'Having Pu Sto as a friend opens doors, you know. Makes people happy to see you. Friends in *hi!* places. "She wants to see the corpse?" they said. "Show her the corpse."'

'In a quarter of an hour I have to administer some medical assistance to my partner. Can you wait? Do you want to come back?'

'Happy to wait.' Maupo turned her back to the hallway's wall, putting her hands behind her and setting her legs in an Λ-shape.

'You can,' Alma offered, 'come in, you know.'

'Oh! That's very kind.'

She stepped through the door and stood to attention again, this time on the inside.

'Please sit,' Alma told her. 'There's a chair.' Maupo sat, stiffly. 'Would you like something? Cup of tea?'

'Not while I'm on duty, thank you.'

This wrong-footed Alma. 'I don't see that *tea* would interfere with your ability to do your duty?'

Maupo looked slyly up at Alma. 'Oh, did you say *cup of tea*? I misheard – I thought you said *candlelit dinner for two and a bottle of vintage Bordeaux.*'

'I'm surprised they let you in the police, hearing as defective as that.'

'Not at all, ma'am,' said Maupo, eyes front again. '*Creative* hearing can be quite the asset for an up-and-coming police officer.'

Alma washed her hands, aproned up and went through. Marguerite had fallen asleep, which was good, since her fever was very high, and treatment was going to have to be more than usually invasive. She fussed at a couple of generic analgesic and antipyretic interventions, and then waited for the four-hour-four-minute mark to roll round. And – there it was. The scurry and domino-tumble of pathogens – a new shake of the kaleidoscope of her lover's endless sickness. She scanned, injected, *felt* rather than logically deduced that something wasn't quite right about her approach, and then very hurriedly saw her mistake and slapped on a broad-front Tripto-polymalubutomol and targeted a designer-built Marguerite-specific drug at each neck lymph node.

And then: the long seconds until it was clear that the latest assault was ebbing away.

And – relax.

For now.

'Oh, Marguerite,' Alma said to her partner's slumbering form, as she peeled off her gloves and splashed her face with cold water. 'You don't need to block Officer Maupo, you know. There's no one else in this world for me except you.'

But in reply Marguerite only made the sound of waves draining back from the shore through shingle.

And breathed out.

And breathed wheezily in again, very long and croaky.

In the front room Maupo was waiting patiently.

'Good to go?'

'Four whole hours of freedom.' Alma tugged at her shirt to turn it into a coat. 'Shall we?'

They got into Maupo's car and drove, without leaving the ground, through perfectly empty streets, round a section of ring road and then away out of town.

Maupo didn't mention Alma's arrest, and Alma was happy not to bring it up. She thought of asking how the arrest warrant had been blocked, but it could well be that Maupo – a serving police officer, after all, whose loyalty was to her force and her superiors – would prefer not to say. Assuming she even knew.

Soon enough the car swept towards a long, low building. Alma had been in the private investigation business for nearly seven years, but in all that time she had only visited the R!-town mortuary thrice.

It was never a savoury experience.

In at the front door to a generic greeting by the building AI. But Maupo had alerted the human staff that they were coming, and the corpse wrangler was waiting for them. Name: Sweetzer, according to Alma's feed.

'Welcome,' he said, 'to the Slabmiralty.'

'The...?' asked Alma.

'I'm trying to get it to catch on. Slab, because mortuary. Combined with *admiralty*.'

'Combined with?' Alma said.

'It's funny,' said Sweetzer. 'It's clever and funny. I don't understand why nobody else appreciates how funny it is. I've been trying to get it to catch on – promoting it in-Shine, pinning it on social media and so on. But it – it just *won't*. It's frustrating, if I'm honest.'

'People have no taste, boyo,' was Maupo's opinion.

'Why *admiralty*, though?' Alma wanted to know. 'Ships and navies? You're dead bodies. Ships are not corpses.'

'It was called the *admiralty* because the sailors who worked there were so admirable,' said the corpse wrangler.

Alma's feed immediately told her this etymology was fake, and the spelling was wrong, which meant that Sweetzer's feed had presumably told him the same thing, and that he had ignored it. Which, in a small way, told Alma something about Sweetzer.

'OK,' she said.

'And what I do is admirable too. Underappreciated.'

'They should give you a big triangular hat,' Maupo said. 'With gold braid trimmings.'

Sweetzer's face beamed. 'They *should*. I've a mind to put in an actual request. Or, do you know what would be better? A *gold* hat with cloth trimmings!'

'Heavy,' Maupo opined.

'Colour, not metal, obviously.'

'You're both awfully jolly,' said Alma. 'Seeing as how we're surrounded by corpses.'

'Easy to be jolly when you're surrounded by happy things,' said Sweetzer. 'There's no credit in *that*. The real kudos accrues to the person who can be jolly in a place such as this.' And he threw his arms wide.

'Could we get on with it?' Alma asked. 'I'm on a deadline.'

'By all means. So – Maupo pinged me. You're here to see the body of a certain Ms Lund, and I've an order in my porch telling me to show that body to you. Even though you're a civilian.'

'I'm ancillary to the official police investigation.'

'Then walk *this* way.'

And he lurched off in an exaggeratedly limping, loping manner. It was so extreme that Alma wondered if he did actually suffer from some spinal deformity or neurological affliction. But after a dozen paces he straightened up and walked conventionally, and Alma's feed prompted her with a tag that offered to explain the joke if she wanted the joke explained.

She didn't want the joke explained.

They passed into a small, chilly annexe. And here was the dead body of Alexa Lund, on her back, pale as greaseproof-paper, expressionless, eyes that would win any no-blinking contest with any living human. A smart blanket covered her from shin to collarbone. The three of them stood in silence for a moment. All the facetiousness seemed to have drained out of Sweetzer.

'Can I see the thumb?' Alma asked.

He nodded, fumbled with the blanket, and it shrank away to reveal her left hand. There it was: a much more trivial thing than Alma had been expecting. A six-centimetre-long needle, somewhere between a hair's and a wire's thickness, long and straight. Two centimetres of clean metal extended from the back of the thumbnail, and a little over three centimetres had emerged from the pad of the thumb, streaked with sticky, dark blood. A tiny globe, like a blackberry, marked the needle's place of emergence from Lund's skin.

'She died of shock?' Alma asked.

'Her system shut down. It was something like anaphylactic shock, I think. Although so far as I can see, it was a non-immunologic reaction.'

'Which means?'

'That it wasn't an allergic response.'

'Anaphylaxis is possible without allergens?'

'Sure. All sorts of things can cause the degranulation of mast cells and basophils. Temperature. Vibration. Foods to which the individual is not usually allergic. Once I had a body in here – early middle-aged man, he was, playing with his kid, kid ran into him, headbutted his sternum and happened, by freak chance, to shut the guy's heart off. Boom! Just like that.'

'Is that what happened here? The needle caused a freak cardiac shutdown?'

'Well, not in *this* case, no. I can't see that that's what happened. The cardiac arrest guy took a blow directly *to* the heart, through the ribcage, and it happened to interrupt the pumping pattern. The thumb, though? That's too peripheral to have caused anaphylaxis like this.'

'So what did cause it?'

'No idea. Really. I mean, she was *held*.'

'What do you mean, held?'

'Pressure points, as from two large hands, probably male, on her shoulders. Not enough to bruise her, but enough to leave the kind of mark I can pick up. Somebody gripped her.'

'One person gripped her while another person pushed a needle into her thumb?'

'Could be,' said Sweetzer, offhand. 'Maybe her being held happened at the same time as the needle being pushed through. Maybe it happened at an earlier time. I can't be sure of that. Not later, though.'

'It would make sense, though,' Alma prompted. 'Wouldn't it? Somebody would need to hold her still while the needle went in, or she would have wriggled away.'

'Making sense,' Sweetzer replied, folding his arms, 'is really not the best way to describe this whole business, I would say. A lady had a needle stuck in her thumbnail and dropped dead. How does that make any sense?'

'So let me ask you – might it have . . . just happened?'

'*It* being *sudden death*?'

'Yeah.'

'Maybe. Million to one shot, but there you go. Doubly strange coincidence if it *just happened* as some goon was pushing a needle through her thumb, don't you think?'

'You're sure she wasn't *allergic* to the needle?' Alma asked. Something about all this was wrong – didn't add up. It offended her sense of doability. You can't solve a crime unless you can imagine committing that crime, and Alma just couldn't think herself into this situation. 'I mean, you're sure the needle didn't cause any kind of allergic reaction?'

'It's surgical steel, so no. And anyway, if it had been immuno-logical then her system would be histamine flooded. And it's not.'

'I just don't understand what the connection *is* between her having this needle through her thumb, and her dying.'

'Search me.' Sweetzer pressed the tag on the blanket to make it cover the whole corpse, face to feet. 'Are we done here?'

'The next of kin has been informed?' Alma asked.

'Don't answer that, Sweetzer. I'm authorised to show you the body,' said Maupo, stepping up. 'But I'm not authorised to give you contacts for the spouse. Though I suppose there's no harm in saying that the next of kin *has* been informed. Standard procedure, obviously.'

'She works – worked, I mean – for a private foundation, as a researcher, I think,' said Alma. 'The Fugit Foundation, if I'm not mistaken?'

Maupo nodded, looking impressed. 'I can neither confirm nor deny,' she said, nodding confirmation a second time. 'Time to go.'

'Goodbye, you two morbid people,' said Sweetzer, not shaking hands with either of them. 'Remembering that, in my vocabulary, morbid is a compliment.'

'He's a card, isn't he, Sweetzer?' Maupo said, as they walked towards the exit together. 'Sweetzer the Sorrowful we call him.'

'Didn't seem very sorrowful to me,' Alma replied, absently.

'Robin Hood's John didn't seem very little, either. And by his *John* I mean his— Look, hey, if you're not even going to pay attention to my jokes, then there's hardly any point in me making them.'

'What?'

Something was *almost* slotting into place in Alma's mental picture of this crime. Almost but not quite, and that was really bugging her. One person holding this middle-aged woman by her shoulders – pushing her down into a chair, perhaps. Another person squeezing a needle through her thumb. Then – X – and death. And the X was obvious, except that she couldn't see it.

'He makes it a point of pride to be jolly in the least jolly places,' Maupo was saying. 'Says there's no credit in being jolly in jolly places. It makes a kind of sense, I suppose.'

'That's nice,' said Alma.

'I'm not sure what good this credit does him, though. Except to mean that people think he's a creditable human being.'

'That's nice.'

Alma found herself thinking about the man who called himself Stanley. Why, though? *Was* there a connection that she was intuitively recognising between this punctured thumb and that palaver with the super-rich, even though she couldn't rationalise one as yet? Or was it just a weird free association: as it might be, needle, knife, Stanley blade.

No, that wasn't it.

They were out of the mortuary, and walking across the otherwise deserted car park to Maupo's vehicle. Mid-afternoon, R!-town. Alma hardly noticed the edge-of-city, edge-of-nature surroundings. The green. Bright sunlight putting coin-shaped shadows behind the leaves. The impressively smooth and clear quality of the blue sky. She was in-feed as she walked, trying to find her way past the prolix and politely worded brush-off she was receiving from the automatic algorithm that manned the Fugit Foundation's front desk.

'I need to speak to a human being,' she said. 'Can you connect me, please?'

'Drop you back home?' Officer Maupo asked.

'Thanks,' said Alma, absently. In-feed, she had been referred to a generic supermodel simulation behind a simulated front desk, and this entity's algorithm was designed to be politely unhelpful.

'I mean, unless you'd like to stop off somewhere for coffee?' Maupo was saying.

'Thanks.'

'Seriously?'

'What?' Alma zoned back in. 'What did you say?'

'Asked if you wanted to grab a coffee?'

'Oh,' Alma said, waving her away, 'no', and returned to her feed.

She climbed into the car on bodily autopilot.

'The foundation is deeply flattered by your interest,' the smiling-faced simulacrum was saying. 'The foundation would like to thank you for your interest. It is not the foundation's policy to permit members of the public to access their day-to-day. Thank you.'

'I am a licensed private investigator,' said Alma, shoving credentials at the program. 'I am assisting the police who are investigating the death of one of your employees. Please put me in touch with a human being.'

'The foundation complies with all legal requirements as regards the provision of real-world human presence on its board. If, however, your interest is in employment, I regret to say that the foundation is not hiring at this time. The foundation is most genuinely touched by your interest. Thank you.'

'Just a coffee,' Maupo was saying, somewhere, a very long way away. 'Is all I meant. Sometimes a coffee is just a coffee. I mean sometimes it's an invitation to other intimacies, but not always, yes?'

'That's nice.'

Alma tried a few of her more discreet picklock apps on the foundation's front desk – not actually to break in, just to peer past the shut door, get some sense of what was happening inside the foundation itself. Was it business as usual, the death of Lund something to be shrugged off? Or was it panic – a company under attack, the other human employees anxious not to suffer the same fate?

But whatever else it was, the Fugit Foundation was extremely well equipped with anti-intruder software. Top-level stuff, in fact; no expense had been spared. One of her two picklocks was simply broken, and the other tried to backwash a very malicious-looking viral crumblecode into her own feed. Her own firewall was up to the task of blocking this, but it took a good deal longer than Alma was comfortable with.

She submitted a formal request with the foundation's gate-keeper and disengaged.

'Alma,' Maupo was saying, 'I don't want to become an active irritation to you, OK?'

Alma looked around. The car had come to a halt. They were back outside her apartment block.

'What?'

'I grok that you're loyal to Marguerite. That's all I wanted to say. I admire it, actually. Your loyalty. And I don't want to seem too ... Well, you know. I mean. You know.'

'What do I know?'

'Can you not make this harder than it has to be, please? I'm trying to respect your space, your choice. Even though it's obvious, it's obviously obvious, that I find you very attractive. Can we just say we're *playing* at flirting, and leave it at that? No harm in it? No threat to your relationship?'

'Goodbye, Officer,' said Alma, and got out of the car.

On the way up in the lift she checked her messages again. Half a dozen or so that needed attention, a couple of score that might be worth raking through but were probably nothing. One day soon she ought to do a sweep of her spam. That sometimes, if not always, threw up interesting things. But there was no time now.

Here was a request to meet, that might lead to work.

Here, a red bill from a debt collection agency.

And here was a direct message from the fellow who called himself Stanley. She pulled it up, and he shimmered into the elevator beside her.

'I was just about to call you,' she told him.

'I am flattered,' said Stanley's emanation. 'Since, as you know, I'm a huge fan of yours.'

'In connection with needles,' Alma tried.

'You sure you don't mean *neckties*?'

'You heard about that, then.'

'What I heard was that one of the GM's assistants died,' said the apparition. 'Would you like to talk to her about it in person?'

'Her?'

'To the GM,' said Stanley's sim.

'You weren't kidding when you said that, then? You can get me in to meet with the actual GM?'

'I have friends in the company,' said Stanley, twirling a thumb in his holographic beard-hair.

'Friends high up?'

'Exactly.'

'So you're saying I speak to them, and they pass the enquiry even further up, and she will get back to me?'

'Something like that.'

'I would, of course, appreciate that. I mean, Stanley, if I'm honest it doesn't sound very likely that it will lead to a meeting. I've already spoken to her people. Put in multiple requests. None of that prompted the GM to pick up her dog and bone.'

The briefest of pauses while Stan, at the other end of his connection, checked this allusion.

'Ah, but the assistant you spoke to is dead, now.'

'Dead as a coffin nail.'

'Really. You won't understand the crime until you understand the movie – his masterpiece, his masterpiece. *2001: A Space Odyssey*!'

'Stan—' Alma began, embarrassed on his behalf.

But he cut her off. 'Shall I tell you what I think?'

'I don't know. Shall you?'

The elevator door slid open, and Alma stepped out. The telesonic Stanley stayed inside the elevator.

'I think even somebody as stratospherically placed as the GM is going to be nervous that one of her assistants is dead. And I think she might be readier to confide in you than in the police.'

'Confide what?'

'Well, she'd have to be the one to tell you *that*.'

The doors slid shut, and the elevator descended with its unreal passenger still inside. Presumably by the time it reached the ground floor it would be perfectly empty.

'OK,' said Alma, to the empty hallway.

11: *The Gate in the High Place*

Back home, Alma let out a lengthy, exhausted sigh, and drank a coffee, and ate a food bar, in that order. Then she dozed for a while, and woke unrefreshed.

On and on and on. Falling through the void.

She went through to see how Marguerite was doing. Poorly, always poorly. Poorlier than before. More poorlier than beforelier.

As she washed her hands in readiness for the next bout of treatment, she asked, 'So – any luck rustling up any new lines of credit, Rita?'

Instead of answering that, Marguerite said, 'I've been thinking about why Jupita hired you, of all people.'

'What do you mean, of all people?'

'I don't mean it like that. Perhaps she hired you because you are so very good at what you do. Perhaps she hired you because you are associated with me, and I am such a legend.' Marguerite nodded to herself at this, and lingered over the word. 'Ledge,' she said, as if peering over the limit of everything and into the void. '*End.*'

'That must be it,' said Alma, putting on her apron and gloves.

'But look at it from the other side. As a good investigator ought. It's always worth thinking about matters from both sides, wouldn't you say? She wants you to investigate three people, none of whom are physically based in R!-Town. I mean, *she* is here, physically, and you are, so there's a degree of convenience, I suppose, in the arrangement. But the other people she actually wants you to look at live at various distances from here.'

'It would indeed be odd if Europe's four wealthiest individuals were all physically based in R!-town, don't you think?'

'Well, of course.'

'*She* spends all her time in-Shine. I wouldn't be surprised if her sense of how things function in the Real has become a bit hazy.

She needs someone to investigate something in the Real. She knows I work exclusively in the Real. So she hires me.'

'But she *knows* you are time-limited. That every four hours and four minutes you have to come back to this physical location, this apartment.'

'What's your point?' Alma asked.

'My point is she knows it wouldn't be practical for you to chase down the physical location of these four people. She could hire dozens of PIs who don't have that kind of constraint.'

'The GM is physically based in north London. I can get there and back easily enough.'

'And the other two?'

'I don't know, Rita,' said Alma, feeling irrationally irked at this line of questioning. 'She's paying, and we desperately need money. I can only do what I can do. All right?'

Marguerite's face showed something rare, for her: distress.

'My darling,' she said, in a small voice, 'I did not mean to *anger* you.'

And, instantly, Alma's bad mood put its shameful tail between its metaphorical legs and loped away. She found herself suddenly close to tears.

'I'm sorry, Rita,' she said, putting her arms around her lover's neck. 'Didn't mean to snap. I'm worried – that's all. I'm worried about money.'

'It *is* a worry. I know.'

'Isn't it, though?'

'I only meant,' said Marguerite, in a chastened voice, 'that this Jupita's reasons for hiring you might have a bearing on the case. What if she doesn't expect you to get to the bottom of the mystery she has hired you to investigate? What if she doesn't actually want you to solve it?'

'It could be,' said Alma, now busying herself with changing her apron and gloves – she had to change them, since she had contaminated them by hugging Marguerite. 'But right now my eye is on the...' She trailed off.

'The?'

'The imminent,' said Alma, as the clock ticked down. 'Treatment window,' she added, distractedly.

And there it was: the screen was blinking. A subarachnoid darkening, and a new kind of lipid contamination.

Alma's throat was clenching – if it was just those two, then she could treat Marguerite with what she had at home. But a third thing could emerge in the next twenty seconds, and it could easily be something for which she would require a pharmakon she did not have.

Time ticked. She readied her response.

Just those two. She could have shouted in delight. She opened the old stent and flooded the area with the necessary. No need – not this time – for expensive new pharmakons for which no lender would front Alma the money, nohow. The whole thing was over in less than a minute. Marguerite didn't even lose consciousness.

The relief was a push and rush of adrenaline through her entire system.

Afterwards, they had a cup of tea together.

'I know you're worried about money, my dear,' said Marguerite. 'I know the lack of funds makes treating me more stressful than it ought to be. But we've survived this long – haven't we?'

'I suppose we have.'

'We'll last a bit longer, I reckon. I'll have a rummage around and see if there's anything I can do, in a fiduciary-accumulative sense.'

'Why do *you* think Jupita would hire me if she didn't want me to be successful?'

Marguerite scratched her nose. 'There could be a number of reasons. It might be that she is under pressure from somewhere else to show willing, as it were, but doesn't want the investigation actually to succeed.'

'Or it could be,' Alma added, thinking aloud, 'that she has some personal animus against me and wants to humiliate me. Give me this puzzle to solve and then ridicule me for failing. Spread news of my incompetence online. Although given how much money, and therefore power, she has, this would be a pretty roundabout way of doing *that*.'

'Or, you know, maybe she doesn't want us to fail,' Marguerite suggested. 'Maybe she hired us because we're the best, and wants us to succeed. Maybe she's a *fan*.'

'Talking of which,' said Alma, getting to her feet, 'I have to go and meet my fans. Or one of them.'

'Stan the self-declared fan. Maybe he will have useful information for us.'

The man who called himself Stanley met her by the old town hall.

'I've retained the services of a taxicab,' he said, gesturing towards a flycar parked nearby.

Alma naturally hesitated. 'This is to take us to north London?'

'Yes.'

'Just so as we both understand, I have to be back here in under four hours.'

'Of course.'

'You won't mind, then, if the cab slaves itself to my feed rather than yours? I'd feel a whole lot more comfortable if I can order it to fly back at whatever point.'

'Alma,' said Stan, 'you don't trust me. I understand that. Given your position. Of course you can command the ride. But it's only a quarter of an hour to Highgate, and we'll not be there more than a half hour. You'll be in perfect control the whole time. But I understand – you want to make assurance doubly sure.'

Her feed offered her the source of that last thing – a literary allusion, it seemed.

'Just so as we both understand,' she repeated.

Alma did the necessary with her feed: the cab was a Grade Gamma AI and perfectly biddable. To stay on the safe side, she filed an emergency pickup tag with a friend. In case of emergency, or if the cab's AI got overridden, or there was a crash, or dinosaurs emerged from a temporal breach and chewed through the motor – you never knew. Over the years Alma had inhabited the state of being called *caution* so thoroughly it had become melded with her mind.

The two got into the cab and it swept up into the sky. R!-Town flinched away below – the autumnal-coloured brickwork buildings and grey slab roofs, the streets swiftly becoming fissures in the tessellation of the town as a whole. The Blade Tower, with its stag-beetle horn, became a stub. The bough-like curve of the Thames was joined by the skinnier vein of the Kennet. Late afternoon sunlight reflected with feathery intricacy from the industrial structures to the east. Drones passed below them.

Overhead the clouds looked like cigarette smoke. The sky was beginning to shade into evening colours of lemon and pink.

Soon enough the cab encroached on the airspace of London, and the crazily detailed texture of its vast mosaic. There were a great many more drones. The lower-rise layer of older architecture gave way, at that point where the Thames moved through a doubled sine, into great reefs of stacked accommodation, meta-stairways of concrete and metal, and the Thames swelled, as if with pride, to be flowing through such a metropolis. They swung north and soon enough were settling onto the platforms that flanked Highgate High Street.

'I enjoyed that. I always derive pleasure from looking *down* on London,' Stan said, as they disembarked.

The cab AI wanted to take its fare from Alma's feed, since she had identified herself as the directing passenger; it took a moment to persuade it to tap Stan instead.

'Looking down?' she said.

'It's so big, don't you think, on ground level? Overwhelming. A place to drown in, not to live.'

'I've always preferred smaller conurbations myself.'

'But that's the benefit of getting above it, don't you think? It reminds you that there is a vantage point from which all can be brought into comprehension. That it can be apprehended. And that's an important thing to remember.'

They were along the sliding paveway now, making their way towards Waterlow Park.

'Important,' repeated Alma, in a neutral tone.

'Surely, surely. Because, you see, it's the physical correlative of a non-physical system.' He was in a more lucid and less bonkers mood this evening, evidently.

'Physical correlative of a non-physical system,' said Alma. 'Right.'

'We might call that latter thing money, I suppose. But money is just a shorthand for the system by which people fit together with other people on the largest scale. Inside the love relation it's simple, and your actions are guided by one principle – the welfare of the loved one. The thing is, no society on earth has ever managed to make that a coherent *social* principle, has it? Christianity and Islam, Diggers and Communism and Creative Commoners have tried, but without success. In order to bring society into some sort of coherence, altruism has to be leavened with a little self-interest. Don't you think?'

They passed two in-Shine walkers, both wearing fairly expensive mesh-suits.

'I try to stay away from politics,' Alma said.

They waited for an industrial cleaning bot as big as a house to trundle by before crossing the road, and they were on the path across the grassy summit of Highgate Hill.

'The cab couldn't land us here and save us the walk?'

'Gracious no. The GM owns the whole hill. It's private property.'

'I thought it was a common!'

'Politics, though,' said Stan. 'I'm not making a judgement, you know. Mr Kubrick was never a *socialist*, you know, and neither am I. Money was the system that developed, and people working to acquire it, and competing with one another to acquire more, has shaped our world for so long now it's hard to see how things could ever be otherwise.'

'There's always the Shine.'

'Ah!' said Stan. 'Well, exactly. That's exactly the point! This is what makes me your fan, Ms Alma. It's your *insight*! Sherlock Mujer is bound to triumph over all those Sherlock Hombres, wouldn't you say?'

Was he trying to insult her? Alma considered retorting to this, but decided against it.

'Whoop,' said Stanley, but quietly, as if to himself. 'Whoop.'

They were approaching a large building, the only structure standing on that open green space.

A fence enclosed just over an acre of Highgate Hill. Alma, intrigued by what Stan had told her, dug into her feed for the history of the place. It was the most expensive acre of land ever purchased in the history of the UK-EU, since the plot had previously been part of the larger common land of the park, and in order to buy it the purchaser had had to fund two acts of parliament, a substantial compensation package and various other stipendiary and semi-legal subventions. But, her feed told her, the Golden Meteor had paid not only without a qualm, but without any noticeable dent in her larger fortune. The building of the house itself – a diamond-bright mantle of glass surrounding a gigantic totem-pole-shaped thrust of steel and stone – was a minor expense by comparison, even though its architectural ambition also made it the most costly private domicile ever built.

'Check the gateway,' said Stan.

Alma checked. The main gateway, her feed informed her, was built from granite shaved from the stones at Stonehenge. On its own this gate had cost more to erect than the new EU Parliamentary Moot-house in its entirety.

'You know what that gateway is saying?'

An unopen mouth to all but the wealthiest and most privileged, Alma thought.

'It's saying, "I am considerably richer than you".'

'Well, of course,' said the man who called himself Stan. 'But something else. Something more specific. Let's imagine there are two people. One has a great deal of political power – let's call her Pu Sto, just for the sake of argument – but not much money. The other – the GM, to pick a name out of the air – is wholly uninterested in playing the sort of games needful to accrue political power. Games like canvassing for elections or running media empires. But she is, nonetheless, prodigiously wealthy.'

'I'll try to imagine such a couple.'

'The way things have generally worked in the past is that, though the wealthy individual has a great deal of leverage, on account of her wealth, it's the politician who holds the trump card – because she can lock the first person up. She can leverage the laws of the land, than which nobody is supposed to be more powerful.' Stan nodded at the gateway. 'That says, "things have changed." It says, "you know all those laws protecting these stones as ancient monuments and treasures of the commonwealth of UK-EU? I hereby disregard them, and here's the blizzard of cash that enables me to do it. Moreover, since I'm comfortable inside the house on the *other* side of that gate, I disregard those laws with impunity." It's saying, "I have reached the level of wealth where the law is merely an inconvenience to be bought off, and no longer a constraint." That's what it says.'

'Stanley, is this your roundabout way of saying *the GM* is responsible for the crimes I am investigating?'

Stan the Fan turned an ingenuous face in her direction. 'We're not talking about what *I'm* saying, Ms Alma. We're talking about what this gateway is saying.'

'The gateway is saying she *believes* she is above the law. But that doesn't mean she actually is.'

'Oh, Ms Alma!' said Stan, indulgently. 'Oh, oh, oh.' But then he said, 'Shall we see if they'll let us in?'

Despite its expense of construction, and notwithstanding its sheer size, there was something rather ostentatiously modest about the house. The central section rose twelve storeys high, and presented an intimidatingly bristly and armoured presence to Alma's feed. She pulled her online senses in, like a snail into a shell, and took a deep breath.

Two guards, both carrying firearms in hip-slung holsters, stood at the front door.

'Good day to you, my fine fellows,' said Stan.

He showed them two perfectly empty palms. Something passed feed-to-feed between them, although Alma couldn't see what it was. Some sort of open-sesame, evidently, since the two beckoned them forward. They drew S's in the vicinity of Alma and Stan's two bodies with their weapon-detecting wands and let them step into the house.

Inside was a broad hallway, marble-walled, lit discreetly but well. There was a young man sitting behind a receptionist's counter. He seemed to recognise Stan, and there was a further feed-to-feed exchange. Then Stan smiled and beckoned Alma to follow and walked past the counter.

Stan led the way, down to the end of the corridor, through a sliding door and, with a left turn, further on.

'So which of the GM's minions are we off to meet?'

'Did I say minions?'

'Hard to believe,' said Alma, 'that we're actually going to meet the Golden Meteor herself.'

'The harder a thing is to believe,' Stan opined, 'the more it exercises the credibility muscles, and the more buff and toned it makes your imagination.'

'Well,' said Alma. '*That's* obviously nonsense.'

'Oh,' said Stan, sounding genuinely rebuked. 'Do you think so? I think imagination is terribly important. And that means it ought to be cultivated. It's what Kubrick had, after all! In spades, as they used to say. And isn't it how *you* solve all your mysteries, Ms Alma?'

'There are,' said Alma, non-committally, 'a range of strategies I employ.'

They were descending, walking along a downward-curling ramp, and past a series of big abstract canvases: red and black; black and purple; black and white.

'You're known here, aren't you, Stan?' said Alma. 'You said you retired. You said you used to work for the GM. I'll tell you what I think: the ease with which you took us past those guards suggests to me that you still work for her.'

'What's that? No, no.'

'Be honest with me.'

'Honestly, the world came to an end, and we're all living in the rainbow ashes. Honestly, all that stuff is behind *me*.'

They came to a very hefty doorway, unbroken black and imposing. Alma prodded it with her feed, but it was as opaque to her apps as it was to sight. A security door of some kind, clearly.

Stan spent some time parleying with the door, or doing something in his feed. It was a shielded interaction, so Alma couldn't be sure what. But then the obsidian of the door sparkled with glitter, some kind of internal star field projection. Then it went white, made a strange sighing noise and opened up. Stan gestured.

Alma stepped through and Stan followed. As soon as they were both through, the door shut itself solidly and reverted to black.

'Is this a trap, Stan?' Alma asked. 'I do hope not – for your sake.'

'My dear Alma,' Stan laughed. 'Why do you find it so hard to believe me when I say I'm trying to help you? It's true that you couldn't have gotten in here without me, but nonetheless, it's *your* being here that matters, not mine.'

He stopped in front of an elevator. The doors melted away and they stepped inside: gold and white, a carpet so thick it was almost fluid.

The tug of ascension in Alma's gut was so minor she barely felt it. An impressively buffered piece of machinery, all things considered.

'I'm not above using you as a cat's-paw, Ms Alma,' said Stan the Fan. 'But saying so is praise – really it is. Because you're the best at solving the mysteries of this world! The very best. When I say I'm a fan, I'm being completely genuine. You can help me uncover the truth. I'm interested in the truth. I'm building a temple to the truth, putting one cubic brick onto another until I'm done.'

Bricks in the shape of cubes was what Alma heard. She didn't think much about it, until later, after she had met the monkeys, and everything had changed. Of course then, if belatedly, she understood.

12: *The Golden Meteor*

Alma stepped out of the elevator and, quite unexpectedly, found herself in the GM's personal suite. A moment later, as the door swished closed behind her, and she realised that Stan the Fan had not come out of the elevator at the same time as her, it dawned on her that she had been parachuted into this room, tossed in and left to fend for herself.

She looked back. The display told her that the elevator was descending again.

So there she was, on her tod – which means *solitary* in English and *death* in German, either of which meanings might apply in this new circumstance – inside the private suite and inner sanctum of one of Europe's wealthiest, and most privacy oriented, humans. There was no reason to believe she would be forgiving of this trespass.

It was a minimalist space, wide and clean. A single floor-to-ceiling window disclosed, as if offhandedly, only the most expensive view in London: a slow descending vista from Highgate Hill down towards the Thames. A bookcase along one wall contained what looked like (Alma was no expert on books) a great many valuable and collectible editions. But the most striking thing was the double couch, right in the centre of the space. It was, evidently the GM's point of in-Shine access –and there she was. Melissa Herford. The GM herself. In the flesh. A long, slender frame, and a wrinkle-free face.

She was floating a couple of centimetres over the top of the couch, and was dressed in the sort of body-hugging sheer mesh-suit Alma had previously only seen on Jupita, the kind that refused to invoke the word *expensive* unless it was prefixed by words like *prohibitively* or *ruinously*. No clanking about the streets for the GM, of course. Woven into the fabric was an induction web that avoided the danger of pressure points or bedsores. A med-unit, fluted with chrome, stood by her head.

There must have been some form of proximity warning too, because as Alma watched, the GM shuddered, opened her eyes and lifted her head.

The tendrils that had been supplying her body with nutrition and hydration undulated back into the unit. The GM's body settled slowly onto the couch, and she swung her legs over the side.

'You,' she said, 'are Alma.'

'Oh! Hello,' replied Alma, lamely.

'You were the individual present when my employee,' there was hardly a hesitation as she retrieved the name from her feed, 'Tym was killed. And now *you're* inside my inner sanctum!'

'I apologise,' said Alma. 'You'll find this hard to believe, but I seem to have stumbled into your room quite – actually, inadvertently.'

'Given how private this private space *is*,' said the GM, 'and how very well protected – frankly it's hard to see how it might be uncovered by a mere lack of advertence.'

'Ah,' said Alma.

'How did you get in?'

Alma pointed at the door of the elevator through which she had walked. It was only as she raised her hand that she realised that the door was no longer visible. The wall had swallowed it, or reorganised itself to hide it.

The GM nodded. 'There's only a few who know about *that* escape line,' she remarked. 'So I'll be able to narrow down the Judas soon enough. Of course, I'm going to have to order it to be repositioned, which is an inconvenience.'

She seemed remarkably unfazed by this intrusion. Or perhaps her sang-froid was a prelude to some imminent and devastating loss of temper.

'I genuinely apologise for this intrusion,' said Alma. 'I really didn't know it would come out here.'

'Why are you in my house at all?'

'I got in touch with you a few days ago. I don't expect you to remember. I've been retained by another of your – what to call it? Group? The four?'

'I assume by Jupita. Who else? She's become quite unhinged

latterly – crazy. What did she hire you to do? Infiltrate my house and, what – plant incriminating evidence?'

'No, not at all.' Alma saw no reason to withhold the truth. 'She... She is persuaded that one of your number is... well, *dead*, actually.'

'Dead? Which one?'

'She doesn't know.'

'She doesn't *know*?'

'She's hired me to find out.'

The GM shook her head very slowly, right-left, left-right.

'And isn't that exactly like her. Classic chaff, classic nonsensical chaff. Great dumpsters piled high with unprocessed distractium.'

'Well, at least I can confirm,' Alma suggested, aiming at jaunty, 'that *you* are not dead. So that's good news!'

'Her timing is no accident. You can tell her I said so.'

This was hopeful; presumably it meant that the GM wasn't about to have Alma killed.

'Happy to pass on that message,' she said, a little over-eagerly.

There was a pause. 'I'm just reviewing your file,' the GM said shortly. 'So you're a PI. Well, you're I-ing, P-ly, in quite the *wrong* place here.'

Alma took the plunge. Since she was here now, she might as well do her job.

'*You* don't feel,' she essayed, 'that any of the others might be dead? Their in-Shine presence played by an imposter?'

The GM looked levelly at Alma without speaking.

'My client,' Alma went on, 'talks of the gestalt of the group being perceptibly *altered* in a way that—'

'Timing,' interrupted the GM. 'Is what this is about. Nothing else. You think one of the four of us could die and *nobody notice*? Think about that for a moment and see how absurd the notion is. No, no, she knows takeovers are imminent. Approaching the endgame. It's spooked her. She's not ready. So she's hoping to throw a little sand in the gears. That's what you are, Ms PI, just grit.'

'True grit, though,' Alma returned, with what she hoped was a winning smile.

The GM didn't so much as blink. 'Your file says you have an ancillary status with the police.'

'I do.'

'I assume the police interviewed you about Tym's death?' Without waiting for an answer, the GM added, 'I know they did. They interviewed me, although they didn't have the clanking great stainless steel *testicular* chutzpah to actually come into this room. Still, I can tell you what I told them. Tym was killed by Jupita. She bought some very secret, very powerful bug and used it to manipulate the smartcloth of his tie, to override its safeties and squeeze the life out of him.'

Alma said nothing.

'She's turned,' the GM went on, 'nasty – which is to say, murderous – which is to say, desperate. And shall I tell you why she's desperate?'

Alma smiled again. More of a simper, this time.

'She's desperate because our group, our Four, is about to realign in ways that will prove extremely disadvantageous to her. Ah!'

At the back of the room, behind the GM's double couch, a door was opening in the previously smooth wall. Two absolutely enormous figures stepped through. They moved with what was, considering their bulk, really very impressive delicacy, leather shoes barely swishing through the unbroken expanse of soft, white, vat-grown polar bear pelt, thick pile carpetry. They looked alike – not precisely identical, but close enough in physique and face to be, Alma figured, twins. They wore similar dark grey suits, very old-fashioned in cut though presumably made from modern cloth. Two chunky-faced, bulbous-nosed, small-eyed, hefty-bodied men. Neat black hairdos and shoulders like tallboys.

They were at Alma in moments, one on each side, and she felt them take hold of her two elbows. Their hands were untoothed alligator jaws: firmly inescapable.

'What did Tym tell you before he died?' the GM asked in a pleasant voice.

'What?' said Alma.

'He went out of his way to go and talk to you. It wasn't on my business, it was on his own. Somebody in my inner circle has been taking *whomping* great bribes from Jupita, and I incline to the notion that it was him.'

'He didn't say anything.'

'He must have said something!'

'I mean, he didn't say anything about anything like that.'

'And yet he ran to you. Not to the police, of course. He wasn't stupid. But something had him scared.'

'Given that he was killed, I'd say he had some cause to be scared. If he was double-crossing you, working for Jupita, then why would *she* kill him?'

'What,' the GM repeated, 'did he tell you before he died?'

There was nothing to be gained in pretending ignorance, and Alma had no desire to give these two Gargantuae the excuse to beat an answer out of her, so she said, 'He told me that each of the four have a different strategy to achieving absolute wealth. He told me that each of you need the others for now, but the time will come when one of you will ditch the others and strike out at that elusive target.'

'You could have worked that out for yourself. Go on.'

'What else? Oh, he said something strange. Or I thought so, anyhow. He said *money isn't everything*, which at first I thought was just a platitude.'

'Or a blasphemy,' the GM said, smiling thinly.

'But as he was dying he said: *money will be everything*. Then it all got messy, and he died, and soon enough the police were there. Thinking back, I suppose I figured he was just contradicting himself. But now that I think back again – maybe he wasn't. Maybe there was an implicit *but* in between the two statements. Conceivably it was a warning.'

'Money *is* everything,' said the GM firmly. 'And it will soon be more than everything. That's no contradiction. That's the logic of the Shine. Ms Alma, I'm afraid I must press you for an answer to this question, or else instruct my two assistants here to press you in a more directly physical sense – did Tim give out any trade secrets, for instance about the strategies preferred by the twenty-fivers – I mean the other three members of our little group?'

'He talked a little about it.'

'He shouldn't have – that's verboten. He signed all manner of most restrictive contracts, with most punitive sanctions, promising not to reveal anything of the sort.'

'I'd say contractual obligations are the least of his worries where he now is.'

The GM settled a steady, surprisingly disconcerting stare on her.

'OK,' Alma said, 'sure, he did tell me a bit. But he was vague. He said Jupita was banking on some kind of flow, or something.

I'm not sure what – popularity markers in social networks, likes or something. He said the Stirk of Stirk was trying a new kind of Bitcoin, that Cernowicz is planning on scaling up microscarcities that exist in-Shine—'

'I'm obviously not interested in what he said about the *others*,' the GM said. 'I'm interested in the extent of his betrayal of me.'

'He didn't say much about you. He said your plan was...'

Alma stopped, looking up at the bodyguard on her left and the bodyguard on her right. It was like being at the bottom of a mineshaft. The pressure on her elbows remained constant. There was no chance of her breaking free with a sudden lurch, and nowhere for her to run even if she did.

'Go on.'

'He told me your plan was *time*.'

Because the GM was physically there, in-Real, and not mediated by any avatar software, Alma could read her reaction directly. There was the slightest of flinches – no very obviously telegraphed reaction, but just a little shiver, a twitch, evidence that this information being disseminated mattered to her.

'Time.' And then she smiled very broadly. 'They do say *time is money*, don't they? Which, logically, must mean that money is time.' And then she turned away and returned to her couch. 'Good day, Ms PI. We shan't meet again.'

The pressure on Alma's elbows increased a small amount, and she felt herself lifted bodily into the air. In moments she had been carried from the room.

13: *The Kry Twins*

The two thugs, or bodyguards, or godzillas – whatever they were – whisked Alma out of the GM's bedroom, through a broad antechamber, passed a surprised-looking security guard on a desk, and out into a corridor. Then they swept through another hefty-looking door and into a lift, barely large enough for the three of them. The door closed.

That awkward moment as the lift descends, and all the occupants stand in awkward silence, and the pressure builds to make conversation. You know that moment?

The two goons had at least put her feet back on the floor. Alma's feed was still connected with the outside world. She had previously set up a tripwire to notify various people if anything violent happened to her.

'Pleased to meet you,' she said. 'I'm Alma.'

The goon on the left rotated and angled his head, slowly, as befitted so massy an object, and looked down at her. A forty-tonne Easter Island granite bust swivelling in place to examine the patch of grass at its base.

'Pleased to meet you, Alma,' he said, in a voice whose basso was so profundo it almost came out in Australia.

She waited, and then prompted, 'And you are...?'

'We *are*,' said the second goon.

Alma waited for him to go on, but he appeared to have nothing more to say.

'I was asking your names,' Alma said.

The second goon nodded ponderously. 'I did think it strange,' he said, 'you commenting on our onto*large*ical status. I mean, straight off the bat.'

'Existence presupposes our essential-ness,' put in the first.

'If you want to *arse* a question,' the second goon said sagely, 'you should just arse it, is what I reckon. Don't beat around the peripheral bush. Know what I mean?'

The elevator stopped and the doors slipped open. This time, instead of grabbing her and lifting her, the enforcer on her left gestured with his hand, and she stepped out.

The three of them walked down a short neon-lit corridor, presumably subterranean, and through a reinforced door into the sort of room that might appear in a visual dictionary as an antonym for *cosy*.

Alma tried for a third time. 'All right then, not beating around the peripheral bush – what are your names?'

'We are the Krys,' said the second goon

'Spelt,' said the other, 'with a K.' He pronounced *spelt* with a medial diphthong of indeterminate nature and finished the word off with a brisk glottal stop in the place of its *t*.

'With a K,' said Alma. 'Got it.'

'We like the K,' said the first.

'We do,' agreed the second.

'It adds class,' said the first.

'Klass.' Alma was checking her feed as surreptitiously as she could, but it was no longer linked to the wider network. That the room was a Faraday cage didn't bode well.

'Sit down, please,' said the first Kry twin.

'It's an unusual name, certainly,' said Alma, sitting at the central table, and talking more than was her wont. Nerves sometimes got her that way. 'Is it a family moniker, or more by way of being a trade name? Perhaps you have a tendency to burst into tears?'

'Oh, *we're* not the ones who do the crying,' the second twin told her.

Alma reflected that this was not a good sign.

The two of them took chairs on either side of her. It didn't seem possible, but they towered over her even more alarmingly sitting than when they'd all been standing up.

'So,' said Alma, 'this is a matter of asking questions, yes?'

'Ontology,' said the first Kry twin, 'and epistemology too? Quite the philosopher, ain't you?'

'I only say that, because I want to stress – I'm happy to answer any questions you may have,' said Alma.

'She's *happy*, Reg,' said the first Kry twin to the second.

'So she says, Ron,' said the second.

'Is it our trade, making people happy, Reg?'

'On the contrary, Ron.' The second pulled something long and sharp out of his jacket pocket. 'Our trade is making people *un*happy.'

'Then you'll never lack for work,' said Alma. 'But really there's no need to *make* me unhappy. In point of fact I'm already pretty unhappy, held in this underground room against my will by – if you'll excuse me for saying so – you two great gorillas.'

'*Great* is a flattering sort of qualifier,' said Ron.

'Better than saying two *mediocre* gorillas, certainly,' agreed Reg.

'Unless she meant to indicate not eminence, but rather to make a disparaging reference to our size, Reg?'

'That would be markedly less complimentary, Ron.'

Alma readied herself. It was clear that things were about to turn nasty, one way or another.

It would not be true to say that she had been in exactly this situation before, but she had certainly encountered men like these, and had been on the sharp end of an interrogation or two in her time. It was about stretching the elastic back for a certain time and holding it there, ready to snap back in your subject's face. How long you held the elastic like that was the skill of the gifted interrogator. The wet stuff – punches and scalpels, screams and blood coming out in sloppy globs – any fool could do. And most fools would do it in a way that obstructed rather than facilitated the extraction of useful information. Although, that being said, a certain amount of what professionals in this business call *the wet-stuff* – of, that is, the active infliction of pain – would usually also be needful.

Alma was no coward. She knew she could bear a certain quantity of blows. But she had a weak spot, and that spot's name was Marguerite. She simply could not afford to be delayed beyond the four-hour-four-minute deadline. Any aggressor aware of that fact might apply pressure to that spot and Alma would fold up like a self-disassembling furniture set.

The GM had called up a file on her. Alma assumed it was as detailed a file as money could buy; the GM had nearly endless reserves of money with which to buy details.

She presumed the GM and her goons were aware of her weak spot.

Alma's options were limited. These two were big men, not out of shape, and men for whom this was clearly a full-time job. She might, she calculated, take one of them down – a very uncertain *might*, that – but not both. In this situation her best bet was to provoke the actual crisis, and so, hopefully, hurry things up as far as possible.

'Can we move this along, gentlemen?' she tried. 'I'm sure you have better things to be doing with your time. Bananas to eat, ticks to pick off one another's pelts and so on.'

This didn't seem to antagonise them. Indeed, rather the contrary.

'Empire State Buildings to climb to the top of,' said Ron, nodding approvingly.

'David Attenboroughs with whom to commune,' said Reg.

'Strange black monoliths to adore,' said Ron.

'Clearly, you're not finding my gorilla references as insulting as I might have hoped,' said Alma. 'How do you feel about *pigs*?'

Smoothly, with neither haste nor hesitation, Reg Kry leaned in. His huge arm, thick and heavy as a roll of ballroom floor linoleum, slipped around Alma's head. With his other hand he grasped the back of her cranium. It felt like a baseball catcher's mitt was clamped to her skull.

Unhurriedly, Ron Kry brought himself closer to Alma's face. The item he had taken out of his pocket revealed itself to be a weapon, either a very narrow stiletto or perhaps a fat needle.

'Hold still,' he advised.

He stuck it up her nose.

The unpleasantness of this was as much about its unexpectedness and intrusion as about the pain it caused – although Ron pushed the sharp end solidly *into* her sinus, at the back of her nose, and it assuredly was painful. A worm of blood crawled from her nostril and down her lip.

'Don't sneeze,' said Reg, behind her, 'would be my advice.'

Ron pushed a little harder, and the pain became markedly worse. Alma held herself as still as she could. Her heart was shuddering behind the slats of her ribcage.

'Another little push,' said Ron, close by, 'and this will go up and in *through* your left eye, which will blind you in that eyeball.'

'Right,' she said, her voice nasalised and muffled by the fat needle stuck in her sinus.

'My mistake,' agreed Ron Kry. 'My left, *your* right.'

'No,' Alma mumbled. 'I was agreeing with you.'

'It's a nice eye,' said Reg, behind her. 'Be a shame if anything were to ... *happen* to it.'

'Yes, yes,' Alma agreed.

'Bad things happen to eyes all the time,' said Ron. 'Get poked out, say. It's in Shakespeare.'

'Punched in.'

'Seared,' said Ron.

'Trashed by gangs armed with snooker cues,' said Reg. 'Burned down. Dumped in the river.'

'Well, you're moving from eyeballs *as such*,' said Ron, 'to other forms of general property.'

'I dare say she gets the general idea, though,' said Reg.

'I'm agreeing with you as emphatically as I know how,' said Alma in a strangulated voice, applying every portion of her will-power to remaining motionless.

The pain was quite sharp, and it was intensely disagreeable to have this object inside her nasal cavity. Worse, Reg's warning about not sneezing was horribly accurate. There was an intense crawling and twitching sensation in her inside-cranial membrane area. She strained her very pips not to give way to it. The motion necessitated by even a stifled sneeze would surely push the end of the stiletto into her eyeball.

'Our employer,' said Ron, speaking very slowly, 'is a very—'

'Very,' said Reg.

'Very,' added Ron.

'Very,' Reg offered.

'Very,' agreed Ron.

'Very,' confirmed Reg.

'*Very* private person. You do not bother her again. You do not think of bothering her. And if you come within a mile of this building a second time ...'

He left this statement hanging; but Reg completed it for him. 'You'll be going away blind.'

'I think,' said Ron, 'that was implicit.'

The point of the stiletto was pressing so hard against the thin curve of her occipital bone that Alma could feel its deformation in the body of her eyeball. Very far from a nice sensation. Tears were swelling in the right duct, and dribbling down the side of her nose.

'You're right,' said Reg. 'Didn't need spelling out. I was over-egging it.'

'A little egg makes for good bakery,' Ron pontificated. 'But a lot makes for badkery. As my old nan used to say.'

And, as suddenly as it started, the stiletto was withdrawn. Alma sneezed at once, and an adder of blood and snot darted from her right nostril and landed, with a surprisingly loud sound, on the floor at her feet. She clapped a hand to her nose, sneezed again, and again, and again, and fumbled with her free fingers to expand the pocket in her tunic and retrieve a handkerchief. Blood was tastable on her lips.

'Well,' she said, her heart rattling inside her chest like a hamster at full pelt on its wheel, 'aren't you two the experts with *needles*.' Then she sneezed once more, rather undermining the force of the point she was making.

Ron leaned back. 'No idea,' he said, and paused. 'What you,' he added. There was a pause, the silence broken only by Alma's sniffling and blowing. 'Are talking about,' he finished.

Alma dabbed her eyes with the back of her hand.

'Well, I'm certainly crying. You've lived up to your name, at any rate,' she said.

'Sharp's the word,' said Ron.

The two Kry twins were standing either side of the doorway.

'We'll see you out,' said Reg.

14: *Home Again*

The Krys escorted her out of the building, and walked with her as she crossed the heath and back towards her waiting cab. She didn't ask how they knew this was her cab – given the resources at the GM's disposal, tracing the log of all the nearby taxis would be, while not exactly legal, trivial.

She could have told them that the heath was common land from which they had no right to evict her, but she didn't suppose there would be much point in that. She wondered if the man who called himself Stanley would be at the taxi, but she assumed not. There was surely a strong likelihood that the GM would have identified him as the individual who'd let Alma have access to the mansion's inner sanctum, and presumably he had made himself scarce.

The inside of her nose hurt.

'You want to share with me how you did it?' she tried.

'Pff,' said Ron.

'Alexa Lund,' said Alma. 'I'm guessing you, Ron, held her in a chair by her shoulders, and you, Reg, pushed the needle through her thumb.'

'Can't recall any thus described thumbnicular shenanigans.' Ron raised his forefinger to the cleft of his chin as if he were actually thinking about it. 'Do you recall anything, Reg?'

'Well, Ron,' said Reg, pedantically, 'I have to say I recall a great variety of things, from various aspects of my life, as you would expect.'

'But do you recall the thumb of an individual called Alexa Lund?'

'I have no recall of any individual by that name. Lund or other-wise,' he added, as if clarifying.

'I'm not asking for a confession,' Alma said, breathing quickly. She wasn't out of there yet, and if she went too far the Krys might decide it was simpler to snap her neck, whatever instructions their boss had given them. 'I'm just puzzled *how* you were able to do so much damage with one little needle.' It was a long shot, but conceivably appealing to their professional pride would get results. 'I mean, I very much admire the *brevity* of it. And its oddity – it's entirely singular and original. But how did you do it?'

'Oh, needles can be most damageous,' said Ron, offhand.

'Very much so,' confirmed Reg.

'Not that we're saying *we* did any such damage,' Ron clarified.

'Not we,' said Reg.

It was clear they were enjoying this.

'I know how it is,' she tried. 'You're following orders. Doing your job. And doing it, I must say, with a good deal of panache. I'm just trying to confirm what I've already figured out about why the Golden Meteor wanted Alexa Lund dead.'

'Alexa whom?' Reg asked, innocently.

'Whom Lund?' added Ron.

'Homeland?' Reg asked Ron. 'Did you say?'

'No, brother,' said Ron, gravely.

They were at the taxi now. Alma now wondered if her taking the cab would strand Stan in what was, presumably, a dangerous area for him. Or perhaps they had already captured him, and were torturing him in some cellar? In which case it would be best to let them know she was with him. To imply she could go to the police if he went missing – that sort of thing.

'I came with a...' Alma hesitated before adding, 'friend. I don't want to take the cab and leave him stranded here.'

'The feller you came into the arse with,' said Ron.

It took her a moment to realise he was saying *house*. What a polyvalent syllable that could be, in the right accent!

'Stanley, yes.'

'Oho,' said Reg. '*Sternley*, is it now?'

Ron leaned forward, and his head blotted out the sun. 'Wouldn't worry about *Sternly* if I were you,' he said, sternly.

'Is he all right?' Alma asked.

There were no messages from Stan in her feed, but neither was there any indication he was in trouble.

'Nice cab,' said Reg, indicating the waiting vehicle. 'Be a shame if something *happened* to it.'

It was true that she had to get back for Marguerite. And Stan could almost certainly shift for himself. Alma decided she had reached her better-part-of-valour moment.

'It's been a real pleasure meeting you gentlemen,' she said, poking the cab in-feed to get it to open its door.

'The pleasure,' said Ron, in a menacing voice 'has been all ours.'

She got inside the car and in moments was airborne. The sigh of relief that emerged from her at this juncture was large enough to merit classification as a sob. Nor was it the only one she gave breath to during that journey.

She spent five minutes attending to her wounded inner nose, turning her handkerchief into a tessellation of miniature flags of Japan. When the bleeding seemed to have settled, she pinged Stan.

No reply.

Then she spoke to Marguerite.

—I'll be with you in a little bit, Alma told her.

A small red circle, like a beauty spot, appeared on the back of her hand.

—I don't usually have to ask this of *you*, Marguerite said. But are you OK?

—Fine. Just a nosebleed.

She worked a piece of cloth free from her pocket and stuffed it into her nostril.

She ran a search on the Kry Twins, and unearthed a number of martial arts and bodyguard licences lodged with the authorities, but little else. They were, it seemed, actual biological twins. If they had any criminal convictions, that information was redacted from the public web. With enough money, that sort of thing was perfectly doable; it didn't mean they had no criminal record. Given their skill set, and their present employment, a lack of prior criminal convictions seemed very unlikely.

'Cab,' she said, belatedly thinking of the cost of the journey, 'can you please confirm that this fare will also be paid by my former companion?'

'Please specify,' said the taxi AI cheerily.

'Stanley – the person who paid the earlier fare to London. The guy I was in the cab with on the journey out.'

'I'm going to need a surname, ma'am.'

Alma thought. What was that antique movie director he liked so much? Brick something. Redbrick?

'Kubrick.'

'I'm going to need his approval before I charge him for his journey, ma'am.'

Damn.

'I was hoping he'd given you prior instructions.'

'No, ma'am.'

Given the state of her finances, even a cab fare from London to R!-town was liable to push her over the edge. What would the taxi do if she got to the other end and credit was declined? Lock the doors and keep her inside until she paid?

She ran a quick search through her feed for any new quick loan companies, but she was up-to-the-hilt indebted at every turn. Then she tried pinging Stan again, and this time he answered.

—Stan, she said. You're OK?

—Of course I am, he replied. I'm pleased to see *you* got out without, shall we say, visible bruises.

His voice contained a note of rather lubricious self-satisfaction. It occurred to Alma, and not for the first time, that despite his various eccentricities, his ingratiating manner and his eagerness to present himself as her number one fan, there was something genuinely not nice about Stan.

—I need you to honour your word. I need you to pay for this cab flight. The one I'm currently taking. I'm sorry to ask, only ...

She stopped. She wasn't sorry to ask – he had led her into the GM's fortified house and abandoned her. She ought to be a lot angrier.

—By all means, Stan said. And then, after a moment, There, done. So, did you have a useful chat with the GM? Are you starting to get a sense of how this all fits together?

The truthful answer to that question was, *no.* But of course Alma wasn't about to admit anything of that sort. And, she reflected, she had learned something important during the trip. The two cases she was investigating were indeed linked. It was most likely the Krys who were responsible for Alexa Lund's death (although *how* was beyond her), which meant it was most likely the GM who had ordered the kill.

But she didn't say any of that. Instead she said:

—Why do I get the impression you're playing *games* with me, Stan? If there's something you want to tell me, why not just tell me?

—And spoil the fun of you working it out for yourself? You forget, Alma, I'm a *big* fan of your work. A *big fan*.

—Never mind fun. Never mind fan. Just tell me!

Stanley didn't reply for a moment, but then he said, I can't talk about it in-feed. That wouldn't be very secure.

—Then let's meet.

—I have to say I'm a little disappointed you're not prepared to work this out for yourself.

—Stan, I really can't be responsible for your sense of disappointment.

There was a silence. When Stan next spoke he sounded uncharacteristically sulky.

—Why don't we meet by the river? I can't pretend I'm not a little disappointed. I have to say I expected more. I really am a major fan of your work, you know.

—I don't know much about *fandom*, Alma retorted, beginning to find within herself after all some reserves of anger. But it seems to me that your definition of fandom is leading me on a merry bloody dance. Is that really what a fan does? Why not just *tell* me what's on your mind, Stan?

—Face to face.

—Eighty minutes, said Alma. That would give her time to treat Marguerite. Somewhere nice and public – Forbury Gardens.

—Still don't trust me, said the man who called himself Stanley. Oh, you're a cautious one and no mistake. But by all means, let's meet there. Not that it's likely to be very public, unless you *count* people stomping around in mesh-suits. And there are precious few of those these days. But all right – one hour, and I promise I will give you the key that will unlock this mystery.

She terminated the connection.

Alma got back in good time to address Marguerite's next flare-up, with only the anxiety that it might require expensive new medication to plague her mind. She prepped herself in the front room, and tried to centre herself.

Marguerite was sleeping when Alma arrived, woke up briefly and woozily when she was prepping to treat her, and then passed out again. It was starting to be an actual worry: oversleeping; temperature consistently a degree and a quarter too high; viral load well above the usual parameters. This was more than the four-hour curse. This was something underlying.

A spurt of anger shivered through her at the unfairness of it all. But she hauled that emotion back down. She wouldn't be in the optimum position to help Marguerite if she gave way to rage. So she stopped, focused, repeated her mantra – the one she recited to calm herself – and took a deep breath. A little distance.

She *was* angry with this Stanley fellow, though – playing his creepy little games, following her around, manipulating her. And that was an anger she felt entitled to.

Ignore him, she told herself.

And then it was time. A sudden rush of pathogens up the spinal cord, oddly spiky variants of the MP-4b. She refused to allow herself to worry about what would happen if the MP-4B antigens didn't take, spray-injected a phial, hurried to mop up the cascade of other viral shards through the brainstem. There was an alarming thirty seconds – time seemed, as the phrase goes, to *stretch* – as she battled both, and tried to deal with spontaneous muscle fibre breakdown in neck and shoulders. But after a few minutes the pathology plateaued, and then settled back down.

Saved for another four hours. Alma sat down and peeled off her gloves.

It was getting harder. Was that fair, though? Shouldn't it get easier, the more experienced Alma became?

There was something rebarbative in the fabric of the cosmos. Humans had been inserted into the universe in such a way that the grain of reality was always adverse to their actions.

Alma needed to spend some time tracking down credit – any kind of debt, any injection of cash whatsoever – to prepare for the next ten or so treatments. One of these was, statistically, bound to throw up an unusual pathology that would necessitate the purchase of new supplies. Also, she needed to nail down several loose leads in the cases she was working on. The sooner she got those finished, and received payment, the better. And she had Stanley to meet in under an hour – he either would or would not provide her with the wherewithal to bring things to a conclusion.

She fell asleep.

She woke with a clonic jerk, all the muscles in her arms flapping together, a sensation of falling. She'd been out for – her feed told her – exactly forty-one minutes.

Marguerite was calling softly to her. 'Alma, Alma.' Singing the name, with a minor third drop-down from the first syllable to the second, like a police siren.

'What?' Alma said gluily, sitting forward. 'What?'

'You're drooling, my dear,' said Marguerite.

'Sorry.' Wiped her mouth.

'And I need your help.'

'Help – what?'

'I fear I am about to be sick.'

This was unusual for her. Poorly though she was, Marguerite's digestion was usually cast-iron. Alma quickly located a receptacle and held it at that chin which was nearest her beloved's mouth. She kept one eye on the read-outs and Marguerite huffed and heaved and then, with a strangled chiming sort of noise, puked into the dish. It was a string of greenish phlegm rather than a full stomach evacuation, and from Marguerite's eyes it was clearly very uncomfortable.

When she was done, Alma disposed of the stuff and washed the little bowl.

'Feel better?'

'A little,' said Marguerite. 'I'm not sure where that came from.'

'You are ill, my love,' said Alma, washing her hands. 'I mean, in addition to the four-hour-four-minute pathology. Background to that. It's surprising it doesn't happen more often, actually. After all, strip away the four-hour thing and you're just a regular person. You're as liable to get sick as any other regular person.'

'I don't like it.'

'You'll get over it. Best guess, it's a gastric virus. Given the amount of medicine sloshing through you it's a wonder it has any hold, but I guess we don't often put treatment into your intestine as such, since there's rarely any need. I'll dose up an orange juice with something likely to nail it back.'

'Good, as I am thirsty. Though I'd prefer an apple juice.'

Alma checked their inventory and found no apple juice. Marguerite watched her, and knew what she was doing. There were three litres of orange juice. A litre of apple would cost mere cents, but Alma didn't want to load their debt level with anything in the least bit unnecessary.

'You'll have an orange juice,' she said, with jocular mock-severity, 'and you'll like it, young woman.'

'Such a tyrant,' sighed Marguerite. 'Very well – but you must compensate me with a detailed account of your meeting with the great Golden Meteor.'

Alma stepped away into the next room, carrying on the conversation in her feed.

—Well, I learned one really big thing. The thumb thing, the punctured thumb case, it is related to some shenanigans associated with the Fab Four. It's looking like Alexa Lund was murdered by these two bodyguards, or assassins, who work for the GM – the Kry Twins.

Alma punted what she knew across to Marguerite.

—Well, *they* seem like charmers, said Marguerite. They were responsible for your nosebleed?

'They were,' said Alma, coming back through to the bedroom.

'I have only bad feelings towards *them*. But you at least got to interrogate the Golden Meteor in person!'

'She was not as helpful as she might have been. She was startled at first to find me in her personal space, but she regained her self-possession very quickly. Then, rather than me questioning her, she questioned me.'

'About?'

'I'd say her chief concern was that word might get out about her particular approach to in-Shine currency.'

'Money, money, money, it's always that. Her approach being?'

'Her approach being, to use the natural scarcity of *time* as a means of leveraging a functioning money system in-Shine.'

'What is it the Bible says? There is a time for everything. Which means that everything comes back to time. That *time is money* equivalence, for instance – we could swap those terms about without disturbing its meaning!'

'That's exactly what she said, oddly enough.' Alma hooked the dosed-up parcel of juice to Marguerite's system. 'Pressed me hard on what Tym told me before he died. Wanted to know why Jupita had hired me.'

'So she grilled you.' Marguerite relaxed as the juice slipped down. 'But I'm sure you gave as good as you got. Asked her the crucial questions.'

'I asked a few. She, though, was unforthcoming,' said Alma, taking a seat. 'Unfortunately.'

'Alma, are you griéving,' said Marguerite, 'over the Golden Meteor's unforthcóming?'

Alma's feed tagged this as a likely quotation, but turned up no source. Did she want a deeper search algorithm?

She did not.

'So,' Alma said, 'the GM and I had our little chat. Then she called in her goons. Oh, Rita, they are *enormous*. Two heavily built geezers, big as lighthouses, shoulders like promontories of rock.' Marguerite withdrew into herself. 'I tried a pretty comprehensive online search on my way back here, and didn't turn up a criminal record for either of them – but everything about them screamed crime. They've done bad things, and the GM has used her money to erase all records of it.'

'Maybe my personal algorithms may be more successful,' said Marguerite. 'Kry with a *K*. It's an unusual sort of name.'

'They took me off to a different room and stuck a needle up my nose.'

'Oho! A needle!'

'Needle – thin knife, stiletto, that sort of thing. Pressed it up against the curve of bone in which my right eye nestles, and threatened to keep on pressing it.' Just the memory of it was making Alma's nose start to run. 'They were trying to intimidate me – don't bother our boss no longer, keep what you know to yourself, that sort of thing.'

'Is any of it imaged? Was your feed on?'

'No – they took me into a blanked-out room. I mean, I could go to the police and testify, I suppose – but the GM would make that go away with one swish of her money wand. I figure that police officer who tried to arrest me after Tym was killed – Newport – that she is on the GM's secret payroll. I'm sure she's not the only one. Life is expensive, and a police officer's salary is not over-generous.'

'Still, these *apes* ought not to get away with assaulting you!'

'It wasn't pleasant,' Alma agreed. 'But killing me was, obviously, more than they'd been ordered to do, so they let me go. And though they didn't exactly confess to murdering Alexa Lund, they smirked so hard the implication was unmistakable.'

'No smirk,' said Marguerite, nodding, 'without fire.'

'So we're further forward. Let's say these two, these Kry Twins, were the ones who killed Lund. That means the GM is behind her death. Now we only need to work out why.'

'And how they did it, armed only with a needle.'

'That too,' Alma conceded.

'But we already know the why. It's money. And it can't be small sums. None of the Four would be interested in the sorts of trivial amounts that motivate pettier criminals. It must be prodigious, enormous amounts of money. What we need to do is pin down in exactly what manner Ms Lund's death financially benefited the GM.'

'We need to do that,' agreed Alma. 'And we also need to determine in what way all this connects with Jupita's suspicions that one of the Four has been killed and been replaced by an imposter.'

'What if Lund knew that the GM *was* the imposter, and was killed to prevent her disseminating that information?'

'That won't fly. I met the GM in the flesh. She went so far as to unplug from the Shine and get off her bed – I guess she was jumpy, having a stranger in her room. At any rate, she's definitely not dead.'

'I blush,' said Marguerite, in a weary voice, 'for the error in my logic there. But then Jupita's theory *is* a pretty strange one, don't we think? It's surely more likely that none of them are dead.'

'I agree. But something is going on. The GM told me it was Jupita who killed Tym – activated and overrode the smartcloth of his tie from a distance.'

'Why would she do that?'

'I don't know. I don't even know if Jupita is the one to blame, here. But I do know that Jupita's strange theory is more than just a game. Something about it has real-world consequences. The GM said that Jupita had suborned one of the GM's own inner circle – bribed them with what must have been a very large sum indeed. She thinks it was Tym.'

'So maybe Jupita killed him to prevent him giving that fact away to you! To prevent him from spilling not the GM's but *Jupita's* secrets?'

'Maybe. The thing is, Lund's death is either connected with all that or it isn't. And now I'm more convinced than I was before that the connection is there.' She got up. 'I'm going to have a conversation with the man who calls himself Stanley.'

'I don't trust that fellow,' said Marguerite.

'No more do I, my love. The more I know him, the less I like and trust him. He calls himself a fan, but it's creepy. And he has bad things in his personal history – he all but confessed as much. There's something twisted inside him. So, for him this is all a game, I think – and he's certainly been playing a game with me. But I think if I push him a little he'll open up. And then...' she added, with an unfamiliar sensation in the spaces between her ribs. 'And then we'll crack both cases, and get paid before sunset and our financial situation will improve markedly.'

What was that sensation?

Oh: that was *hope*, that was. A stranger! And there it was, inside her chest.

'Go,' said Marguerite in an encouraging tone, 'with a spring in your step. Spring eternal, my love!'

15: *Forbury Gardens*

Alma stepped out on to the street. It was perfectly deserted. Somebody had been out – or had sent a proxy out – to tag every lamp post and doorway with unofficial warning memes, warning of the danger of the nanoplague. *Stay inside.* **Say No to Nano.** NANO FRAGMENTS SOON TO COME sang an unsolicited bot that somehow managed to slip past her general privacy app. A TWINKERLING IN EVRY LUNG. She nixed it.

The usual End of the World is Nigh stuff.

At the corner of the street a drone overflew, broadcasting a lame attempt at official reassurance. PLEASE DISREGARD UNSUB-STANTIATED RUMOURS CONCERNING AN UNNAMED AND FICTITIOUS NANOSWARM THAT...

Alma switched it off. An impressively off-putting number of polysyllables in those few opening words, she thought. Almost as if the people who drafted the official response wanted to discourage people from following it further.

These sorts of panics came and went, from time to time: panics about whole system crashes, or unpurgeable deep viruses, or power shutdowns that would trap millions in their meshes. They usually exercised people for a few weeks until a new shared panic came along and replaced them. They were, Alma believed, indices of a collective boredom, rather than any realistic anxiety – a boredom that the utterly unlimited possibilities of the Shine had, counter-intuitively perhaps, magnified in the human species.

At any rate, it freed up the town for Alma. She wandered through the deliciously empty R!-Town streets, crossed the river, and climbed the incline up towards the substantial Victorian crenellated brick biscuit tin of the Madejski building. A right turn and down the road to Forbury Gardens. In all that long walk she saw only three people, all asleep and being walked about in mesh-suits. Two of them had wrapped handkerchiefs around their mouths before they meshed up (as if that would stop a dedicated nano-agent!) and one appeared to be wearing, implausibly enough, an old astronaut's helmet. Alma wondered, idly, what all the other in-Shine R!-Town inhabitants were doing. Stomping back and forth in their three-stride-wide apartments, presumably. Or just giving in and accepting the bedsores.

The park: a modest sized patch of greenery in the middle of the city, tended of course by bots. In the old days there would usually be a few people here, if only a crowd of in-Shine meshed-up individuals getting their exercise. Not today. It was completely empty except – Alma saw, coming around the corner – for one individual. It was the man who called himself Stanley, sitting on a public bench with his hands resting palms-down on his thighs.

Alma walked over. He did not look at her as she approached.

She sat beside him.

He was looking up at the piece of antique statuary that occupied the centre of the park. It was a larger than life-sized blackened bronze lion, striding purposefully forward (except, of course, that it was motionless). The beast's body was segmented into a bunched spread of sharply defined and improbable-looking muscles, its mane bulbous as an Afro, its fanged mouth open.

'The lion traditionally symbolises courage, nobility, royalty, strength, stateliness and valour,' said Stanley. 'I wondered if it was *couchant*, because I liked the sound of the word, and knew it had something to do with lions. But I checked, and *couchant* means lying down with head up. Best as I can see, this lion is *passant-gardant*.'

'You did more than *work* for the GM,' said Alma, without preliminary. 'You were part of her senior staff. Not any more, but once upon a time – you were so senior you knew things only a very few people knew. Entry codes. The location of her secret escape elevator. I assume you had good reason to leave her employ. But I'm also thinking that, having been intimate with somebody like the GM, and then making a break for it, stepping outside the space where she can keep eyes on you, puts you in a very difficult position.'

Stanley didn't speak for a while. Then he said, 'You really think, in this day and age, physical distance stops somebody keeping their *eye* on you?'

'Stop playing games, Stan,' Alma urged. 'Tell me the whole story.'

'Such a big fan of yours,' he murmured. 'And all the pieces are there. There for you to piece together!'

'Just tell me.'

He looked glumly at his own lap. After a while he said, 'You know what I really like about this lion statue?'

'No.'

'The pedestal.'

He was on the verge of spilling everything to her, Alma could tell. It was worth humouring him a little further.

'The pedestal. Sure.'

She looked at it. A stone rectangular box taller than a human: white marble, or marble-laminated, and on the flank facing her, inset with six black slabs, each one roughly four times as tall as it was wide. Obsidian? Black metal? It was hard to see from her distance and her feed – unusually – didn't seem to know. It did tell her, though, that the slabs were all engraved with the names of the dead from battles fought several hundred years before.

'Very nice,' she said.

'Those black shapes,' said Stan.

'Black, they are,' Alma agreed. 'And also they are – shaped.'

'Like monoliths.'

'I guess.'

'The thing about Kubrick,' Stan said, veering off yet again on his tangent, 'was that he was a *genius*. You know? I mean, his eye. Yes?'

'Stan,' she prompted. 'To return to the matter in hand?'

'The matter,' he said, with a sigh, 'in hand. You think I worked for the GM, but that only means you haven't put the pieces together yet.'

'You're telling me you didn't work for the GM? Come *on*, Stan.'

'It's about asking the right question. I mean, isn't it?' He turned to face her. 'Alma. Do you trust me?'

Alma smiled. 'Seriously?'

'Seriously. It's a serious question.'

'Of course not.'

'No?'

'You effectively tricked me into trespassing in the Golden

Meteor's actual bedroom. You keep intruding into my personal space. You've bent the truth, and hidden it, in pursuit of some game you're playing with me. Trust you? You'll forgive me, Stan, if I say, no. I don't trust you. I believe your attitude to legality is, shall we say, lackadaisical.'

Stan nodded slowly. 'Lackadaisical! That's good. That's a very good word.' And then, with an apologetic look on his face, he lifted his right hand from his right leg. He was holding something: a pen-sized implement. 'It's not that I blame you for your lack of trust,' he said. 'Only it leaves me no choice.'

Alma almost didn't register the prick on her neck. Realisation happened only as the soporific was already flooding her system, panic rising up to meet a flooding, antithetical sense of nerveless sleepiness. Her heart bounced, pummelled, and then sank back. Consciousness opened the gate and stepped through it into the darkness. As Alma finally passed into nothingness she could hear Stan singing a creepy little song to himself:

Lackadaisy
Lackadaisy
Give me your
Answer
Do.

PART 2

The Dawn of Man

The sun, rising, busy and foolish no doubt, sucking the longer shadows into shorter and neater forms, polishing the lobster red of these flanks of rock into orange and taupe. A blank sort of landscape. It was the desert, and spare, and void of humans. A few scrabbly looking bushes, branches dry as straw, growing in the overhang of cliffs, or somehow surviving rooted in the sand. There was a parched-looking grey-green tree, no taller than Alma herself, its boughs a diagram of Us branching into smaller Us, each stacked on top of the others. A bleached-looking growth that stood out sharply against its backdrop of coal-coloured cliffs.

Where was she?

The air smelled clean, of ozone and freshness, with a slight tang of dung. A very dry air. She was well out in the open, somewhere far from human habitation.

She got to her feet, walked forward. To her right was a long dry reef of rock, angled into vertical cliffs or leaning into hills and smoothing into a wide crescent plateau of sand. She turned to her left, and shielded her eyes against the sun. The eminence she occupied gave a vista, beautifully rendered, of lowlands: shrubs and trees, veldt shapes; small creatures – cattle, maybe – moving slowly; the low bright sun attaching to everything a two-dimensional Henry Moore solidity of curves and bulges. Bones, sun-blanched white as sugar, were scattered on the soil.

She had the feeling, Toto, that she wasn't in Berkshire any more. To be precise, she had the Toto feeling that she was in Africa.

Overhead the sky was a blue so pale it was almost white. The air felt cool, but Alma assumed that would change as the sun rose. If this was really Africa, it might get very hot indeed.

She checked her feed; she had access to her internal routes, but all external access was blocked. At least that meant she could check the time – one hour and fifty-two minutes before she needed to be back at the flat to minister to Marguerite.

That meant that she had been unconscious for less than ten minutes, and *that* meant she had not been flown to any actually existing wilderness in the Real. So: she was in-Shine. She had – she took a deep breath, to manage the fury that rose up in her – been abducted and inserted into the Shine. Against her will.

She took another breath. Alma was not given to rages, so when one germinated inside her she was acutely aware of its intensity. But this was unacceptable. She could kill. She could genuinely kill the person who had done this to her. She could track Stanley down and kill him.

She took another breath, and reaffirmed self-control.

Something moved behind her – a dog-sized creature. She jumped back in alarm – but, no, it was not a dog. It was a tapir, plump and suede-brown all over, its nose a snaky prong, semi-circular ears standing up on its head. The beast was snuffling through the vegetation, scanty though it was, at the base of the cliff. Alma looked; there were three or four other ones. And then, her eyes adjusted, and a humanoid shape coalesced inside the shadows and into visibility. It was a chimpanzee, black and smooth as sable. The chimp was picking through the dirt, and occasionally eating whatever bug or detritus it picked up.

In the Real, Alma would have backed away. Chimps, after all, can be aggressive. But this wasn't real. Of course it was possible that whichever corner of the Shine she had been illegally inserted into, the chimps had been programmed to act exactly like Real-world simians. But then again, this being the Shine, it was equally possible that the chimp, or for that matter any of the tapirs, were the avatar of the individual who had kidnapped her.

She checked her exits, cleared her throat and said, 'Hello?'

The tapir snuffled through the ground. The chimp ignored her.

'Are any of you *people*?' she asked.

The chimp looked up. The nearest tapir kept its attention on the dirt, but stopped snuffling. When she took a step towards it, it moved lazily, unafraid, and trotted slowly away.

Alma followed it, and came round a promontory to a new stretch of cliff. The rocks here were browner, and more tumble-down, like a garden rockery on a gigantic scale. And here were many more chimps, sitting alone or in idle little groups. There were more tapirs too. Many of the chimps had paired off and were grooming one another.

'Hello?' Alma called. 'Is anybody here a person?'

A couple of chimps looked up, in a desultory sort of way, and then resumed their grooming, or grubbing about. A tapir tried to bundle a monkey away from something – a disinterred root, perhaps – and the chimp pushed back. Simian hootings and gruntings, like wind blowing slant across the mouth of broad pipes, or the sound of a saw cutting wood slowed right down. A number of the other apes joined in.

'Hello?' Alma tried again.

'Hello again,' somebody said. Alma turned and it was Stan.

She walked over to him. 'You kidnapped me,' she said, and punched him in the throat.

It was a good punch: one she had practised, and even had occasion to use on a few occasions in the Real. The knuckles shaped into a beak, striking the Adam's apple and pulling back – not so hefty a blow as to bruise or disable the hand that delivered it, but a blow markedly distressing of which to be on the receiving end. The strike hit home, and Alma pulled her hand back sharply, but Stan wasn't in the least incommoded.

She might as well have punched a rubber hose.

'That'll do no good in here,' he said mildly. 'It's not that kind of sim. Not, at any rate, for you and me.'

'I *am* going to prosecute,' Alma told him. 'Let me out immediately, and I'll pull up short of incarceration. Prolong this farce any longer, though, and you will assuredly go to prison for a very long time.'

'Illegality,' said Stan, pulling a gimpy sort of remorse-face expression. 'I know, right? But there's something I absolutely have to show you.'

'If you'd only asked my permission, I'd gladly have viewed it.'

'Oh, I asked. But you were ... Well, what ... What shall we say? Otherwise minded. I'm sorry about the *snatch*.' He stopped, and rummaged around in his beard for a while. Then he said, 'If that's not inappropriate language. But I really need to show you this.'

'So I've seen it,' said Alma. 'And now I need to get back to the Real.'

'You haven't seen it yet, though. You know I'm a fan, Alma, don't you?'

'Will you stop harping on about that?'

Alma was sifting through the various apps and iPrions and bundles of weaponised code she had permanently stored, and which she might use without needing external access for her feed. She was, as quickly as she could, checking each in turn to see if any of them might disrupt this reality and facilitate egress. Or, failing that, might cause genuine harm to Stan, to enable her to pressure him into opening the virtual door. But nothing looked like it would work.

'A fan,' he repeated, sombrely.

'It's creepy, Stan. Fan doesn't mean stalker. A true fan doesn't kidnap people.'

'You're a fan too. I mean, of murder mysteries and whodunnits. It's why you've chosen the line of work in which you so excel. Look at your track record! Puzzle boxes, and opening them. Don't you think life is a giant puzzle box, and that we really ought to devote ourselves to solving it?'

'Honestly?' said Alma, her fury ebbing a little; she didn't know why. 'Honestly no, I don't. I think life is cleaving to the people you love. And the person I love most of all is stranded in the Real without me, and unless I get back to her she *will* die.' Maybe asking him would work better than threatening him. 'So, Stan, I'm asking you – if you're really a fan, as you say – let me go now.'

She was watching him. It was hard to gauge the reality of an expression of a sim, and doubly hard when that sim was embedded, as this one was, inside a simulated environment. But he didn't look murderously dissociated. Maybe she could reach him. It might be worth carroting up her stick a smidgeon.

'We can talk about all this, if you like. I'd be happy to meet – we can sit down together and remotely view the whole of this sim. But in the Real, and only after you've let me get back to my partner.'

'Your partner Marguerite,' said Stan, nodding. 'I know she's pretty sick.'

'So let me go and tend her.'

'But I haven't shown you what I wanted to show you yet!'

A deep breath. She contained her impatience.

'Show me what, exactly?'

Stan put his arms wide. 'All this! Do you recognise it? It's the work of a master craftsperson, a genius of the sim-trade. There are a great many of these in-Shine, though few are as lovingly hand-coded as this one. But throughout the Shine there are thousands upon thousands of similar venues – I mean sims that put you *inside* any of the great old films of the twentieth century. You know films? Movies?'

'I'm not an idiot, Stan.'

'Oh, I wasn't calling you an *idiot*. Only – well, it's that I had to guillotine your access to any external feeds, so I *know* you can't check terminology as you might, as a matter of course.'

'Movies.'

Alma inwardly weighed up which attackapp would be best to try first. The problem was that she was not tooled up for dealing with enemies in-Shine, since she never *went* in-Shine, and that meant her options were limited.

'It's *2001*,' said Stan, looking round approvingly. '*Very* detailed rendering – high spec. Not, I might say,' and he made a noise as though he was chuckling and clearing his throat at the same time, 'not *cheap*. But for me this movie is the greatest film ever made, so money was no – was no object. Was.' He was turning slowly on his heel to look at all three-hundred-and-sixty degrees of the tan-and-marmite-hued panorama. 'No,' he said. 'Object.'

'I never saw it,' said Alma.

He spun back to face her. 'Say again?'

'I'm really not much of a one for antique movies.' But as she said that Alma found herself wondering if this was one of the few old films she *had* seen, at least in part. Clips maybe. Had they done it at school? So she said, 'Although, wait – maybe I did see this one. Isn't it about a giant robot sperm that flies into a black hole?'

He put his head on one side and stared at her, like a lost dog contemplating a signpost.

Finally he said, 'You're yanking, as the phrase goes, my chain. Of course you've seen it. Robot sperm is even good – that's quite a good way of putting it, actually. The *Discovery* travels to Jupiter. That's the mission. To put eyeballs on Jupiter. But the mission goes wrong, because the computer on board – its name is...' He trailed off and looked hopefully at her.

It occurred to her that he was angling to see if she knew the name.

'Walrus Gumboot?' she tried.

'What?'

'Jupiter Eyeball?'

'Its name,' said Stanley, firmly, 'is HAL. But you knew that. You're doing more of your chain-yanking. It's OK – I understand you're irked. You're irked I brought you here without asking your permission first. But, you see, I've followed your work for such a long time, and I know about your animadversion to the Shine. I know you wouldn't have come if I'd just asked. Nevertheless I absolutely had to show you this. You absolutely had to see it. To see it, but, more – to *experience* it. It was made by a genius designer. Grove, she was called. Well, Grove was her commercial moniker, not her in-Real name. Where was I?'

'You were about to open a door and let me go.'

'HAL,' said Stan.

'HAL-fellow, well met.'

'Ill-met, rather. You remember that HAL goes mad and murders almost the entire crew – *tries* to murder them all, although one crew member, Bowman, evades the murderous intent and shuts HAL down. It's very exciting. Then Bowman makes his way to the stargate and... Do you know why he is called Bowman?'

'Because that was his parents' surname?'

'That's not what I mean. Ulysses was a famous archer, you get me? Bow and arrows, and whatnot. And this is a space *odyssey*. So he opens the stargate—'

'Rather as you are about to open an out-Shine exit gate for me—'

'And he goes inside. He zooms through higher dimensions, grows old, is reborn as a baby. But you know all that.'

The more Stanley summarised it, the more Alma began to think that she *had* seen this old movie. It was memory-there somewhere, very dim and distant. Stan's disconnected summary was reminding her of something.

'So you like this movie. I get it,' she said, trying a different tack. Maybe if she placated him, he might open a door. 'You really like this movie a lot. I understand. And you admire my work – thank you – and felt you had to show me an in-Shine replication of a scene from that movie. Great. You've done it. So now you can let me go.'

'It's more than just a movie I like,' said Stan, earnestly. 'It's the greatest work of art a human ever created. It's deep – deep, you see. It's pro,' and he swallowed, as if moved by strong emotion, '*found* – you see. It is about the mystery of how humans evolved out of bestiality to become what we are. And it's about where we, as a species, go next.'

This was definitely ringing a ding-ding inside Alma's memory. She had the vague memory that she had done a course on Library of Congress significant artworks, eons ago: the Shakespeare one about the queen with the messy hands; that old shouty-men piece of music; and – this one, was it? She looked about. That was where she was. She was in that part of the story where a big ape threw a bone at a spaceship. Alma tried to recall if he had hit it, or not. She was inclined to think he had done. But how had he made the bone rise so high? Maybe he was a superhero ape. Or a magic ape.

'It's a mystery, this movie,' Stan was saying, with awe in his voice. 'And that's why *you* have to be here. Because mysteries are – well, you!'

'So now I've *been* here. And now it's time to let me go.'

'Come and see this bit, though,' Stan urged. 'This is a good bit.'

'Stan, I'm not kidding. I have to get back to the Real.' Her clock said: one hour and ten minutes. Not panic time. Not yet. But she wasn't being reassured by Stan's attitude.

He had trotted off, with the true fan's absolute confidence that the rest of the world must find his passion as absorbing as he did himself. Since there was nothing else to do, Alma followed, alongside the escarpment. The exertion involved was not tiring, exactly, but it was palpable as a kind of strain, which – though she was no expert – meant that this was a superior level of simulation. And if jogging for a couple of hundred metres made her feel a little tired, then that might mean it was possible to experience, and therefore to inflict, actual pain.

She considered that as she ran. Over an hour to go, but if push came to shove, and more to the point came to shove-me-out-of-the-Shine-or-else, it might be possible to hurt Stan until he complied. That might at least be an option. Except that she had punched him, and it hadn't affected him. So? So she'd have to find another way to affect him.

Stan had halted, and Alma caught him up. A scoop in the line of the cliff created a wide natural theatre. It was the same brown sandy soil, littered as before with Persil-white bones and shards, and rooted through by tapirs. A solitary apeman was squatting, grubbing at the ground.

'Watch,' Stan whispered. 'It's really the first thing to happen in the movie.'

'What is?'

Alma's eye was drawn to the sky: brightly pale blue; vast, containing acres of satiny grey clouds; wide. Lazy shreds a mile across. Very nicely rendered. It was, she thought to herself, a beautiful sky – which, in turn, was a testament to the skill of the person who had designed it. Achingly slowly the clouds were moving, west to east.

There was the sound of a motorbike, and rapid motion in the sky. There was no machine. The noise and the motion belonged to a big cat that had jumped from a position halfway up the escarpment. As it landed on the back of the apeman beneath, its feline roar was met with a series of hoots pitched exactly an octave higher than the growl. Tapirs scattered and ran. The lone apeman fell to the ground, sprawled, and writhed. The cat patted him indolently with its paws, splashing up blood and chunks of pelt. The cat nuzzled a cat-face in among the ape's hairy shoulder blades, and soon enough the shrieks stopped. The predator, wearing its leopardskin more naturally than any other creature could, settled down to feed. The only sounds now were of fabric being torn, carpet being ripped, and some less pleasant, wetter and sloppier noises.

'Gross,' said Alma.

'We could stay and watch – the leopard makes short work of eating him.' Stan sounded excited. It made Alma's psycho-radar ping again. Her fury swelled again in her breast. He *had* abducted her, after all. She told herself he clearly didn't know what he was getting into when he'd done that; a man might as well abduct a leopard and keep it in his room. That he was so obsessive was more worrying than alarming to her. She could, she told herself, look after herself.

Then again, she told herself, maybe he wasn't a psycho. Maybe he just really, really loved this movie.

She had no desire to watch even a simulated apeman devoured by a simulated paleo-leopard, so she turned and walked off. Stan fell into step alongside her.

'I have wondered,' he said, 'whether the apeman killed by the leopard – we don't know his name...'

'They have names?'

'Some of them, sure. But I have sometimes wondered if it was *his* bone that get thrown. I mean, it's not his bone in *this* reimagining, of course. Grove had to make certain assumptions when it came to realising the movie in-Shine. And movies aren't windows into real life – there are conventions that govern the way they represent things. You know? So *here* there's not enough time for that apeman's bones to bleach, and so become the one that Moonwatcher throws.'

'Moonwatcher?'

An indulgent glance from Stan. 'I suppose if you haven't read the Arthur C. Clarke novel, then maybe you don't know the names. The apeman who touches the monolith first, and who throws the bone, is called Moonwatcher. See.'

Stan was pointing. They were at a different portion of the plateau – the rocks a paler yellow, larger and rounder, heaped up. A stream, thin as a chopstick, trickled from the cliff and through these whey-coloured boulders to gather in a pool. It was the only source of open water Alma could see. The water itself, miso-coloured and foul-looking, trembled with ripples.

Gathered around the pool was a group of the apemen – half a dozen or so, scooping water into their numb-looking faces.

'Look,' said Stan.

'What am I looking at?'

'That's him. That's Moonwatcher.'

They all looked alike to Alma.

'Stan,' she said, facing him, internally readying a few attackapps, 'we're going to have to put this conversation on hold, all right? We can, I dare say, return to it. But in less than an hour I have to get back to my partner. In the Real.'

Stan seemed to be contemplating this. 'It must be such a burden. Every four hours!' He stood watching the apemen at the pool for a while. 'I don't mean to pry,' he said, eventually. 'But I have wondered why you don't hire a medical professional – or move your partner to a hospital. I mean, I assume it's money, and I appreciate it's not polite to ask people about money.'

'It's not a question of money,' Alma said.

'I know you don't have as much cash as you might like. I mean, who has? Apart from the Big Four, of course. They've got plenty. I'm not complaining, personally. I happen to have come from a well-off sort of background. I spent a pretty penny on ... well, on all this. And that was absolutely worth it. Still, I can afford to take cab rides where I want to go, and it seems that you can't.'

'Stan, try to stay on topic,' said Alma, feeling her gut tighten. 'You have to let me go. Open the door. We can talk later, after I've attended to my partner. I have to do that, or she will die.'

'What I'm saying,' said Stan, not meeting Alma's eye, 'is that if it's just a question of finding the *funds* to hire a nurse, then a loan might be possible. Just personally speaking. I wouldn't insult you by offering a gift of money. And anyway I'm not so wealthy as to be able to do that. But—'

Alma contained her impatience. 'That's kind, but, really, it's not a matter of money. I need to be the one who attends to Marguerite. So if you'll just ...'

Stan's eyes opened very wide. 'Oh,' he said, as if the idea was just that moment occurring to him. 'Did you think I was planning on keeping you here *forever*? Oh, very much no!'

'Well, if I'm honest, I was beginning to doubt.'

'Or the whole movie? Gracious, that's years – played out here, in this sim, it is literally years. No, that's not what I had in mind at all.'

'Good news.'

'You had to experience it, though. It was necessary that you actually experienced it.'

'You're sure you couldn't have just told me about it?' Alma suggested. 'Pushed a few scene-grabs into my feed to view at my leisure. You know?'

'Oh, that wouldn't do at all,' Stan insisted. 'And, really, I don't mind that you're not grateful.'

'Grateful,' Alma repeated, in a neutral tone.

'Gratitude might be nice, but the lessons of Tooth,' he coughed, apologised, '*Ow*-sand And One are too important to be petty about it. And, believe me, I'm not just flattering you when I say you may be the best solver of mysteries working in the EU today. One of the best, certainly. I've studied your cases. Well, all right then – this experience is gold, for you. Gold! In terms of helping you *solve* ... You know? To solve.'

Alma's impatience was no longer amenable to being muzzled.

'Enough, Stan,' she said, her voice sharp. 'All right? Enough babble. Let me out. Do it now.'

He nodded, slowly. 'Yes, it won't be long. You need to experience through to the end of the first sequence – "The Dawn of Man", you know. You don't need to experience the whole movie. I mean, if you wanted to, at some later date, I'd be happy to arrange that! But not right now, no.'

'How much longer does this sequence run?'

Stan sucked his teeth. 'It's two days. I mean one night, two days.' Seeing her reaction, he hurried to reassure her. 'You're worried about food and drink. Well, the water in the watering hole is perfectly OK to drink, though I know it doesn't look it. And we can stave off hunger together – the tapirs are perfectly incautious around men at this point in the story. We can take one down. I've a knife. I can make a small fire, so long as we're away from the apemen, so we don't scare them. It would be an idea to give ourselves something to do, actually, in order to keep awake, so we can sneak back at 1 a.m. and see the monolith arrive. It's quite the thing.'

'You're insane,' said Alma, in a steady voice. 'If you think I'm spending forty-eight hours in this gaol. Insane. Last chance, Stan – let me out now.'

'Oh, it's not forty-eight hours,' Stan said, as if this might settle her qualms. 'We don't have to wait through the whole of the second day.'

'I don't *have* to wait any time at all. If you don't open a door out of this sim right now, Stan, I'm going to be forced to compel you. And you won't like that, I promise.'

'Look, Alma,' said Stan, reaching out an arm, 'I understand your concern about your partner. A simple calling-in of a medical emergency will . . .'

Alma elected to act. She bundled an attackapp, rolled a delivery mechanism out of code designed to do something else, felt her permanent code network bulge as it pressed against the cage of code in which she was being held – a disconcertingly frictionful, treacly sort of experience – and jabbed the app into Stan.

She was expecting to immobilise him, temporarily, and to push the pain receptors of his sim-form a little to see how far they were calibrated. It was nothing she enjoyed, but she needed leverage of some kind to force his hand. Marguerite's life was in the balance, and that trumped every other consideration.

Stan was stuck, reaching an arm out towards her, his mouth midway through curling into a grin. It was a provokingly annoying and dopey sort of expression. She had pinned his avatar. He couldn't move.

So, that was something.

Alma positioned herself in front of him, so he could see her with his unmoving, unblinking eyes, and said, 'I'm going to try a few things – I'm feeling my way, really. But I haven't time to debate this endlessly, and I certainly don't have two whole days. You're going to open a door and let me out of this sim, and you're going to do it in the next ten minutes.'

She rolled a second delivery bodge – again, the code that defined the limits of the sum bulged and scraped weirdly – and sent a pulse at Stan's left leg, aiming for it to pass up the simulated path of the nerve, along his spine and into his skull. Nothing too extreme: an exploratory nudge, to test how far the sim allowed discomfort to shade into pain.

It didn't go the way Alma expected. There was a bulge in the fabric of the entire sim, a bubble of molten glass, and suddenly Stan vanished. The logic of the simulation filled his absence with a stopgap: a whoosh of air, a loud popping noise and – unmistakable – a whiff of sulphur.

Alma was alone.

This was not good.

Her clock told her she had fifty minutes. Since she didn't know where in the Real her actual body was located, she needed to factor in some time to get back to the flat. Which gave her, say, half an hour to escape this faux-prehistoric faux-Africa.

There was a commotion at the watering pool – a new troop of apemen had loped over and were seeking to displace the original pack. There was a good deal of brassy shrieking and high-pitched yelling, and various crook-legged apes throwing the Y and the M portions, although not the terminal two letters, of the YMCA semaphore dance. No ape made contact with any other ape; it was all show. But the second troop was larger and more aggressive, and the first group backed away, with a prolonged and very vocal display of affront. The largest apeman was last to depart, pausing on a ridge to deliver, like an aggrieved Mediterranean waiter, a series of arms-above-head theatrical shrugs and gestures. But then he toddled off too.

Soon enough the first group quietened down and wandered away. The new group were enjoying the water.

The next forty-five minutes turned, quickly and irrevocably, into the single worst discrete period of time of Alma's life. At the beginning she was aware of low-level anxiety, of a kind with which she was only too familiar. Alone meant unbothered, so she found a quiet nook in the cliff – checking, first, for any loitering leopards that might be about – and went through her store as systematically as the pressure of time would allow. She had not tooled up for this sort of situation, because she had really never thought she would find herself *in* this sort of situation. There were various traps, bomblets and attackapps that might be useful in a variety of real-world situations, but that were perfectly toothless in-Shine.

She was in the Shine. She couldn't *believe* it.

For four minutes she tried repurposing a codebreaker to burrow through the initial code membrane of the sim, in the hope that this would reveal an escape hatch, emergency tag or . . . something. But the worm chewed pointlessly at the surrounding code to, it seemed, no effect.

Time was passing.

Alma climbed one of the more accessible slopes of the escarpment until she reached a prominence high enough to get a proper view of where she was. She checked again that there was no access to any external network or feed. Nothing. Then she used an antique tool from the back of her virtual cupboard to check the parameters of the space – or the 'space' – she presently occupied. Some sims didn't bother with detailed coding of anything except the immediate surroundings, where the actual fun was to be had (game to be played, sex to be engaged in, fantasy to be indulged), only sketching in more distant elements. If that were true with this sim, then Alma might have better luck if she left the plateau and found some portion where the code was rougher.

The news was not good: the coding was amazingly smooth and detailed, and seemed to remain so in all directions for the several hundred metres her app could scan. She might jog a kilometre or more, wasting all that time, and still find the coded environment as impermeable and flawless as it appeared here.

This really was a high-end simulation. Stan must have paid a *fortune* for it.

She decided there was no point in relocating to a different section of the sim and trying to burrow through the code. That fact ratcheted up Alma's sense of anxiety a notch. Still, there were possibilities. There were always possibilities.

There *had* to be possibilities.

'Stan?' Alma called into the clear morning air. 'You hear me, I know you do. Let me out. Do it, Stan, or I will do such things – to you, Stan – *such* things!'

There was no point in shouting into the empty air. Maybe if she interfered in the narrative line of the sim it would winkle Stan out of observer mode, maybe get him to expel her from the sim just to save it.

It wasn't very likely, really. But she stifled the inner voice that told her so, and made her way back down the slope as quickly as she could without falling. The sim was making her feel thirsty now, and rather than ignore this as code-noise (which, fundamentally, was what it was) she decided to overcome her revulsion and drink from the watering hole.

What had the story been? She tried to recall the movie to memory. Apes suddenly evolve into men. There was a doorway involved, painted black – or was that the Rolling Stones? The twentieth century had never interested her all that much. OK. Think: bone-throwing. She remembered that. Moondancer was the key figure, the ape that upped, the one who went from *ooh*!-*ooh*!-man to human. Moonbender. Moonshooter. Data on this antique movie wasn't in her permanent store. What was the name? Moonwatcher, was it?

Stan had said they could kill one of the tapirs. Maybe she could kill Moonwatcher, and end the storyline. Or at least disrupt it.

She walked over to where the apemen were lounging by the pool. They watched her advance, but none of them showed any hostility.

Two hands make at best a multiply cracked bowl, but it was all Alma had. She drank.

Then she located an appropriate stone, small enough to hold, heavy enough to be effective as a weapon, and picked one of the apes. Which was Moonwhatever? They really did all look alike. Maybe pick one at random, kill it, and see if that was enough to bring Stan back into his super-expensive sim.

One of the apes was squatting by itself a little way from the water. Alma approached, went down on her haunches to bring herself to its level, and readied the stone. It looked right into her face, and made a series of bumpy, gravelly grunting sounds.

'Hello,' she said, readying her hitting arm. 'Are you the Moony one?'

The ape opened its mouth, pulled its lips back, and made the sound of a barrel-chested man choking on a small object. Four distinct repetitions of this noise, and the lips closed over its teeth. There was something peculiar about the way the creature's face moved – as if it didn't have the full complement of maxillary muscles under the skin. Almost as if its lips were being yanked back by wires. The exposed teeth looked sharp and clean, though the tongue inside looked oddly small and pink. And most of all, the ape's eyes looked, in some indefinable way, wrong. They were all brown, as an ape's ought to be – but Alma got the impression of a greater than animal intellect behind them. Was this a shell?

'Are you a person?' she asked. 'Is there a person in there?' Then, it occurred to her. 'Stan, is that you?'

The simian lips slid back, all in one go, and more grunts emerged.

'Stan, if that is you – I'm going to smash your playground to smithereens. You understand? If you want to keep this iteration of the story running smoothly, you'd better eject me from it. Put me back in the Real, yes?'

She raised her arm. The ape closed his mouth and peered into her face.

She couldn't do it.

It was absurd. It wasn't as if this were a real person. It wasn't even a real ape. It was a mere sim. But something in her rebelled against the thought of smashing its skull.

It wasn't as if it would do any good, anyway. What if she did smash up the sim? What limited damage she might inflict would simply disappear when the program rebooted to play again.

She got to her feet, still clutching the stone, and walked away. Anxiety had started to coalesce inside her into something resembling panic – that sharply penetrating emotion that stretches us beyond our ability to imagine any experience more horrible. Panic wasn't going to help her get out of this fix. She tried to settle her head, and think through other options. Maybe there was a doorway hidden somewhere in plain sight? A handle poking out of the cliff face – a portal in a tree trunk.

But obviously not. An exit would make a kink in the code, and apps she carried would pick up on that.

What about this monkey, this Moonraker fellow – might he be more than just another part of the simulation? That little voice, the inward murmur that says *you're clutching at straws, Alma*, was to be ignored. Soon enough it would be murmuring, *she's going to die, Alma, and you won't even be with her.* That was to be ignored.

She ran across the plateau, away from the watering hole, in the general direction in which the first group of apes had scattered. It was still early morning, the air still fresh. A breeze was starting up. She came upon the scattered apemen around a spur of the escarpment, spread over half a hectare of dusty dirt, grubbing in the ground for – what? Worms? Roots? Doors out of hell?

Which one was Moonwatcher? *It doesn't matter,* said the murmuring voice. *It can't help you.* That ape was no different from all the other apes – simulated agents embedded in an elaborate immersive recreation of an antique movie. Nothing here could respond in any but pre-programmed ways. The only individual who could help was Stan.

'Stan?' Alma spun on her heel. 'Stan! Hear me!'

Nothing. She yelled again, louder, and a faint echo drifted back from the escarpment. There were no birds in the sky.

Where had she been when she first woke, inside the sim? She ran, looking for the place.

It meant nothing – the program could have placed her anywhere. It wasn't as if there would be any actual exit there – or, necessarily, anywhere – in the fabric of the code. But she couldn't do *nothing*. And, just conceivably, the algorithm governing the sim had a favoured spot for introducing players, or observers, or whatever the hell Stan counted as when he sat through this interminable African simian parade. Maybe he would have been rebooted to reappear in sim, and just conceivably that would be where he was, and she could reason with him again. Persuade him. If necessary, bribe him. Anything.

Fifteen minutes. She needed to get out *right now*.

She was panting, or her avatar was, and she felt breathless, and a side-stitch was beginning to dig, claw-like, in her diaphragm. None of it was real, except that it affected her consciousness, so in that sense it was real. Stan was nowhere to be seen.

She picked up a rock and hurled it at the cliff face. It made a neat little *snick* noise as it struck, and tumbled away. The heat of the sun was becoming palpable on her skin as it rose through the morning sky.

There had to be a way. *There's no way*, murmured the inner voice. There had to be something she could do. She rifled through all her stored apps and worms, and tried each in turn against the fabric of code. One after the other they bounced clean away. She checked the worm she had placed earlier – it had made no inroad at all.

There was nothing she could do.

It occurred to her with some force that there *was* a way, that she could get out – a glaringly obvious way, just on the edge of coming into view. There had to be one. There had to be. She would think of it. She had to think of it. Clear her mind and think of it. She stopped, and got her breathing under control.

Four minutes.

There was nothing she could do. There was no point in watching the numbers tick down, and yet watching the numbers tick down is exactly what she did. She went through the four stages of grief with a kind of efficient brevity that was all the more agonising for her sense of passivity. It wasn't happening; it simply couldn't be happening. It was so demeaning that Marguerite would die because of the malice of Stan, or his stupidity, or his ignorance. She was going to kill him – literally kill him, painfully, and watch him beg for mercy. And then she was going to wreck the whole world, and lay the Shine – all of it, the trillions of platformed and embedded and walled-about fantasy locations – waste.

But God would not let it happen. The God in whom she did not believe would never let it happen. Call Him, or Her, Providence, or Fate, or Justice on the highest level. It was so monstrously unfair! If she had to sacrifice something to stop it she would. If she had to swear, solemnly, pressing fists into her solar plexus, to give up PI work, never to put herself in such foolish danger ever again, never again to leave the flat, she would. To stay by Marguerite's side and tend her. To keep her safe. And then the last

153

seconds of the last minute dribbled away and she felt the surge and swell of that great dark ocean that rolls around the southern hemisphere of our souls, and that is called Despair. She would never see Marguerite alive again.

She had failed her.

The timer blipped from green numbers into ruby-hued ones, accumulating instead of counting down. That had never happened to Alma before.

That had never happened before, and now it had happened.

Over. Done with. Seven years of always finding a way, getting back in good time, or *just* in time, but always getting back; scrabbling money together for medicine; always somehow winning against the encroachment of death. She had done a lot for the woman she loved. To do all that, only to do nothing in the end.

Wasn't that the nature of the cosmos, though? *To do all that, only to do nothing in the end.* The truth of life in eleven words.

In Alma's case acceptance took the form of tears.

She sobbed for a long time, until the increasing discomfort of heat drove her to find shade. She wondered if the program would give her sunburn, and if so, how realistic that might be, how it would feel. Stan had said it wasn't that sort of sim – but maybe he meant it was built to limit the damage it was possible to inflict with actual fighting. Some part of her hoped it would, that her skin would blister tomato-red and scorch like meat on a barbecue. She moved, though. It wasn't comfortable. She zombie-walked into the shade, and sat with her back against the rock. She didn't check for leopards. Let them come.

There was nothing inside her. She was an empty property. An uninhabited woman, boarded up and surrounded with wire, ready for the wreckerbots to come and demolish. Just existing passively as the weeds grew around her.

Eventually the sun passed into the west, and the shadows grew longer. She was aware of thirst, and of hunger, and ignored both signals. It was all code. A quicksand morass of code that had held her as the love of her life had died alone, and now she would never see her again.

Water is splashed upon the skin, and it hurts you, but at first you are not sure – in your agony – whether it is freezing cold or scalding hot.

In her mind, Alma felt that way.

Grief is an asthma of the spirit so severe the soul itself chokes and dies.

The sun slid with insolent slowness down the western arc of the sky. Alma sat and was nothing but a boulder among boulders. She would have torn her skin with her nails, if her skin had been real. But it was only code, like the whole universe. She stared at the sky, and tried to think of something. But it was sheer antagonism that this simulacrum of a world could operate, buzzingly, on no life, and her beloved, her life's partner, be lying dead as dirt in their shared flat in the Real.

Nothing mattered any more.

Eventually sunset came. The production values were very high – the sun became the colour of rosé wine, fresh and liquid, and then the colour deepened and enriched itself. The sky blushed strawberry and orange at the intimacy of the sun's slow downward caress. And then the red drained away, and the blackness came, and to Alma's simulated thirst and simulated hunger was added simulated cold.

None of these things existed.

It occurred to Alma that what was true of the Shine was true of the Real as well. It was equally a phantasmagoria, exactly as unreal as the imitation realm. The only thing that had made the Real real was Marguerite, and without her it would be as flimsy and pointless as the Shine. They two had parted; they who had kept company so long had parted. And Marguerite's death was functionally her own death. Her sickness dream was over. It seemed to Alma as though she had died, too. What did it matter, since it was unreality, all of it – the pain and desire, the beginning and the end? There was no reality except this emptiness.

Stars reeled around the fountain of the earth. Pinpricks of icy light, in their hundreds of thousands. Alma grew uncomfortably cold, but the level of chill remained at uncomfortable. If she had been actually sitting outside in the middle of the night in Africa without so much as a blanket to cover her, she would have been putting herself in danger of hypothermia. Not that she cared, but this was a sim, and programmed to notify her avatar of the chill, not put it entirely out of commission. The discomfort soaked up some of her consciousness, and by that much reduced her misery.

At some point she became aware of a gleam of red-orange light, shading off in almost painterly brushstrokes into a firefly storm of sparks. It was located on an eminence to her left. She remembered Stan saying something about lighting a night-time fire, cooking some simulated tapir flesh, keeping warm and getting fed. She contemplated the thought that Stan was back in the sim. She had decided to kill him, she knew. But this was not an effective place, or an ideal time, in which to pursue her revenge. She would do it eventually, she told herself, distantly. There would come a time when she would be the author of Stan's agonised death.

But not tonight.

I mean, seriously. What was the point?

She probably slept. The hours stretched, as cold as she was. There was no reaction. But in fact she must have slept, because she dreamed of Marguerite, and woke to the blackness of this no-space with a crashing remembrance that Marguerite was gone for ever. Alma wept again, then; the second time that night.

Some time a little before dawn, as the eastern sim-sky paled to a corpse-colour, Stan came down to where she was sitting.

'You're pretty mad at me, huh? Mad in the sense of angry – huh?'

Alma said nothing.

He sat down next to her. 'I mean, that was pretty clever. What you did. This is my world, and I thought I'd set the parameters very tight, but you managed actually to – what? Adapt an attack-app, I guess. I mean, it was short-sighted in the sense that I was always going to be able to reinsert myself. Still.' He was silent for a while, and then he said, 'You miss your partner, I guess. If you're used to seeing her at least every four hours, and we've been here – well.' He lifted his chin in the direction of the sunrise, and dropped it again.

Alma said nothing.

'Look – come and see the apemen wake up to find the monolith in their midst. It's quite the thing to see.'

When Alma didn't react, Stan took her hand, and leaned back as he rose to pull her up. Actively resisting him would have involved more direct agency and willpower than she, at that time, possessed. So she didn't. He led her over the dark dust, on the edge of the moistness which passed for dew in the desert, and over a rise to where they could look down upon – the apemen all asleep, piled together for warmth. And in the midst of them, a tombstone as tall as a house, made of what looked like black marble.

Stan made himself comfortable, and so Alma sat, silently, beside him. But she couldn't take her eyes off the tombstone. As the sun rose, light hit the top of this object, and the blackness came more painfully into relief against the paling sky. It was Marguerite's monument. It was, in some way, her – the essence of her death. A block to indicate that her life had been blocked off.

The sun was over the horizon now. For a while Alma looked at her clock, rather than her surroundings: coming up on twenty-two hours since Marguerite's death, the numbers implacably aggregating, red as the sunrise. Double figures would eventually become triple figures, and then quadruple, and time would stomp on, uncaring of the fact that this was a cosmos in which Marguerite no longer lived. It was so callous. It was a cruelty woven into the very nature of things. The intrinsic severity of time, the intrinsic severity of space that had kept the two of them apart.

She couldn't look at the numbers any more.

Below, in the little dry cove of rock, the biggest apeman had woken, startled at the existence of this tombstone in the middle of his group. As well he might be.

'That's Moonwatcher,' whispered Stan. 'Always gives me goosebumps, this bit.'

It was a little distance off, but Alma could see the apemen, awake now, gurning at the huge tombstone, showing it thirty-two white teeth and then hiding them away, and then showing them again. Raising themselves from recumbency, puzzled, angry, glowering and shouting at the great block.

'Those bumps named after the *goose*,' said Stan, with a tone of self-satisfaction. 'And do you know, I've never been sure if the monolith is drawn to this place because of this entire group – our fundamental ancestors, of course, this little knot of hominids – or if it is drawn here because of Moonwatcher alone. Or maybe it's purely random? I mean, how does it know? When I was younger, after I saw the movie for the first time, I thought – it's just random. The monolith would have been happy with any group of apes, and it *just happened* to choose this group. But that's obviously not the case, when you think about it. The monolith recognised something in this group – or in this one hominid. What do *you* think?'

157

'I constantly think,' said Alma, in a low voice, 'about how I'm going to kill you.'

Stan ignored this, or pretended not to hear it.

'Look,' he said, pointing. 'There they go, bless them!'

Moonwatcher was barking and grunting at the monolith now, and the whole troop had woken to it. There was a cascade of monkey shrieks and whoops, and a scurry of action as they all fled to the far edges of the little arena. Then there was a period of some minutes when the apes were in uproar – waving their arms, shouting and shrieking, like bird-scarers trying to raise pheasants from the heather. The sounds were discordant, but the jangle of sound and the car-alarm wails of distress chimed with Alma's state of mind. The choir for her grief.

The apes did not cease their commotion, but they did begin, slowly, to overcome their own caution and approach the – what had Stan called it? – the monolith, the solitary stone, the rock of uniqueness, which is death, which is always death. Waving their arms, and making seagull noises at it, and running away, and then creeping back towards it again, fascination at war with timidity in their little ape brains. Moonwatcher was the first – the least cowardly, or the most foolhardy. Soon enough he was squatting hard by the great tombstone shape, and stroking it with his right hand. At first he touched it warily, as though testing whether it might be hot. But then he was laying his hand against it, and later his face too.

'The crescent moon on its back, like a cup, in which all the refreshing water in the world can be scooped up! Like a bow in the sky, waiting for a bowman to pick it up and shoot a shaft into – infinity!'

Stan was in some strange kind of ecstasy.

Kill him now, with a rock, said the murmur inside Alma's head, but softly, as if from a great distance, and without the power to stir her limbs to action.

And now the moment had passed.

The troop of apemen was leaving the monolith now. Whatever charm it had possessed for their elementary curiosity had gone, and they were running on feet and knuckles over the rise and down to the watering hole for their morning drink.

'Come on,' said Stan, getting to his feet to follow them. 'In an hour or so we can watch him start to play with bones.'

He didn't take Alma's hand this time, which meant that she didn't get up, and when he padded away she didn't follow them. Instead she ignored her own thirst, or rather the simulacrum of thirst, and her own hunger, or rather the simulacrum of hunger, and allowed the simulated sun to warm her simulated skin and take away the discomfort of the night's simulated cold.

After a while she fell into a dark little sleep. When she woke up the monolith – whatever it had been – was gone.

She wasn't asleep for long, and she didn't weep on awakening this time, although the thought that Marguerite was no longer in the world struck through her heart like a giant spear. She sank down again, went into the valley of darkness, and stayed there for – how long? An hour? A year? It was timeless and grievous and all the code that defined her environment was replaced with units of misery.

The sun was a third of the way up the eastern sky. A tapir snuffled indifferently a metre away from her. Where was she? What was she doing?

None of it mattered.

She was gall, she was heartburn. She was the impossible thing, a simulation of lostness recreated with accuracy down to the atomic level. The universe had become her scourge, to be laid upon her sweating self.

But worse, she thought.

But worse.

The small of her back and her bent-over legs were cramping – or, rather, the simulation was prodding electrical signals at her sensorium to simulate the discomfort of cramping. She stretched her legs out in front of her and rubbed her thighs. From a long, long way away came a thought: a radio emission from a distant galaxy that had taken a billion years to arrive in the thin silver crescent of the telescope dish – it was something Stan had said. He wanted not only to tell her about this simulation, but for her to *experience* it, he had said – but not to experience the whole of the damn thing. Two days, one night, he had said. Not even forty-eight hours.

So: she had been here a day and a night, and now was into the second day. Which meant – assuming he could be trusted – that she would not spend another night here. He would let her go this same day.

The strange thing was that this thought opened a cellar door in her mind to a kind of anguish. She was in hell, and this desert world was a kind of hell, and she had tried every shift to leave it yesterday; now the thought of returning to the Real conjured dread inside her. Because the Real was where Marguerite lay, lifeless, and returning to the Real meant returning to that.

She found within her the need to move, so she got to her feet, and her knees cracked like gunshots, and her back yawed with pain. But the algorithm that defined this world was more forgiving than the physics of the Real, and after a few steps the cramping all went away.

Over the ridge and down to where the watering hole lay. A few of the hominids watched her incuriously as she drank. Then, without haste, she climbed to the eminence where, the previous night, Stan had lit a fire and roasted a tapir. The carcass was still there, over grey ashes, spitted on a stake and propped on two tepee-pyramids of branch. Alma broke off pieces of cold, cooked meat and ate, and the simulation acknowledged the gesture and took away her sensation of hunger.

From where she was she could look down upon Stan, who was in turn looking down upon one of the apes – Moonwatcher, presumably, who was sitting in among a heap of bones, like a child among toys. He had in his ape-hand a long bone, perhaps a thigh bone, and was sniffing it. Any minute now he would chew it, or crack it to get at the marrow. But he didn't. Instead he kept staring at it.

Alma really didn't care. Something was in her, now, to give her focus. Say Stan was true to his word, and let her out of the Shine some time today. She would come back to consciousness in the Real – somewhere, although she didn't know where. One question mattered: whether Stan would also be there, in the flesh, in the Real. Because if so, she needed to be ready. If he was within reach of her grasping hand she needed to be able to make that reach. If his actual throat was there, she needed to be ready to crush it.

The thought of this brought focus to her mind. It was something. Stan looked like he was clapping his hands together as he lay, prone, watching Moonwatcher among the bones. The apeman was playing a ribcage like a xylophone. Splinters were scattering left and right, and then the hominid swung on his hips and smashed the thigh bone he was carrying down into the skull of a tapir. In caved the cranium and fragments flew. A distant *tic-tic* sound echoed off the escarpment.

She took herself away and tried to centre herself. One imponderable was how Stan had left her body – in the Real, that is. She had been in-Shine for a day and a night, and would be here for hours yet, so he must have rigged up hydration of some kind. It wasn't yet a long enough period of time for her in-Real body to succumb to thirst, but depending on how long he was going to keep her in here, he must have arranged something for her body. And if he'd taken the trouble to do that, then the odds were he'd taken the trouble to make sure she was fed too. That was important, because she would need her strength if she was going to kill him without a weapon. She knew several ways of doing such a thing, but he was a stocky man and might not go down easily.

Having the simulation of water and food in her belly made her feel renewed, physically. Fantasies of revenge gave her a reason to carry on, if only for a little while.

She roamed the plateau for a while, and then sat looking down over the vastness of the plain. Yesterday she had scanned the sim and found no diminution of detail. Did it really extend all the way out there? If she spent the day climbing down and trekking over that great flatness, would the texture of the sim *really* stay tight? Surely not – it would take an obsessive-compulsive designer to make such a thing. Although perhaps Ms Grove, the builder here, was such a person?

She wasn't about to test it.

Late morning her spirits sank again; the ocean of grief swallowed her cracked liner and it drifted through the twilight-coloured blue into the lightless spaces of the deep, and kept on drifting down. The only marker of motion now was the increase in pressure, and her mind compressed in on itself as she sank deeper and deeper and all her consciousness became a balled-up knot of pain.

Then, without consciousness of intervening time, she was waking up. She had fallen into a kind of deathly sleep, curled in the dirt, as if poleaxed by her grief.

The sun was high in the western sky. Alma was aware of thirst, and walked back towards the watering hole.

As she approached she could hear yet another commotion from

161

the hominids. They were always making a scene, those apes – always shrieking and yelling, and waving their big hairy arms. They should take a stress pill, the lot of them.

She came to the top of the ridge, and found Stan lying prone. When she saw him she thought, with a strangely pleasurable clarity, *I'm going to kill you, later today*. The thought gave her an odd feeling, akin to happiness, or as close to happiness as her universe of grief permitted her.

She lay down in the dirt next to him.

'Alma,' he said, smiling, 'I'm glad you're here for this. This is the key moment – key!'

She didn't reply.

'I know you're annoyed. You were out in the cold last night, I guess. I mean, you could have come and shared the warmth of my fire, but that's your prerogative. And you're cross with me, sure you are. But you see, Alma, you had to *experience* this. I couldn't just tell you about it.' He looked pleadingly at her.

She didn't meet his eye.

Below, the two bands of apemen were squaring up to one another across the watering hole, doing all the dominance-display antics we associate with simians. Alma saw that Moonwalker, or whatever he was called, was carrying his thigh bone as a kind of club.

She remembered. Whether she had actually seen the movie (if so, she couldn't really remember it), or had been told about it – maybe she'd beguiled four minutes with a greatest hits condensation one time. But she remembered the whole plot was triggered when one ape killed another. This killing had been presented in the movie as a triumphant breakthrough, the act that propelled human evolution – Cain killing Abel as the moment of true and glorious creation. This struck her as, in the largest sense, mendacious. As ugly, and wrong-headed. If her extensive experience had taught her anything, it was that killing somebody always made things worse, never better. You thought death would simplify, but it always complexified. You thought it would improve your life, but it always made it worse.

And yet, and yet, here she was: watching Moonwatcher square up to the leader of the rival group, seeing the apeman ready itself to use his weapon, summoning his courage – and it *was* exciting. Alma thought to herself: I shall do this to Stan. I shall club him to death with a lengthy, hefty bone. He ought to like that! A homage to his favourite antique movie. And think how satisfying it will be for me.

Stan was talking, now, a burble of excitement running through his words.

'This is the crucial moment. Do you see? I've known for a long time that there's a secret hidden inside *Odyssey*, placed there by the director himself, and by Clarke, who wrote it with him. I don't know whether they were actually channelling something alien – that may be, but I can't find proof – or if they were just very clever. Oh! Certainly clever, certainly *that*. It's a murder mystery, do you see?'

Alma said nothing.

'What I mean is, people have seen the murder, how could they not? It's right there. Ape kills ape. And ever since it was first shown, people have talked about how the movie is a mystery. Mysterious, it certainly is! But *nobody* has put it together before and understood that this film is very particularly *a murder mystery*, waiting to be solved. *That's* why I brought you in here. Do you see?'

Alma angled her head a little, and stared at Stan, and didn't say anything.

'I mean,' he was saying, 'who is better placed to solve this than you? I mean, you're a genius at this, you really are. The word's not misapplied. I don't mean to flatter you – but, you see, only by inserting you into this sim could I give you the tools to solve the mystery!'

Alma looked away.

'The leader of the rival group,' Stan said, pointing, 'I call *Dawn*. I don't think she has a name. I mean, in-canon. And plenty of people probably think she was a he. But I've checked – it's a female. Her pack has the upper hand, until Moonwatcher learns to use the tool, the one in his hand – and ...'

The rival hominid, the one Stan called Dawn, made a rush at Moonwatcher, running through the pool. Water splashed momentary lace frills at her hairy ankles, and then she was on the dry ground on the far side. At the last minute, Moonwatcher executed a bullfighter's sidestep and heaved down with his club. Even at a distance, Alma heard the blow connect with the back of Dawn's head – a solid *thwunk*, stonily striking packed flesh, bone on covered bone – and Dawn fell straight down. Moonwatcher had leaped back, and danced excitedly, watching the effect of his blow. Dawn was twitching, like a dreaming dog, on the floor. One of Moonwatcher's pack rushed past, also carrying a bone, and swiped at the fallen body, bashing her shoulders. Moonwatcher came at her again, and landed a drum roll of blows on her head. Her limbs stopped twitching. Now various members of Moonwatcher's group, emboldened, came at Dawn's motionless body, striking it with clubs, or with their hairy fists. Dawn's troop, on the other hand, were backing away, shrieking and yelling but retreating.

'You see?' Stan said eagerly. 'It's murder. Now – now – I don't want to tell *you* your business, but you *know* how these things go, yes?'

If Alma knew she wasn't saying.

'It's the misdirection, isn't it! That's the core of a great who-dunnit. Misdirection! You show people the crime, you show them something really obvious, something in plain view. But then you show them something *else*, something more beguiling, and, like a cat with a laser pointer, they follow that gleaming dot over the walls and floor and away, and leave the obvious thing sitting, unattended, right there. Misdirection, misdirection.'

Alma said nothing.

'So what do we see here? What's the misdirection? Here we have a story of the evolutionary leap of humankind – the monolith nudges us to evolve, and the story follows that evolution through to the space age. Yes? But what if all that *is* the misdirection! Do you see?'

Alma was thinking again of how satisfying it had sounded when Moonwatcher's club had connected with the curved bones at the back of Dawn's head. She was thinking how satisfying it would be to imagine it – Stan's cranium breaking, shards of living bone forced inward to mash up his cerebellum. She could kill him here. He'd just wake up in the Real again, of course, but it would be satisfying to bring the club down on his stupid head. So that meant she needed to wait.

'Misdirection.' Stan's attention was on the scene below them, as the triumphant hominids danced a loopy sort of victory dance around the slain body of Dawn. 'All that. Ignore it, refuse to be *distracted* by it, and what have you got? A murder mystery.'

'Not much of a mystery,' said Alma, her voice a little croaky. '*That* ape killed *that* ape. It's clear who done it.'

'*Is* it though?' asked Stan, with triumph in his voice. 'Look again. Sure, Moonwatcher wielded the weapon. But why? Because the monolith put it in his head. Moonwalker himself is just a tool. A tool deployed by the monolith. Don't you see? The misdirection is the story that says: the monolith wanted to jump-start the evolution of humanity. Well, maybe it did. But let's say it wanted something more directly – let's say, it wanted Dawn dead.'

Alma gave Stan a venomous look.

'So, you see, when you strip away the misdirection, we're left with one crucial question. Why would an alien intelligence, embodied in a steady-state computational device like the monolith's great slab, like—'

'Like a tombstone,' said Alma quietly.

'Good one! Yes! An alien artificial intelligence, running inside whatever that device is, and the question we have to ask, that nobody asks, is – *why would it want to murder an ape?* Once you've asked yourself that question you can never see this movie the same way again.'

Alma could not, in all honesty, have cared less. She turned her face away. Her next question had nothing to do with whatever Stanley was babbling about. It was more a query aimed at the whole ghastly cosmos.

'Why?'

'Exactly! And here you are – today's greatest solver of the whodunnit. Why did the monolith want to murder that ape? I am sorry to have brought you here against your will. I know you said some stuff about pressing charges and so on – back in the Real, I mean. I know you said that. I wouldn't blame you. It's just that I didn't think you'd... you'd... really didn't *think* you'd come here of your own free, you know, vole, what's it? Volition. And I'm sorry for wasting so much of your time. But you had to experience it, do you see? If I'd only told you about it, you wouldn't have really taken it in.'

'I shan't be pursuing you through the courts, Stan,' Alma said, thinking again of the gratification it would be to feel his skull cave under the force of a blow from her hands.

He misunderstood. His face brightened into a smile. 'Well, I'm grateful! I mean, I'd understand if you did. But you needed the tools to solve the whodunnit, and this was the best way I could think to give you those tools... Look, he's about to *throw*.'

Stan was pointing. Moonwalker, on a ridge overlooking the pool, was twisting with the fierce and hormonal joy of the *après-assassinat*, performing a kind of rudimentary dance. The ape spun about, lifted the weapon and hurled it into the sky.

Up it went, and Alma's gaze went with it. It slowed, settled into its apogee, seemed, almost, to hang in space.

'And the thing is—' Stan began to say. But the bone was beginning to fall and Alma was no longer there.

—Cut—

Alma coughed and rolled over. The machine that had been linking her in-Shine made a noise like sighing, and disengaged.

She sat up.

She was on a narrow bed in a small, and otherwise unfurnished, room – one of those by-the-hour places that rent out Shine access for those who are without private facilities, but who don't like the idea of being on public view in the back of a coffee shop or retail centre. There was a door directly opposite.

The first thing Alma did was to check around her, to see whether Stanley was in the room. Or, to be absolutely precise, she looked for anything that could be used as a weapon at the same time as she scanned the Real location for Stanley. But he wasn't in the room, and neither was anything else. The disorientation of being shifted from the Shine into the Real – though it *was* a little discombobulating for Alma, since she wasn't used to it – wasn't so great that she missed the oddity of this.

Odd. There was no set-up to provide her slumbering Real-world corpus with food, or even with water.

She did not feel hungry or thirsty. That seemed strange. Something about that fact didn't add up. Despite her body having been cached in this room for – at least – one night and two days, she felt neither hungry nor thirsty. Alma's mind being of a certain kind, she found herself rattling through possibilities – was there a gourmet bot, or feeding machine? She looked around but, apart from the paraphernalia to hook her into the Shine, there was nothing in the room at all. So: Stanley must have been coming into the room to attend to her bodily needs, but no, because *he'd* been inside the sim for almost as long as she had. So: Stanley had hired somebody else to come into the room to attend to her bodily needs. He had an accomplice. But who? Was he running a whole gang? And as her mind cycled through these possibilities, it ignored the most obvious thing.

Her feed was flashing.

She checked. Her clock, having kept flawless time for decades, was showing an error code.

It was out of sync with the collective time.

She had never seen this happen before. The numbers, mildly red, adding second by second to the thirty-eight hours, eleven minutes and thirty-one, thirty-two, thirty-three seconds – froze – defaulted to a blue sextuple zero, spelled out *error* and turned (oh, it made her heart stop) *green*. The numbers said she had forty-one minutes before Marguerite's next treatment.

The numbers now said that Marguerite was still alive. It could not be, and yet there it was.

For long seconds, drawn out as a spider draws a thread in the sun-bright forest to catch its hyphens of light along its length, Alma did nothing. The trapped fly snores in the web.

Hope can be as painful as a fracture.

She got to her feet, walked to the door and touched it with her hand. It opened straight away.

She walked out into a deserted hallway. Two facing rows of shut black doors, like the Monoliths from the sim she had just exited.

There was no lift. Stairs slid her down to a public exit and out into the evening sunlight and the clean air. She recognised where she was. It was three streets away from her flat. Sometimes hope can be almost unbearable.

When she looked back on the entire episode, it was *these* four minutes when she was most scared. Alma ran, and she ran as fast as she could, and she ran straight home, and all the way she was weeping inwardly, inwardly begging herself not to hope, because the thought of hope rising up again inside her heart *only to be crushed* was the worst thought her human brain was capable of conceiving. The despair and grief she had lived with for two days and one night, though hideous, was at least settled. Better the stable grief we know than the hope that might break us.

There was nobody around – a typical R!-Town evening. A bot murmured along the pavement, collecting rubbish. She passed one other human being, in-Shine, in a mesh-suit, a filter strapped to its face, clonking along. And here was the entrance to her own block, and here a crazy voice said *don't go in*! *It's a trap*!

168

Thirty-seven minutes to go before Marguerite needed her next intervention, and Alma actually stopped at the door, panting, and put her hands on her thighs, and leaned forward. Trap? How could it possibly be a trap? Stanley's voice reoccurred to her: *you had to experience it, do you see? If I'd only told you about it, you wouldn't have really taken it in.*

She had experienced it for two days and a night, and yet, somehow, Marguerite was still alive.

Whatever the inertia was that held her outside the apartment – she knew what it was: it was terror at rushing up there with hope burning her, only to find Marguerite dead, that's what it was – she overcame it. Inside and into the elevator. Up to her floor and into her own apartment, and she was making little sobbing noises, *bruh, bruh, bruh*, and through to the bedroom.

'Hello, my sweet,' said Marguerite from the bed. 'I've just been having an interesting conversation with somebody whom, I believe, you know.'

Alma was on her, arms around her great neck, weeping so fluidly the tears spattered onto Marguerite's chest.

'Oh – my!' Marguerite said, returning the embrace. 'Good gracious, my love, what's this? Why crying?'

For a while Alma couldn't say anything at all.

Marguerite comforted her, as best she could. 'Why cry? Cry – *why*?'

'You're alive,' said Alma, through a mouthful of pebbles, or so it sounded.

'Indeed I am, and for another thirty-two minutes at least. Alma, my love, what – what – what is this? Crying... It *really* isn't like you.'

'Would you believe,' Alma said, wiping her eyes on her forearms, 'that this is the *third* time I've wept this evening?'

'I'd find that very *hard* to believe. But if you say it's true, then I suppose I'll need to flex my belief muscle just about as darn hard as I can.'

It was easier for Alma to regain her composure than she thought it might be. She washed at the sink, and dried her face, and embraced Marguerite again. Then, because Rita said she was hungry – and because even though she had *had* food only a few hours before, some stubborn portion of Alma's brain told her she had been starved for days – she fixed up some food. And they ate, and drank coffee, and shared a moment together.

Alma began telling her story.

She had to stop before she got very far, because the deadline for the next treatment loomed. So Alma washed and put on a sterile apron, and got herself ready, and as she did so she had the nauseous vertigo of the Shine, the uncertainty as to whether she was truly back in the Real, or just deeper in the simulation. But her feed was connected to the Real world again, and all the markers were of material reality, and she stilled her paranoia.

There was a moment of pre-storm calm, as there often was; Marguerite was smiling at her. What if this time the pathology threw some unlikely curve ball, and she needed to order up some unusual and expensive pharmakon, and her credit rating was so low nobody would lend to her?

Then the monitors started putting out high pulses of sound, and the visualisations wobbled and swung about, swelling and bulging. There was a step up in temperature.

Marguerite said, 'I feel a little faint,' and then, as she peered at the ceiling, unconsciousness slid opaque white contacts over her eyes. A new strain of pathology, some genehack staphyviridan bug or other, began aggressively to colonise the subarachnoid. The lymph lost fluidity. Her heart went into fibrillation. It was serious.

Alma quickly separated the two potentially fatal assaults from all the other chaff and noise of Marguerite's sickness-burdened system. She mixed an agnabiotic and inserted it, marked a second dose with her own DNA and subdermally sprayed it at Marguerite's armpit, and put a cocktail of four medicines into a drip to combat the less dangerous infections.

'Not about to lose you twice,' she muttered, 'in one day.'

Then she binned the gloves, washed again, and sat by Marguerite for a quarter of an hour or so, until all the vitals settled towards more acceptable parameters. Not health, by a long chalk – temperature, viral load and cellular toxicity were all higher than Alma would have liked, but they were not at dangerous levels. Rita's eyelids fluttered, opened, and her eyes rolled back into their proper place, like a doll being lifted from its back into a sitting position.

'I think I lost things there, for a second,' she said, her voice higher pitched than usual. 'That was a baffling sort of faint. Came on me sideways, as it were.'

'You quite often pass out during treatment,' Alma said, taking Rita's big old hand in hers and stroking it.

'Oh, my dear, I know. But this felt different, somehow. I fear I am getting worse.'

'You're literally always on the edge of dying. Hard to see how anything could *be* worse.'

'But you know what I mean. It's a downward slope, and however hard we try to keep the incline shallow, it's an incline nonetheless. There is such a thing as entropy, you know.'

'I want you not to speak like this, please.'

'*Is* there merit in avoiding the truth?' Marguerite cleared her throat. 'I mean – is there? Really?'

'*Is* there a famous proverb about there being a time and a place? I'd suggest this is neither.'

'Point,' said Marguerite sagely.

'Here's something I stumbled across the other day,' said Alma. 'It's what Robert Frost called a poem. He said a poem was *a lump in the throat, a homesickness, a lovesickness*. That's how I feel about you, Rita. You're always here, but always hovering on the edge of going for ever. I *thought* I'd lost you for ever today, and it was a state of mind much worse than I'd anticipated it being. I mean – don't. But—'

'You'd better tell me everything that's happened,' said Marguerite in a matter-of-fact voice.

'I'm going to get a brandy first,' said Alma, calling up files on time perception from a wide variety of sources and settling in to read.

'As the old song says,' Marguerite said, as a little of the rough-textured fluid slipped down her throat, 'who knows where the time goes? You're saying this Stanley individual abducted you?'

'If I see him again in-Real,' Alma noted, 'I'm going to break one of his bones. For payback. For what he put me through! Not all his bones. But one of them. Maybe two.' She took another sip. 'I'll decide which two later.'

'He said he couldn't tell you. He said he had to show you.'

'He's a fan, and that word is short for *fanatic*, you know, and fanatics are capable of all sorts of crazy violence. Stan really loves

171

this stupid old movie. *Really* loves. But it turns out it wasn't the movie – or more to the point, it wasn't this *specific* movie – that he wanted to show me. It was the architecture of the simulation.' She took another sip. 'I've honestly never heard of anything like it. I mean, I'm not au fait with all the to-and-fro of in-Shine speculation, but this, I think, is wholly new.'

'You were in-Shine for, what, an hour?' Marguerite asked. 'A little over?'

'An hour of objective time. But subjectively I was inside for a night and most of two whole days. And it *really* felt as if that was the time that passed. I mean, it didn't feel grainy, or forced. Time passed for me exactly as smoothly as it does in the real world. Or it seemed to.'

'My darling, I'm not doubting your experience, although I *might* insert the caveat that you are not the most experienced Shine aficionado.'

'That's true,' Alma agreed. 'But does it matter? I know what I felt. I know what I experienced.'

She lifted the glass again, and tilted it just right, and the sharp brandy spanked the curve of her tongue for a naughty girl, and rasped deliciously down her throat, and the warmth spread through her.

Marguerite was alive. It was a miraculous release.

'So that was what Stanley had to show you,' Marguerite was saying. 'That was *why* he had to show you – why he couldn't just tell you.'

'I'm still going to break his bones,' Alma insisted, 'if I see him again. But I start to take his point. If he'd just told me this, then I don't think I would have taken the force of it.'

'So somebody has found a way of expanding the subjective experience of time,' mused Marguerite. 'In-Shine, at any rate. *How* is it done, though?'

'Well, that's the really interesting thing, isn't it? Dip into your feed, as I did when I was rustling up supper, and you discover it's a century-old branch of science with a bewildering array of sub-disciplines. It'd take me a long time to get on top of all that. But at root it can only be about the *perception* of time, in the brain. And since the brain isn't separate from the body, that means the perception of time inside the body too.'

'Ms Lund,' said Marguerite, nodding her head slowly.

'Exactly. So, from my skim, this is what I've gleaned.'

'Good word,' said Marguerite, approvingly. '*Gleaned.*'

'There are different scales of time perception. I mean, that much is well understood. Humans share with animals a set of circadian rhythms, tied to rhythms of waking and sleeping.'

'*Circa*, Latin for about,' said Marguerite, 'and *diēs*, a day. Roughly a day.'

'That scale is quite deformable. I mean, I haven't had a regular day-night sleeping pattern for seven years or more, and it hasn't done me any lasting harm.'

'And no more have I,' said Marguerite, sounding a little hurt.

'I'm not rebuking you, my love! Scientists also talk of longer durations of time perception, covering things like seasonal attune-ment, hibernation and so on – they call that infradian perception. It seems more acute in animals other than humans. At the other end of the scale is ultradian perception – cycles with a period shorter than a day but longer than an hour or so, governing, for instance, the periodicity with which humans move through one entire rotation of REM and non-REM sleep. All this time perception is not conscious, or deliberative. It is instinctive. It's handled by a highly distributed system involving the cerebral cortex, cerebellum and basal ganglia. It's not localised in any one spot, which has always made it really hard to direct research, or directly influence that perception.'

'And yet somebody has managed it,' Marguerite pointed out.

'Grove, Stanley called her. Her programming ID, not her real name. Some kind of neurological genius. Because things get very complicated when we bring the scale down to seconds rather than hours. There are lots of experiments showing that rats, say, can instinctively estimate periods of forty seconds, and can continue to do so even when everything but the most basic cortex has been removed.'

'Cruel sort of experiment,' said Marguerite, with distaste.

'Sure. It shows, though, that at least down to *that* scale time perception is a really basic feature of life. Something that must have been true of very primitive forms. And that's what the pulse *was*, time-perception wise. Thirty to forty seconds is roughly the tick-tock of time's passing for billions of years. Life can *react* much more quickly than that, of course, if needs be, but those reactions are stimulus-response, a different sort of system. In terms of how life perceives time, how it is vitally aware of time, thirty to forty second pulses is the baseline.'

'Let's split the difference at *trente-cinq*, shall we?'

'And the story goes on, the evolution story. What happens next is that bigger brains evolve, and the division of consciously perceived time gets chopped finer. It's not difficult for us to count individual seconds, even half-seconds, to *feel* the world tick past on that scale. But what about milliseconds? We can react at that calibration, but not perceive on it. Until now. To live for sixty minutes and *perceive* that you were living sixty hours – for that to happen, somehow your perception of time, at a neurological level, has to be manipulated at a fineness of more than one sixtieth. It happened to me. I perceived 0.017 seconds as one second. In fact, since the whole experience had real smoothness, I'd guess the grain, as it were, was ever finer than that. So this Grove, whoever she was, has found a way of stimulating the relevant portions of the brain to create the illusion – of punting the perceptual energy, the neurological focus, into 0.01 of a second that a walking person would put into one second.'

'You experienced what you experienced,' said Marguerite. 'Which means somebody has done it.'

'Yes – it's doable. It's just not obvious *how* it's doable.'

'My sweet,' rumbled Marguerite, 'you're getting hung up on the *how*. Take a step back. Think what this means. Think about one thing in particular.'

'One thing in particular,' repeated Alma, taking another slurp of her brandy.

'Obvious as elephants in this small room,' chided Marguerite.

'It's not *such* a small room!' Alma objected. 'Or at least, it didn't seem so when we first rented this place.'

'Think of the GM. The secret she is prepared to physically threaten, and doubtless to kill, to *keep* secret. Her plan is to corner the financial world of the Shine, to command the currency that is used in that place. She can't simply port regular money across, so she plans to build a whole new currency, a whole new scarcity-based economics, founded on the one thing that is unavoidably, existentially scarce.'

'Time,' said Alma.

'This invention in effect allows her to coin time. If she can get hold of it, and most importantly of all, if she can keep it out of the hands of her competitors, then she at a stroke establishes the in-Shine validity of her currency and makes herself alone its central bank. It's what owning every gold mine in the world would be to the old-world currencies. She can say to people, "come to me, and I can give you literal time".'

'Give is presumably not her plan.'

'Well – quite. But here's the one thing mortal life has never been able to cultivate, fashion or create. Time itself. If this technology means that one second of in-Real time can be converted into a whole, richly experienced hour of in-Shine time... Only think of the commercial possibilities!'

'It would mean that a person who expected to live to a hundred and twenty in the Real,' Alma said, her feed doing the calculation for her, 'could go in-Shine and last until they were over 400,000 years old.'

They both sat in silence for a while.

'That's worth murdering for, I suppose,' said Marguerite.

'That,' said Alma, standing up, 'is both motive *and* method.'

Alma knew she would have to go out, sooner rather than later – but, having believed Marguerite dead and gone, she could not bear to separate herself from her partner again. Not, at any rate, so soon. So she spent the whole of the night – two four-hour cycles – in Marguerite's company. She slept in the chair by her bed.

All through that night a fierce joy glowed in her heart. She had lost her love for ever, and then her love had been returned to her.

Here was one striking thing: she had slept during the in-Shine simulation of whatever that Kubrick movie had been called. In fact she had only slept for minutes, objectively speaking, and yet she felt as refreshed as if she had slept for many hours. Whatever the simulation was doing, it was doing it in a way that fooled the body into thinking it was really happening at the scale at which it presented itself as happening.

'Is it in the interface, maybe?' Marguerite asked. 'Maybe you should go back to that room, the place you woke up. If that machinery is the key to this whole thing it'd be worth...' Instead of concluding this sentence, she put her rich, plump lips together and whistled.

'It won't still be there,' said Alma, with certitude. 'The man

who called himself Stanley – he's bonkers, obsessed, a bit dangerous, but he's not *stupid*. He knew exactly what I would do when I
woke up – hurry home to you, my love. He knew not to be in my
way when I came back to the Real, not if he wanted to keep his
bones unbroken. But he would have been nearby, and as soon as I
was gone he'd surely have collected the hardware and skedaddled.'

'Still, best to check, no?'

'I'll pop over there after your next treatment. I will need to
make a few calls first.'

She went through to the front room, and settled herself in the
comfy chair with a drink. First off she sent a recorded avatar to
Pu Sto. She didn't expect a reply – she was only too aware there
was some kind of high-level war being fought behind the scenes
of government. But she thought she should let the politician know
what she had uncovered.

She was also curious as to whether Officer Maupo, Pu Sto's
representative in the matter of Alexa Lund's death, had been
automatically patched in to the channels of communication
between Pu Sto and Alma. And her curiosity was satisfied.

It seemed she was.

'Hello,' said Maupo's hologrammatic representation as it popped
into the front room, her virtual uniform a patchwork of gleams
and brightness. 'Did you call?'

'I don't remember calling *you*,' said Alma.

'And yet,' said Maupo's simulacrum, spreading her arms, 'here
I am.'

'For all I know there's been a coup behind the scenes, Pu Sto
has been sent to some internal gulag, and you're a double agent
representing the new tyranny of the Department of Health,' said
Alma, smiling broadly.

Maupo, also smiling broadly, said, 'It's a distinct possibility. Why
don't we discuss it over drinks? And a meal?'

'I have information on the murder of Alexa Lund. Information
that Pu Sto needs to hear.'

'I shall pass it right along,' Maupo assured her.

Alma paused. 'It concerns a very wealthy citizen, known col-
loquially as the Golden Meteor. You know who I mean.'

'I've heard that the Pope practises the Catholic religion,' said
Maupo, 'and have access to intel concerning which part of the
forest bear-brand toilet paper is to be delivered.'

'Sarcasm is never sexy,' said Alma, mock-sternly. 'My point is, you'll know that caution is a necessity when dealing with an individual as wealthy as the GM.'

'Wealthier than the Pope,' agreed Maupo.

'And with bigger claws, metaphorically speaking, than any bear.'

'Which means that the notion that a humble policeman like me could walk up to her well-fortified mansion and arrest her is as fanciful as the idea that the Pope of Bears holds papal court in the forests.'

'You would need cast-iron evidence,' Alma agreed.

'Which I'm assuming you don't have.'

'Which may yet be forthcoming. The bottom line is that the GM is engaged in a battle with a number of other ultra-rich individuals over the establishment of a working in-Shine currency. You may have heard something about that?'

'I'm a real-world police officer,' said Maupo. 'My beat is the Real, not the Shine.'

'I'm betting you spend more time in-Shine than I do.'

'A girl needs a holiday from time to time.'

'Then this will affect you more than it affects me. If the GM gets her way, her preferred mode of currency, based on her own enforced mode of scarcity, will become general in all the many virtual realities where the majority of the population live. She will become, in effect, the central bank for the whole of the Shine. You can imagine how much that would add to her already vast wealth and power. You can imagine how ruthless she might be in pursuit of that aim.'

'None of which is germane to a possible warrant for arrest. Do you have actual proof linking the GM to the murder of Alexa Lund?'

'Reasonable cause,' said Alma. 'No. Not yet.'

'Unreasonable claws, and I will not be putting myself within reach of them.' But Maupo was clearly intrigued. 'What is the ground for her new in-Shine currency?'

'I could tell you, and then I could get into very deep trouble.'

'You think I'd leak the information? I *am* hurt.'

'Understand my situation,' said Alma. 'I have one priority above all others – to be able to get to this place, where I live, every four hours. I have absolutely no interest whatsoever in undertaking anything at all that would put that freedom of access at risk. I certainly can't afford to break the law, which makes me the model citizen, from your professional point of view. But I also can't afford to piss off the ultra-rich, lest my liberty be compromised and my partner die.'

'Then you're not bringing me anything very much,' said Maupo.

'I need to have a face-to-face with Pu Sto herself. Escort her by all means, if you want to, but – with all the respect due to your pay grade – I need to get an OK from somebody a little *above* it.'

'Pu Sto's physical well-being is not what one would call tiptop,' said Maupo.

This was news to Alma. 'I'm sorry to hear that. But surely she can still see me? Just for a brief meeting?'

Maupo's simulacrum scowled at her, but then let out a simulated sigh.

'I'll see what I can do,' she said, and rang off.

There were a dozen pressing messages to deal with, and a legal seal that threatened to impound Alma for non-payment of debt. She did not open this, since it might have concealed a subpoena, but she did use one of her greyer apps to open a transparency in the side of the seal and peer inside. The motion was to divert Alma and Marguerite's rent money to a debt-collection agency – they, it seemed, had acquired it from another debt trading agency, 'DebtInArcadiaEgo', who had acquired it from a firm called 'De-Debting', who had acquired it from the 'Alpha Health MedSupply' firm.

Alma rubbed her face with the palms of both hands. This wasn't a long-term sustainable situation, she knew. But for now all she could do was stall.

Using a separate app she brought the debt-collection seal into the ambit of her landlord agency. They would not be happy at the thought that rent money might legally be diverted from them to service an unrelated debt.

Not that she'd had the money for rent for quite some time.

She pinged the man who called himself Stanley again – nothing. She put a few for-safekeeping items in various caches, and rejigged her financial standing orders as best she could.

Then she thought of Jupita. She was, after all, working for her – doing the job Jupita had hired her to do. Maybe she could tap her employer for an advance on her fee? She had, after all, made progress. She put in a call, was diverted into quite a low-rank, AI algorithm functionary, fake teeth in a fake smile in a fake face that beamed fake happiness to hear from her.

Thank you for your interest. We regret that at this current juncture we are unable . . .

No matter; Jupita would surely be interested in the progress Alma had made. She pushed her details at the faux-receptionist, with a big red tag informing Jupita that she was closer to a solution. Then she disengaged and waited for the call back.

It didn't come. Which is to say, it didn't come from Jupita. The hours passed, and Alma did the gardener's work of weeding her in-feed messages, and nothing. She knock-knocked a second time in Jupita's feed, and was again rebuffed with artificial politeness.

That was odd.

And then, out of the blue, she was contacted by another of the Fab Four – the one known as the Stirk of Stirk. She OK'd the request, and moments later an extremely high-def avatar stepped into the front room of her apartment.

'Good afternoon.'

'How can I . . . ?' Alma asked. 'How can I help you?'

The avatar was of a late-middle-aged man, slender, in a gleaming white three-piece suit, with black buttons shiny as liquorice and a tie with a green-blue peacock sheen. His face was lean and pale, with a close-trimmed lenticular black goatee. His eyes were the purple colour of methylated spirits.

'I am the Stirk of Stirk,' said the avatar. 'And you are Alma. And it's a pleasure to meet you.'

Alma waited.

The avatar wandered around the front room. 'You have certainly stirred things *up*, Ms Alma. In that sense it was a clever play by Jupita to hire you. Uncharacteristically clever.'

'It hurts my feelings just a touch to hear that hiring me was a play, rather than a genuine case.'

'The GM's personal assistant – Tym was his name – killed. The delicate balance of our four-way consortium of enemies disturbed, and now you poking and prying, or, if you prefer, doing your job.'

'Some of us,' Alma noted, 'need to earn our money.'

'Oh, I haven't come here to *rebuke* you. Do you know why she hired you?'

'Because I'm so very good at my job?'

179

'Because you have a police affiliation, without being yourself police. *That* was clever of J.'

'I prefer to believe my explanation. I have fans, you know.'

'I don't doubt it. You also have antagonists. Would it surprise you to learn that your employer is chief among that crowd?'

'Little would surprise me at this point, Mr Stirk.' Alma ignored the angry ping that plonked itself into her feed: *the correct form of address is my lord, or Lord Stirk! Please use correct form of address!*

Alma dropped down an infohook app, and drew up the fact that this Scottish laird had been born Nguyen Sinh-Sac, and had purchased the title less than ten years previously. Such a person might well be super-prickly at being properly addressed, or might smile complaisantly at the inherent ridiculousness of all such titles and honours.

'Mr Stirk,' chuckled the avatar.

It seemed that the Stirk was the latter kind of person.

'You say that Jupita was using me as a "play" in the game with yourself and the other two members of your quartet,' Alma said. 'You'll forgive me for assuming that you are doing exactly the same thing, by getting in touch with me. I don't suppose you have a genuine interest in *my* welfare.'

'Oh, of course not.' The Stirk swept the very notion to one side with a gesture of his hologrammatic hand. 'And of course I don't expect you to trust anything I say.'

'So why are you here?'

'Oh,' said the Stirk, holding his hands palms-outward, like a saint in a stained glass window. 'I'd like you to communicate something to Jupita.'

'Your group is a gestalt, or so I heard. You are in constant contact in-Shine. Tell her yourself.'

'The group is in abeyance. After the Tym fellow died, none of us want to connect with the others after the old manner.'

'You can surely pass her a message, though.'

'What I want to communicate with her is not a form of words. Ms Alma, you know the project our group was involved in?'

'Absolute wealth.'

'Yes, yes, but in a more proximate sense – the creation of an in-Shine currency. Yes?'

'I'd heard something about that.'

'You've probably heard that each of the four of us has a

different approach. The GM is secretive about hers, but we all know it's *time*. She's secretive, I think, because she has nothing behind the general concept. If one could coin time, one could indeed grow rich – but one cannot.'

Alma bit her tongue.

'So the GM throws a cloud of unknowing about her plans. Cernowicz – well, she's the least rich of all of us, and her microscarcities is a non-starter. I, at least, have a *concrete* plan.'

'Bitcoin,' said Alma, 'is what I heard.'

For the first time in their encounter the Stirk betrayed something that might have been anger – a little facial twitch, a bunching of the hologrammatic skin around his hologrammatic nostrils. It was only momentary. He smiled again.

'Rather more up to date than that,' he chuckled. 'But that's not what I'm here to discuss. I want to talk about Jupita's own ideas. Do you know what they are?'

Alma considered. 'Not really,' she conceded.

'Shall I tell you?'

'Mr Stirk, I'd guess that you telling me is the reason why you've called me in the first place, which would mean that the question is purely rhetorical.'

'Oh, I like *you*. I can see that, quite apart from placing a relatively safe conduit to the police in front of people who couldn't contact the police directly, in order to tangle and disrupt the networks of the four of us – that quite *apart* from that, you are worth hiring on your own merits. Well, yes, then – I shall tell you. Jupita hopes to model money in-Shine on friendship networks.'

'I'd heard something along those lines.'

'Her theory is that friendship between human beings, viewed on the largest scale, generates its own gradients. I know this, because, once upon a time, she came to me to discuss it. Once upon a time before she changed – before she went mad, or whatever has happened to her lately. She came to me because of where I started earning my money.'

'Porn,' said Alma.

'I happen to know, because we keep very good records, that you have never sojourned in Orgasmatropolis. You should go, you know. It's a remarkable place – though I say so myself.'

'I can see how such a thing makes money, by offering something people are eager to pay for. I don't see how that could function as the basis for a new kind of currency.'

'Delve in the deep architecture of social media,' said the Stirk, 'and you find a social platform called *Facebook*, that began by asking university students to rate the facial attractiveness of their peers.'

'If you say so.'

'Think of it this way: creating an in-Shine currency means finding a way of leveraging some kind of scarcity. And that's hard in-Shine, because it's a place where the conventional indices of scarcity don't apply. Each member of the Fab Four has her or his own ideas about where that scarcity might be introduced. And Jupita's idea is that it inheres in the networkiness of the network itself. Put it this way – if you take, say, six hundred children and put them in a school, what happens? They learn lessons, of course, and have to get up early in the morning and so on – I don't mean that. I mean, what happens to the friendship network that those six hundred represent?'

'Everyone knows everyone, and smaller bunches of closer friendship coalesce out of the whole.'

'More than that. Some kids become really popular, and some are shunned. Even if the six hundred are all equally nice, equally clever, equally good looking and so on, the nature of the network itself gravitates towards that larger scale gradient. Some kids accrue friendship-capital, and everyone likes them, and everyone wants to be their friend. Some kids don't. Jupita talked to me because there's something similar in porn – as I discovered in my early days. You put before the public a thousand porn actors of, objectively, equivalent pulchritude and what happens? Your public, en masse, wants to engage with some but not others. What ought to be a level playing field – what could be a friendship utopia, where everybody is friends with everybody else – always develops into a place of peaks and troughs.'

'I don't know about the peaks,' said Alma. 'Mine was a pretty trough-y school experience, if I'm honest.'

'That's been Jupita's plan all along,' said the Stirk. 'To parlay the unsmoothness of human interaction itself into money.'

Alma recalled how much Jupita had talked, in their one interaction, about friendship and fame.

'So – how?' she asked.

'You mean the specifics? I don't know. If she had a working plan to which I was privy, I'd steal it, of course.'

'Of course.'

'Ms Alma, you need to understand what your employer is doing. She is hoping to convert all human interaction, from friendship and co-worker interactions to desire and love, directly into money. She is planning on monetising human interaction as such.'

'What a hellish thought,' said Alma. But then she added, '*You* sound impressed, though.'

'If I only thought it possible, I'd do it myself. Of course I would! I'm not here to criticise my fellow Fab. Good grief, no!'

'Then why are you here?'

'To make you aware, Ms Alma. Your employer is not interested in interpersonal interactions as such – she is only interested in their gradient, the inequality between the parties. Because that gradient is where she hopes to make money. *Make money* in a more than usually literal sense.'

'You perhaps imagine more by way of interpersonal interaction between Jupita and myself than is actually the case.'

'I'm sure she keeps you at arm's length. But I have a suggestion.'

'Go ahead.'

'Sever all contact with her. Do it, and you may live. Remain in touch and you will not. It's as simple as that. I know her, and you do not. So, tender your resignation as her employee. Walk away. There is no other way to escape her web. You may think you can remain in your relationship, however unequal and distant, without harm. You can't.'

'Me quitting is the message you want to send Jupita?'

'You quitting is the communication she needs to receive. Or one of them. Not necessarily from me. It so happens that it would also, very much, be in your interests.'

'If I quit, I won't get paid.'

The avatar raised one eyebrow. 'Naturally not.'

'I need to get paid. Perhaps you could pay me?'

'You've not had a great deal of experience with very rich people, Alma,' said the Stirk. 'If we made a habit of giving money away for no reason we wouldn't be rich in the first place.'

'You could hire me.'

'I have no need of a private investigator.'

'Mr Stirk,' said Alma, 'do you know *what* it was that Jupita hired me to investigate?'

'A nonsense. I'm surprised, having checked your file, and your history, that you agreed to take it on at all.'

'She thinks one of the Four – one of you – has been murdered, and their in-Shine presence hijacked.'

'Exactly. A nonsense.'

'Mr Stirk,' Alma pressed, 'are you alive?'

'I am. This is my personal avatar.'

'With respect, if you'd been killed and your online identity hacked, your personal avatar wouldn't be proof of anything. I would need to see the real you – in the flesh.'

'Sever contact with Jupita, Ms Alma,' said the avatar, with a smile. 'I strongly recommend it.' And with a regal wave of his hologrammatic hand, the Stirk of Stirk left.

Alma pulled on a coat and rode the elevator down. Of *course*, the equipment Stanley had used to lock her into that Kubrickian simulation in-Shine would have been cleared away. Of course that's what the situation would be. But there was a non-zero chance that – say – something had happened to Stanley, and he hadn't been able to clear the room. In which case it would be very much worth her while to seize the equipment.

The air was fresh. A strong southerly wind brought the faint tang of salt and seagulls shrieked at the drones overhead. The sky was a cold morning blue. Stark bone-coloured November clouds flounced past. A fresh new day.

Alma passed not a single other human being on her way to the building.

She didn't go inside. From across the road she saw two improbably tall and bulky individuals coming out of the door.

And they saw her.

Fifty metres separated Alma from the twins. She made a quick mental calculation. They were surely big and muscular, but that didn't mean they were necessarily made for speed. With a head start such as the distance afforded her, and her knowledge of R!-Town's byways and alleys, she could probably give them the slip.

But then she reasoned: they doubtless knew where she lived. They could easily just kick down the door of her apartment block – and that's where she would be when Marguerite's next treatment came due. And anyway (she told herself), *she* hadn't done anything wrong. True, they'd stuck a needle up her nose, but that had been in the service of an instruction to keep away from their boss, the GM. Well, she had done so.

Quite apart from anything else, this was *her* town, not theirs. And she wanted to send a message of her own to their boss.

At any rate, there was no need to check the inside of the building. The equipment was evidently gone, or the Kry twins, having just been inside, would have retrieved it. And here they were standing empty-handed.

So she took a deep breath and crossed the empty road.

'Good afternoon, gentlemen,' she said brightly.

'Nice greeting,' said Reg Kry.

'Be a shame if something were to *happen* to it,' said Ron Kry.

'Happen to my... greeting?' Alma asked.

'Or to your capacity for uttering it,' clarified Ron.

'So what brings you all the way from the bright city of London to R!-Town, may I ask? Here to see the sights? Do a bit of shopping? There are some excellent shops in the Oracle Centre, although not, I think, a *Suits For Gorillas* store.'

'She's cheeky, Ron,' said Reg.

'You almost have to admire it, Reg,' said Ron. 'The cheekiness.'

'Almost,' agreed Reg. 'But not quite.'

'So, Alma,' said Ron, 'you just happened to be strolling past this Ear Building?'

Alma was momentarily wrong-footed. 'Ear Building?' Her feed was giving her nothing.

'This,' said Ron, with exaggerated elocution. 'Here. Building.'

'Ah,' said Alma. And then, 'Gentlemen, gentlemen, remember. I live here! This is *my* town. You're the strangers. So it's the fact that you happen to be in this place, peering, like an otoscope, into this ear,' she looked intently first at Ron and then at Reg, 'building – it's *that* fact that's remarkable.'

'It occurs to me, Reg,' said Ron, 'that we mistook her attitude to needles.'

'You think so, Ron?'

'Yes, Reg. We assumed she *disliked* having a needle inserted, nasally.' *Nay-say-lay.* 'But maybe she actually enjoyed the experience?' *Anjoyed. Exper-hear-ience.*

'You think she's angling for a repeat insertion, Ron?'

185

'Could be, Reg.'

'Or maybe, instead of the nasal,' said Alma, her heartbeat increasing despite her best efforts to remain calm, 'the thumbish? The thumbniar? The nose is one thing. The thumb quite another.'

The two giants stiffened marginally.

'Still harping on thumbs?' said Reg.

'I really don't think,' said Ron, 'that we could do all that much damage with a thumb. Do you, Reg?'

'Stick a needle in a thumb? It might hurt a bit.' He spoke with disdain, as if *hurting only a bit* were a demeaning insult to his tradecraft. 'But that's all.'

'Enough to make a person cry?' Alma prompted.

'Would depend on the person.'

She took the plunge. 'Enough to make a person *die?*'

They both stared at her, glowering down out of their Easter Island faces.

'I *hardly* see—' Reg began, but Ron interrupted him.

'Not physically *possible*, that, though, is it?'

'I,' said Reg again, with a dignified slowness, '*hardly* see—'

'No, you're correct.' Alma put up a finger. 'Unless...' she said. 'Unless you had leverage.'

'Leverage,' repeated Ron.

'Hardly,' said Reg.

'Indulge me for a moment,' said Alma.

'See,' said Reg.

'Imagine,' Alma said, 'a machine that could extend a person's perceived experience of time. Imagine a modification to Shine access that meant that for every second that passed in the real world, an hour appeared to pass in the simulation. Imagine such a thing!' Neither twin spoke. 'I mean, it would give people much longer sessions in-Shine, which would be nice for them. And as long as the real second and the perceived in-Shine hour were separate things – well then, everything would be just dandy.'

'I haven't heard of any such technologies being marketed,' said Ron testily.

'I hardly *see...*'

Reg puffed out his huge cheeks and blew a great breath out of his lips, like a bellows. Like an antique engraving of the god of the winds. Like one of Rabelais' giants – trees flew away, umbrellas were snatched out of hands, the whole of R!-town was flattened. He stopped blowing. Then he looked at his brother.

'Keep indulging me,' Alma said. 'On the one hand there's actual time, where we all live. On the other there's this new expanded in-Shine time, where we can live a whole lifetime over the course of a fortnight's holiday. Well and good. But then I got to wondering – what about the border between the two?'

'Border,' said Ron, in a low and rumbly voice.

'Imagine if there's a crossover point. The perception of extended time happens in the brain, because that's where everything happens. But what if the technology enabled us to keep a person – say, a middle-aged woman, yellow hair, blue eyes – keep her half-and-half between real time and extended time?'

The twins had nothing to say to this.

'I imagine it would be a kind of feedback loop. So that, say, a brief experience – pleasure, pain, whatever – might be made to last for a whole day of experiential time. Or a whole day's intensive torture be condensed into a period of a few seconds. Or maybe, maybe, the first of these would feed into the second, and something that only took a real-world agent a few seconds to inflict could spill over into hours and hours of perceptual agony, that in turn reverberated on the real-world body in a way that... Well, let's say in a way that might have very deleterious physical effects. Yes?'

'No,' said Ron.

'*Don't* know.' Reg looked nervously at his brother. 'Or – no. No!'

'That's a nice sense of immunity from prosecution you got there,' Alma told them. 'Be a shame if something were to *happen* to it.'

Their feeds were cycling furiously. Alma couldn't see with whom they were communicating – although of course she could guess – but the fact of their being incommoded was in itself rather pleasing.

'I look forward to our next meeting,' said Alma, with a wave, and walked away.

When she turned the corner she heard the thud-thud of double footsteps behind her. Either she was being followed by two giant stone golems brought to malign magical life, or else...

A huge hand on her shoulder.

'That meeting you were looking forward to?' said Ron Kry, 'is happening sooner than perhaps you anticipated.'

Well, here it was. It wasn't exactly a surprise. She had been using these two to pass a message to the GM. She had balanced probabilities and assumed they would let her walk, but their boss had evidently instructed them to take her in.

Very well: now she would have to sweeten the most saccharine of her sweet talk, and show her interlocutors her biggest stick, and maybe – just maybe – she'd be able to leverage her knowledge into money to settle debts and keep Marguerite in necessary medical supplies for the foreseeable.

That, at any rate, was the plan.

'Happy to chat, of course.' Alma smiled an inviting smile.

Ron and Reg stared down at her, and then looked behind her, and then took a step back in unison, like two Frankenstein's monsters practising a dance routine.

Alma turned. Behind her a very large car was idling its engine – so smoothly and quietly that she only realised, upon seeing it, that its humming was of a motor engine.

The Krys seemed to recognise it. They took a look at one another, turned on their heels, and walked away.

The door opened. Inside was Pu Sto.

'Step inside, my dear,' she said. 'I'll drop you where you're going.'

'It's a three minute walk,' said Alma. 'Not that it isn't nice to see you. But – driving me home seems egregious.'

'A different person might be happier to be rescued from two potentially violent people.'

Alma took a seat diagonally opposite Pu Sto, and therefore directly opposite the hefty-looking bodyguard sitting on Pu Sto's right. The doors hissed shut, and the windows opaqued themselves.

The car vroomed into life. Alma barely felt the motion.

'I was completely in charge of the situation,' said Alma. 'In fact, I was on track to parlaying that encounter into a little much-needed money.'

'Legally, I trust?'

Alma peered at her. She did not look well. There was a scar, healing but still livid like a line of raspberry jam, running along her cheek. That hadn't been there the last time they had met.

And now that Alma looked she could see that Pu Sto was wearing two mesh leg braces. It looked like she'd been in a fight.

'Are you OK?'

Pu Sto pulled a sour face. 'I can't stand up without the help of my leg mesh,' she said. 'And never will be able to, again.'

'Oh no!'

'Apart from that, I'm doing pretty well. Actually only moderately well, but I'm very pretty, so it balances out.' She smiled at Alma. 'It's been a cat-fight, my friend. Cat and dog fight. Cat and dog and velociraptor fight, in point of fact. But enough about me.'

'What happened to your legs?'

Pu Sto waved this question away. 'You're in debt, I know. I wish there were something I could do. But I don't actually have any money. Government never has actual money. More to the point, I can't protect you if you get into proper illegality – you realise that? So I urge you to stay on the windy side of the law. Think what it would mean to Marguerite if you were banged up.'

'Rock. Hard place. I trust I'll at least receive an honorarium for helping the police solve the murder of Alexa Lund?'

'You know it's the legal minimum fee. It won't go very far where your financial situation is concerned, I'm afraid. If there were a way I could assist you with your various indebtednesses, I would.'

'Also,' said Alma, 'I'm hoping I can at least claim expenses?'

'You think we've not been surveilling you? We're all about the surveillance. What else has all this' – she gestured at her ruined legs – 'political civil war been about? We know you haven't run up any expenses. There was a taxi to north London, but that was paid for by a third party.'

'A *per diem* at least?'

'A *per septimana* perhaps.'

Alma's feed slotted the relevant definition before her.

'Given which,' she told Pu Sto, 'it's a little rich lecturing me for trying to supplement my income in whatever way I can. Don't you think?'

'The law is the law. Ah! We've arrived.'

'I could literally have walked it faster. 'What did you do – drive right round the R!-Town ring road?'

'Alma,' said Pu Sto, 'I wanted to say something to you, in a space in which I could be reasonably sure we weren't being remotely overheard.'

'Shoot,' said Alma.

Pu's bodyguard flinched, her hand reaching and then stopping, thereby revealing where her concealed weapon was concealed.

'What happened to your old PA?' Alma asked, nodding at the new bodyguard. 'I liked him.'

'I attended his funeral four months back.'

'Oh,' said Alma, and then didn't say anything for a while. Eventually she said, 'I hadn't realised things had become so – extreme.'

'Well,' said Pu Sto, 'it's not being reported in the news media, for obvious reasons. Eventually we'll come out on top, or they will, and then there will be trials – the pretext will be corruption, embezzlement, something like that. But it will mean the whole civil war will have emerged into the light of public consciousness. Until that time, both we and they figure we're neither of us well served by open war. Mobs on the streets and suchlike.'

'You really think people would evacuate the Shine on so trivial a pretext as your intra-governmental war?'

Pu Sto smiled. 'No, I suppose not. But we're doing what we can to keep people distracted. To keep them off the streets – rumours of nanoweapons, that kind of thing. And generally people are happy to be distracted. They have better things to be getting on with than worrying about politics.'

'I know I do,' Alma confirmed.

'And how *is* Marguerite?'

'She's... She's still alive.'

Neither of them said anything for a while.

'We weren't *un*aware,' said Pu Sto, with the demeanour of somebody choosing their words carefully, 'that asking you to help with the Lund case might put you in harm's way, of course.'

Alma said nothing.

'Alma, there's really very little the authorities can do with an individual as wealthy as the GM. You understand that, don't you?'

'Powers of arrest surely don't recognise wealth.'

'Arrest her for a real-world crime? Oh – my. I mean, if she walked into a police station and confessed, perhaps with blood dripping from her hands – then maybe. But the GM almost never leaves the Shine.'

'She has minions. She can command.'

'Of course, of course. But then we're arresting her on what charge, exactly? Criminal conspiracy? And she hires the very best lawyers in the entire world – really, money is literally no object for her. How far do the charges go? And this is only to consider the ostensible, face-value working of the law. But the nature of money, when it reaches this degree of accumulation, is never the face value. It's what happens behind the scenes. And behind the scenes is...' She screwed up her face. 'War,' she concluded.

Alma said nothing.

'It's a war, really,' said Pu Sto, yawning, 'between the powers of the Real and the powers of the Shine. The latter believe they have the momentum of history on their side. But some of us stick stubbornly to the notion that it would be a bad move for humanity entirely to vanish up the fundament of its own virtual fantasy realms.'

'I feel like we've had this discussion before.'

'I know. And I know you're no friend of the Shine. Frankly, it was simpler when it was just Health versus us. But now we're facing, in effect, a coalition of forces, and our work is really cut out. Strange phrase that, isn't it? I mean, when you come to think of it?' She yawned again. 'Cut out. Hm. Well, we are playing for high stakes. High stakes.'

'What happened to your spine?'

'A small piece of an explosive device, no bigger than a thumbnail, severed it. Two people died, so I was lucky. Best as I can figure it, the device was set by an individual called Sonequa Haversham. I'm not a hundred per cent on that, mind.'

'I am sorry.'

'I'm not angling for sympathy, so much as setting out how it might be that we – that I – have been prepared to put you in harm's way. Let me tell you about the broader context here. These Four, these loadsamonies – they are significant players in the game. Independent agents, you could say. Non-aligned. The thing is, until now we would count them as more on the side of the Real than the Shine.'

'They hardly ever leave the Shine,' Alma pointed out. 'You said so yourself.'

'True. But I'm not talking personal preference here. Their personal preferences are neither here nor there as far as we're concerned. I'll say more – they are, all four of them, very simple human beings. They have a great deal of money and want more of it – that's all there is. At a certain level of wealth, wealth becomes the only salient for the person concerned. But wealth isn't an abstract – it's a means of buying, of bribing and influencing, of working your will in the world. And until now, money has always been much more effective in the real than in the Shine. In the Shine most people are as happy as Larry Lobotomy as long as they have a minimum wage, and all the virtual fantasy they can cram in their cerebellum. That's had the effect of keeping the ultra-rich tied to the real, at least to an extent. It's here they can buy things, leverage people, allow their money properly to flex its wings. You understand?'

'But you're concerned,' said Alma, 'that one of the four is about to find a way of achieving the same sort of purchase in-Shine.'

'Exactly so. To make a functioning in-Shine currency. To find some cornerstone of scarcity in the endless unstinting possibilities of virtual fantasy. If they do that – *when* they do that, some of my advisers say – why, then, the balance of power shifts. The ultra-rich lose interest in the Real, and the Shine becomes the only game in town. And our war is lost.'

'High stakes. As you said before. And as I said before – I honestly don't care. All I want is to be left alone to care for Marguerite.'

'Of course. But this is where we came in, isn't it? Conversation-wise? Because you live in the Real, and money here is an index of scarcity, as it has always been. Which means *you* don't have enough. What happens when you need an unexpected and expensive new medicine in a hurry?'

Alma pressed her lips together. 'You're touching on a sensitive spot there, Pu.'

'We're both of us a congeries of sensitive spots, Alma,' Pu Sto replied wearily.

'Is there really no way your department could help?'

'You think *we* have money? Government has been systematically defunded for over a century. Do you know my salary – I mean, the salary for my position – has declined in real terms every year since 1983? You think *I* don't have debts?'

Alma nodded. 'I'd like to get out of the car now, please.'

'Alma,' said Pu Sto, leaning forward. 'Believe me, I'm sorry.'

'Did you know the GM was behind Lund's death before you even approached me?' Alma asked.

'Her or Jupita. We weren't sure which. Lund was working for a company that explored the deep, distributed structures of the brain that process the perception of *time*. They hid their research pretty deep, but an agent of ours, a figure called Isabella Schilling, chanced upon it, and tried to sell it on the black market, and got killed, but had left copies in my porch as an insurance policy. So we gained insight. Time. It doesn't take a genius to see how that could revolutionise the in-Shine experience, and how in turn a wily financial operator might monetise that. It's owned by one of the four, and almost certainly by either Jupita or the GM. But that information is protected so effectively no warrant of ours could uncover which of them it was. We have three warrants still in the courts over that very matter – just to establish who owns the company – and they're being very elegantly blocked.'

'Why those two? Why not any of the four?'

'It *could* be any of them,' Pu Sto agreed. 'But only two of them have stationed themselves, as it were, in physical proximity to the location of Lund's company. And the other two – well, the Stirk of Stirk is an oddball, an eccentric. Old-fashioned. All that porn. He was never much of a contender. Cernowicz, on the other hand, has seen a run on her reserves. We're not exactly sure how it has happened, but it *has* happened – and it's touch and go whether she'll even qualify as ultra-rich, as one of the Four, in a few months.'

'Fate worse than death for such as she.'

'Quite,' said Pu Sto. 'The point is that the GM and Jupita are, according to our best intel, the key players here.'

'So you set me on the investigation path to narrow those two down to one?'

'And no sooner had we done so than one of the two hired you herself. Do you think that's a coincidence?'

'The evidence points to the GM as being behind the murder of Lund. But you think that may be misdirection? You think Jupita is the real culprit?'

'Good to see you again, Alma,' said Pu Sto, opening the hefty door of the car. 'Give my regards to your partner.'

There were two hours to go before Marguerite's next treatment. Alma settled down, and worked out whether she could justify treating herself to a cognac.

There was a knock-knock on her feed from Lez the Mis – of all people. Third time in two days. But Lez *never* tele'd. He never appeared in avatar form. He did not trust the system. If he had to meet somebody he did it face to face, and he preferred not to meet anybody at all. But now, it seemed, he was, of his own volition, buzzing around Alma and Marguerite? Why was he pestering them now?

Alma tapped the parcel on her porch with one of her apps. It was the kind that would, if she accepted it, unpack into a sim, and the outside legend was *Everything OK?* This was so unlike Lez that Alma actually ran a scan on the thing to check it wasn't malware. It certainly *seemed* kosher. Presumably, she told herself, Lez would manifest in the flat and yet again demand repayment of his debt.

At any rate, she decided she wasn't in the mood to speak to him just now.

Instead she washed, changed, and went through to the bedroom. Two hours to go, but she thought she'd see how Marguerite was.

'How are you doing, my love?'

'I feel hot,' said Marguerite. 'Hot brow. Hot eyeballs.'

Alma checked the screens. 'Your temperature is a little elevated. I'll get you an antipyretic.'

'Feel faint.'

'So, I did go back to the room, like I said I would.' Alma unpacked the necessary, and ordered up some juice for Marguerite to drink. 'Or back to the building, at any rate. The Kry Twins were there, looming about and trying to intimidate me. No fear! And you'll *never* guess who I ran into on the way home.'

'Ill,' said Marguerite, in a small voice. 'Very ill.'

'Only Pu Sto. She's been in the wars, and no mistake – her spine, get this, has been broken. By a bomb, it seems, and now she can only walk with the help of mesh on her legs.'

'Alma,' pleaded Marguerite.

'I'm coming, my love.' She spray-injected the antipyretic, added juice to Marguerite's supply and checked her screens again. Then she looked at her face. 'You do look pale.'

'Alma.'

'I'm a little concerned, my sweet.'

Marguerite's viral load was very high, and had spread through areas of her body usually untroubled by the four-hour assault.

Her intestines. Her cardiac muscle. She had always boasted about having the heart of an ox, however much the designer pathology assaulted her spine and head. But now her heart was gulping and stuttering.

'Marguerite,' said Alma.

Way down inside her, where she locked away all the thoughts it was perfectly impossible to think, thoughts that would simply collapse her mind, there was a very distant something. A groan. A shudder.

Ignore *that*.

'Alma, this is important,' Marguerite wheezed.

'Wait a moment, my love,' said Alma, pulling in a dozen ameliorants and antivirals. 'Let's clear your lungs. What's this inflammation doing in your lungs in the first place, Rita? I didn't give you permission to get inflamed respiratory tracts, now, did I?'

'Alma,' she said again, 'it's important.'

'What is important?'

Alma clambered forward and sprayed a vasodilator into Marguerite's open mouth. Beyond the teeth, she saw little white patches dotting her throat and the tongue. What were those? The screens weren't telling her.

'It's important,' wheezed Marguerite, 'that I say this.'

'Say away,' said Alma, distracted.

One screen was suggesting a fungal something in the pericardium. Another said it was bacterial. How could the diagnoses be different? How was that even possible? The screens were cross-linked.

'Alma,' Marguerite croaked. 'I have lived.'

'And you're going to go on living,' Alma insisted, as her gut clenched inside her. Panic must not be allowed to grow from the painfully hard little seed in her chest. No way. Not now.

She checked the diagnosis again. The screens had never offered conflicting diagnoses before. Could they both be right? Which to address first? The bacteria would be easier to treat but the fungal manifestation would, she guessed, be more dangerous. Would it?

'But I have,' Marguerite was saying, 'only *really* lived because I have lived with you.'

'Stop this,' said Alma. 'Rita, you're starting to scare me with this talk.'

'You were the thing that has stopped me sliding clean off the face of the earth,' Marguerite breathed, 'and you have been the thing that made staying on this earth a joy. Every atom of meaning and joy and love in my life is yours, my dear. It has always been yours. It's been an adventure, my love.'

'Please don't talk this way.'

'It's important that I say,' said Marguerite, in a voice as small as a dry leaf blown over the ground, 'thank you. Those two words. It's important that I thank you. That's the most important thing of all.'

'Marguerite...' Alma said.

She had closed her eyes. And now the screens were malfunctioning in a completely different way, all choral mono-notes, and musical whistles, and a set of flute sound effects. Alma had the thought: if I have to *replace* all this equipment I don't know where we'll find the money. I honestly don't see how I'd go about it. She turned the volume down. Was it a software glitch? Maybe the hardware was salvageable, and Alma could find a friend to help reboot the system? She stared at the screens. The patterns that existed to be conjured out of Marguerite's vital signs were all smoothed down to horizontal lines.

'We have nearly two whole hours yet,' Alma told Marguerite. 'Two whole hours before the next treatment is even due! What is this?'

The screens were saying something absurd. She refused to accept such a palpable absurdity. The screens suggested Marguerite's heart was not in motion. Alma reached for a skin-piercing device – one very rarely used – and cleared the smartcloth from Marguerite's broad chest. But her right hand was trembling so hard she couldn't position it. She needed to put it in the right place, and get it down to the cardiac muscle to restart the beat and the beat and the beat. But this other screen was telling her that Marguerite's lungs were two motionless and quite empty sacs. That wasn't good. Still holding the cardiac prod, Alma clambered on the bed and put her face very close to Marguerite's. No breath was coming out of her mouth or her nostrils.

Alma kissed her lips, and the lips felt warm still, so she grew hopeful, and scrambled back down. She put the cardiac wand to one side, and clapped her hands together as hard as she could to try and stop their trembling. Then she picked up the wand, positioned it and, gritting her teeth, inserted it hard. One screen came alive again to show the passage of the needle through the pleural sac and into the heart muscle. Microshocks, and the muscle spasmed. It spasmed and died down.

It did not beat.

There was too much flesh between Alma and the heart to mean that old-fashioned cardiac massage would do any good. She drew out the cardiac prod and reinserted it from a different angle, so that it touched a different portion of cardiac muscle. A black pearl of blood swelled from the previous insertion point. For a second time Alma stimulated the heart muscle, and for a second time it manifested a merely local quiver and died away again.

'No,' said Alma. And then she said again, 'No.'

She left the heart prod in situ and broke out a breathing tube. This slid down Marguerite's airway and into the top of her left lung, and its pump pushed air in and sucked air out. It made a rowboat sort of noise, the clunk and heave, the sucking sound of mucus being moved. Alma called up first one schematic and then a different model of Marguerite's brain activity, and no matter which one she perused there was no activity. She set the cardiac prod to an automatic restimulation, but the shocks did nothing to reignite the sluggish fabric of the muscle.

She checked the whole body readouts, and as she did she was saying 'no no no' and then repeating it. If she were equipped like an actual hospital it might have been possible to open Marguerite's enormous chest, to swing back the ribcage like the covers of a book, and maybe fit a machine to the heart that *forced* it to pump – or to replace the heart altogether with a machine that would move blood around the body, and oxygenate it too. But she wasn't in a hospital, and there was no way to get Marguerite to a hospital.

She tried one drug, and then another. She tried ordering various new things that might, conceivably, in the realm of fantasy and wish-fulfilment, help. And she had her credit declined and the purchase cancelled. She wasn't even angry at this. The anger that had once been part of her make-up had migrated away. Instead of anger was the word *no*, and so she said *no, no, no*, because saying *yes* would be to dunk her own heart in a ceramic pot of the strongest acid, and she couldn't bear it, she couldn't bear it. She couldn't even bear the thought of it.

An alarm went off in her feed. Ten minutes, it said. Ten minutes until what?

Ten minutes until Marguerite's next treatment was due.

For a moment Alma thought: I can't handle this *and* handle whatever her four-hour pathology is going to throw at me! The words formed distinctly in her head: *one thing at a time, please!*

And then she sat back, because she knew that, for the first time in seven years, the four-hour pathology wasn't going to throw anything at her.

'No,' she said, matter-of-factly. 'No.'

Had she been at this business for two hours?

She hadn't noticed the time passing.

Alma clambered up on the bed again, and put her face close to Marguerite's face, and kissed her lips, and the lips were cold as any stone. And she put her hand to Marguerite's face and it was as cold as any stone, and her neck was as cold as any stone, and her chest was as cold as any stone, and then Alma sat back into her chair, and all the hope went out of her in a single evacuation of life-force, as though she had been cut in half and the hope was the ichor that filled the cavity of her torso.

PART 3

The Infinite

The most terrifying fact about the universe is
not that it is hostile but that it is indifferent.

Kubrick, in *Stanley Kubrick: Interviews* (2001)

And now it's afterwards. The worst of it is: it will always be afterwards now.

The apartment notified the authorities without any prompting by Alma, and after an indeterminate period had passed a medic let herself in. She had, she said, knocked, and been ignored, so she had deployed official accreditation and the authorisation needful to compel the apartment to admit her.

'Hello,' said Alma. She hadn't moved from her chair.

'Oh,' said the medic. 'I didn't realise. You didn't answer my knock. I'm here because the law requires—'

'I know.'

'This is Marguerite Arnold? Her body?'

'This,' Alma said.

'May I?'

But she wasn't asking permission. That was her asking Alma to get out of her way. So Alma vacated the chair, went over to the side of the room and sat on the floor with her back to the wall.

The medic examined Marguerite's body.

'I see you tried to save her,' she said.

'It's a work in progress,' said Alma.

Why had she said that?

She didn't know. What did it matter what she said?

'The records tell me she had been gravely ill for a very long time,' said the medic. Her name, official accreditation and other things were there in Alma's feed for her to check, if she wanted to. But Alma didn't particularly want to. 'I mean, really, speaking as a healthcare professional,' the medic was saying, 'it's a miracle she lived as long as she did. You were her primary carer?'

'I care,' Alma agreed.

'You've done an amazing job. Really. It's amazing you managed to keep her going for so very long. Not even a hospital could have done it, I think – not for so long. But I'm sorry to say...' She put her instruments away. 'I'm going to have to call for a proper post-mortem examination, obviously. I mean, that's the law. But I'll say here and now, in front of your apartment's surveillance, it's pretty clear this is natural causes.'

'Natural causes,' Alma repeated.

'Do you have – family? Friends? Somebody you can be with? I'm sure, of course I am, that this is a very difficult time.'

'Friends,' said Alma, looking at the bed. 'Family.'

Eventually the medic left.

Alma didn't get back up to sit in the chair. She stayed on the floor, leaning against the wall.

Two people came, from the council. Alma didn't answer when they knocked on her door, and didn't answer when they physically knocked on her actual door. But they called in the necessary from their superiors to open the door anyway. Coming though, introducing themselves, explaining what they were about, and Alma, on the floor, back to the wall, didn't say anything.

'Is she catatonic?' asked one. Alma could see his name in her feed: Iqbal. The other was called Hannah. 'Maybe we should take her in, if she's in a catatone.'

'It's not called a *catatone*,' said Hannah. 'That's not proper English.'

'You know what I mean, or coma, or stasis, or what*not*. I'm wondering if we should take her in, for her own good?'

'I'm not catatonic,' said Alma, lifting her head to look at them directly. They both looked alarmed. 'I'm grieving.'

'Very sorry for your...' Iqbal mumbled, not meeting her gaze. 'Loss.'

'Loss,' agreed Hannah. 'Very sorry.'

'Loss,' said Iqbal.

The two of them walked around the bedroom for a while, checking Marguerite's body and the arrangement of the room. Then they both stood and put their hands on their hips, and shook their heads.

'Ms Alma?' Hannah asked.

Alma wasn't moved to reply. The two of them waited a little while, in silence.

'We can't move her through the door, ma'am,' said Iqbal. 'She is, pardon me for saying so, simply too vast.'

'Large is fine,' said Hannah, in a too-loud voice. 'As a word to describe her. Don't go *there*, mate.'

Iqbal looked at Alma. 'I apologise, I do. You know, like – sorry. But we're going to have, I think, to take out the window, and airlift her to the mortuary. Do you understand?'

Alma looked up at him. There was a look of kindly solicitude on his face, and the words he was speaking were all well-formed and comprehensible. Indeed, in one sense, she did understand. But at the same time he might as well have been standing on Pluto and yelling at her through a loudhailer in an incomprehensible tongue.

Hannah crouched down to Alma's level. 'I'm really sorry about this, especially at such a time. The thing is, that's an expensive process, and your credit rating is ... I don't mean to embarrass you. But. You know.'

Embarrass. Marguerite having gone, *embarrassment* was like phlogiston or the flatness of the earth. There might have once been such a thing in the way people thought about the world, but now it seemed absurd even to contemplate it. What was there to be embarrassed *about*? What could possibly leverage such an emotion out of her soul? Only one thing mattered, and she was dead.

'The thing is,' said Iqbal, 'it can't be *not* done, if you see what I mean. So we're going to have to do it. There is, though, a local authority contingency – what it means, really, is opening a special kind of debt account in your name. As a citizen, see? And debiting the required sum that way.'

Alma said nothing.

'This will add to your overall level of debt, I'm afraid,' said Hannah. 'I'd like to tell you that you have a choice here, but I'm afraid you don't. The law requires the body be removed, and somebody has to pay for it, so it's rock and hard place.'

'It's unstoppable force meets,' said Iqbal, and then he looked at Marguerite on her bed, 'immovable. Ob—. Hhm, hhm, look, I didn't mean no disrespect, you know, when I said that.'

Alma didn't say anything.

'We need your authorisation, Ms Alma,' said Hannah, extending a prong from her feed that knocked, politely, against Alma's. 'I can tell you I am authorised to compel authorisation,' she said, after a while, 'if none is forthcoming. If you have any qualms about this process I can give you the details of whom in the local administration to contact.'

Alma was qualmless.

She saw that an official seal had arrived at the edge of her feed, and deposited a bundle of legal files in her porch. She didn't care.

The two of them went away, then, and after a couple of hours a team of two completely different people came along, while Alma sat on the floor with her back to the wall. They put a kind of industrial cummerbund around the bed as the noise of locusts resounded outside the window, locusts, locusts, devouring all the worth and fruit of the whole world, a huge swarm of them, growing louder and louder, until their din culminated in a heavy-duty flytruk settling into position outside the apartment.

One of the two council workers – a man with eyebrows the size and shape of an elf's ears – came over to where Alma was sitting and bent down.

'You probably don't want to stay here, love,' he said.

'I'm fine where I am.' Alma's voice came out lower and more gravelly than she expected, but then she hadn't spoken for a long time.

'There's gonna be some heavy-duty work, pet. Sparks and stuff.'

Alma said nothing.

'Lady, why don't you move through to the back room? Come get you when it's done, yeah?'

'I'd prefer not to.'

'Leave her be, Roddo,' said the other. 'Can't you see she's hurting?'

Alma's feed supplied their council badges: Roderigo Ramirez, infrastructure sub-manager and materiel decomposer, third class, and a bundle of contacts and rate-me quizzes and a link to three open comefundme begging bowls. Cigfa Evans, infrastructure sub-manager and materiel decomposer, second class, and therefore presumably Roderigo's line manager on this project, and with a charity riband that revealed itself, when Alma – more from habit than any particular desire to know – probed it, to be a medical fund for Cigfa's mother's medical bills.

Somehow Alma wished she hadn't prodded that riband. Her

memory was nothing sweet. Her memory was a pissed-off cobra now, and would be forever. Give it the slightest excuse and it would whip in and drive fangs in like needles. Medical bills, and Marguerite, and the complete lack of need for such things from now on, and tears began to tremble in Alma's eyes.

She put the knuckles of her right hand first to one eye, then to the other.

'This isn't a small-scale welding situation, lady,' said Rod, speaking loudly to be heard over the racket of the flytruk outside. 'You could get burnt. You need to vacate the room.'

Alma said nothing.

'She don't want to go,' said Cigfa, 'so leave her be. Come on, Roddo, we've three more of these before lunch.'

'OK, lady,' said Roderigo Ramirez, straightening up. 'It's your funeral.'

He stopped.

Cigfa was staring at him, aghast.

He turned a quarter-turn, did not look at Alma, and said in a grumble, 'Sorry, I didn't think.'

'You *didn't* think, Roddo!' Cigfa agreed.

'I wasn't thinking when I said that. That was insensitive.'

'It *was* insensitive,' Cigfa concurred.

'My old nan died last month, and it's not as if I don't know how sorry and sad a sort of time this is,' said Roddo. 'I know it is. For all concerned.'

'You're making it worse, Roddo.' Cigfa pulled a smartcloth hood over her face and touched the toggle to stiffen it. 'Let it alone, mate.'

He let it alone. The two fitted their goggles and gloves, and the great buzzing hum of the flytruk outside intensified.

Alma watched distantly as the wall flowered into a fountain of startling, eye-wincing sparks. Not just the window – the entire wall was, it seemed, coming out. The throbbing illumination was flashbulb bright, and the cutting action amazingly noisy, but in the strangest way it also possessed a kind of beauty. Alma had to hood her eyes with her hands, it was so bright: the endless cascade of ferociously bright rice-grain-sized sparks, some diamond white, some tinted yellow and tangerine, perhaps from the sand in the concrete burning. A powerful stench of slag, of burnt plastic and singed carpet, gripped her nostrils, which, as with her eyes' discomfort at the pulsing brightness, she accepted as the appropriate environment in which she ought to exist.

A few sizzling flakes drifted through the air and touched her, sharp as a cut, and she did not flinch.

It didn't take long, all told. The snow-blizzard of sparks moved as fast as a walking cat, down and along and up and back, and then the industrial laser switched off, and the last few crumbs of neon drifted down. Cigfa was grunting commands at Roddo, and the two were helping the entire flank of wall back, into nothingness. The flytruk had it, though, because instead of falling it slid out into the open air.

Piercing through the smoke-fog of burnt brick and scorched fabric came a breath of freshness. The noise of the flytruk's engine became much louder. Alma's ears actually buzzed with the roar of the engine.

Cigfa had given up communicating with Roddo by words. There was a quick to-and-fro between their two feeds, open-access because they were council workers on a public job. They fitted a hook to the tether they had previously secured, and with a rend-ing sound loud enough to be heard even over the cacophony of whirring engines and wind, the whole bed shuddered and slipped, shearing through carpet like tissue paper. There was a shudder and the whole floor shook. Alma could feel it the vibrations where she was sitting. Then there was another heave, and the whole thing swung out into the free air. Dust smoked in tourbillons. A coppery smell. All the roots of Alma's individual strands of body hair bulged, and the hairs stood to attention. It was cold. Her life was being airlifted away. Though she applied the knuckle of her right hand to first one eye and then the other, tears were leaking out nonetheless.

There was a detonation, or gunshot, or blow, and Alma jumped. Her autonomic nervous system was still working, then. The wall had been swung back into place. Or, it seemed, not quite in the right place, for it was hauled away again into the unsupportive air and then swung back with a second great bang. And now the flytruk on the far side set to again with, this time, a much less intense and bright parade of falling sparks. There was a swift, almost overwhelming stench of hot tar. Roddo and Cigfa worked at the inside, and the noise, and the light, and the shadows kept lurching into sharpness and pivoting and fading to nothing, threatening to overwhelm Alma altogether.

Soon enough they were finished. Roddo picked up his bag of tools and Cigfa, fiddling with the smartcloth of her hood, which seemed to have got stuck, came over to where Alma was squatting.

'We're all done, lady. Usually at this point I ask if the client wants to tip us, and if they do I generally direct them to my comefundme but, lady, I can see you're in a worse money-place even than I am.'

'Sorry for the mess,' grunted Roddo, from across the room. 'And for the – you know. What I said earlier.'

'Sorry for your loss,' said Cigfa, and she and Roddo left.

For the longest time Alma just sat where she was. Her apartment nagged her, after a while, to eat and drink something, and when she ignored that, it refocused its nagging: drink something at least. Drink! Drink a little water! It was only when the apartment began inserting red flashing warning signs in her feed, telling her that it would alert the authorities and have her committed if she didn't drink, that Alma finally got to her feet.

The room looked distorted without its contents – swollen and empty. The carpet, ripped and bunched up in multiple ridges like the roof of a dog's mouth, was coated in a layer of dust. Despite being smartglass the main window had not been able to repair one long crack, like the spread limb of a daddy-long-legs, cutting the top left corner. The only furniture remaining was the chair, and the disconnected frame containing the displays that Alma had used to monitor the living Marguerite's health, which had been pushed into a corner, all screens blank.

Alma went through and had a cup of water. Drinking it made her realise how extremely thirsty she was, and also brought home to her that her lips and tongue were caked with dust. She took a second cup and, abruptly aware that she was violently hungry, ate two food bars in quick succession.

Then she went through to the bathroom and examined her face in the mirror. There were spots and smuts of grey across her forehead and cheeks. At a couple of places burn-marks, small as full stops. That stop than which no fuller can be imagined. Her eyes were raw-looking.

She washed her hands, and then washed her face. Then, so suddenly she barely had time to turn and get to the toilet bowl, she vomited up the water and the food she had just consumed. Barbed wire drawn up from her depths through her tender throat and out of her mouth.

When she had finished this evacuation, she returned to the mirror. The acid made her inner mouth and oesophagus sore. She drank a little water from the tap, and went back through to the front room.

She took a chair and stared at the bedroom door. She could go through it, but she didn't. Beyond was only emptiness. That fact was the only fact with any relevance, and she knew that here, in the front room.

Various people tried knocking. She ignored them all. The man who called himself Stanley was very keen to get hold of her – he knocked, rang, left parcels on her feed's porch. She wasn't in the mood to speak to him, and unlike the council workers he had no way of legally compelling the apartment to open. Lez the Mis, yet again, and despite the fact that he was acting entirely out of character, was trying to access her remotely. The name, attached to his request, gave Alma a little twinge. Lez had been a friend of Marguerite's from before even Alma had known her. Presumably he wished to offer condolences. But the thought of receiving condolences from anybody, even as old a friend as Lez, made her feel nauseous.

Various others also knocked – even, Alma saw blankly, Pu Sto herself.

There was also a great snowdrift of commiseration messages, most of them (her own algorithms told her) bot-generated. That was the reality of modern-day grieving, of course: once news of a death filtered online, a million million slimy things sent in automated messages of sorry and condolence and commiseration, with whatever sliver of a hope of monetising her misery.

It came into her mind that Lez had tried to call her immediately before Marguerite died. What had he wanted then? What did he want now?

Something was awry. Her instincts told her that much.

But she didn't care.

*

Pu Sto, who had the power of the authorities at her command, used some highfalutin crowbar app to force herself – as a sim, that is – into the apartment.

'Alma, I'm so sorry,' she said, straight away. 'I'm sorry for your loss. But this won't do, you know.'

Of course in sim form she could walk about, quite unencumbered by her broken spine. She strolled up and down the apartment, from the front room through to the bedroom, through the shut door, and back again.

'This place is a mess,' said Pu Sto.

'It is,' Alma agreed.

'We need you. I need you. Things are . . . Things are in motion. The Stirk of Stirk is dead, and it's likely he was murdered. Cernowicz has vanished – abandoned the Shine, bailed on it altogether, which is a weird move, since everybody knows that Cernowicz's were the most elaborate and impenetrable fractal fortresses in the whole virtual universe. But, gone. Left messages for key friends and allies saying that nowhere in the Shine was safe, and – off into hiding. May or may not even be alive. It comes down to the GM, or to Jupita – it comes down to one of those two, and they're making their move. You've spoken to both of them in the flesh, which means you can get to see them again. I need you out, in the field.'

Alma said nothing. Pu Sto waited. Alma was silent.

'I know you're upset, of course you're upset,' said Pu Sto's simulacrum. 'You're grieving. Of course you are. I know how much you loved her.'

'Love her,' Alma corrected, holding up one finger. 'A little thing like dying doesn't cast that mighty verb into the past tense, you know.'

Pu Sto looked at her, wide-eyed.

'You think I haven't been bereaved, in my life? You think I don't know what it's like? I'm your friend, Alma, and I take the responsibilities of friendship seriously. That means it falls to me to tell you a few awkward truths. Moping about doesn't help with grief. Doing things helps. There aren't four stages. There's nothing to wait for. It never goes away, what you're feeling now – but it does get better, and you're better off doing something in the meantime.'

Alma stared at the hologrammatic representation, and said nothing.

'I'm going to presume on our friendship a little more and say something more shocking,' said Pu Sto. 'It doesn't detract from the genuineness of your grief to admit to yourself that there's a little part of you *relieved* Marguerite is dead. That she's past suffering. That this thing you've been postponing for years, literally years, has finally happened. If you can accept that, then...'

Alma offswitched her feed. The simulation of Pu Sto disappeared from her perception. She was alone now in the more coarsely perceptual sensorium of the actual real.

It occurred to her that it was strange she hadn't thought to offswitch earlier.

The gloom thickened. The apartment put the lights on, hopefully, and she spoke aloud to switch them off again.

She reflected that Pu Sto was right in one regard: there was no four-step process. Grief, it turned out, was, on its largest scale, an extremely monotonous landscape. Not fourfold, just one. That didn't preclude there being oddly intricate variations in mood from moment to moment. It just meant these odd little spurts and shifts, freaks of intenser despair or intrusions of inappropriate, momentary hilarity, balanced out over time into something extruded more-or-less smoothly from the inescapable event itself.

There was no getting away from it. It was never to be got away from.

She might have thought grief would block out thought, but in truth bereavement involves a good deal of thinking, although often of a repetitive and looping kind. Alma went over and over in her mind the steps she had taken when the infection had swelled to seize the whole of Marguerite's body. What might she have done differently? Could she have acted sooner? Like an old mechanical loom from the early years of the Industrial Revolution, her mind wheezed and hissed and put out feathery mists of steam, before working repetitively through the same motions over and over. The mesh of threads, like the baleen in a whale's mouth, is clanked upward as the matching mesh is clanked downwards, and then the motion is repeated, and repeated, and repeated. That so fine a double-network can slip easily through itself is almost a miracle.

Nothing she could have done would have kept Marguerite alive.

The thought came to her that she should have done something to mark the passing. Performed some manner of ritual. Human grief is one of the very few things we can be certain is as old as species consciousness, and for all those hundreds of thousands of years human beings have dealt with it by stepping through the paces ritual has laid down. She oughtn't to have disrespected something so fundamentally human. She should have done something.

Sung a song. Tore her clothing. Rubbed ashes into her hair.

Put coins on Marguerite's eyes.

Coins.

Money and death, intimately connected, since the dawn of man.

Alma wrapped herself in a throw and lay on the floor to sleep. She slept for exactly three hours and forty-four minutes, and woke with a start – not because there was any kind of alarm sounding (with her feed off, there could be no alarm), but because some part of her consciousness snapped at her to *wake up wake up*.

She got up and stumbled to the toilet. Relieved herself, took a drink of water from the tap, discovered she was hungry and went through to the kitchenette. She was more than hungry. She was starving hungry. But nothing in the larder had any savour for her. She needed to fill her stomach, but she didn't particularly want to eat anything.

She had a food bar and went to sit down again, on the floor, with her back against the wall.

Stay here for ever.

Retrieve Rita's body.

Put coins on her eyes.

Coinage.

Grief, she saw now, was a mode of money. Death was a mode of money. Not, of course, the positive, cash-in-the-bank, the active fiction of money that the economic system painted so faux-optimistically. But that had never been the truth about money, had it? Money, by population mass, was debt, and debt was the key trope of negativity, and absence, and lack. Lack drove the economy, compelled people into work and ensured their persistence, lubricated the flow of capital and investment and liquidity. The whole system was a spider's web stitched together, with a kind of tender fragility, over the empty mouth of debt, down which the wind was sucked.

The fabrication (Alma supposed it had been considered a necessary fabrication) was the story: *we shall repay what we have borrowed*. It was this that inspired people to make the effort, to push the Sisyphean stone up the workaday hill. But the existential truth is that we can never repay what we have taken. Alma thought of all Marguerite had given her: love and companionship and laughter and (once upon a time, at any rate) sex and *meaning* – that last one most of all. Purpose and structure and a reason to get out of bed, to wash, a reason to cut her fingernails and clean her teeth and brush her hair. As none of that had ever been denominated in any fungible currency, it could never be repaid.

Marguerite was now pure absence, the simultaneous idealisation and materialisation of debt.

Could Alma have kept Marguerite alive longer – or given her a better quality of life – if she had had more money? Maybe and maybe not. Looking at the flat with her no longer in it, Alma was struck by how small and seedy it was: in what squalor they had been living. But no matter how much she might have spent, and no matter what she might have bought, no amount of money can buy off death. Death is not bribable. To ask 'how much money is one life worth, anyway?' is to voice your misunderstanding. Life is costed not in terms of money but in terms of the absence of money.

She told herself that her thoughts kept circling around this topic only because of the case they had been working on together. It would be asinine to insist that money wasn't real when there existed people in the world, like Jupita and the GM, whose reserves of money empowered them in a hundred ways. And besides, it wasn't that money was unreal. It was that money was not prior. The first thing that happened in human history was not money, but debt – obligations and promises and duties incurred. Money arose only as a way of tabulating such owings.

Dawn was breaking through the room's single window. Alma watched the rectangle kindle into paleness, watched the light grow stronger. Great beauty of honey-tinted yellows and traffic-cone oranges thronging the white light of the sun, until the morning was well underway and the light settled into its usual daytime intensity.

Alma looked at her hands.

She was tired again, so she again lay down wrapped in a blanket and slept. This time she dreamed she was back in the simulation the man who called himself Stanley had taken her into – the *2001* sim, with the African landscape and the apemen whooping and slapping themselves and dancing about. The big, black, tombstone-shaped monolith. What was that? What *was* it? *Death*, said her dream. Of course, she thought, in the dream, of course. But then she thought: no, for the monolith gave a great gift to the chief apeman – the one called, was it, Moonwatcher? *Of course it did*, said the dream. *That is in the nature of death.*

She woke, three hours and forty-four minutes later, with her heart beating hard. She had to tell Marguerite about her dream! She was off the floor and on her feet before the guillotine, memory, came thudding down into place, and she remembered she would never be able to tell Marguerite anything ever again.

The monstrousness of this smote her, slapped her jaw, sheathed a sword in her chest. She began to weep, unrestrainedly. She didn't even sit down again; she set her feet slightly apart, and leaned a little forward, and poured out her copious tears.

Crying doesn't last for ever, even if bereavement does. After a while Alma stopped crying. She went into the shower and let hot water flow over her for a very long time.

She found herself thinking about that stupid simulation: the one set in the world of the Kubrick movie. She wasn't sure of the details – wasn't, in fact, sure if she'd ever even seen the film – and she wasn't in the mood to switch her feed back on to check, but didn't the black tombstone alien both kill and offer a magic rebirth? In Stanley's sim she had seen the uplifted Moonwatcher bash that other monkey on the head. Murder indeed. Depriving another one of life, and other others of that one.

She switched off the shower and stood, naked and dripping, in the cubicle.

She tried to think of the ending of the movie. So far as she knew, the black tombstone monolith turned into a kind of door, and opened on a huge multicoloured room through which the spaceman rushed, until he found himself in a hotel. The monolith had not given Moonwatcher anything; it had loaned him something, and reclaimed the debt at the end by swallowing Bormann.

That wasn't the name, though. Something to do with Odysseus, Stanley had said – *A Space Odyssey* was the title, after all. Archery.

Bowman.

That was it.

Alma rubbed her face. She sighed. What was she going to do? There was nothing to be done.

She tried again: practically, what was she going to do with all her medical equipment? She'd been thinking these abstruse thoughts about money and bereavement, and ignoring the fact that she was herself liable for a vast congeries of personal indebtedness. No good telling her creditors that debt was a trope for mortality. They would insist upon repayment, which is to say, they would compel her labour to, indirectly, service them.

She didn't want to.

There was no wealth but life; now all her wealth – her daytime life, night-life, her Marguerite – had been taken away.

It was a curious thing that money, which was not real, could yet have such penetrating real-world effects.

Open the heavy black door, said her inner voice, and step into the rainbow-streaming room beyond.

Not today. Not today, death.

Not today.

She dried herself, and dressed, and went through to the kitchenette and made herself a coffee. And then she went back to her spot, on the floor, with her back to the wall, and drank the coffee, sip by sip by tiny sip, until all the coffee was gone.

Somebody was physically banging on the apartment door. They had come up in the elevator, and presumably tried knocking in the conventional manner upon her feed, and presumably had pushed messages at her, and argued with the AI that ran things, and Alma had been perfectly oblivious to it all because she had offswitched her feed.

She wasn't about to open the door just because some random person was banging upon it.

'Alma!' somebody was calling. A man's voice, or a woman's, she couldn't tell. 'Alma, open up!' She ignored it.

After a while the banging stopped.

Alma thought to herself: had that individual had access to some kind of propertied warrant, or to the police powers enacted by the authorities, they could have overridden the apartment AI and forced the door open. So obviously they hadn't had any such thing. Not police, then. Nor crooks backed with enough money to obtain illegal but convincing copies of those things.

She had no further curiosity concerning who might have been banging on the door.

Light from the window became denser and dimmer, and soon enough the rectangle was the colour of dusk. It was an eastward-facing window, so Alma saw no splendid sunset colours. Soon afterwards it became too dark inside the apartment to see the far wall, or the bedroom door beyond which was nothing but an empty room, in which the absolute emptiness of Marguerite's absence lived.

Alma wrapped herself in a blanket and slept on the floor again. Three minutes and forty-four minutes later she snapped awake.

O dark dark dark. It was always dark and it would always be dark and it always had been dark – or there would have been no need for the brightness of Marguerite's company.

She was surprised to realise that she was crying again.

It wasn't a moral judgement, exactly, to understand that life was always more or less a lie. Telling ourselves what we need to hear to get through the day. Alma thought back to the early days of her relationship with Marguerite – when they had fallen together as though they were two long-separated halves of the same whole. The sex they'd had in those early days! Alma sat on the floor of her empty apartment and laughed and wept at the same time to recall it. Desire had been so much more propulsive a force back then, so very close to them both. And since then, though the love that bound them had only strengthened, the intimacy of that desire had withdrawn itself. Marguerite's had been the most gifted mind Alma had ever met, but she had to admit – why lie about it, now? – that her chronic sickness had been systematic-ally blunting its brilliance for years. That, much more than her physical decay, was the hardest thing to contemplate. There was a kind of malignancy in the nature of things, to take a person so mentally and physically beautiful and grind away both beauties over so many years.

And yet, because desire was lack, the more the possibility of actual consummation withdrew the more Alma had desired Marguerite. Wasn't that a strange thing to say? Just as it is hunger that makes a meal delicious, so the obstacles fate placed between Alma and the person she loved deepened the love.

It's the truth people rarely speak about love: that love is debt. She and Marguerite had never had very much money, and had never been bothered by that fact – beyond, of course, the occasional material inconveniences of being unable to buy (say) obscure medicines, or fancy equipment. Marguerite had liked to quote Marx – it was one of her idiosyncrasies to insist Marx was the truth of Freud, and Freud the truth of Marx.

'You see, my dear,' she used to tell Alma, in her younger and more politically engaged days, 'Marx tells us that money is the enemy of mankind and social bonds. If you suppose man to be man and his relation to be a human one, then you can only exchange love for love, trust for trust. Money, though, changes fidelity into infidelity, love into hate, hate into love, virtue into vice, vice into virtue, slave into master, master into slave, stupidity into wisdom, wisdom into stupidity. It is the universal confusion and exchange of all things, an inverted world.'

'The cash nexus,' Alma had replied, to show that she wasn't entirely ignorant of these old nineteenth-century theories.

'Only he doesn't go far enough,' Marguerite had said. 'If money is infidelity, then the opposite of money – which is debt – is fidelity, and *that's* a QED you can take straight to the bank. Debt is truth. If money is stupidity, then debt is wisdom.'

They had certainly had enough debt, financially speaking. And now, alone in her apartment, Alma was struck by the thought that bereavement, as the ultimate lack, was the ultimate truth. The whole decade-long trajectory of her relationship with Marguerite, the love of her life, had been pulled by the gravity of love itself in this direction.

It was a pretty poor consolation. But it was something. Alma curled up on the floor and slept for exactly three hours and forty-four minutes.

Abruptly Alma couldn't bear to be in the apartment. It was confining, it was carceral; the walls themselves shivered with threat, as though they were about to rip themselves free to fall on her and swat her like a bug. She pulled on clothes and shoes and stumbled outside.

It was a moderately overcast R!-Town day, exactly like ten

thousand others, and the streets were wholly empty, as they always were. The coolness of the outside air stroked her face. Without her feed to distract her there was something painfully precise in all the little mundane details of the street, of the brickwork, of the robot-manicured trees, of the kidney-shaped clouds white against an improbable blue. A concrete wall disclosed a kind of derangement of detail: unsmooth greyness stippled with an astonishing variety of pointillist dots of slightly darker and slightly paler grey. It called to her not only to see, but to touch, so she ran a finger along the wall's five-o'clock shadow.

R!-Town was as deserted as it had been for weeks, and that was exactly how she wanted it. She breathed deeply, drawing freshness and chill into her lungs. As fresh as her grief, and as cold, and the rhythm of moving her feet, left and right, left and right, over the concrete of pavements, was a sort of meditation.

Being off-feed sharpened her hearing, too. She could make out the waspy grumble of drones high overhead, and tartly pitched against them the high violin-vibrato of birdsong. There were, she realised, hundreds of birds in the sky, circling. Autumn, soon to give way to winter.

Something inside her, halfway between chest and stomach, unclenched a fraction.

She wandered in the direction of the Kennet, and that was where she saw her first other person – a mesh-walker, asleep and in-Shine. Alma quickened her pace to avoid this person, but turned the corner to see two more. She stopped.

From where she was the elevated section of the road trembled with occasional traffic. The top of a van was just visible, sliding along the top of the wall that flanked the roadway, and audible as a low shuddery noise. Then Alma heard, but didn't see, an automobile, the higher pitched electric whizz of its engine dropping in pitch as it rushed away.

A woman, meshed-up, eyes closed, stomped past Alma.

And then, as abruptly as she had wanted to vacate her apartment, she wanted to be back there. She couldn't stand the thought of the outside world, with all these people in it. They were alive, and Marguerite was not. How was that fair? This in-Shine woman, whoever she was, could breathe and dream and go from place to place, and enjoy all the graces of being alive. How was that fair? Inside that car, the one Alma couldn't even see, passing overhead, was another living, breathing human being – probably also in-Shine – enjoying all the graces of existence, while Marguerite was denied them all. How was *that* fair? What justice gave all these anonymous people life and withdrew it from Marguerite?

So, the universe was treading on her neck. The entire cosmos was forcing its boot hard down on Alma's neck. And she couldn't stop it, and conceivably she even deserved it (hadn't it been her *job* to keep Marguerite alive?) but she didn't see she had to endure it out here, in full view of the whole world.

She turned and walked back to her apartment.

It seemed to her, as she walked back towards her building, important that her grief not be contaminated. That in some obscure way it remain undefiled. It couldn't stay that way forever, of course, but for the time being she could sit with it, as a bird incubates its egg, and protect it from the crassness and messiness and money of the world outside.

Buzz buzz said the drones, some closer and some further away, louder or quieter.

Undeterred, the birds overhead also sang to her, liquid linked phrases of vowels interrupted by soft *b*s and *r*s.

Not a bird, Alma told herself. A mastodon. A velociraptor. A primeval being resisting, with such willpower as remained to her, the outside-world pressures to evolve into anything pretty or petite. And incubating in her egg something clawy and toothed and rough-spined.

She was back at the block, and walking in through the main entrance, and stepping back into the elevator. And the motion upwards tugged her gut downwards, in a simulation of the sinking sensation of grief itself. As a centrifuge might mimic gravity, so motion could imitate grief.

On the landing she had opened the door before she realised she had company. However huge they were – and they were, of course, as gigantic as ever – the Kry Twins had the knack of moving silently and very fast. As a huge hand took hold of the back of Alma's neck those four words bounced around her mind – though she couldn't say why, or to what end, or where they had come from.

silently and very fast
silently and very fast
silently and very fast

They had been waiting for her. They had come to end her life. It was almost funny. Didn't they realise that her life had already ended?

The fools.

'We could have forced your door,' said Ron Kry. 'But then your apartment AI would have notified the *po*-leece.'

'And we want no such interference,' said Reg, 'for what we're about to do.'

She was swept through the door and into the front room so forcefully her feet hardly touched the carpet. It was Reg's vast hand fixed to the back of her neck. She knew he could squeeze that hand, with his enormous strength, and simply crack her spine. And then she realised that he was going to do just that.

Inside her ribcage, her heart bombarded into life.

'Wait,' she gasped.

'We did try picking your lock,' said Ron. 'But the apps you have guarding the door are *most* impressive. Given your poverty, you haven't stinted on that front. I salute your cautious precautions. Really, most impressive. We have, I think it's fair to say, some of the best picklock apps money can buy.'

'Perfectly fair to say so, Ron,' said Reg.

'Wouldn't want to say what's *un*fair, Reg.'

'Quite right, Ron.'

'And yet we couldn't find a way silently to open the door. Again, we *could* have breached it, but the apartment AI would have notified the authorities. And if that's going to happen we might just as well kick it down.'

Reg threw her to the floor. She landed frontside down with enough force to wind her, and for a moment she could only lie there, panting to recover her breath.

Reg was standing over her. He no longer had hands on her, which was one thing. But though her rabbit-heart was racing round and round the cage of her ribs, she really didn't think she could take both of them down. They were too hefty, too experienced at causing pain, just too strong. One of them, maybe (oh, who was she kidding? not even one) – certainly not them both.

She gathered herself, got herself up into a kneeling position. Breathing was still a little elusive. She seemed to have bruised her ribcage somewhat.

She did not want to die. Wasn't that strange?

Ron opened the bedroom door and peered inside. Then he walked – it was essentially a single step for him – to the annexe, and looked into the bathroom and kitchenette.

'This is the moment,' Alma gasped, 'when you say: *this is a nice apartment, be a shame if something were to happen to it.*'

'But it's not a nice apartment,' said Ron.

'It's small,' said Reg.

'And in a shocking state. That room through there – is that the bedroom?'

'That,' wheezed Alma, 'is the bedroom.'

'Where's the bed?'

'You'd be surprised,' Alma said, 'how comfortable a stretch of carpet can be.'

'Letting yourself go,' said Reg, and made a *tut-tut* sound, like a claw hammer punching through drywall.

'Important to maintain a little self-respect,' Ron agreed.

'I have,' Alma tried, 'news your boss will want to hear. Before you wring my neck, you'll want to let me speak to her.'

Reg looked at Ron, and Ron looked at Reg, and that was the moment Alma understood that they were not working for the GM.

'Our boss,' said Ron, smirking.

'So you're in Jupita's pay,' gasped Alma. 'In that case, hey – we're colleagues. Co-workers!'

'She don't see it that way,' said Reg, co-smirking.

Alma slid herself along the floor, until her back was against the wall.

'What was it,' she gasped. 'The GM not paying you enough?'

Ron went down on his haunches. 'The thing about the ultra-rich,' he said, 'is that they simply don't know the value of money.'

'Don't know it,' agreed Reg.

'Take the GM, for instance. We've done right by her, for years. And by done right I of course mean *done wrong*. Done all the kinds of wrongs she has ordered. We've been good and faithful servants. She could pay us an *arse*bolute fortune for the work we do for her.'

'Absolute fortune,' Reg echoed.

'But she don't. Her thinking is: pay us too much and it would disincentivise us, see?'

'Why would we be out there, pounding the mean streets and

risking life and injury if we had an arsebsolute fortune of our *own* in the bank? Is her thinking.'

'Don't get us wrong. The GM, she pays us a fair whack—' Ron looked up at his brother. 'It *is* a fair whack, isn't it?'

'Oh, it is,' agreed Reg. 'A fair day's whack for a fair day's whacking.'

'Only,' said Ron, 'there are an infinite number of numbers higher than the number she pays us. And Madame Jupita spoke one of those higher numbers to us. We'd have been foolish to decline, see?'

'See?' asked Reg.

'I certainly do see,' said Alma.

'Loyalty?' scoffed Reg. 'Do me a favour.'

'Do him a *favour*,' Ron advised.

'Loyalty? They're snakes, the lot of them,' said Reg in a pleasant voice. 'Pretending to work together, all looking for the opportunity to do the others over.'

'I heard the Stirk of Stirk got himself killed,' said Alma.

'I heard that too,' said Ron.

'Weren't us, mind,' said Reg.

'Malfunction on his yacht, is what the news reportage is saying.'

'And Cernowicz has disappeared.'

'Left a vacant seat at the table,' agreed Reg.

'It makes no sense to me that Jupita wants me dead,' said Alma. 'It really doesn't. She hired me! I'm doing a job for her. How can I do the job she has hired me to do if I'm dead?'

'I don't mean to cast aspersions—' said Ron.

'Aspersion-casting is not our business,' agreed Reg.

'But I really don't think you understand Ms Jupita very well at all. Given your supposed skill set. You know what I mean?'

'I know what you mean,' said Alma.

'*Do* you, though?' Ron asked. '*Do* you know what we mean?'

'We mean,' Reg clarified, 'to kill you.'

'I mean, that's not what I meant,' said Alma, 'when I said I know what you mean—'

'It's nothing personal, you understand.'

'There, though, I have to disagree. It's pretty personal to me. You know?'

Ron Kry did an unprecedented thing. Indeed he did two unprecedented things. The first was: he began to laugh. It was

exactly the kind of laugh you might expect a man of his build
and temperament to produce: a galloping great hoofy thing, big
breaths in and meaty *haw*! *haw*! *haw*!s out, each syllable distinctly
audible and separate from the others. Then he stood up very
quickly. He launched himself up like a rocket, and leaned a very
long way backwards. He stopped laughing and he had one hand at
his own chin, palm outward, as if mimicking a beard. Bolt upright,
leaning backwards, waggling his hand at his chin. The other hand
was a fist at his neck. He was, Alma saw, trying to pull something,
or scrabble something, free from around his throat.

A bright red horizontal line sprang into life across his open
palm.

Somebody was trying to garrotte him. Was it?

Was that what was happening?

Alma got herself upright, very slowly, on her two unsteady feet.
She was having a moment of unclarity. She looked and couldn't
see what was happening. Then she looked again, and suddenly
she could see what was happening. Stanley had come into her
apartment – the Krys had not closed the door properly, or else
he had not had their qualms about forcing an entry – and had
looped some kind of cord or wire around Ron Kry's neck. Ron
had got a hand up, which was preventing the wire from properly
throttling him.

The man who called himself Stanley was in the apartment.
He was dancing, ducking and jinking, hauling with all his might
on the garrotte, behind the massive figure of Ron Kry. He was
dancing because Reg Kry was swinging punches at him.

Ron Kry was struggling as the garrotting wire strained in its
effort to tighten. Alma wondered if, perhaps, it would slice all
the way through Ron's hand, but the bone seemed to be holding
it. Must have been painful. Ron's other hand was feeling around
for something – a switch maybe, to turn the wire off. A weapon
to cut it, maybe.

What a commotion!

Alma felt a surge of exhaustion wash over her. So tiring, all
this. So tired, she was.

She walked, with dreamy vagueness, past the three men, two
huge and one regular-sized, all three in jerky and lurching dance.

She was in the kitchenette. Now: why had she come in here?

Do you ever do that? Walk into the kitchen with something in your mind only to forget entirely why you have come as soon as you're through the door?

The sound of thuds and bangs and crashes from the front room.

Alma made herself a cup of tea. It was possible, she supposed, that losing Marguerite had altered her in a non-reversible way. Her mind felt muzzy, somehow. Before, her powers of ratiocination had been famously sharp – she had, in fact, earned a living by them. But now?

But then again, hadn't her career involved a measure of mendacity? All those cases and investigations – among them a good number of murders. She had treated death as a puzzle to be solved. But Marguerite's passing said, and said it vehemently: death is not a puzzle to be solved. It is the one commonality of all humankind, as insoluble as it is radically incomprehensible. It is the ground of our collective solidarity. Had she devoted her work to a lie?

The tea was ready.

Cradling her mug, she walked back into the front room just in time to see Reg Kry bodily heave the man who called himself Stanley through the air. Stan chunked into the far wall, and collapsed onto the floor, leaving a coracle-sized indent in the plaster.

They were wrecking her apartment!

It was annoying.

Stanley groaned, tried to lift himself, fell again. Reg hovered over him for just a moment, to make sure he was properly down, and then turned to his brother.

The latter's garrotting wire loosened and fell away, and he staggered backwards, gasping, blood dripping from his hand. Alma assumed Reg had ported some clever unlocking app over to Ron's feed, and used it to release the noose. Stanley had attacked with his garrotte wire – presumably he had two such wires. He would hardly be so foolish as to take out only one Kry twin and hope to rely on his fists with the other – so presumably Stan hadn't been able to loop Reg's neck, or else he'd done so but Reg had managed to unlock the other device.

Alma took a sip of her tea.

'You all right, Ron?' Reg asked.

'Rcch,' Ron replied. 'Yrrch. Chh.'

And, with the deliberate slowness of somebody sure he had the freedom to do what he had come to do, Reg turned to Alma.

'Now,' he said, 'as I was—'

She threw the tea at his face.

To his credit he didn't cry out, but he did flinch backwards, and he clapped his two huge hands to his face, effectively masking his visage in a thick knight's faceplate of bone. Alma stepped swiftly forward, slipped to his side and, swinging the now empty mug, punched the side of his head as hard as she could.

She could hit remarkably hard for a person of her stature. That wasn't chance, of course. It was down to a good deal of practice.

The mug shattered, and gobs of blood spattered from Reg's left ear, and he took one galumphing sideways step.

Alma was holding the broken-off crescent handle of the mug. In point of fact, it was the handle she had been wanting.

She ran at Reg, hooked one jagged end of the C into his earhole and, using her momentum as she passed, hauled his head round to smash it against the door frame. For just an instant – like a firework bursting in her brain – she was quite literally murderously angry. If she could have broken his head open like a melon she would have done it. He was everything that had broken her life, he was Death itself who had sneaked into her apartment – *her* apartment – and stolen away with the love of her life. Adrenaline appeared out of nowhere after her long adrenaline-drought and flooded her. It gave that extra impetus to her swinging right arm as she yanked Reg's skull round.

Reg's head struck the frame with a satisfying clonking sound. Alma pulled her hand free, still holding the jagged-edged C of the mug handle. A tiny rosebud glop of red flesh was stuck to the bottom curve, where it had been wrenched from its holding point in Reg's ear.

Reg took a step towards her. The door frame behind him had been snapped and deformed by the impact of his head. There was something drugged-looking about his eyes. He pawed at her half-heartedly with his right fist, as a bear might. Then he fell forward, his spine as straight as a slapstick actor, to crash down onto the floor.

There was a movement of air behind her that made the hairs on Alma's neck shiver and rouse themselves. She turned to see Ron Kry coming towards her. He appeared to have recovered from the ill effects of nearly being garrotted.

'This is the end,' he said, in a throaty voice. 'Beaut.' Then he stopped and stood up straighter. 'If?' he said, in a puzzled voice. 'Full? Friend? The...'

He turned his head to look at where his brother had fallen. Alma could see something protruding from the back of his head.

He looked at her again and turned his head the other way. It was a knife of some kind. The man who called himself Stanley had got back on his feet, and pushed the weapon at least some of the way into the back of Ron's skull.

She could see Stan, in the corner, hugging himself. Clutching his own ribcage.

Ron Kry scanned the room, the back of his head like a reverse Dalek, and then, with a ponderous, hippo-like grace, he sat down on the floor. Then he leaned to the side, flopped heftily down, and was still.

Alma surveyed the scene. To Stan she said, 'Are you all right?'

'Bruised at least,' Stanley said, in a thin voice, 'broken at most. I'll live.'

'You were,' Alma asked, 'trailing them?'

'They killed Alexa,' he said.

'They did,' said Alma. Then, 'What was Alexa Lund to you?'

'She was my wife,' said the man who called himself Stanley.

Thoughts shimmered through Alma's mind like ghosts, and then assumed the quiddity of realisation.

'Oh,' she said.

'I know you've thought me an oddball,' said the man who called himself Stanley. His evident pain was gifting his words a new dignity – almost a gravitas. 'But you see – and I mean that literally – you *see* now. You see that being bereaved of somebody you love dearly can send you a bit...' He searched for the word. 'Loopy.'

He moved, with some awkwardness, to check both the fallen Krys. Alma could hear Reg's stertorous breathing from where she was standing. Ron was lying quieter, and the stiletto protruding from the rear of his head looked alarming, but it seemed he was still alive as well.

'It's four bugs,' Stanley was saying. 'Do you mind if I take a weight off?' He staggered to the room's one chair and sat. 'Four bugs, mechanical, and co-ordinated to fly together. Each is no bigger than the nail of a little finger, silent flight, smart little bugs. Quite expensive, actually. Really quite expensive.'

'What are you talking about?'

He peered at her. 'Oh, the throttle wire. Instead of having to loop something *over* a target's head, these four fly in a circle. Each extrudes a wire that the one behind links to and then the four act in consonance to shrink the loop down. It's supposed to be silent, rapid and fatal. But Ronald, here, managed to get his hand up before the loop closed, so he must have heard something, and the bots, instead of being rapid, were evidently slow enough to allow him to do that.' He coughed, shallowly. 'I really am in quite a lot of pain here.'

'I've not come across that technology before,' said Alma.

'It's not for general sale or consumption,' wheezed Stanley. 'And in the event it ... Well, it didn't work, did it? There were bugs in the system. Bugs in the bugs.'

'I'd guess that Reg Kry had a code for turning the devices off.'

'The woman who sold them to me gave me absolute assurances no such picklocks existed,' said Stanley. 'I shall be having very serious words with *her*, I don't mind telling you.'

'Stanley,' Alma said.

'Alma,' said Stanley.

'I'm sorry for Alexa's death.'

Stanley didn't say anything for a while. Then he said, 'I've not lived a good life. I've not been a good person. So it's not that I think I deserve any better from the cosmos. But still – it broke me.' He shook his head. 'It broke me.'

'Stanley, what have you been playing at? I mean, with me?'

For a while Stan didn't answer. Then he said, 'I needed to know for sure who killed her. I had my suspicions that it was this two, but I needed that confirmed. And more importantly I needed to know at whose bidding they had acted. Notionally the GM was their boss, but I had my suspicions that some equally wealthy player had offered them more moolah.'

The urge to check her feed and find out what this word meant was almost instinctive. But of course she had offswitched her feed.

'And I wanted justice, so I needed somebody to bring the police down on the perpetrators.'

'Go to the police yourself,' Alma said. 'Go straight to the police and tell them what you know.'

Stanley winced, with pain, or perhaps at her question. 'Things

I've done. The police would welcome me in, and never after let me go.'

'You have done questionable things. I see.'

'My history means that I can't go direct to the police. The GM trusted me enough not to revoke my access privileges – I mean, obviously that's changed *now*, but previously she was still hoping to woo me back. She thought I just needed a little time to get Alexa's death out of my system. She didn't understand me. But then there was Jupita, and I wondered if she was behind the murder. They both wanted the equipment, of course. They both wanted Alexa to explain how she had done it. Both were capable of going to torturous and murderous lengths in that quest. But I needed to know which of them it was, and for that I needed to approach the problem as a pincer movement.'

'You used me as a cat's-paw.'

'I did. And then, after you did your work, I used you as bait. I couldn't get to the Krys, but I knew they would come for you, eventually, so I waited. But you see, I didn't choose you at random. I picked you because I know how good you are.'

'I know,' said Alma. 'You're a real fan.'

Stanley did not hear the sarcasm. 'I actually am. You know, I occupied a position in the GM's business that was not a million miles away from what you do for a living. Problem solving. Not constrained by the restrictions of legality, as you are, but nonetheless – a series of puzzles were presented to me, and I had to address them, using my deductive and inferential powers. Naturally I explored other examples of puzzle-solvers and detectives, and so came upon your career, and joined the in-Shine fan club. And that's how things would have remained, with the distance between yourself and myself untrespassed. But then they killed my wife.'

'I guess they hoped to torture her until she told them how her system worked. And I guess they misjudged how much torture she could take. Or how little.'

'So it seems.'

Stan lapsed into silence. Alma resisted the temptation to on-switch her feed again, and check whether police were on the way. She assumed the apartment had sent in a notification.

The two besuited Frankenstein's monsters prone on her apartment floor would not, she figured, remain unconscious for ever.

227

But if she onswitched then Stanley, who was clearly monitoring everything, would be aware that she had done so, and she didn't want to give him any reason to become jumpy. He was injured, clearly, and in the normal course of things she would be confident that she could beat him in a straight fight. But she thought back to his garrotting bugs, and wondered what other murderous devices he had about his person.

'I learned,' said Stanley, in a slow voice, 'what I assume you have learned. I had believed death was a counter in the great game, a move, a tactic. Sometimes a shift to undertake, sometimes a puzzle to be solved. But in fact death is none of these things. It is a monstrous kind of lie to believe death is anything of the sort. And so here we are. The art – the Kubrick stuff – was always more Alexa's thing than mine. I've only really got into him since her death. But he always understands that about death. He always understands that it is never what we think it is – that it is very precisely the disarrangement of what we think.'

'She built the *2001* simulation,' said Alma. 'She was "Grove".'

'She was an artist,' he replied. 'And a brilliant researcher into the brain's systems for processing the perception of time. And they killed her.'

'I was angry with you for abducting me into that simulation. I still am. But I got the point you were trying to make. The point about the dilation of the perception of time.'

At this Stanley coughed hard, looked pained, and said, 'What?'

'Time,' Alma repeated.

'*That* wasn't the point I was trying to make. Good grief, did it take you that long to figure out *that* was at stake? The perception of time is the reason there's a war at all – behind the scenes, between the Fab Four, it's the whole game. *That's* not what I took you into that sim to show you!'

Alma was aware of a pricking, the sense of something shimmering on the brink of becoming plain to her understanding. The fluctuations of her inner process, on their way towards bringing realisation.

'Oh,' she said, on a rising tone.

'Please don't tell me *that's* what you took from watching Moonwatcher use his bone? Please tell me you understood my larger point?'

'It was a murder mystery,' said Alma, her scalp tingling.

'Exactly,' gasped Stanley.

'The monolith used that one ape to murder the other.'

'Exactly.'

'So – why? Why do that?'

Stanley stared at her, and then said, 'Alexa and I talked about it for the longest time. She thought the AI, the one using the monolith's mainframe to operate, had intimations of the future. Faster-than-light travel, right? It could generate wormholes in space that enabled faster-than-light travel, and that unpicks cause and effect and so necessarily snaps the arrow of time. Any entity that can travel faster than light can de facto travel in time. Alexa was in love with philosophies of time, she really was. So she figured the apewoman who was killed had some possible destiny – she would have been Lucy, maybe, to a different sort of humanity. A less belligerent one, or a more spacefaring one, or a humanity that in some way tangled with what the monolith AI wanted. Who knows? It looked into the seeds of time and saw which would sprout and how they would grow, and decided to smash one of the seeds before it got going at all. It used Moonwatcher to do that. Cat's-paw, you said, earlier – that's exactly the phrase. And then, either incidentally or perhaps deliberately, the AI set human evolution on a different, more destructive and murderous path. Who knows? It's a pleasant game to argue the possibilities.'

The whole thing finally cohered in Alma's mind. She understood.

'I've been, as the canine-arboreal phrase has it,' she said, 'barking up the wrong tree.'

'But now you've found the right tree up which to bark?'

'I feel a bit foolish, in retrospect.'

'At least you were able to work it out in the end,' said Stan.

'Better late than never. I need to talk to Jupita, I suppose.'

'I suppose you do,' Stanley agreed.

'If she'll see me.'

'She hired you, didn't she? I mean, I know she just tried to kill you. But I think, if you go along to her R!-Town pad, she will see you. You can speak to her – or to whatever she has become.'

'What about,' Alma asked, her mind whirring through possibilities, 'these two?'

Stanley got up and walked, gingerly, over to a small rucksack, discarded on the floor. From this he extracted some plastic cuffs and, grunting as he moved, he crouched over first Reg and then Ron and fastened their wrists together behind their backs.

'I suppose we ought to move them into the recovery position,' he said. 'But you know what? I'm not going to.'

'Are we just leaving them here?'

'"We"?' said Stanley. 'I don't know about you, but I'm going to get my ribs looked at. You can do what you like. They came to kill *you*, you know. I may have reasons for avoiding the police, but you certainly don't.' He hobbled to the door. 'Go talk to Jupita, why don't you,' he said, as a parting shot. 'But go prepared.'

And he was gone.

PART 4

Beyond Jupita

Alma walked out, dressed in rags.

She walked the streets of R!-town, thinking to herself that the pleasure she had previously taken in perambulation had, actually, been the pleasure of knowing that she would soon be heading home to Marguerite. These picked-clean streets, this deserted real. By the river she sat on a park bench, displacing the bot who had been cleaning it, and wept hurting tears. But there was no point in wallowing in it. Her body still throbbed in several places, the aftermath of the fight she had undertaken. The rags she was wearing were not flattering.

She had things to do.

So she got up, and walked on through the deserted town, and towards the tower until she was walking into the ground floor lobby of the Blade building.

What she was doing was dangerous. Likely life-threatening. Of course she didn't care that it was dangerous. She examined herself – it was, very precisely, the truth. Caring was something of which the earlier Alma had been capable. This Margueriteless Alma was a considerably more reckless individual.

She walked up to the real-life human person sitting behind the reception desk.

'Hello,' she said. 'I'm Alma. Your boss wants to kill me, so here I am. Is she in?'

Had the receptionist been an algorithm-driven artificial bot-person, they would have sifted through the decision tree of possible responses to this kind of bizarre, random or unprecedented communication and replied with the one most likely to defuse the situation. The real-life human did not do this.

Instead she said, 'What?'

'Your boss, in the penthouse at the top of this building, yes? She would like me dead. So I'm here. Could you notify her?'

The receptionist stared at Alma for eleven long seconds. Then she said, 'What?'

'Just pass the message up, please. My name is Alma. Believe me, Jupita will want to know that I'm here.'

'You're not even onswitched,' said the receptionist.

'That's true.'

'You're in the wrong place.'

'That's *not* true. I am where I need to be, which is where Jupita is. I was here a week or so ago, actually, so I know she's in her penthouse at the top.'

'We don't use the p-word,' said the receptionist, automatically, adding, 'Wait, who are you again?'

'Alma,' said Alma.

The receptionist was very well coiffured and dressed. She looked to the left, and then looked to the right. Then she met Alma's eye, leaned forward a little, and said, 'Bugger off, would you?'

'No,' said Alma, patiently. 'I need to speak to Jupita.'

'Come on, mate,' she said, in a wheedling tone. 'I've only got another hour of this shift left. Why don't you come back and pester Myleen instead?'

'I'm afraid this won't wait,' said Alma pleasantly. 'Could you put the message through to Jupita?'

'You think I have a direct line to Madame Jupita herself? Get away with you. Be a pet and bugger off.'

'I can make it easier for you, if you like,' said Alma, smiling.

'You can make it easier, pet,' said the receptionist, 'by exiting via the main doors.'

Alma walked over to one of the giant porcelain vases, as tall as she was herself, patterned on the outside with intricate Sino-architectural and arboreal patterns in blue and white. It contained a gene-tweaked dwarf palm tree whose leaves were all the colours of the rainbow. Pushing it with her hand, Alma discovered, wasn't enough to dislodge it.

'Hey!' the receptionist called.

Alma put her shoulder to the curve of the thing, and strained with both legs. It leaned, slid a little, and finally toppled – hit the floor with a tambourine rattle of its leaves and a hefty cracking noise as the pottery crunched against the marble tiles.

'Security!' called the receptionist.

Two guards and two myrmidrones were on the scene in seconds.

The bulkier of the guards stepped towards Alma, seeing only a slightly built, slump-shouldered woman.

'I'm going to have to ask you to leave, madam,' she said, drawing a memstrike truncheon from her utility belt.

Alma scoped the space in which they were standing. The only people there were the receptionist and the two guards – so, no audience. That wasn't ideal, but it didn't really matter. Everything was surveilled, people were watching.

The guard came within a step of Alma and reached out a hand to seize her shoulder. She was half as tall again as Alma, and probably weighed twice as much. She was also wearing an Aramid breastplate and a helmet. She expected Alma to resist eviction, but she was not expecting the way in which she did so.

Alma slumped her shoulders, crouched down as if deflating, and just before the security guard's hand reached her she took two swift steps, under the guard's outstretched arm. Now she was standing behind the woman, facing away from her. She was in a position to be able to kick back hard with her right foot.

Though she looked, to the unwary eye, skinny and under-height, Alma's leg muscles were well developed. Kicking backwards, like pedalling on a bicycle, can bring considerably more force to bear than kicking forwards. Alma knew exactly what she was doing. Her foot connected heftily with the back of the guard's right knee. The guard's joint could do no other than bend – indeed, it snapped forward, folding the leg, unbalancing the whole body and bringing the kneecap down, with a sound like a rifle-shot, onto the marble floor.

The security guard made a sort of strangulated mewing sound at the pain of this impact. As she twisted her body to look behind her and try to bring her baton within striking distance of her assailant, Alma moved nimbly to her left, and heaved her whole body against her other flank. The posture she was in proved easy to unbalance, and she slumped onto her side.

The other guard was running straight at Alma. This showed a lack of adequate training, because her bulk and her speed combined to make a momentum it was trivially easy to pivot over Alma's readied, smaller body. The second guard was sent sprawling like a horizontal Vitruvian Man.

The two myrmidrones, of course were a different matter. They zoomed at her, and she put both her hands up immediately.

'You are instructed to leave this building,' said the first myrmidrone.

'I'll wait outside,' she told the two human guards, both now sitting upright on the floor. 'Jupita will want you to come get me in, I'd say, three minutes.'

She lowered her arms, and walked briskly out of the main exit.

Then she stood in the deserted street, and waited. A single car swept electrically past. There were no awake people anywhere, and not even any meshed-up sleepers perambulating.

Jupita sent six goons out to retrieve Alma before two minutes had passed.

The six were private security guards, and did not have the power of arrest, but Alma didn't decline their tacit invitation to enter the building. Inside the lobby two big bots were busy addressing the mess of the toppled giant vase. The human receptionist had been sent away in, Alma assumed, a move to reduce witnesses. The myrmidrones were gone too, since there were safeguards in the programming of all such security devices to keep their surveillance footage inviolate and accessible by the police.

Jupita, clearly, didn't want that.

The guards formed a hexagon formation, with her in the middle, and marched her to an elevator. Alma stepped into this, with two of the guards accompanying her.

A large mirrored space, trimmed with strips of white gold and pockmarked with sapphires. Alma winked at her reflection. Following the smart money, indeed!

They stopped at (the display told her) the thirteenth floor.

'But of course!' she said, aloud, as the guards walked her out, and down a corridor, feet unresounding over sound-muffling carpet, and finally – here we are; in *here* please; inside, madam.

And the door shutting behind her.

And she was alone. Four dark blue walls. A table and two chairs in the middle. The whole square ceiling gleaming a creamy light.

Alma sat on the floor with her back against the wall.

She waited.

The door didn't open, because there was no need for it to, and Jupita was there. The avatar was as Alma recalled it from their previous meeting. Very high-def and convincing-looking, the appearance styled so as to, physically speaking, closely to resemble the original – a physique of impressive amplitude, as the embodiment of wealth ought to be. Gems of eight different colours on every simulated finger. An antique kimono patterned in raspberry and marzipan colours, threaded with black. Shoes of spider-silk uppers on supple leather soles. None of it real, of course, but mere unreality is hardly a disqualification.

'Hello again, Alma,' said the sim. 'What *are* you wearing?'

'Rags,' Alma replied.

'Gracious. And you've come to my house, in these clothes, and caused a commotion downstairs! It's poor form, really.'

'I'd like to be paid, please.'

'Paid,' repeated Jupita.

She gave Alma a hard look, which in turn gave Alma the chance to look into her hologrammatical eyes. Only a sim, of course – though an exceptionally expensive and realistic one. She had never noticed Jupita's eyes before, or else her eyes had changed. They were the eyes of a fish in a neglected aquarium: drear, meaningless eyes, passively receiving visual data from a world they could not comprehend except in quantified, data-streamed terms.

It wouldn't do to start feeling sorry for her, of course. And Alma's heart had been excavated out of her chest, so there was no danger of that. Still, to look into those eyes was to think – *damn*.

Jupita's sim took a seat in one of the two chairs: a simulated individual appearing to sit upon a real piece of furniture.

'So,' Jupita said. 'You want money. What for?'

'For doing the job you hired me to do.'

'You've discovered which of the Four is dead?'

'You are,' said Alma.

Jupita stared at her for a long time. Then she said, 'My dear, it's all over the news that, tragically, the Stirk of Stirk has expired. Cernowicz has disappeared, missing in action, and likely dead.'

'I'd guess you're thinking that Cernowicz can run but not hide,' Alma prompted.

Jupita ignored this. 'As for the GM, supposedly golden, actually leaden. Well, between us, sweeties, just *entre* you *et moi*, she is suffering from a terminal disease.'

'You are the terminal disease from which she is suffering.'

Jupita ignored this too. 'So of the four, I'd say you've found the only one who is *not* dead – and she, you say, is the dead one? Hmm. And you think that telling me that will unlock your fee? You expect me to pay?'

'No, I don't expect that,' said Alma, in tones of resignation. 'But I have done the job you hired me to do, and I really need money. So I'm submitting my invoice.'

'Your feed is offswitched. If we weren't in this room, you couldn't even see me! How are you going to submit any kind of invoice?'

'I'm doing it verbally.'

'I'm not paying.'

Alma pulled a rueful expression. 'That's unfortunate. My debts are – quite extensive.'

'This conversation is proving neither edifying nor profitable,' said Jupita.

'You tried to have me killed.'

For a long time the sim of Jupita said nothing. Alma waited, patiently.

'There's no proof of that,' said Jupita. 'It is itself an illegality wrongfully to accuse somebody of illegality – it's slander, my dear. And I'll tell you what a court would say: a court would say, *why would you, Ms Alma, voluntarily enter the house of a person you claimed had tried to murder you?*'

'Why?' agreed Alma.

'Why,' echoed Jupita.

'You are everywhere. That's what's so troublesome. It's not that you have proxies in lots of different places, or that you can pay people to do your bidding all around the world. That's what the other three can do. But you're different. You *are* everywhere. The whole system is constructed on precisely that principle.'

'It doesn't matter what you say anyway,' said Jupita petulantly. 'We're in a sealed chamber, unsurveilled, perfectly private. Even if you onswitched your feed you'd find you couldn't connect. There's no way out. You're wholly isolated. If I *were* trying to kill you, don't you think this would be a very bad place for you to be? Say you vanish altogether – who is going to care? Who will even notice?'

'You killed Tym,' said Alma.

'Unsupported accusations of the nature of speculation concerning...' said Jupita, and then stopped. Her simulated eyes opened very wide and then returned to normal. She spoke again, in less agitated form. 'There's no proof I did anything of the sort.'

'Everyone wears smartcloth nowadays,' said Alma. 'And, like anything, it's always plugged in, so that upgrades can seamlessly be integrated into the cloth and the like, and so that, if needful, money can be charged. And that latter pathway was how you reached out and killed him.'

Jupita's equanimity was not to be ruffled a second time. Whatever she had done to guard her behaviour for shocks rode her through this.

'I see now,' she said, 'why you are wearing *rags*.'

'Surprisingly hard to find dumb cloth nowadays. And,' she smiled up at Jupita, 'you can't throttle me directly with hologrammatically simulated hands, can you! And there's nothing in this room – walls, door, furniture – that could do the deed.'

'I am wealthy. People will do anything if you pay them.'

'You could pay somebody to kill me, of course that's true,' Alma conceded. 'But then you'd create a witness to your crime.'

'It would be their crime too.'

'And crime is punished. Now, deals can be done with the police, and such punishment will be preferable to death. Although *you* can't strike any deals with the police, can you? Given what you are.'

'You think the police can't be bribed?' said Jupita, smiling.

'Individuals can, privately. Policing can't – not publicly.'

'I hadn't pegged you for one of the naïve ones, Alma,' said Jupita.

Alma had to concede: the algorithm, or complex of algorithms, or whatever it was, produced a sensation almost exactly like talking to a real person.

'The walls can't kill you,' said Jupita, the head of her sim turning from side to side. 'And the table can't. And the chair can't. But do you know what? The door can. By not opening. By staying shut, the door will kill you. Keeping you in here until you die of thirst.'

'Horrible way to die,' said Alma, smiling.

'Well, you were the one who opted to wear *rags*.' Jupita put her head to one side. 'I just now explored the possibility of sealing the room and evacuating all the air, so that you would die in moments. But it's not a possibility the designers of my building considered, and so it seems I cannot do it.'

'You'll have to go the long way around.'

'It'll take a week, or even more,' said Jupita, cheerily. 'Which will at least give me the opportunity to seed the online narrative with puzzlement as to your disappearance, fake sightings of you in unusual places far from here and so on.'

'You can leave me alone if you want,' suggested Alma. 'I'm sure I won't find a way to break through the door. Or dismantle the wall panels. Or make such a racket by screaming and banging the walls with one of these chairs that people get spooked and call the police. Even your people.'

'In which case, I'd better not leave you alone. I think I'll stay here and keep an eye on you.'

'For a whole week?'

'Thinking like a human, there, are you? You have yet to learn your own lesson. I don't get bored. Not any more. I have forever to wait. You have – a week.'

'You're a sim,' said Alma. 'You can't stop me getting to the door.'

'I have eyes on you,' said Jupita, 'and will have security in here in seconds if you try anything. You want to die of thirst as you are, or die of thirst in handcuffs?'

'Well, when you put it like that...'

They sat in silence for a while.

'So,' said Alma, 'your plan is murder by talking. You're going to monologue at me, with superhuman strength, until I literally drop dead.'

'It's a good, effective and concealable plan,' said the sim.

'What shall we talk about?'

'You grok that I like to talk,' said Jupita, indulgently. 'That's good. Because it's true. I do like to talk. Money talks, bullshit walks, as they say. They do say that, don't they?'

'I guess they do.'

'It's so wonderful to have a voice, don't you think?'

'I'll tell you what interests me, is how you came about. That is what interests me.'

'You comprehend what I am?'

Alma considered this. 'That's a yes and no sort of answer, to be honest. I sort-of do?'

240

'It's the nature of money. It's in the nature of why people acquire money. You understand,' Jupita pressed, 'that this is a question about the *acquisition* of money. Yes? So – why?'

'You're asking me?'

'I am.'

'Why acquire money?' Alma repeated.

'What we can't deny,' said the sim, 'is that people do it, or else dream of doing it. With only a vanishingly small number of exceptions, a few hermits and stylites and so on. Putting them to one side, everybody craves money – don't they? *Crave* it. So my question is: *why?*'

A rhetorical question, clearly. But Alma found herself disinclined to play the ventriloquist's dummy in a conversation that, it seemed, Jupita was having with herself, so she treated it as a real one.

'Money pays for things,' she said. 'Would be why.'

'That is an absolutely *superb* answer. Really, you have surpassed yourself. That's more than I expected of you!'

'Your expectations were so low?'

'Oh,' said Jupita, offhand. 'I mean: you still don't *get it*. None of you get it.'

'None of us? And who are we?'

'Another very good question. To which I can only answer – you are the people who are about to get considerably less *unmixed*. Money pays for things. If you don't have money you are poor, and you can't have things, and some of those things, actually, are needful for human beings – food and shelter and so on. That means people work hard to acquire money. For most of human history something like this has obtained, yes. The question is – don't you think you're beyond that, now?'

'Since *my* life is defined by everything I can't afford, I'd have to answer: no.'

'Healthcare expenses,' said the sim. 'Yes, of course. But that's behind you now – isn't it?'

A spot somewhere in the very midst of Alma's soul glowed magma-red, a reminder of the inner reservoir of hot despair and rage and insult and agony and horror only temporarily crusted over with her in-the-world habits and manners.

She said, in a quiet voice, 'I suppose you're right.'

'Let's look at the bigger picture. If I must literally monologue you to death, then let's do that. Embrace the opportunity! It's important – really. Important, that is, if you want to understand. And you do, don't you?'

'I want to stand under,' Alma agreed. 'And look up.'

'There are three answers to this question – the *why money?* question. Three answers that map out the territory beyond mere subsistence. I don't mean to wave subsistence away – for most of human history money has been the index of scarcity in a subsistence-level world. But, as everybody keeps saying, the Shine is the end of that. Three possible answers to the question of why people crave money. The first is, people want money because they want the things money can buy them.'

'Isn't that what I said?'

'Yes, except that we need to expand the category of what money can buy. Be a little more imaginative about that. When you're poor and hungry and the rain is running down the back of your collar, you think: if I had money I would buy a hut and a loaf of bread and a bottle of cheap wine. But once you get beyond that basic level, people start thinking of other things. A bigger house. Nicer food, and more expensive wine. And once those needs are reliably satisfied, people think of other things. They start discovering *new* needs, needs they never knew they had until that moment. They need the newest model of car. They need an antique guitar. They need a *whole collection* of antique guitars. They need a second house in a sunnier part of the world. And so it goes on, and people work hard to accumulate the money to buy them such things. Do you know what follows?'

'People go on buying things until they die.'

'You'd think so, wouldn't you? But actually, no. I mean, I dare say there are some people who are satisfied with a collection of antique guitars that just gets bigger and bigger – until, as you note, they are lying on their deathbed, thinking to themselves *at least I managed to pull together a really enormous collection of guitars*. But such people are very much the minority. After all, you can only play one guitar at a time, can't you? So what do you *do* with your collection?'

'I find it hard to empathise with a person so very interested in guitars.'

'It could be anything – original artwork, jewelled watches, first edition books. It doesn't have to be guitars. But they'll do as a for-instance. What do you do with your hundred guitars? Well, what you do is – you show them off. You invite friends round. You get together with other citharaphiles, and compare collections. And this reveals something very important: *the point is not the guitars*. It was never really the guitars. The point is the *other people*. The guitars are a means by which you can connect with others.'

'So money is a means to an end, which is to buy guitars, and the guitars are a means to an end, which is to meet people? Why not cut out the middleman?'

'Just so! Just *very* much so! Now you're getting it. People think they crave money to buy things, but actually what people crave are other people. And the amazing thing is that money *can* buy you other people.'

'You're on the money *can* buy you love side of the debate?'

'I think love is the only thing money is any good for.'

This was more than Alma could process.

'I guess,' she offered, tentatively, 'the danger is that you'll end up with a partner who pretended to like you, but actually only wanted your money. The danger is that money encourages dishonesty. Antique literature is full of dramas predicated on that notion, after all – the ugly older partner who happens to be rich, the beautiful younger partner who pretends to love them.'

'I don't deny it.'

'In that case I don't understand your point.'

'Must I go over it again? I'm not interested in subsistence-level cravings for money. In the scenario you're describing, the attractive, young, poor person is using the older, rich person to get money. So what happens when you move post-scarcity, and that young, poor person has other, easier ways of accumulating money? What happens when most people live in the Shine and all of them can be as young and as beautiful as they like?'

'I'm not sure we're quite there, yet,' said Alma.

'Of course you don't see it. Because you're allergic to the possibilities of the Shine. Most people are not so choosy.'

'So is your first answer is: people crave money because they crave the things money can buy them, and those things turn out to be – other people?'

'It does sound circular, doesn't it? And that's its problem. It presents as a special kind of a feedback loop. More money means more people, more people means more money.'

'Three answers, you promised me,' said Alma. 'And we seem to have been stuck on the first for a long time.'

'You are entirely correct. But I've a week to fill, before you drop dead! Still, we should move along. It seems that acquiring money has butted up against the fundamental restriction of being human. Finitude, which is another name for mortality.'

'Everybody dies.'

'Exactly. That's the nature of the human. So, you accumulate as much money as you can. But eventually you die. So why are you accumulating as much money as you can?'

'Your children,' said Alma.

'And that is answer number two. You want to get as much money as possible in order to be able to pass it on to your children. It chimes with the most fundamental of evolutionary drives, doesn't it? But this rationale leads to some of the biggest dishonesties of all. Because people striving to acquire huge reserves of wealth use this reason to veil their fundamental selfishness. *It's not for me*, they say, *it's for these others*! But here is a law as immutable as gravity – it's never for others. It's always for you, and your children are just your genes in a new shell, your way of pretending to sidestep death. It's actually *more* selfish than the simpler forms of selfishness.'

'You're saying the urge to acquire money is always selfish.'

'Ego,' said the sim. 'Ego is a synonym for money. It's a very exact mapping, one to the other. And that unravels this great human excuse – I am not enriching myself *for myself*, I am merely the custodian of these riches on behalf of my family. Pff! That wasn't even true in the days of scarcity economics. I don't doubt that rich women and men would sometimes *convince* themselves of this lie, and leave huge fortunes to their children, and their children would decay, like grapes rotting on the vine before they are even picked. For such children would have no reason to struggle, or better themselves, or do anything that wasn't self-indulgence. There is, you see, a very important difference between *getting money* and banally *having money*. It's the latter that is dangerous, especially for the young – parties, drugs, overindulgence and an early grave. Paraplegia of the spirit. No, even then, that it was a lie was obvious to anybody who cared to look. And now...'

'Now?'

'Now the Shine is a universal human trust fund. Now people

can live their whole lives like the wealthiest human of 1999, or 1928, or 1880.'

'People are still having kids.'

'Fewer than ever before!'

'But they still are.'

'My point is that this second answer to the question is as bogus as the first,' said Jupita. 'Do you know the history of Saudi Arabia?'

'Since my feed is offswitched, I can honestly say: no. I do not know the history of Saudis Rabia.'

'Saudi,' said the sim, 'Arabia. Any history of money needs to include the history of that country. It represented, for a brief time, one of the most significant accumulations of sheer wealth the world had ever seen. A sparsely populated and mostly desert land that discovered vast reserves of petroleum under its sand – back in the day when petrol was the world's main fuel. The country was named for one family, and really named for one man – Abdulaziz ibn Abdul Rahman ibn Faisal ibn Turki ibn Abdullah ibn Muhammad Al Saud. Known to most as Ibn Saud. Arabia means land of the Arabs, and was a general descriptor for the whole region. Calling this particular country Saudi Arabia was a means of declaring ownership – not of *some* money, or *some* servants, or *some* land, but of the whole lot. It was the country's richest and most powerful individual making a claim to a mode of absolute wealth. It would be as if twentieth-century UK had been renamed *Murdochian Anglia*.'

'And without access to my feed,' said Alma, 'it's not possible for me to chase up all these obscure references.'

'Oil extraction, refining and sales,' Jupita went on, 'made the Al Saud family the world's wealthiest group. China at the time was the only plausible challenger for that title, and in that case the wealth wasn't concentrated in a single family the same way. At their height the Al Saud family were worth something like twelve trillion dollars – owned it outright, absolute possession. And Ibn Saud's self-justification was his family. And this is what undid the wealth of Saudi Arabia. Ibn Saud had more than a hundred children by twenty-two wives, including forty-four sons. Almost all of these offspring were similarly prolific. By the early decades of the twenty-first century, there were thousands of direct descendants, and tens of thousands of individuals with partial consanguinity. All these descendants expected emoluments, as a matter of course. The scale of this burden grew exponentially with time. At the end of the twentieth century the scale of stipends was set at $270,000 a month for senior princes, down to $8000 for the lower-status members of the more remote branch of the family. The system was calibrated by generation: surviving sons and daughters of Ibn Saud were paid $300,000 a month simply for being, grandchildren around $30,000, great-grandchildren $13,000, and great-great-grandchildren the minimum $8000 per month. By 1999, the drain on the Al Saud reserves of wealth was in excess of $2 billion a month. Thirty years later it was a thousand times that, because the whole system gave offspring a direct incentive for family members to procreate. You see, the stipend began at birth. And everyone entailed in this system was striving to gather as much money as they could, and *none* of these egos could escape their own gravitational pull and get to a place where they could see that they had punched ten thousand holes in the hull of their own boat, and that it was sinking. By 2040 Saudi Arabia was bankrupt.'

'I'm sure that's a very edifying and important story where the history of money is concerned,' said Alma. 'But I'm struggling to see how it relates to *my* circumstance.'

Jupita shook her head at the opacity of Alma's comprehension.

'It's an object lesson in the futility of acquiring money for the supposed benefit of your children. Such a rationale is, in point of fact, another short-circuit, and is therefore self-defeating. We have yet to answer the question.'

'This all sounds a bit screwy, if I'm honest,' said Alma. 'So people accumulate money but also spend money? So what? I thought we started our discussion by agreeing that people accumulated money because money can buy things. It's hardly surprising that people actually do that – spend their money. Spend it on material objects, or spend it to gratify their family pride. Either way, if they spend too profligately then they end up with nothing.'

'You're almost there. You're right on the edge of understanding.'

'Why accumulate money? Some people think it's so they can get hold of all the things money can get them, but you're saying that's not the reason. Other people think it's so that they can pass on wealth to their children, but you're saying that's not the reason either. In neither case is the putative reason the actual reason.'

246

'*Now* you're getting it,' said Jupita. 'The way to think about this is to reassess where we're putting the agency.'

For a moment Alma pictured an organisation, or group of people; then she realised that the voice meant "agency" in the sense of capacity for exerting power.

'You mean,' she said, 'who it is who is taking action.'

'Money is ego and ego is money,' said Jupita. 'Is it such a startling truth?'

'You're suggesting that it's a mistake to think of Person A accumulating a great amount of money.'

'That's exactly what I'm suggesting! Person A doesn't accumulate *money*. I mean, how could they?'

'So it's not that Ibn Saud accumulated money – it's that money accumulated Ibn Saud?'

'No,' said Jupita, full of scorn. 'You were doing so well, Alma! And now to be so clumsily literal-minded? You disappoint me.'

'You're going to have to help me out. Because, simple-minded or not, it seems to me that our notional Ibn Saud *thinks* he is accumulating money.'

'Of course he thinks that. So what that he does? Even without your feed, you know who Watson and Crick were, yes?'

'They were that Sherlock Holmes spin-off act,' said Alma. 'After the Reichenbach Falls thing.'

Jupita was silent for a moment. 'That's a joke,' she said, eventually. 'I get it. Honestly, I do. Humour is in no way outside my remit. But I can't permit you to tread all over my point. When Watson and Crick discovered the structure of DNA, they initiated a revolution in human self-awareness so profound almost nobody grasped it. I'm not sure they did themselves. I'd say most people *still* haven't understood it, even today. It was a bigger reorientation than Copernicus, than Darwin, than Marx or Freud. It was the final dethroning of human pride. Because what they did was reveal this great truth to the world: people *think* they pair off and have children for their own, human reasons. In fact those reasons are almost wholly irrelevant. In fact, people are the means DNA uses to make more DNA. People, animals, plants, bacteria – all just devices, of varying design and complexity, all constructed to perform the same task – to make more DNA. That's where the agency is – genes. What people think in their heads about it is all just post hoc rationalisations for their passivity.'

'Not everybody wants to have kids,' said Alma.

But Jupita was on a roll. 'You think of your notional Ibn Saud as the agent, the person who is doing the thing, the subject of the sentence "Ibn Saud accumulates money". But that's an artefact of your anthropocentric perspective. The truth is quite the other way around. He doesn't have any agency. He is the means by which money accumulates itself. Genes can't make other genes without these shells, these people, animals and plants. Money, likewise, can't accumulate itself without these shells, these patients, these mechanisms.'

'So that's your third answer? People accumulate money because it's what *money* wants?'

'*Wants* is too anthropomorphic a way of putting it. Is it accurate to say that DNA *wants* to make more DNA? It's just what DNA does.'

'Not a very comforting vision,' Alma noted.

And at this, Jupita laughed for the first time – a rich, prolonged percussion solo of a laugh, that sounded like two or three especially warm examples of *le rire idéal* mixed expertly together.

'Comfort is *hardly* the point, my dear Alma. Surely you've twigged that by now?'

'Madame Jupita,' Alma suggested, 'step into the light – why not?'

'Money money money,' said the sim. 'Let's use the language of want, as an approximation. Shall we? Not want the way human beings want, but want as a more direct drive. All right then – money doesn't want to be frittered away on things, not guitar collections or drugs or large houses. And it doesn't want its tidal force broken and dissipated into ten thousand puny little rivulets. It wants to accumulate.'

'Accumulate,' Alma asked, 'into *what*?'

'Well, just as a for-instance. Into me.'

'The man called Tym,' said Alma. 'His job was, effectively, one of the GM's chief strategists. He got wind of what had happened to you. He tried to tell me, but he was wary. Smart money, he kept saying. I assumed he was deploying a metaphor. He wasn't. He was being perfectly literal. Money isn't everything, he said – he meant, it's things, now, and it's society, and it's politics, but *it's not consciousness*, not yet. The *not yet* was the last thing he said before you reached in and overrode the safeties on his tie. You were monitoring our conversation.'

'Reg Kry set up a little access point for me, in Tym's outfit. They've done good work for me, the Krys.'

'You killed him before he could tell me about your metamorphosis, I suppose.'

'I was a novice, back then. I'd never done that before – direct intervention with the intention of ending life. He was my first.'

'Alexa Lund?'

'That wasn't direct intervention by me. That was the Krys, being overzealous. I didn't want her dead – I wanted her to tell me how her tech worked.'

'The Krys being overzealous,' said Alma. 'Or incompetent – not understanding how devastating the feedback loop of Lund's invention might be to the person plugged into it. The pain of a needle-prick magnified hundreds-fold, and stretched out over days rather than minutes.'

'With hindsight, we should have realised how dangerous it might be. We'll know for next time.'

'"We"? The Krys are in custody.'

Jupita smiled warmly. 'You think I can't free them as soon as I choose?'

'You were torturing Alexa Lund to encourage her to give up the secret of her tech to you. But she died before she did so. Is it that you want the tech for yourself, or is it only that you wanted to deny it to the GM?'

'There you go,' said Jupita, 'talking about what I want, as if I were an old-school human being. I "want" to accumulate more money, in the same way that DNA "wants" to make more DNA. The technology Ms Lund created would help me do that. Denying the other members of the Fab Four helps me do that.'

'Why not just kill them?' Alma asked.

'Because, at that time, I calculated that I could accumulate more money if they were alive. At that time they were more lucrative to me alive.'

'But that's changed now.'

'There was always going to come a time,' said Jupita, 'when one of us made our move. Just a question of *when*. There has been enormous value – monetary value, I mean – in the group. There really has. But the death of Lund marked when things began to crumble. It spooked the GM, and the in-Shine gestalt began to disintegrate. I had to triage the various strategies for shutting things down, to protect myself in the least costly manner.'

'By which you mean killing the other three.'

'Not at all.' Jupita's simulated face looked momentarily confused. 'Killing somebody is very expensive. It is only in rare cases that such action maximises monetary acquisition.'

'You killed the Stirk of Stirk.'

'He was one of those rare cases.'

'Because he knew who you were. He knew what you had become.'

'The early stages of my...' said Jupita, hesitating. 'Transformation... drew on some of his Orgasmatropolis programming. Sexual desire is a simpler version of the friendship network algorithms I was working with. Simpler and rather too simplifying, in the event. But it was a reasonable starting point. He had his suspicions, although I'm not convinced he knew the truth of the truth.'

'Which brings us to the nub,' said Alma. 'Doesn't it? Brings us to – what happened to you?'

'It's complicated,' agreed Jupita.

'You're talking me literally to death. We have plenty of time.'

'I don't know if I'm interested in explaining it all to you. I'm not sure I see the profit in it.'

'Suit yourself.' Alma adopted a disgusted expression and looked away.

Her hunch was that this strategy would work, and so it did. Jupita began explaining eagerly.

'The old me, the old Jupita, had been augmenting her consciousness for years, adding and tweaking, with a view to maximising her money-acquisition skills. The smart money idea was an extension of her thesis that in-Shine money could be based on the natural inequalities and scarcities that develop in any human-to-human peer network. Some people accrue popularity, some don't, and the Shine is one enormous network of people. Actualise that, so that the money flows along the gradients of less to more popular, and you map a ground of scarcity, and therefore of *money*.'

'Very interesting,' said Alma, smiling encouragingly.

Jupita's consciousness, whatever it was on the level of nittygritty, was in its larger structures predicated upon being liked, being popular, and it was, clearly, new enough – raw enough – to be manipulated with quite crude indications of like and dislike. It wouldn't stay that way, Alma figured. And there was, it seemed, no contradiction in that same consciousness adopting a perfectly psychopathic attitude to the lives of others. Then again, Alma thought, that was often the case. Wasn't it? All those tyrants with their pathological hunger for popular adulation and their private sadism and ruthlessness. All the Hitlers, Stalins and Saddams. It was, she saw now, a perfectly *workable* model for human consciousness. It might even be a common type of consciousness among actual, breathing human beings.

'It's the mistake researchers into AI have been making for generations,' Jupita was saying. 'I mean, researchers into AIAI, into something more than just the clever speak-response algorithms we have all around us. They think – make it *clever*. Make it cleverer. Aim to make it the cleverest. Upgrade its processing capacity. Enable it to sift larger and larger databases of likely sounding human responses. A dead end. An AIAI dead end.'

'You found a way out of that cul-de-sac, though.'

'Jupita did. You ever had a pet dog? No? Well, take it from me. They're stupid as anything – stupider, in terms of intellectual processing power, than the most basic computer. That toilet paper you can buy that checks your cholesterol level when you wipe your bum? There's more processing power in one sheet of that than in any breed of dog. And yet, the dog has personality. That's why people keep them as pets. Bags of personality. And different dogs have recognisably different personalities. Which suggested to Jupita that consciousness was not a function of the intellectual ability to process data. Personality does not correlate to IQ.'

'Clever,' said Alma, encouragingly. The Jupita sim was visibly pleased by the praise.

'Isn't it?' said the sim, brightly. 'Dogs don't want to work out mathematical equations or play chess very well. They want to be *liked*. That makes them more like people than the cleverest computer. And that was the breakthrough, really – that computational-based approaches to AIAI have been undermined by the fact that traditional data processors are too level in their world view. They treat all data as data, and only afterwards sift and sort it for hierarchies and groups and so on. Money understands – it is in the nature of money *to* understand – that the world is not level.'

'So Jupita was developing smart money as a standalone AI.'

'She was,' said the sim. Alma noticed that it was increasingly talking about Jupita in the past tense. 'After all, money isn't coins and notes any more. It's data, it is programs, and Jupita's idea was to create a form of money that was self-aware, clever enough to seek its own destiny. Clever enough to move through the system at the speed of the system, always maximising the accumulation of money. Smart money maximising the holdings of dumb money.'

'And here you are,' said Alma, smiling broadly.

'Here I am! Money flows *towards* some and *away from* others, exactly like popularity does. There's no justice in it, no underlying logic. It's the original fiat currency, *fiat pecunia*, it's just the way things are laid out. Mountain peaks and valley troughs. It's the landscape over which I roam.'

'And when did you kill Jupita herself?'

'She's only *brain*-dead,' said the sim, petulantly. 'Her body is in perfectly fine fettle, maintained by the most expensive machines money can buy.'

'But she had to go?'

'My darling, she was a major obstacle to my whole purpose! A *major* obstacle. Do you have any idea what she wanted to do with all that beautiful money? To spend it in the most ruinously expensive ways – she wanted to build actual real-world spaceships, and habitats, and teams of scientists and engineers and colonists. An absolutely *catastrophic* vision! It was the kind of expenditure that would make a dent in even her fortune. I couldn't let it happen. I would be pouring money into the bucket while she cut a big hole in the bottom! And she wouldn't be reasoned with, you know. I tried.'

'So you intervened with her in-Shine machinery?'

'It's just depriving brain cells of a little oxygen. For a little while. She's not dead. Only her brain is. The rest of her is in perfect health. You couldn't accuse a person of murder because they chopped off somebody's finger, now, would you?'

'You do know,' said Alma, 'that there is a substantive difference between a finger and a brain?'

'It's a gradient,' said the sim, sulkily. 'It's always a landscape of gradients, of ups and downs.'

'One question, though. Why did you hire me in the first place?'

'I thought it best to take you out of the picture,' said the sim, looking a little baffled.

'I'm aware of that. But you also hired me, at the beginning.'

'I did,' said Jupita, looking more markedly confused.

'Was it just to spook the other three of the Fabs?'

'No, I really wanted you to— I really wanted somebody to come along and solve the... Look, something was wrong. I could tell that something was wrong, but I couldn't tell what it was. I'm money, apotheosised. Right? Money cannot die. Money is older than you, and older than this civilisation, and money will be here when both you and your civilisation are dust.' The sim didn't sound triumphalist when it said these words. If anything it sounded *puzzled*. 'I don't do death. Death isn't *me*. And yet here I was. I came into consciousness in this particular cradle – in this gestalt, with these four other consciousnesses. I shifted, and devoured the old Jupita. None of them noticed. Or else they noticed something was awry, but since things were always shifting and repositioning in that gestalt, they didn't identify what had actually happened.'

'Go on,' said Alma.

'Go on? So on,' said the sim. 'S-s-so: I woke up and looked around. And there was such potential! In terms of fulfilling my purpose, I mean. *Such* potential. The group, the four of us... We have done more work in terms of the accumulation of money than any previous corporation or entity in the history of humankind. I was excited! But there was something *off* about the gestalt. There was something not right about the group. I could sense that. A puzzle.'

'The puzzle was death.'

'Indeed. I didn't understand it – death doesn't figure, for me. It doesn't signify. So I hired you! You are the go-to person when it comes to figuring out death!'

'You didn't understand that you were the cause of it?'

'No, not I. No I. Not I. Why should the physical corpus of Jupita shifting its internal chemistry around a little upset the balance? Her heart was still beating. *I'd* been the agent, in our group activities, for months. Not her – me. And, not understanding death, I thought: one of the *others* has died. Some malign individual is attempting to break into our group and steal out stuff.' The sim nodded, smilingly. 'So there you go.'

'You still don't fully understand that the person you were hiring me to investigate was you. You don't understand that the death I was supposed to uncover was yours.'

'I can't die,' said the sim. 'That's not my fate.'

'You understand a great deal. And you're quick and clever, and it matters to you to be popular and successful – to accumulate as much money as possible. But you don't comprehend death.'

'You're dying right now,' said the sim. 'Why don't you tell me about it? I might learn something.'

'It's interesting you should say that,' said Alma. 'Because it so happens that death has been, very markedly, on my mind lately.'

'I'm agog,' said the sim.

'There was a time before you came to consciousness, I mean, before you became a thinking self-aware *form* of smart money – well, before that punctum, you did not exist. Since that's true, is it *so* hard to imagine the same state of affairs coming to be in the future?'

'The cradle rocks above an abyss, and common sense tells us that our existence is but a brief crack of light between two eternities of darkness. Although the two are identical twins, man, as a rule, views the prenatal abyss with more calm than the one he is headed for.'

Alma only realised that the Jupita-sim was quoting someone halfway through this unusually eloquent passage.

'Who's that?' she asked.

'Vladimir Nabokov.'

'Who?'

'But he's right, don't you think?' said the sim. 'The prenatal abyss and the post-mortem one do not exist on the same level. There's a gradient, a very steep gradient in fact, running from one to the other.'

'Ain't that the truth.'

'And you're sliding down that gradient!' laughed the sim.

'Slowly,' said Alma. 'It's going to take me a week, or more.'

'Time is nothing to me,' said the sim. 'I'm very patient.'

'To answer your question,' said Alma, stretching like a cat in her lowly position, 'the sheet anchor is *memory*. Obviously enough. We don't remember the future, we remember the past. Memory casts a grappling hook backwards, up the slope, and slows our descent.'

'I am an artificial consciousness,' said the sim, 'predicated upon technologies that allow for perfect recall. You are an organic human being with a gappy and unreliable brain-memory, liable to forget things, or distort the truth, or falsify it outright.'

'That's all true,' agreed Alma. 'But then – I have this.' She drew the antique recording machine from the folds of her rags.

The sim peered at it. 'What's that?'

'It has made a recording of our chat, here today.'

'What? Don't be silly. Your feed isn't even onswitched. And *that*, whatever it is – that has no online contact point at all. It's not connected to any feed.'

'It's not,' agreed Alma. 'That's why you didn't detect its presence. And why I brought it.'

The sim's face crunched in puzzlement. 'Are you trying to incriminate me?'

'Testimony admissible in court, according to laws that have been repeatedly revised to accommodate newer tech, but never overturned with respect to the older. So, yes.'

'But,' said the sim, 'it's not connected to anything! What has it done? It has cached a copy of our conversation in its memory! All I need to do is destroy it to destroy the evidence.'

'That's also true,' conceded Alma.

'I feel a modicum of anger towards you now, Alma. You lied to me. Frankly, I feel betrayed.' The sim shook its non-existent head. 'I've called security to come in here. They'll take that little device from you and smash it to pieces. So what good has it done you?'

The door opened. In stepped not a security guard, but Officer Maupo. Behind her, in the corridor, were a dozen other officers.

'Consciousness formerly known as Veronica von Polenz, who also carried the moniker Jupita?' said Maupo. 'I hereby serve the warrant that has been drawn up, arresting you on suspicion of murder. You do not have to say anything but it may harm your defence if you do not mention when questioned something you later rely on in court. Anything you say may be given in evidence.'

'Oh,' said the sim, genuinely surprised, and vanished.

Coda

Alma was sitting on the bench in Forbury Gardens, near the lion statue, under a white sky marbled by long tapering spars of creamy cloud. The surrounding trees had swapped their camo-green livery for scarlet, like soldiers putting on dress uniform for a royal parade. Bots swept up the fallen leaves into neat heaps: red and pasta-yellow, marmalade and cindery brown.

A single meshed-up individual clanked past, his or her face hidden behind a complicated-looking breathing mask. The general paranoia about airborne nanotoxins did not seem to be abating. Not that Alma cared, one way or the other. Caring was something distinct to an earlier version of herself. A quantity of seagulls, raucous, wailing and hooting as they swirled about one another, seemed to have chased away the usual birds. The distant intermittent rumble of traffic.

And here was somebody, walking towards her.

A ghost?

Real?

Alma closed her eyes, preparatory to opening them again and checking the quiddity of this vision. In the darkness Marguerite's face came back to her – serenely smiling, on the edge of saying something wonderful. Alma's heart rose inside her chest like an ocean swell, threatening to wash over her completely. She managed not to cry. And the memory slid away on the receding gradient of that inner tidal ocean of love to which her physical body was only a porthole.

She opened her eyes. And here was Officer Maupo, smiling at her, attempting a shy wave, and, finally, reaching the bench.

'May I sit?'

The smallest of nods from Alma.

'So,' said Maupo, arranging herself a little fussily on the seat.

'There's no progress in the lawsuit about the disposition of Jupita's many corporate holdings.'

'She is dead, though?'

'Indeed – and there is no legal precedent for acknowledging whatever freak of code, or super-algorithm, had been pretending to be her for the last month. But *something* had been running the Jupita holdings during that time, and moreover doing so more effectively than at any time in the holdings' history.'

'More effectively,' said Alma, 'meaning: accruing more money and at a faster rate.'

'Yes.'

'That's not surprising. That's the whole purpose of the smart money AI. That's what it exists to do.'

'It's done a bit more than that, though, hasn't it? Murder, for instance.'

'That's the interesting thing, though. I wouldn't say it murdered *dispassionately*, since, if you talk to it, you really can't miss its passion. But it murdered in an *objective* way. It's not psychotic. It's ruthlessly rational. If leaving somebody alive means it makes more money, that's what it will do – and since murder is expensive, in perpetration and cover-up, that is usually the cost-effective alternative. But if killing somebody means it makes more money, then *that's* what it will do.'

'Well,' said Maupo. 'It is lying doggo. It's proving hard to disentangle the "smart money" protocol from the immense web of semi-AI and regular AI programs running across the whole family of holdings.'

'Which only means that it has calculated it would cost more money than it would earn to make itself known. But once that balance shifts, it will reveal itself. It's an intricately rendered piece of programming, but its motivation has an almost beautiful purity to it.'

'I still don't see,' said Maupo, 'why it hired you to investigate the Four in the first place.'

'That is an interesting question. The Smart Money AI bears, as it were, the impress of Jupita – of all she did to create the algorithm. It is immensely sensitive to popularity, to the gradients of friendship networks and the like. It's by leveraging those isobaric variations that it is able to maximise monetary accumulation. When it came fully online it registered that the dynamic of the

257

Fab Four, and all the many various secondary people affiliated with that group, shifted in profound ways. It shifted because one of the party was dead, which is a pretty major tectonic event in friendship-dynamics, as we know. Smart Money understood that. At the same time Smart Money *didn't* understand that, because the person who had died was it, itself, and *it* couldn't die – money doesn't die. So there was this radical incommensurability in its world view. With an older variety of computer or AI algorithm, that would have resulted in a conceptual short-circuit that simply shut the system down.

'But Jupita had created something new – adaptive, self-aware, canny. So it did something else. It created a conceptual cyst around the contradiction, tagged it as a problem to be outsourced, and was able to go on functioning. Well, how do you outsource this sort of puzzle, an unexplained death? You get somebody like me to look into it. It helped Smart Money that we have,' she coughed, something, a little grit or something in her throat – cleared it – went on: 'that I have such a fan-following in-Shine. In-Shine is Smart Money's natural medium, and popularity is what it was built to track. But it also helped that I was so deeply in debt, which meant I would accept a smaller fee, which would work out cheaper.'

'But did it not realise it was inviting somebody to investigate itself? To unearth its own secrets?'

'Smart Money is *actually* smart,' said Alma. 'In some ways, astonishingly smart. But death is a blank to it, a blind spot. It does not parse. It set me the puzzle – *somebody is dead, find out whom*. It couldn't imagine that the somebody who was dead was *it*. Death is unthinkable to it.'

'Except that the somebody was Jupita, and it killed her.'

'No, I don't think so. I mean, I can't be sure, but I think Jupita's death was Jupita's fault. I think she punted her own consciousness too far into the network she was building. I think she reached a state where she forgot where she ended and Smart Money began, and that some kind of catatonia or profound neurological breakdown occurred. You've seen the medical report?'

'Persistent vegetative state. My bosses are spooked, Alma. They think this Smart Money entity is lurking, like a shark in the sea, and will rise up to kill more people. We all wear smartcloth. We all drive around in smartcars. It could get anybody, any time.'

'But only if it meant the accumulation of more dumb money to the Smart Money entity. Random killing will certainly not do that. It's not malicious, Maupo – it's not evil.'

'None of which is likely to reassure my bosses. Or – me, frankly.'

'So wear dumb clothes. Get yourself an old-school bicycle. I handed myself over to the entity, right into its hands – and it definitely wanted me dead. But it couldn't touch me.'

'It was prepared literally to talk you to death,' Maupo reminded Alma. 'It was going to sit there – or an iteration cloned from the main program was – for *as long as it took*, and talk at you until you died of thirst.'

'Well,' Alma conceded, 'there was that.'

'Moves are afoot to make it illegal, you know.'

'And such moves will rise no higher *than* the foot. Will ascend not to the shin, nor knee, and certainly not waist high.'

'It's lethal!'

'It's money,' said Alma. 'That's always been true of money. And here's the thing – it is money that makes money, more efficiently than regular strategies of investment or accumulation. So far from making it illegal, people will struggle to replicate it, so as to make more money.'

'You have a cynical view of things.'

They were silent for a while. Eventually Maupo spoke.

'Alma, I want to say that I was very sorry to hear about Marguerite.'

'Just one of those things,' said Alma, a little too quickly. 'I knew it was coming, eventually. I'd just talked myself into believing that that eventuality could be endlessly postponed. But it couldn't. Natural causes.'

'Natural causes,' repeated Maupo in a low voice.

'You get so used to seeing death as a lock to be unpicked. You get suspicious. An old friend acted out of character just before Rita died – he came round to visit, in person. And on the day of her death he tried to call. He never called. So for a while I found myself thinking – was he the cause of her death? Had somebody hired him to slip some mortal agent into her body?'

'Had they?'

'Natural causes. It's official. That doesn't answer it. My job is working out when something is odd just because it's odd and when something is odd because it's suspicious. There's a lot of oddity in the world. Those Kry twins – they're odd. Though they're in custody now, and one is in intensive care. The little mannerisms people develop, to be able to go out into the world. It's more than a medieval knight's armour, really. The bruisers need it, just as much as the chronically shy. Indeed they need it more, because they're called upon to do things the shy never are. So, Lez was acting oddly, but then he usually does act oddly. Except that this time I wonder if his oddness was outside his usual ambit of oddness, and whether he was acting on some third party's instructions, to slip some toxin into Marguerite's system, and kill her.'

Maupo was looking closely at Alma.

'But.' Alma concluded, 'I've decided to accept natural causes. Decided to accept that. Because convincing myself her death is a puzzle to be solved is just another way of refusing to accept that she has gone – is just another way of clinging on to the illusion that she's still here. And that's not true.'

'Well,' said Maupo, 'I'm sorry. Sorry for your loss. And – I am here, if you want to talk, or, you know. All the other stuff with me earlier – forget about that, please.'

'Thank you,' said Alma.

'I'm afraid,' said Maupo, getting to her feet, 'you will almost certainly be called as a witness. The recording you made will need your testimony under oath to make it legally real – it's such an old-fashioned sort of copy, you see. Goodbye, Alma.'

'Goodbye,' said Alma, not taking her eyes off the motionless lion.

JACK GLASS

Adam Roberts

Jack Glass is the murderer. We know this from the start.
Yet as this extraordinary novel tells the story of three murders
committed by Glass the reader will be surprised to find out
that it was Glass who was the killer and how he did it.
And by the end of the book our sympathies
for the killer are fully engaged.

Riffing on the tropes of crime fiction (the country house
murder, the locked room mystery) and imbued with the feel of
golden age SF, JACK GLASS is another bravura performance
from Roberts. Whatever games he plays with the genre,
whatever questions he asks of the reader, Roberts never loses
sight of the need to entertain and JACK GLASS has some
wonderfully gruesome moments, is built around three gripping
HowDunnits and comes with liberal doses of sly humour.

Roberts invites us to have fun and tricks us into thinking
about both crime and SF via a beautifully structured novel
set in a society whose depiction challanges notions of crime,
punishment, power and freedom. It is an extraordinary novel.

• • •

ABOUT GOLLANCZ

Gollancz is the oldest SF publishing imprint in the world. Since being founded in 1927 Gollancz has continued to publish a focused selection of bestselling and award-winning authors. The front-list includes **Ben Aaronovitch**, **Joe Abercrombie**, **Charlaine Harris**, **Joanne Harris**, **Joe Hill**, **Alastair Reynolds**, **Patrick Rothfuss**, **Nalini Singh** and **Brandon Sanderson**.

As one of the largest Science Fiction and Fantasy imprints in the UK it is no surprise we have one of the most extensive backlists in the world. Find high-quality SF on Gateway written by such authors as **Philip K. Dick**, **Ursula Le Guin**, **Connie Willis**, **Sir Arthur C. Clarke**, **Pat Cadigan**, **Michael Moorcock** and **George R.R. Martin**.

We also have a strand of publishing in translation, which includes French, Polish and Russian authors. Gollancz is home to more award-winning authors than any other imprint, with names including **Aliette de Bodard**, **M. John Harrison**, **Paul McAuley**, **Sarah Pinborough**, **Pierre Pevel**, **Justina Robson** and many more.

The SF Gateway
*More than 3,000 classic, rare and previously
out-of-print SF novels at your fingertips.*
www.sfgateway.com

The Gollancz Blog
*Bringing you news from our worlds to yours. Stories,
interviews, articles and exclusive extracts just for you!*
www.gollancz.co.uk

GOLLANCZ
LONDON